PRAISE FOR NUALA O'CONNOR

Praise for

Becoming Belle

"O'Connor offers a stunning historical reimagining. Her eye for details, including Victorian dress, food, and technology, enhance her mastery of character and inner dialogue."

—*Library Journal* (starred review)

"O'Connor has the thrilling ability to step back nimbly and enter the deep dance of time—this is a hidden history laid luminously before us of an exultant Anglo-Irish woman navigating the dark shoals and the bright fields of a life."

—Sebastian Barry, award-winning author of *The Secret Scripture* and *Days Without End*

"*Becoming Belle* is a glorious novel in which Belle Bilton and nineteenth century London are brought roaring to life with exquisite period detail. In her portrayal of Belle, Nuala O'Connor delivers a seductive study of a complex and fascinating woman who deserves the stage provided for her in this wonderful book."

—Hazel Gaynor, *New York Times* bestselling author of *A Memory of Violets*

PRAISE FOR

Miss Emily

"Lovely. . . . *Miss Emily* pulls us in from its first limpid lines and then detonates with an explosion of power—much like Emily Dickinson's poems. The novel captivates with its high emotions and rich images. Hope, Ada comments, 'may be small and bald at first, but then it gathers feathers to itself and flies on robust wings.' So, too, does O'Connor's quietly soaring novel."

—*Washington Post*

"A beautifully imagined account of an unlikely bond."

—*People*

"O'Connor is a gifted writer; not only does she bring a believable sense of poetry (clay is 'deathly cool around my fingers') and self-assurance to Emily, she is also capable of conveying complex feelings succinctly, a talent shared by her historical heroine."

—*Publishers Weekly* (starred review)

"A gorgeously rendered tale about a friendship between the real-life poet Emily Dickinson and the fictional Ada Concannon, this book is a celebration of relationships and art."

—*Globe and Mail* (Toronto), Best Book of the Year

NORA

ALSO BY NUALA O'CONNOR

NORA

A LOVE STORY OF NORA
AND JAMES JOYCE

∽

NUALA O'CONNOR

HARPER ● PERENNIAL

NEW YORK • LONDON • TORONTO • SYDNEY • NEW DELHI • AUCKLAND

HARPER ● PERENNIAL

A portion of this book was originally published as "Gooseen" in *Granta*, June 16, 2018.

P.S.™ is a trademark of HarperCollins Publishers.

FIRST EDITION

Designed by Jamie Lynn Kerner

Library of Congress Cataloging-in-Publication Data has been applied for.

ISBN 978-0-06-299172-0

21 22 23 24 25   LSC   10 9 8 7 6 5 4 3 2 1

For Finbar, as ever.

Wherever thou art shall be Erin to me.

—JAMES JOYCE, "NORA," *ALPHABETICAL NOTEBOOK*

Yet man is born unto trouble, as the sparks fly upward.

—JOB 5:7

NORA

MUGLINS

Dublin
JUNE 16, 1904

W E WALK ALONG BY THE LIFFEY AS FAR AS RINGSEND. THE river smells like a pisspot spilling its muck to the sea. We stop by a wall, Jim in his sailor's cap, looking like a Swede. Me in my wide-brim straw, trying to throw the provinces off me.

"Out there are the Muglins Rocks," Jim says, pointing out to sea. "They have the shape of a woman lying on her back."

His look to me is sly, to see if I've taken his meaning. I have and our two mouths crash together and it's all swollen tongues and drippy spit and our fronts pressed hard and a tight-bunched feeling between my legs. His hands travel over my bodice and squeeze, making me gasp.

"Oh Jim," is all I can manage to say and I step away from him.

"You have no natural shame, Nora," he says, and he's coming at me now with his thing out of his trousers and in his hand, that one-eyed maneen he's no doubt very fond of. It looks, I think, like a plum dressed in a snug coat.

"No natural shame?" I say. "Don't be annoying me. Do you think because I'm a woman that I should feel nothing, want nothing, know nothing?" But I dip my nose to his neck for a second, the better to breathe his stale porter, lemon soap smell. Span-new to me.

Jim squints and smiles. I kneel on the ground before him, my face before his tender maneen, glance up at him; Jim drops his head, the better to see my mouth close over it. The taste is of salt and heat, the feeling is thick and animal. I suck, but only for a spell, then I draw back and peck the length of it with my lips. I stand.

"There," I say, "there's a kiss as shameful as Judas's and don't tell me it isn't exactly what you wanted, Jim Joyce."

A groan. He wants that bit more, of course, but that might be enough for today, our first time to walk out together. We kiss again and he lingers in my mouth, wanting to enjoy the taste of himself on my tongue. His paws travel over me, front and back. Oh, but he's relentless. So I unbutton him, put my hand into his drawers, and wrap cool fingers around his heat. A gasp. I work him slow, slow, fast until he's pleasured, until my fist is warm and wet from him.

"You've made a man of me today, Nora," Jim says, a coddled whisper, and I smile. It's rare to have a fellow say such a thing and I feel a small bit of power rise up through me, a small bit of joy.

I wipe myself with my handkerchief and Jim fixes his clothes. I hold out my hand and Jim takes it and together we walk on.

THROWAWAY

꩜

Finn's Hotel, Dublin
JUNE 20, 1904

A HORSE CALLED THROWAWAY WON THE GOLD CUP AT ASCOT. This I'm told by a man whose hotel room I'm cleaning. The man shouldn't be in the room while I'm here. Or I shouldn't be in the room while he's here. One of the two. But I'm so shocked by his attire that my brain can't decide which it is. The man is wearing only an undershirt and, though it's long, he appears to have no drawers on and he's talking to me as if he's in a three-piece suit crowned with a hat. I stand like an *óinseach* with a rag in one hand and a jar of beeswax in the other, trying not to gawp.

"Throwaway!" the man says. "Can you believe it?"

The man doesn't sound Irish. He may be English. Or perhaps even American. His arms are white beneath a fur of black hair. The strands look long enough to plait. He has a gloomy expression, a father-of-sorrows way about him. His bare legs are bandy and fat, like a baby's. I feel my face scald hot, so I turn my back to the man and look for somewhere to put down my rag and polish.

"A twenty-to-fucking-one outsider," he roars and I jump. "And all my money thrown away on that damned nag Sceptre."

He starts to laugh and it's a mirthless sound. Then he goes

quiet and I hear a click; I turn my head to see the man start to hack at his wrists with a razor.

"Sir, sir!" I shout.

But he keeps slicing at his arm until he draws red and I run to him. There's not enough blood to fill a fairy thimble, in truth, but he holds up the dripping wrist and cries and shivers as if he might die. I take hold of his shaking arms and sit him on the bed, and I run to try to fetch the porter for he will surely know what to do. But, as I hammer down the back stairs of Finn's Hotel a voice trails behind me, calling, "Throwaway runaway! Throwaway runaway!" on a long string of cackles. I open the back door and in apron, cap, and all I run and run and run until I can go not another step. At the river Liffey wall, my stomach lurches and I empty my breakfast into the water and watch it float off to the sea.

IRELAND

❧

Finn's Hotel, Dublin
JULY 16, 1904

To Jim I am Ireland.

I'm island shaped, he says, large as the land itself, small as the Muglins, a woman on her back, splayed and hungry, waiting for her lover. I'm limestone and grass, heather and granite. I am rising paps and cleft of valley. I'm the raindrops that soak and the sea that rims the coast.

Jim says I am harp and shamrock, tribe and queen. I am high cross and crowned heart, held between two hands. I'm turf, he says, and bog cotton. I am the sun pulling the moon on a rope to smile over the Maamturk Mountains.

Jim styles me his sleepy-eyed Nora. His squirrel girl from the pages of Ibsen. I am pirate queen and cattle raider. I'm his blessed little blackguard. I am, he says, his auburn marauder. I'm his honorable barnacle goose.

"Nora," Jim says, "you are syllable, word, sentence, phrase, paragraph, and page. You're fat vowels and shushing sibilants."

"Nora," Jim says, "you are story."

GOOSE

❧

Galway
MARCH 21, 1884

I WAS BORN IN THE UNION WORKHOUSE IN GALWAY. NORA JO-seph Barnacle they called me.

Mammy was a spinster—twenty-six years old already when Daddy lured her into matrimony, promising their life would bloom and rise like the bread he baked for a living. But the only thing that bloomed was Mammy's belly and all that rose was Daddy's hand to his gob with the next drink and the next. When I was three, and my twin sisters were born, Mammy sent me to live with her own mother, Granny Healy, in her quiet houseen in Whitehall.

"It can't be helped that you're a Barnacle," Granny said, "but always be proud of your Healy and Mortimer sides."

But still, as I grew, she liked to spin tales for me over bread and butter and bitter tea.

"You're a seabird, Nora Barnacle. Born from a shell." She eyed me over the rim of her china cup.

"Not born from an egg, Granny, like other birds?"

"No, not from an egg at all, loveen. A shell. For the barnacle is a rare and magical goose."

"I like magic." I tried to sip my tea the way Granny did, heartily but with grace. "Where does the shell come from?" I asked.

Granny leaned closer, broke a piece of currant cake in half, and put it into my mouth. The rest she chewed herself and she looked over my head, out the window into Whitehall, as if she'd forgotten me.

"The shell, Granny?"

"Well, girleen, that's the most peculiar thing of all. That shell you came from grew like a fruit on the branch of a noble tree that stood by the Galway Bay shoreline. The shell-fruit got heavier and heavier until it dropped into the sea. There it bathed in the salty water until it bobbed ashore at Salthill."

"Do you mean *our* Salthill, where we walk the prom?"

"The very place."

I sat before Granny and imagined a pearly shell lying on the shore, nobbled like the conch Uncle Tommy gave me.

"Go on, Granny. Tell me more."

"This beautiful shell burst open on the shingle at Salthill and inside there was a dark-haired baby, serene and curious. The baby smiled and smiled, and she had one droopy eye that gave her a wise and holy look." Granny leaned forward and put her cool finger to my eyelid.

"Me."

"Yes, my lovely Nora, it was you." Granny set down her cup. "Your mother was walking the Salthill prom that day and, when she saw that fine shell, she tripped down to the beach. She clapped her hands when she found a baby inside, smiling up at her. She was so happy. Your mother picked you up and brought you home, her little barnacle gooseen."

I settled back against the rungs of my chair. I lifted the china cup to my mouth and let the tea scald my tongue.

"All that trouble I took to be born," I said. "All that falling from a tree and bouncing on waves and landing onshore and bursting from a shell to be scooped up by Mammy."

Only to be sold off like a goose at a fair, I now think. *Might it not have been better if I had come more naturally*, I ask myself, *to have entered the family with some portion of stealth? If I had managed that, maybe Mammy would not have given me away to Granny. If I'd managed that, maybe I'd still live among my sisters and brother and be part of everything in the house in Bowling Green. Maybe, if I'd come into life more naturally, Mammy would love her Gooseen well.*

HEARTBALM

❧

Finn's Hotel
AUGUST 1904

MONDAY AND I LIE ABED, THINKING OF JIM, WHEN I SHOULD be up and getting into apron and cap. But divil I'll get up until I've let my imaginings play out. My hands wander under my nightgown, I slip a finger into my crevice and press; I knead my bubbies and let my palms slide over my nipples, while keeping Jim's sweet face fixed in my mind. He's all I need in my head.

Last night, when we walked to Ringsend, he told me he was called "*farouche*" by a lady he knows, one of those moneyed ones, no doubt.

"*Farouche*, Jim?"

"Wild, savage."

He seemed hurt by the word. "Sure, isn't your savagery one of the best parts of you?" I said. "Isn't it what makes you the man you are?"

And he pushed me against a wall and whispered my name into my ear over and over and called me by his names for me: Goosey, Sleepy-eye, Blackguard.

He said, "I will make you my little fuckbird," and my reason slithered to pulp when I heard that and I kissed him with all the fierce light of my body.

༺ ঙ ༻

JIM HAS ME WRITE LETTERS TO HIM, BUT MY THOUGHTS ARE STIFF on the page—I'm not fond of writing; words don't slide off my pen the way they do for him. I left school at twelve, like most people, and haven't had much call to write more than a few lines since. But Jim wants to know what I think of when we're apart, to bind us closer, but it seems to me all I think of is him and does he want to read letters that are all about himself? Perhaps he does.

I slip from the bed, gather my paper and a book I'll use to help me write the letter—I need it, truly, for I don't know what to be saying and am sitting here chewing my fingers and gawping at the blank paper. After much scribbling and mashing of spoiled pages, I come up with a few lines:

Darling Jim,

At night my soul flies from Leinster Street to Shelbourne Road, to entwine with yours. Jim, I can't bear to be apart from you and my mind conjures and caresses you every minute of every hour that I do my work fixing beds and waiting tables, as if my heart will dry up without the balm of you to oil it. This is love, Jim, it is constant and racking and true and I will see you, my precious darling, tonight and we will hold hands and rejoice that we found each other of all the people in Ireland. I bless the day you first accosted me on Nassau Street with your serious face and sailor's cap and dirty shoes, and I thank Our Lady that I could see immediately, from your polite manners, that you were a good man. And I bless the day we first walked out together—the sixteenth of June is etched on

my soul. I am lonely without you, Jim, believe me to be
ever yours,

Nora

I scramble into my uniform and web it, lightning quick, to catch the post for I want Jim to read my words this morning; I hope he likes them. He's right about jotting things down, it does make me feel closer to him. The letters are heartbalm.

MOUTH

〜

Dublin
AUGUST 1904

JIM HAS A MARVELOUS WAY OF SPEAKING. IT'S NOT ONLY THE lovely words he knows, a whole dictionary of them inside his mind, it's his voice. It goes up and down but keeps itself still and contained, too. Jim sounds like a man on a stage, giving a speech. He could be saying any old thing and still he comes across as if he's rehearsed lines and is now delivering them. Every sentence that falls from his mouth does so at the right time and in the exact right way. I see it as a God-bestowed gift that he has. And, because his voice is a fine one, like an orator's—a Thomas Kettle or a Charles Stewart Parnell—you can't but believe everything he says.

The girls I work with in Finn's call Jim "posh" and they can't believe he's with me.

"You'd think the likes of him would be with one of his own kind," Molly Gallagher said to me one day.

"But amn't I good enough for any man, Molly?" I said, stung by her.

"You are of course, Nora," she said, linking arms with me, but I could see the doubt in her face.

In truth, I too find it hard to credit that Jim would choose me above the educated ladies he knows, those Sheehy women and the rest. They, like him, have a grand air about them and they sound so fine, like creatures from another world. My voice, in comparison to all of them, is that of a honking goose, loud and fast and spilling out of me. But Jim tells me I sound "melodious" and longs to hear me speak.

"Speak to me in your western tongue, sweet Nora," he says, when we lie atop Howth Hill, letting the cool dusk wind lap over us. I love to be by the sea with him, bathing in the salty air.

"What do you want me to say, Jim?"

"Tell me," he said softly, "the siren songs of your soul. Let me hear the melodies of your mind, my little Galway rogue."

That's the way he talks. From another man, the things he says would come across daft, but Jim can sound like a poet and a politician, both at the same time. He has the perfect voice for himself, for who he is, a thing to admire and love about him. And yes, I do love him, I do indeed. I know it already because when I'm not with Jim, it's as if I carry the whispering ghost of him wrapped around me. I feel him gone from me as if part of my body were taken. He never leaves me, head or heart. And is that not the sweetest of God-bestowed gifts?

Today, though, he chastises me.

"What sort of a letter was that, Nora?"

"How do you mean, Jim?" I roll on my side to look at him.

He pets my hair with his fingers. "It didn't sound like you at all."

I dip my eyes and pout my bottom lip. "I don't know *how* to write like me."

He tips my chin upward. "Yes, you do. Write as you speak, Gooseen. Isn't that why I like you so much? Your gorgeous Galway voice and your funny little tales."

"I'll try, Jim," I say, though I haven't a notion how I'll do what he asks.

SONG

Dublin
AUGUST 24, 1904

I HAVE THE NIGHT OFF WORK AND JIM'S FRIEND VINCENT COS-
grave comes to Finn's Hotel to walk me to the concert rooms in
Brunswick Street. Jim will sing there tonight and I'm fit to burst I
am that proud of him.

"I will go on ahead of you, my little pouting Nora," Jim wrote
to me last night. "Dire performance nerves will not permit me to
see you before I sing."

Outside Finn's, Cosgrave offers me his arm and I hesitate, but
then I take it. He saunters like a man following a hearse so, after a
minute, I withdraw my hand and increase my pace.

"Where are you off to so fast, Miss Barnacle?" says he. "You're
like yon stallion Throwaway, belting out ahead of me."

I laugh. "That horse, Mr. Cosgrave, seems to be the only horse
I know."

He smiles. "Why's that?" I shake my head. "Ah, go on," he
says, "tell me."

"Well, all right, I'll relate to you how I first heard of Throwaway." I slow down until Cosgrave falls in beside me and I tell him
all about the man in the hotel with the razor and his distress over
that very horse winning Ascot. Cosgrave laughs and I laugh, too,

though it was alarming at the time. "Throwaway!" I bellow, just like the man.

"And did you tell Jim that the fella was in nothing but his undershirt, inside in the room in Finn's, Miss Barnacle?" Cosgrave asks, reaching for my arm; there is a wicked pull to his mouth, a class of leer. I step away from him. "Oh, you didn't reveal that to darling Jim? Naughty Nora." He waggles his finger under my nose, then grabs my hand, and tries to kiss it. I snap it back.

"Mr. Cosgrave! Jim Joyce wouldn't be happy with these antics, after asking you to escort me."

"Jim Joyce, Jim Joyce," he mocks. "I have it up to my neck with the same Jim Joyce. And you, Nora Barnacle, know little about him. That fella may tell you he adores you, but it'll never last. Mark me. Joyce is mad, for one thing—who wouldn't be, that had to live with his father? Mr. John Stanislaus Joyce, the disappointed, drunken snob."

"That's no way to speak of Mr. Joyce. You know little about it." But I'm struck that Jim gives me few details of his family life except to sigh bitterly about his father from time to time and the plight of his sisters and brothers who live at home still.

Cosgrave leans his head in close to mine. "And your Jim, you should know, is also a man of particular urges and very fond of his trips to the particular houses of Tyrone Street."

I don't like his tart manner and I can feel my skin heating inside my dress; I don't even know the man and only agreed to be escorted by him as he's Jim's good friend. "I think you've said enough for one day, Mr. Cosgrave."

"Well, Miss Barnacle, not quite—the biggest thing is that Joyce is a class of lunatic. Stone mad." He taps his forehead then points into my face. "Remember I said that."

Cosgrave pulls back and stalks on ahead of me. I follow behind him to the concert rooms and he doesn't let another pip out of him, for which I'm very glad; it suits me better not to listen to his bitter, slobbery talk. The outright cheek of him, talking to me in that way. Jim is mad, indeed! But it occurs to me that I'll have to ask one of the girls in Finn's what goes on in Tyrone Street, though I fear I already know.

Jim's brother, Stanislaus, is at the concert. He comes to me in the foyer at the interval where I'm drinking a peppermint cordial, standing alone with my back to the wall, Cosgrave having disappeared with himself. I recognize him the second I see him though we haven't met before. Stannie is both like Jim and not like him—he is slim and serious, in the same way, but blockier and shyer and his hair is more bountiful.

"Miss Barnacle," he says, quietly, offering me his hand, "Stanislaus Joyce."

"Oh, Stannie, I thought it was you," I say, shaking it. "I didn't think I'd ever get to lay eyes on the best brother in person, Jim never stops talking about you." I sip my cordial from pure nerves at meeting one of Jim's relatives. "But how did you know who *I* was?"

"I confess I've seen you with Jim on occasion, across the street in town."

"And you didn't wave or come to us? For shame, Stannie!" I laugh.

He blushes and I'm alarmed. "Oh, it was lightly meant, I'm sorry. It's very lovely to meet you at last, Stanislaus Joyce."

I grab his hand in mine and shake it again, but he takes this as a dismissal and walks off, leaving me alone with my peppermint in my hand and, I feel, a silly, surprised set to my gob.

MY FACE ALMOST BURSTS FROM SMILING, I'M SO PROUD OF JIM. There is not a man who can talk like him and now, it's clear, not a one who can sing like him either. Even when the pianist bursts out crying like a babby and runs from the stage with nerves, and Jim has to provide his own piano accompaniment, he doesn't falter. Down he sits and plays like an angel. Out of his mouth come the sweet words about the Sally Gardens and taking love easy. I know that he's thinking of me as he lets the notes roll and rise—my own heart rolls and rises with him. I would go to the side of the earth with Jim Joyce, for sure. And I'd drop off into black, starry space in his arms if it came to it.

EYES

⟐

Dublin
SEPTEMBER 1904

JIM HAS GOAT-BLUE EYES, CLEAR AS SALTWATER, EYES ELEC-
tric from the jumps of his fierce mind. My eyes are mud in comparison, but Jim says they're like mountain pools. He says I have
the eyes of a saint, a virgin, a pleasing plaster Mary.

"Go on out of that," I say. "A blessed statue?"

"Your eyes are quiet like the Madonna's," he says. "Even when
your hand tickles me to pleasure, your eyes stay molten and melancholic." He rubs his fingers across his forehead. "My own eyes,
alas, ail and fail. I'll be blind by fifty, I wager. Blind as biblical
Bartimaeus."

This is the way Jim talks. He got education, away in Clon-
gowes Wood school in County Kildare and then in Belvedere
College and the university, here in Dublin. Places for boys from
moneyed families. He even went to Paris to study doctoring but
came home when his mother was sick and ready to pass away. His
pappie had colossal hopes for Jim, but the same man drank those
hopes away, Jim says. Money is *all* in fine schools and colleges,
and when it's gone, you're out on your ear, no matter how grand a
sentence you can spin.

Our heads are puddled together in the marram grass, mine and

Jim's, and the Irish Sea is a nearby shush. We have different heads. Jim's is full of song and story, questions and schemes, bothers and dissatisfactions. Mine, I think, is full of other things: songs, for sure, but mostly memories and, most important now, feelings. I'm happy to lie in his arms and kiss, feel the soft heat of lips, his hands roaming into my drawers, mine into his. But Jim loves to talk and muse and go on about everything; he's always bothering himself, trying to figure things out.

"Do you think the tenor John McCormack can hold a tune as well as I can?" he says.

"No."

"Did that bowsy Cosgrave try to hold your hand when he chaperoned you to the concert rooms to hear me sing? Did he try to kiss you? Or worse? Be frank with me now, Nora."

"He did not."

"Did you think Stannie looked at you queerly that time you met?"

"Ah, Jim. What is it you're trying to say? Queerly? Your own brother!"

"Do the other girls who work at Finn's Hotel have boyfriends?"

"They have."

"Are they free with them?"

"I don't know."

"But don't girls talk about everything, Nora?"

"They do, I suppose."

"So, are you lying to me?"

"Ah, shut up, Jim, for the love of the Lord, and kiss me again."

He leans in and I take his tongue between my teeth and press until he laughs. He pins my wrists over my head and bores his own tongue deep into my mouth, poking at every tooth and lapping all around until I'm liquid with the madness of it. Our breath comes fast like horses after a race and we roll in the marram and the sea gives her siren call and the air is keen and fresh. We finish kissing, mouths bruise-soft, and lie on our backs to watch the cloud shapes roll above us in the blue: here a cottony ship's masthead, there a stippled mackerel. I take Jim's hand in mine and squeeze it.

All my loneliness for Galway is gone. Since I took up with Jim, Dublin has opened her arms to me, taken me to her breast. My jackeen Jim. He's cut from Dublin as sure as Nelson's Pillar was. But still he talks of getting away, of leaving all behind; he sees a lit-up future far from this country. I daren't ask if I can go, too; I'm hoping he will invite me.

I roll sideways to look at him: the wrinkled linen jacket, the dirty plimsolls, the clever eyes, stilled now under sleepy lids. He looks serene and innocent, yet he's the same man who stole one of my gloves and took it to bed with him and told me after that it lay beside him all night "unbuttoned," as if I could believe that. I'd say that same glove saw plenty of skittery movement! I gaze now at Jim and wonder what Mammy would make of me lying on the seashore with a glove-caressing jackeen's fingers roaming into my garters and beyond. What would she say to my hands powering over his prick, snug inside trousers? She'd be polluted with rage, to be sure. And Uncle Tommy? Well, he'd beat the thunder out of me and no mistake, like he did over Willie Mulvagh. After seeing me with Willie, Uncle took out his stick and left me purple and raw and running for the first train out of Galway. Yes, Mammy and Tommy would be galled to their bladders if they could see Jim and me now, carefree as birds, love wrapped snug around us like a shawl. And I find I do not care.

MEMORY

❧

Dublin
SEPTEMBER 1904

Though Jim is jealous of any other man whose mouth has met mine, he makes me talk of the two dead Michaels, Feeney and Bodkin, and poor Protestant Willie, who Uncle Tommy objected to so strongly. Jim loves details and takes meaning from everything: dates, songs, tiny occurrences, objects. Mostly Jim wears me out with his investigations into my life before I met him, but I play along anyway, to please him.

"Tell me again about Feeney," Jim says.

Jim and I are once more walking by the sea, this time at Sandycove where his friend Oliver St. John Gogarty lives in a squat tower. I let the breeze lap over my face and remember Michael.

"He was never a robust young fellow, there was something of the lamb about him."

"Lamb?"

"What I mean is Michael was pale-faced, sunken. Always a little sick. But he was gentle and he could sing well."

"Feeney sang for you often, I suppose." His nose wrinkles.

"He would sing 'The Lass of Aughrim' and linger over the saddest parts."

"The pair of you were thwarted, Nora, a bit like the lovers in the song. Go on."

I sit on the seawall. "Ah, Jim, you have me repeating myself like some doting crone. Haven't I told you all this before?"

He sits by me and takes my hand. "I like to hear these things, they're good yarns. Tell me again about the night of the rain."

I spurt air between my lips to help me keep my patience. "I was in bed one wet night, the wind howling, when I heard stones hit my window. I looked out and there was Michael Feeney, under the tree, shaking with the cold. 'Go home, you'll catch your death,' I said. 'I don't want to live if I can't see you, Nora,' he called back. I ran out to Michael and embraced him and went back inside. A week later he was dead. It was terrible. Only a gossoon of seventeen."

"And you think you were the cause of his death."

My heart babbles in my chest. "He shouldn't have been out on such a squally night. He was ailing." I drop my head. "And then when Sonny Bodkin was taken by TB. Well."

Jim puts his arm around me and squeezes; his look is impish. "Nora, my little man-killer."

I shrug him off. "It isn't funny, Jim. Dying is not one bit funny."

"It's not, Nora. Death descends so lightly but it's the hardest thing of all."

Long-gone Granny Healy floats across my vision like a blot in my eye, but as she does in my dreams, she merely smiles. Jim's face slackens and I know he's probably remembering his dear mother just as I'm thinking of the only woman who was a real mother to me.

We sit together on the seawall, letting the jounce of the waves, their gray-green light, soothe and calm us while we conjure the dead.

WANDERER

❧

Dublin
SEPTEMBER 15, 1904

I'M A WANDERER, NORA," JIM SAID TO ME WHEN I MET HIM FIRST just three months past and it has proven to be true. He flies from lodging to lodging, now with this friend in Shelburne Road, now with that one in Sandymount. He doesn't want to live with his pappie and the family for they draw on him like leeches, he says. The way it is, Jim finds it hard to settle in one spot and people, generally, annoy him; he finds their oddities hard to deal with.

"I've enough foibles of my own without having to figure out other people's," he told me once.

"People are strange, it's true for you," I answered but I thought about it for days, the business of him not getting along with others. I can muddle through with most people and, I think, life's easier on those who can.

At the moment Jim is staying with his friend Gogarty in the old tower by the sea. It's a bit of a trot from there to town, so I see less of Jim and that pains me. I prefer to be with him every day for I feel complete when we're about each other. Therefore, it's a lovely surprise to find him outside Finn's when I step out for a minute of air on my dinner break.

On seeing me, he tosses away the cigarette he's smoking. "Nora, I summoned you with my mind and you came." He steps forward and grabs my hands and his look is feverish.

"Jim, what in heaven is the matter?" His lovely blue eyes are bloodshot and the lids swollen. "Have you been weeping, my love? Has something happened?"

He pulls me along by the wall, away from the hotel door, to talk; his sharp glances to left and right unnerve me. "Nora, I want to get out of Dublin. Life is waiting for me, if I choose to enter it."

I dip my head—made quiet by his confession. He talks so fondly of his time in France and I knew, I suppose, from things he'd say, he wanted to go back there, but I hoped I'd be enough to keep him fixed to Ireland.

Jim lifts my chin with one finger and asks a question I hoped for but did not expect. "Nora, will you come with me?"

"Away with you? As man and wife?"

He shakes his head sharply. "No, Nora. I won't be bound by any church. Does that make you want me less?"

I take my hand from his. "No." I hesitate. I know Jim has no time for priests or churches, but what would become of me if we go off together, unmarried? I'd be stained, spoiled, unable to return to my life here. "But will we ever marry, Jim?"

He shivers and looks to the ground. "I'm not sure I'm a man for wedlock."

I nod and stand where I can see the entrance to the hotel, in case the manager sticks his head out and sees me. It would be a great adventure to go with Jim, away from all we know, but I'd like to marry even if he would not. I might, it occurs to me, cajole him into it by and by. It wouldn't be proper for a man and woman to be together in life without marrying, after all. I'll surely convince him to wed if we go abroad together, if only in a quiet little way. Jim's head still hung, his teeth begin to chatter, and the look around his eyes is that of a hunted man.

"Jim, something has you rattled and raw. Are you going to tell me what it is?"

"I walked from Scotsman's Bay, through the night, Nora, to see you and ask you if you'll leave this place with me. Please say that you will."

My heart pummels my ribs—I mean the world to Jim as he does to me. He walked through the dark hours just to see me. "You were up all night? You have the look of it, right enough." I've never seen him so shaky, even after one of his big nights of drinking with his friends.

Jim drops his head into his hands and groans. "Will you answer what I'm asking you, girl?"

I wrap my fingers around his and pull his hands down. "I'll leave Dublin with you, of course. I'd go anywhere with you, Jim." My heart bullies my rib cage, but I mean it—I want to be with him more than I want anything else.

"Do you understand me, Nora? Do you know what this means?" His eyes are frantic.

"Yes," I say, "yes."

A tiny sob escapes his throat. "Oh, Nora, thank you." Jim kisses my hand then lights another cigarette with shaking fingers. "Gogarty shot at me last night, in the tower."

"He shot at you?" My astonishment is total. "With a gun?"

"He had Trench, that awful Hiberno fiend, staying. Trench said he dreamt a panther was about to kill him and the damn fool pulled out a revolver and shot a bullet across the room. Not to be outdramatized, Gogarty snatched up the gun and shot at my side of the room, knocking a clatter of pans on top of me where I lay. I knew then I could not stay another night with Gogarty. He's a class of troll, like so many of the men I know, and crazy besides."

I bless myself. "Dangerous is what Gogarty is. It's lucky you're not stone dead, Jim. If I see that craythur I'll give him a tongue-lash like he's never heard."

Jim chuckles and grabs me around the waist. "You look un-commonly beautiful, snapping like a dragon in your white cap and apron, Nora Barnacle. Perhaps when we leave you will pack that little uniform in your trunk?"

I push him off. "Behave yourself, James Joyce."

Jim jigs his legs—he's shook after his ordeal, it's clear; he brings his face close to mine. "Nora, I went to Byrne—the only sensible man of my acquaintance—and asked him if we should go abroad and he said I should not hesitate to ask you and that if you said yes to me, I was to take you as soon as I ever could."

I dip my head; I don't know Byrne at all, but it pleases me that he spoke for me. The hotel door opens and a band of guests wafts out onto Lincoln Place. I will shortly be missed.

"I have to go back in, Jim. If I'm caught idling out here with you, they'll string me. And dock my wages. We'll need every penny."

He puts his hands on my arms, turns me to face the hotel door, and pushes me playfully. "Go," he says. "You've promised to come away with me now and that can't be undone."

"It can't and it won't," I say, blowing him a kiss.

"I knew there was one who understood me," he calls after me as I run to Finn's door; I turn and wave to him before dipping inside.

While I dust mantelpieces, tuck sheets, and clean toilet bowls, my breath freezes for moments at a time imagining two bullets pinging across the tower and the horrible fright Jim got. The peril Gogarty put him in. My insides tumble and throb with relief to know that my Jim is safe and that soon we'll be together properly, just we two, and no one on God's earth will be able to interfere with us. Smiles break across my face as I work and I can't stop them; they come in unbidden waves and I welcome and savor them, along with the giddy ratter-tatter of my heart. We are *going* away! We are going *away*!

EXILE

❦

Dublin
OCTOBER 8, 1904

THE OCTOBER SKY OVER THE NORTH WALL IS EXOTIC AS plum flesh, yellow bleeding to rose. I'm in a borrowed coat—Molly Gallagher's best—for I have none of my own, and I know not if Switzerland is warm or cold. And, though Jim has been to Europe before, he cannot say one way or the other. The gold of the wedding band he bought—and shoved onto my finger outside the jeweler's, not in any church—winks on my finger, distracting me from looking out for Jim below on the dock. His pappie and some of the family will see him off; Jim's father believes he's traveling alone. No one of mine is here to wave to me for I told no one I was leaving.

The air is salt-sweet and cool, the portholes beam light into the dusk. The deck throngs with those aching to stay and those, like myself, aching to go. My legs and my will seem determined to take me farther east and farther again. Away from Galway, away now from Dublin to the Continent, to Zürich, where Jim has secured a teaching post.

Jim comes aboard at last and I see him dip through the crowd, straining his neck to find me where we agreed to meet. "Jim!" I call, waving my hand high over my head. "Jim!"

His face collapses in relief and he comes, drops the trunk he's been struggling to drag, and embraces me.

"This is it now, Nora. *Nulla retrorsum.* No going back."

"Then we'll face forward, my love."

We turn to the open sea and all that lies beyond; standing side by side, we watch twilight descend. Jim's fizzling, giddy, smoking cigarette after cigarette. He tosses the butts to the gulls who keen like mourning women. The boat begins its slow move away from the dock.

"We're off now, Nora."

"Yes, Jim, we certainly are."

We stay at the ship's rail, our backs to Ireland. "Good riddance to the old sow. No self-respecting man stays in Ireland," Jim says. "There is nothing more natural to the Irish than the leaving of their home. All the better to weep for her," he says. My guts churn and I start to cry. "Oh Nora, Nora, have I alarmed you? Are you sad to go, my darling?"

I shake my head. "I'm all right, Jim, I'm grand."

It's not that I'm pained, it's more like a wash of ease and certainty basting my heart. Jim and I are alone together at last. Away from Galway and Uncle Tommy and Mammy. Away from Dublin and Cosgrave and Gogarty, and Jim's pappie and brother, Stannie, and the rest of his large, grasping family. It feels good to leave them all behind on the island.

I weep and the salt of my tears buoys me, as sure as if they were the sea and I a bouncing lump of jetsam. How can I explain that I'm happier than I've ever been? Happy that Jim has let me share this journey, that we will be joined now, if not in marriage, at least in trust. I look at Jim and laugh, tears still bubbling from my eyes. He pulls me close to him and laughs, too. Yes, I'm happy. I am as easy and free and content now as a goose on the wing, looking for a soft place to fall.

MONEY

❧

Paris
OCTOBER 9, 1904

THE TRAIN IDLES INTO GARE SAINT-LAZARE AND IT'S A CAV-
ernous and somber place. It's been a long couple of days, in
London first, to pursue a publisher who didn't want to be netted,
and on then to Paris, long hours of trains and boats, dust and stuffy
heat and cold. The Saint-Lazare station is a gloomy cathedral over
our heads, and I begin to tremble for I'm only now opening my
mind to what we've done. Jim says we're married, but in truth,
we're not, and I'm at his mercy, with not one other soul to protect
me. What scarce money we had between us is all but gone.

Outside the train station, Paris tinkles with wealth: the buildings glint light and women saunter in white dresses, smart and
contained, their children and dogs as neat as themselves. In my
borrowed coat, of serviceable black, I feel a drab, slovenly creature
in comparison. We haul the trunk and suitcase to a park near the
station and I flop onto a bench, clenched all over, and hungry and
fagged from traveling. My courses, too, have me low; my bleed has
begun, it feels, to spite me and make me tireder yet.

Jim drops down beside me and pulls my head to his shoulder.

"I'm that weary, Jim, I'd sleep on a mantelpiece if I was let."

He smokes a cigarette and I can almost hear the churn of his mind. "Sit here, Nora, my darling, and wait for me. I'm going to go and borrow a few bob from my old Paris friends."

I grasp his arm. "Ah, don't leave me, Jim. What if someone tries to accost me?"

"Shout at them in English, Nora. They'll leave you alone."

I look at our luggage. We can't both go and we need money. "All right then," I say.

"That's it, my sleepy-eyed girl. Take your rest and I'll return, quick as quick." He kneels on the ground to look into my eyes and I push a smile onto my face. "You're pale as milk."

"My courses have come on."

"Ah. Your boot is pinching you. That's what my sisters say." He kisses my nose. "I won't be long."

My boot is pinching me. Your boot is pinching you. Those words rollick through my brain like the beat of a train across tracks. My head flops into sleep. *My boot is pinching me. Your boot is pinching you.* I don't know how much time passes; only the noise from carriages and horse-clop keep me half conscious. *My boot is pinching me. Your boot is pinching you.* My head droops like a doll without sawdust and skitters upward when another vehicle passes outside the park. Hunger pangs waken me fully and I hold my stomach and wonder what we'll do for food and I wish for Jim to come back. I count to a hundred, first in English, then in Irish. *A haon, a dó, a trí, a ceathair, a cúig* . . . How will we survive without money? . . . *a sé, a seacht, a hocht, a naoi* . . . Why didn't I put by more money when I was working? . . . *a deich, a haon déag, a dó dhéag* . . . When I reach ninety-three, Jim rambles through the park gate and I let out a whimper of joy.

He comes toward me, flapping three notes. "Sixty francs," he squeaks and lists the names of people he saw or didn't see— Douce, Doctor Rivière, Curran, Murnaghan—and who gave him what. I nod as he recounts their help, but I'm only concerned with the money.

"How much is that really, Jim?"

"Plenty," he says, and the knots that've been tightening in me loosen a little.

We ride a carriage to Gare de l'Est and Paris unfolds around us, a glimmer of a place that I wish to linger in, but we must press on. I send a postcard of the Eiffel Tower to my mother, with a few short words to let her know I've gone abroad. In case she might be fretting.

Jim and I take the night train to Zürich and arrive there on the eleventh of October, a full three days since we left Ireland. And for the first time ever we will share a bed in a place called Gasthaus Hoffnung, which translates, Jim tells me, as the Guesthouse of Hope.

HOPE

❧

Zürich
OCTOBER 11, 1904

I FIDDLE WITH MY GARTER STRAPS IN THE BATHROOM OF THE
Hoffnung, my fingers suddenly useless as sausages. My cheeks
in the mirror are pink, as if from a slapping, but it's just that I'm
hot and agitated, excited too. I unpin my hair so that it cascades
down my back and draw a few noisy breaths to balance me out.

I hope I can be good for Jim, enough for him. We've never
lain together fully and, though we delight each other with hands
and mouths, what will the real thing be like? I shiver. He's waiting for me in the bedroom down the corridor. Jim is no stainless
innocent—he told me about his dalliances with wayward women
in Monto's kips and around Tyrone Street. *But isn't that what unat-
tached boys and men do*, I scold myself, *go to those who lie down for a
living?* Jim did it from a tender age and, though it cut me at first to
think of the baseness of the trysts, I understand why he went. Men
need to have a release, even young ones. Women just have to make
it up on their marriage night.

I often saw those kinds of girls in Galway; we laughed at them,
selling their ripe bodies for bread. Now I know they have hard
lives—dirty auld fellas and eager strips mauling them, morning,

noon, and night. I also know that Jim expects me not to be like those women, to display a certain amount of virtue while satisfying him fully, and I hope I'm able to do just that.

I take up my brush and go at my hair with a mad fury—I need to hurry along. At the sink, I wash days of grime from between my toes and splash soapy water between my legs. The blood of my courses has slowed its flow and I'm glad of it. I hear Jim cough a few times and realize that he's signaling to me. I struggle out of my corset—Jim calls it the breastplate for he's irritated he can never get past it. Over my head I pull the nightgown I bought in Pim's for this very occasion. The smell and feel of the untouched cotton sends a ripple through me that makes me go lax and taut at the same time. I knot my discarded clothes into a bundle and walk the corridor to our room.

Jim has a single candle lit. He's sitting up in bed with a shocked, hopeful look on his face. "Come closer where I can see you, love," he says and I step forward. He holds out his arms to me and recites softly:

> . . . *may these two dear hearts one light*
> *Emit, and each interpret each.*
> *Let an angel come and dwell tonight*
> *In this dear double-heart, and teach.*

"Oh Jim."

I drop my clothes bundle and rush to him; he shoves back the eiderdown for me to crawl in beside him. We fall on each other in a frenzy, hands grasping and mouths finding the best places to land: necks, lips, ears. Our breath comes in joyous pumps, our lungs and mouths doing spontaneous work. Jim rolls me onto my back and slowly lifts the hem of my nightgown from ankle to knee to thigh, all the while keeping his ice-blue eyes to mine. I grin and he smiles back, then he drops his head between my legs. I puddle and swoon when the tip of his tongue reaches the tip of my sex. He sucks, he nibbles, he licks. His groans are heated, animal, his breath and spit hot on me, his tongue now hard, now soft. I buck forward, I guide his mouth and sing out with lust. Jim slides up me and his mouth is on mine, hot and slick and salty, and he has his maneen in his hand, to guide him inside. It doesn't take more than one jolt and he's in and tearing through me. My nightgown is rucked around my neck, half strangling me, and I struggle out of it and Jim's mouth is around my nipple, fast as a starving babe. His suckling swoons my back upward and he pounds farther into me and it's as if his maneen might come out of my throat. We're locked together, the dear double-heart of the poem he said to me, and we buck and thrust until we're both riding the same mad wave, somewhere outside of us but also deep within us, and it's the strangest, most beautiful place I've ever been. I roll him onto his back and straddle him.

"Fuck up, love," I whisper. Then louder I say it. "Fuck up, my lover."

Jim cries out and I feel his flood inside me and I pull back so I will feel its heat outside of me, too, and he clamps his mouth around my breast until I, too, am shuddering like an animal. He flips me onto the bed and slides his naked body down mine, so his face is below again to feel the gorgeous madness breaking through me on his mouth.

We are stilled. Our skin soaked, salted and a-tingle. Our breaths come slower. Jim lifts his head to me and laughs.

"You're my little fuckbird now, Nora."

"That I am, Jim."

I laugh and hold out my hands to him. He slithers up beside me and we kiss and giggle and hold each other, we talk and touch and love through the night until we're altogether spent. We sleep.

WORK

❧

Zürich
OCTOBER 12, 1904

WE CAN'T UNGLUE OUR EYES FROM EACH OTHER AT THE breakfast table. I nearly burn my tongue on the hot chocolate, I'm paying so little heed to everything except the man before me. The crisp and buttery pastries are a mild distraction and we eat a fair few between us, but all the while we stare at the newness we find in each other. Herr Döblin and his staff flicker at the edge of our attention, serving us, tidying tables when the other guests finish their food and leave. After breakfast we tumble on the bed with our clothes still on, kissing and pressing at every scrap of heated flesh we can lay bare without stripping entirely. But, eventually, Jim pulls away and jumps to the floor.

"I hate to leave you, Gooseen, but the world of work calls."

"Don't be long, Jim," I say, flicking up my skirts to give him a flash of my drawers. He leaps on me again and slots a finger inside me making me gasp. He probes his tongue in all parts of my mouth then hops up again and leaves, all groans and grins as he backs out the door.

I know he has to go to meet the man at the Berlitz school, to learn the particulars of his teaching job, but I'm lonely for him already and have nothing truly to do. I sulk on the bed for a few minutes, then I haul myself up and out, to look at this strange city of Zürich.

I dawdle down Bahnhofstrasse and stop to stare at the lavish displays in the shop windows, everything span-new and neatly arranged, breathing riches through the glass. I lean in closer to ogle the things that look good enough to taste: kid gloves flimsy as altar bread; a plum *devoré* velvet gown that I crave as a child craves sweets; hats with grape clusters and plumages a foot high. Jim says they call this "licking the windows" in French and I can see why; my nose is so close to the glass that my breath makes a steam patch. I fashion a *J* in it with one finger and walk on.

I wander and think about Jim, glowing with the memory of our loving. My heart and my sex, both, tighten and slacken in welcome throbs. But it seems to me that, despite everything between us, all regard and all lust, Jim does not know the meaning of love, or what it really is. Oh, he loves me, of that I'm certain but, for all his fancy wordage, he refuses to name what we have as love, he hesitates to define it that way.

Last night, after the first time, he spoke French to me. "*Tu es touchée*, Nora," he said. He had to tell me that it meant I was no longer untouched, no longer a virgin.

"It might be easier to say 'I love you,' less mysterious."

He rolled away. "How you ladies love to talk of love."

"There are different kinds of love, Jim," I said. "Mother love, lovers' love, sisterly love."

That made him shrug and light a cigarette. I've never met such a man for stubbornness in his ideas and positions; if Jim gets hold of a notion, the devil himself couldn't wrestle it from his grasp.

This morning I pressed him again. "Do you love me, Jim?"

"If love is wanting the beloved one to be happy then, I suppose, what we have is love," he said.

"You see, Jim, you said 'beloved.' The word *love* is trapped within the longer word."

A little shrug of the shoulders and I wanted to strangle him, in truth, for not just saying "I love you, Nora Barnacle." If only to settle my heart.

"I want to answer you honorably and truly, Nora, and if you question me, and then don't like what you hear, well, that's your own lookout."

He's a singular man, to be sure, my Jim.

I MAKE MY WAY BACK TO THE GASTHAUS HOFFNUNG AND GO UP to our room, thinking I will rest awhile before Jim gets back and then I'll be ready for him, naked in the bed, as a surprise. But when I open the door, he's here ahead of me, smoking a cigarette by the window. He doesn't turn.

"Jim?"

"There's no job for me in Zürich, Nora. It was all a lie."

I close the door behind me, my heart thumping now. "What do you mean, love?"

"I was conned out of my money by that English agent I wrote to; she had nothing to do with the Berlitz school. There was never a position for me here."

"Damn the woman." I knead my fingers. All I can see is our adventure in Europe over before it even began and me returned to Ireland in shame. I gather my nerve, for his sake and for my own, and go and slip my arms around him from behind. "We'll be all right, Jim."

He turns and places his Turkish cigarette between my lips and I drag hard on it. "We will be all right," he says. "I won't let you down, my little goose." He kisses my forehead. "The man from the Berlitz is sending out a call to their other European schools;

I badgered him until he agreed to do so. I'll be accommodated someplace, he says, he's sure of it."

"Might we be sent back to Paris?" I cross my fingers behind my back.

"It'll be Switzerland or Italy, more likely."

"Well then, that's it, Jim. I don't mind as long as we're together." And I really don't.

"Nor do I, Gooseen." He unpins my hat and lifts it off, the better to kiss my neck and unbutton me from my clothes.

ONWARD

~

Trieste
OCTOBER 20, 1904

JIM SCRIBBLES ALL THE WAY TO TRIESTE ON THE TRAIN—HIS story set in Dublin about a man called Stephen Dedalus—and I look out at the scenery that's better even than a moving picture. The mountains are steeper than those in Connemara and blacker, and the lakes are so flat and glassy it's like you could walk across them. I keep calling out to Jim to look at this wooden house and that snowy peak, but once he's into the writing, he goes off to another place and can barely hear me.

Once more, on landing in the town of Trieste, Jim escorts me through an echoing train station to a park. We have only our suitcase now—Herr Döblin at the Hoffnung in Zürich agreed to mind our trunk.

"Why must I wait in a park again, Jim?" I whine.

"It's best if I go to the Berlitz school alone." He jiggles his hands in his pockets. "Who would have guessed when we left Dublin that we'd end up in Austria, Nora?" he says, his tone light.

I turn my head from him in a sulk. "Are you embarrassed to be seen with me, Jim Joyce?"

He sits beside me. "You know that's nonsense, Nora. It's just that the school is not expecting a married man, so I have to ease the way, that's all."

"Well, you have no wife, Jim, do you?" I want to rile him.

"You know exactly what I mean, Gooseen."

"I suppose," I say. "At least go and buy me a bit of bread before you disappear, to stop my stomach eating itself."

Jim does as I ask, then goes off to the school. I gobble the bread and sit on my bench. A sailor walks by and stares at me and I pull my glance from his. Back he comes and points at his chin.

"What?" I say harshly, hoping my tone will get rid of him. He points again at his face then at mine.

"*Pane*," he says. "*Bröt*."

What is he saying? I shake my head vigorously to dismiss him but once more his finger jolts forward; it mustn't be rude to point at a stranger where he comes from. I swipe at my chin with one glove and a large crumb of bread comes away on it; I flick it to the ground. The sailor smiles and I nod my thanks, but I don't return his smile for he may think I want to encourage him. He frightens me a little, his eyes are needy and sharp. I turn my head away and am glad when he walks off. I watch him go and shift myself on the hard bench for my legs and behind are getting numb.

The hours tick by and no Jim. I watch the shadows of the trees slither and change. No Jim. I observe birds hurry from branch to branch and hear their trills and calls that are like conversations and I long to open my own beak and join in, though my song would be a lonely lament. Still no Jim. I say a Hail Mary, muttering the Latin words the way Granny did, and the nuns in the convent, too: "*Ave Maria, gratia plena, Dominus tecum.*" I repeat the prayer three times in a row, thinking I can make a charm of it and that, on the third go, Jim'll walk through the gate. But, no, there's no Jim.

The air grows cool and dusk descends. I want to cry, but the tears won't get past my fear of this strange place and the bigger fear that Jim won't return to me at all. I'm a woman alone in a strange land and anything might happen to me. Men come to the park to stroll and smoke and talk; some gawk at me like nosy children and I keep my face forward, trying to look as if I've just arrived to the park and mean to leave shortly. I'm so busy ignoring the men that I don't see Jim when he finally dashes up beside the bench, making me jump like a scalded rat.

"Mother of God," I yelp, but I throw myself into his arms. "Where in heaven's name were you, Jim? Don't leave me like this again." And then I notice the sorry state of him, he's wretched. "You look terrible, Jim, where were you all those hours?"

"Oh, Nora, you'd scarcely believe where I was if I told you." His eyes hop wildly in his head. "I was arrested, Nora," he says.

I snort. "Ah now, don't be codding me."

"I swear on my mother May Murray's grave," he says. "I saw three English sailors falling drunk around the Piazza Grande and a carabiniere was shouting at them and they couldn't understand. So, obligingly, I stepped in to mediate for the sailors. The policeman—clever shite—asked me to go with him and the Englishmen to the station to interpret for them and that, Nora, is where Aughrim was lost."

"He threw you in a cell!"

"*Sì*, Nora. *Esattemente*!"

"Oh Jim."

He pushes his hand through his hair. "They summoned the

British consul at my request and he was a typical specimen of that breed: accused me of being a criminal. 'I am a Bachelor of Arts of the University of Ireland,' I said to him. 'I am a teacher of English at the Berlitz school!' Eventually he saw sense but the little slieveen was snotty as bedamned. They're a cold race, the English, Nora, no mistake."

"Such a scrape, my love." I take his fingers in mine and ask what I most want to know. "And what news of your job, Jim? Are we set up with a room?"

He rubs my hands and sighs. "There's no work in Trieste, either, Nora. I've been duped again, curse the lot of them."

"Jesus, Mary, and Joseph." The bread I ate goes to clots in my stomach; I bless myself. Oh, what will happen to us now?

"Stouten your heart, Gooseen. A man named Artifoni who works at the school means to help us. He's a decent fellow, he felt sorry for me, I think, and took me aside to talk and I confessed we were two and that we're unwed. Artifoni says we must say we're married, everywhere we go, to avoid upset."

"We will so, Jim, if that's what needs to be done." I twist the wedding band on my finger and feel a small push of hope. Perhaps the lie will take root and we'll soon be properly wed.

"Artifoni says he'll send me to Pola; he guarantees me a Berlitz job there, though the spokespersons for that school are slippery as eels, as we've seen. Artifoni told me of a boardinghouse we can go to tonight."

"And where's Pola, Jim?"

"Seventy or so miles beyond here, my darling."

My gut bubbles. "It seems we'll never find our settle-spot." I look at him and realize all I can do is trust him, for what choice do I have? I'm at his mercy. "Well, Jim, what's seventy-odd miles when we've come so far?" I say cheerfully, though my insides are curdled.

Jim stands and offers me his arm; he hikes up the suitcase with his free hand. "Good girl. We won't worry, Nora. We'll be right in no time, I promise you."

ARRIVAL

Pola
OCTOBER 1904

W E ARRIVE TO POLA ON A BOAT, THE SUITCASE GAPING AND bulging with dirty clothes for it has to hold Jim's things as well as my own—not that we have much; we're missing the trunk left behind in Zürich—Jim for his notes and papers about the Dublin book that he's writing, me for a change of clothes. Sure, even if we had the trunk, we'd have had to break the lock, for Stannie has not yet sent on the key that Jim so cleverly left behind in his pappie's house. Is it any wonder I sometimes style him Simpleminded Jim?

But the money he now earns at the Berlitz school is good and we're snug in our tiny room in Via Giulia. It has a kitchen and pots and pans so at last I can cook some plain fare rather than relying on the sloppy food here that turns my guts. Jim has to sit up on the bed to do his writing, but what harm? Once he's at it, he's at it and I don't think he'd notice if he was on a raft drifting out to sea when that pen is flying across pages. He wastes a fierce amount of paper.

THE DAYS ARE STICKY, WARM WITHOUT END IN POLA, EVEN INTO the night, and we both suffer from insect bites. No sooner do I feel a pinch on my skin than the spot begins to puff up; I even get bit on my eyelid and Jim says, "You look more like a pirate than ever, Nora."

"I feel like a slug," I reply, squinting and winking at him from my bulgy eye to amuse him. I love to hear Jim laugh. He makes me sick with laughter when he chases the mosquitoes around the room with a candle, trying to burn them out of our life.

"Feckers!" he roars.

"Ah, stop annoying yourself, Jim."

PEOPLE HAVE A PRETTY WAY OF LIVING IN THEIR BUILDINGS ON the Continent. A big door on the street leads to a courtyard and around it are ranged the rooms, up over the storeys. It means everyone has a bit of green to look out on, without the bother of tending it and, also, that the rooms are quiet because the noisy street is far away. Oh, but the heat! Will it ever end? Jim and I sweat like navvies and our new friends, the Francinis, laugh because, they tell us, *il sole*—the sun—is only working part time at the moment.

"You will be ten times hotter yet, Signora Joyce," Alessandro Francini says, "a hundred times! It makes me wonder how you westerners will ever survive the Austrian summer." Francini shakes his head and chuckles to himself; Jim and I dab at our clammy foreheads and inspect our mosquito bites.

Francini works with Jim. Like us, he and his wife ran away to be together and they already have a child, a little boy. Signora Clotilde Francini Bruni has been kind to me, though she only speaks a little English and she shows me how to make a poultice with lemon juice and basil, to paste onto our swollen red bites. I have warmed to her, though we can't say many words that the other will understand.

"I teach you," she says, pointing to her mouth.

"To cook?" I ask. "I can cook Irish food."

"My wife means to help with your Italian, Signora Joyce," her husband explains.

"I'd rather learn it from you than anyone else, Clotilde." She nods happily and shows me how to paste the green muck we've made together onto my bites. It smells good enough to lick off and swallow down. I pat a scoop of basil-lemon mulch onto each bite. "Damn these insects to Hades."

Clotilde smiles. "*Zanzare*, Signora Joyce."

"Mosquitoes," Jim says to me.

"*Zanzare*," I repeat. "*Zanzare*."

PURCHASES

❧

Pola
NOVEMBER 1904

WE'RE LOOKING BETTER THAN WE HAVE BEEN, JIM AND I, despite the absent trunk. I can scrub our things at the sink and the blazing sun has them dry in a finger snap. And, the way the water is here, when I wash my hair it glistens like polished copper. Jim's good pay—£2 a week!—means we have, finally, a bit to spend. I regret not saving a farthing at Finn's Hotel, over all those months, frivoling it away on frocks, hats and gloves, and bottles of lavender and violet water to smell nice for Jim.

Anyway, he looks smart now and I'm better and brighter myself, despite the dress that is ready to fall off me it's that worn. I bought a hair tongs and, as long as I don't burn his scalp or ear, Jim's happy to let me wave his hair, so that it is en brosse in the way of the other gents around the school. He got a new brown suit—on tick—for teaching in and a loose red tie to wear with it. He's going to the dentist once a week; his teeth have been cockeyed since he was an infant, he says, and what better place to get them fixed than the Continent? Jim is stouter from large bowls of minced meat and pasta—he thinks he looks "mannish"—and I'm rounder, too, probably from bread and potatoes for they're all I can stomach most meals.

Jim is extravagant by nature and sees money only as something to be got rid of. To scrimp where I can, I buy a little machine and with it I roll Jim's cigarettes. I have the occasional one myself when I want the peppery pull of the smoke in my throat. For a few pence, I can make seventy cigarettes, with the good Turkish tobacco we like, and Jim is proud of my economy.

Today, I'm lying on the bed with the shutters closed against the broil of the sun, waiting for Jim to get back from teaching. I'm bored and lonely, and I bash my fist into the pillow with annoyance and toss around a bit. I have a few Italian words, thanks to Clotilde, but I find it impossible to arrange them into good sentences. Last night I told Jim I was lonesome and he said, "No one is alone who has a book in their hand," and he gave me George Moore's stories to read. I tried to get through a bit this morning, but it was *not* a satisfying experience, so I tossed the book away.

I hear Jim coming up the stairs. He starts to sing once he enters the courtyard and every day I follow the song into the hallway and up, up, up until he comes into our room. Today he's singing the song about the lost key, so I know Jim is in good form. He flings open the door and belts the last line.

"*Ancora un litro di quel bon!*" He stands and, with a flourish of his arm, props a tiny pair of spectacles onto his nose. "*Ecco!*" he calls and comes closer for me to inspect his face in the dim light.

"You got eyeglasses, Jim!"

"*Pince-nez*, Nora. Pinch-nose." And he takes my nose between his fingers and tweaks it. Then he takes off the glasses and perches them on again, to show me what he means. "Pinch-nose. *Pince-nez*."

"They'll be a great help to you, Jim, and they look very handsome on you too."

He bows. "I thank you, my lady. And what has occupied you since breakfast, Nora?"

I point to the book on the bed. "That yoke."

"Do I detect dissatisfaction with the venerable Moore?"

"The man doesn't know how to finish a story, Jim, so I didn't read any more than the one."

Jim snorts. "Moore no more. Not to worry, my dear, we'll find you a stack of penny dreadfuls." He picks up the book and reads: "'She wished to live for something; she wished to accomplish something; what could she do? There was art.'" Jim squints and repeats, "There was art." He puts down the book. "Nora, this *pince-nez* may just save my life," he says.

ROW

❧

Pola
NOVEMBER 1904

I'M MAKING A FINE STUDY OF IGNORING JIM IN THE CAFFÈ MIRamar. Useless Jim. Bold Jim. Bad Jim. Money-squandering Jim. Last night he didn't come home and I couldn't sleep ten minutes at a time for worrying about him. I made a raggy mound of the bedsheets trying to sleep, but also trying to stay awake to hear his step. I had him out in the bay floating between the men-o'-war; I had him bruised, bloody, and broken in an alley; I had him dead altogether and in a grave and myself abandoned and wretched in Pola, with no family to turn to. He lurched in, drunk, as morning broke, but I was a haggard heap from worrying and I roared at him.

"Where the divil have you been? I was worried sick."

I was relieved to see him, yes, but he was bandy-legged from grappa and whatever else he'd thrown into his belly. Still, at me he comes, falling onto the bed and pawing at my front, as if I'd let him on me in that state.

"My lovely Nora," he cooed. "My only Gooseen. My blue-eyed queen."

"Get away from me, James Joyce," I said. "You're three sheets to the wind and you smell like a midden."

"Oh, the full moniker, the full Joyce," says he. "I must be

in trouble. But you forgot my other names." His head wobbled. "James Augustine Aloysius Joyce. Now, have that for a mouthful. Oh Jaysus." He snorted and tried to kiss me, but I pulled away. "I love you, Nora Barnacle," he said, "oh, how I love my Gooseen."

"Is that so?" I said. "Well, if you did, you wouldn't leave me deranged off my head with worry."

Jim rolled onto his back and, there and then, fell fast asleep. I pushed and poked him but he wouldn't wake so I lay down again myself, annoyed with him, yes, but relieved too that he was back safe. We both spent most of the day in bed and, in the afternoon, Jim had to get up and make our hot chocolate himself, for I refused to rise or talk to him.

Now we're at the Miramar and I'm keeping my gaze straight ahead, on the iron bridge out the window, and he is determined to soften me so that I won't embarrass him in front of the other English teacher from the school, Mr. Eyers, who is due any moment. Eyers is the one, I wager, who happily leads Jim astray; Eyers is fond of absinthe and high talk and he looks at me like I'm dirt on his shoe.

The *Daily Mail* is on the table before me and I would like to pick it up and read, as is my custom at the caffè. But my chest is clamped tight and I'll sit here until Jim apologizes in a way that sounds real, that means something. I feel him press my hand, but I refuse to look down. He waves something in front of my face and I snatch it. A piece of paper with his handwriting. I don't read it. I stare ahead.

"For the love of Jaysus, Nora, will you just look at what I wrote?" he says.

I don't give him the satisfaction of meeting his eye; I hold the paper up before me and read his words:

"I am beginning to tremble, Nora. When we go home, I will

kiss you a hundred times. I suppose I annoyed you by stopping away last night . . . Please look at me as you always do or I will be forced to run up and down the caffè like a rabid dog."

My stoniness cracks and I snigger at the idea of Jim romping through the Miramar like some crazed pup. I keep my gaze forward but slip my hand into his and squeeze it.

"Thank you, Nora," he whispers.

"I was worried out of my brains all night, Jim," I say, unable to keep the fret from my voice. "Don't ever do that again."

"I won't," he says.

"And do you love me?"

"You know well that I do."

I smile at him and lift my newspaper and Jim does, too, and we begin to read.

EXPECTANT

❧

Pola
NOVEMBER 1904

MY STOMACH SWILLS LIKE WATER DOWN A DRAIN AND MY head on the pillow is leaden. I grunt and sigh and tell Jim to get up without me; I know he's itching to get to his writing, anyway, before he goes to the school to teach. Across the pages his hand goes every morning, *scratch scratch scratch* with his nib, and his face takes on a concentrated, faraway look. Now, instead of getting his papers to start, he props onto one elbow and peers into my face.

"Nora, are you all right?"

"That pasta I ate last night, little as it was, is threatening to heave out of my gullet onto this bed," I say, letting out a groan that would rouse a graveyard.

We had gone to the Caffè Miramar to eat because our potatoes ran out and I was too tired to walk from Via Giulia to the market, buy them, walk back, peel and boil them. In the caffè I ate a tiny bowl of *pasta al pesto* and then belched and gurgled all the way home after it. My innards were bad and I felt altogether out of sorts. Now the smell of that pesto comes back to me, and the sharp, green taste of it, and I retch. Nothing comes up.

"I'm in a savage mess this morning, Jim."

"I think you're in a peculiar way, Nora, that's what it is."

"Ah, what do you mean?" Spit pools in my mouth and my whole throat fills with a sourness that is starting to feel familiar; I've had it the last few days. "It must be the food," I whisper. "All that garlic. Or I took something here at home that was on the turn. Milk, maybe."

"Three days in a row? I think not, my love. Don't we buy fresh every day?"

Jim lies back on the bed beside me. His arm brushes against my breast and I shove him away.

"Oh, don't tip off me, my nipples are stiff as pegs."

For once I can't bear Jim to touch me; the thought of his mouth on my breast makes me angry, somehow; the stuff of my nightgown is irritation enough—when it scratches against me, I want to scream. Jim leans close again, his breath mucky from old wine and tobacco, and I lurch away. This time, what little is in my stomach hurls up through me, out of my mouth, and onto the floor.

"Ungh," I cry, sweat oozing between my eyebrows, down my back, under my breasts. "Oh, I'm moidered, Jim. I'm in bits altogether."

Still, I make to rise from the bed to clean the sick, but he gets up first and wipes the floorboards with a rag. I lie back and will myself to sleep for it's only in oblivion that I don't feel unwell.

"Nora, I tell you, you're in a peculiar way."

"Why are you riddling me, Jim? Tell me what's wrong with me."

"For the love of Lucifer, girl, you're pregnant!"

My eyes snap open; I clutch my belly and moan. Oh Jesus, oh God, oh Mother Mary. I don't want him to be right, but as sure as shit stinks, he *is* right.

"Oh, Jim, the poor little one-een. We're not even married and we've barely a pot to piss in. How on earth will we feed a child?"

Jim laughs and sits on the bed. He points to my front and I lift my nightgown out from the neck to look down at my breasts, mauve nippled and taut, and I can't help but laugh, too, though, in truth, I'm well and truly vexed. I can only imagine what Mammy'd say to see me unwed and with a baby on the way.

THE DAYS ARE COOLER. I SIT IN THE COURTYARD SOME MORNINGS and watch the landlady's hen bustle about like a shopper busy at market. It burbles and scuffles in the dirt and hops under shrubs and I wonder if it means to lay. I follow it for I want to see the egg come out. Stannie sent Jim some pages from a midwifery book and they showed a baby inside a woman—as if the stomach had been cut down the middle. The baby was upside down and the writing told, in fancy words, the way the baby gets out.

"Like a bird laying an egg," Jim said, when we studied the pictures together.

"This doesn't look possible," I said, turning the pages this way and that. The pictures seemed to say that the baby's huge head would push through my tiny opening, but how could that be?

I follow the hen now and crouch down. Its feathery backside pulses, as if breathing, then puckers like a bad-tempered woman's mouth and I see the bumhole stretch and start to bulge, pink and wet. I grimace; I don't like the look of that at all. But I can see the top of the egg peeping through, speckledy and skin-colored, and I'm mesmerized. The hen grizzles a bit and pushes, and out plops the egg, quick as quick, and it's wet all over, but within seconds the shell dries and there sits the egg, ready for the pot. A little miracle.

"Well, now," I say to the hen who is burbling away, "you're a marvelous little thing."

I look around to see if anyone else is in the courtyard and if they've seen what I've just witnessed. There's no one. But Jim is home from the school today, propped up on our bed at his writing, and I dash up the stairs to tell him.

"Jim, the landlady has her hen out there and he's after laying a lovely egg."

"*He*!" Jim giggles. "He?" He laughs loudly. "Jaysus, oh Jaysus, Nora, you're a royal entertainment. My funny girl."

"What, Jim?"

"Nora *mia*, we can assume, I think, that the hen is female."

"Ah, what do I care?" I say. "That bird laid a gorgeous egg, all by itself, that's what I know. He just went and did it, easy as that. The same way the baby will come out of me."

Jim pulls me onto the bed and kisses me and it's a heated one, a kiss with hunger in it. He sets his pen down, pushes his writing pages off the bed, and pulls me onto him. His hand up my skirt and in my slit has me dripping in seconds and I move my body over his fingers and we look at each other, ready to begin.

PRIEST

❧

Pola
DECEMBER 1904

SOME DAYS WE'RE PURE IDLE AND THOSE ARE MY FAVORITE days, for the loneliness for company doesn't drag on me then. Today is one of them. Jim has no classes and his writing isn't pressing on him, so we're going to spend the day together. The weather is colder and so, too, is our flat, but we wrap up, prop ourselves in bed with hot chocolate, and Jim sings to me and I sing to him. He has the face of a saint most of the time, but when he's at a song he looks like an angel.

The baby growing inside me has me tireder than ever, but I forget about all that when Jim stops here with me. He's not that fond of the teaching and likes a day without it.

"Tell me again, Nora, about the Galway curate with the wandering paws." Jim can never hear a story only the once.

"All right then," I say. "I was sixteen and working as a porteress at the convent. This priest was new and young, Father Flannery was his name, and he had black curls, like a child's. He came to hear the nuns' confessions and I was always the one who opened the door to him and he'd grin and shake my hand. He had lovely manners." I smile to remember him then, as I first knew him. "Then one day, Father Flannery invited me to come to tea at the presbytery and I agreed, though I knew well enough not to tell the nuns."

"They'd have had your guts."

"Most likely, Jim." I sip my chocolate—it has cooled now and I take a gulp and hold its milky sweetness on my tongue.

"Go on, Nora." Jim puts on his *pince-nez* and leers into my face, with his tongue lolling, pretending to be the priest. "The next bit is my favorite part."

"Don't I know that, Jim Joyce?" I tap him on the nose to stop him acting the maggot. "Well, when I got to the presbytery the fire was blazing and the Father had lovely sugar-topped biscuits all set out and a pot of tea warming. The place had a far finer setup than we had in the convent."

"Go on, go on, get to the part."

"Ah, Jim, let me tell it my own way." I drink my chocolate; he can wait now.

"The priest and I sit opposite but near each other, at the fireplace, and next thing Father Flannery shunts his chair closer to mine until our knees are touching. 'You're an uncommonly lovely girl, Nora,' says he and reaches out to touch my hair. 'Such beauty.'

"'Thank you, Father Flannery,' says I, for it's rude, Granny taught me, not to acknowledge a compliment.

"Then he holds out his arms and says, 'Come here to me, Nora, till I give you an auld hold.' And I've been told, too, never to disobey a priest so I climb into his lap where he wants me and he's crooning 'You're such a lovely girl, a sweet colleen' into my neck and I don't know what to be doing or where to look even."

"And could you feel the cockstand growing beneath you, Nora? Did you rise up to the ceiling on it?" Jim cackles.

I shake my head because Jim knows the story as well as I do. "Father then starts creeping his fingers up my leg, under my skirt, and his hand pauses at my garter then goes sliding up my thigh. My cheeks are burning and I know what he's doing is not allowed, so up I jump off his lap.

"'Oh, Miss Barnacle,' says he, 'is it time for you to leave?' And he has his hand over the bulge in his drawers and he tries to stand up and walk toward me.

"I say, 'Yes, Father. Sister Aloysius is expecting me back to the convent this instant.'

"His face is redder than a turkey's and he says, in a strangled voice, 'If you tell about this in confession, Nora, don't say it was a priest who mortified you. Say it was a man. Only a man.'

"And I nodded and ran from the place and he wouldn't ever meet my eyes after that."

"The dirty old get," Jim says and he's grinning like the newly insane, because he loves to hear of other fellows who tried to have their way with me and failed, for I suppose it makes him feel I'm his and his alone.

CHRISTMAS

❦

Pola
DECEMBER 1904

JIM IS FOND OF HIS FAMILY, ESPECIALLY STANNIE, IN A WAY that I'm not fond of mine; they're close, I suppose, because they grew up jowl to jowl. He writes to his brother often and I watch him now, composing one of those letters at the table, and the way he takes such pains over it and laughs now and then, and mutters to himself. I suppose, because I didn't live in the house with my sisters and brother, they're as strange a crew to me as distant cousins; I don't feel much of a backward pull to them.

"You miss Stannie," I say.

Jim lifts his head from the letter. "He's the only one who truly comprehends my writing and my mind."

"I understand you well enough." I'm put out at not being Stannie's equal.

"You understand me like no other, Nora, in so many special ways, but you don't care a rambling damn for art, my darling."

I shrug my shoulders, a little prickled, though I know he's right. "You and Stannie are highfalutin', Jim, because of your schooling and I'm lowfalutin', I suppose, because of mine."

He sniggers. "There's more than education in it, Nora, but you mustn't fret. You're perfect for me and that's all that matters.

I cannot abide educated women—they're stiff as corpses and their gloom is contagious." He holds out his hands and I go to him and he pulls me onto his lap. "You are another thing entirely. The most precious thing."

"But you need more than me to talk to, Jim. More than your students, too. I know that."

"Don't worry your head, my little goose."

I chew on my finger. "Why don't you ask Stannie to come here?" I say.

Jim drops his head back to look at me fuller. "To Pola?"

"Well, why not? You'd have him to talk to and he's not happy in Dublin, is he? Your father makes him responsible for the whole lot of them at home, it's too much."

He tuts; his pappie's endless scattering of money on drink, and its effect on the family, agitates Jim royally, though not enough to be abstemious himself, it must be said. Though at least Jim's drinking less often than before.

"Maybe I *will* suggest to Stanislaus that he comes. Would he, I wonder? He hates Catholic countries more than I do, he mightn't warm to Austria."

"He'd never fit in the flat," I say looking around.

"Oh but, Nora, I never told you! Francini and Clotilde have offered us a room in Via Medolino. It slid from my mind last night and I meant to say it this morning, but I got distracted."

"Really, Jim? Oh!" Their flat is warm and large; I get a vision of us all there, sharing a table and laughing, and I like that picture.

"Clotilde says it's too cold for you here, in your delicate condition, and they have a free room with a stove in it and even a desk for me to write at. How could I have forgotten? They surely will have another small room that Stannie could take."

"They might," I say, though I'm doubtful. Sometimes Jim just barrels into things without pausing to think much; in one way it's what makes him exciting to be with but, in another, it wears me out. Still, the thought of a stove and the comfort of warming air thrills me. "When can we go, Jim?"

"Anytime, they said. We are welcome anytime."

WE HAVE CHRISTMAS DAY WITH CLOTILDE AND ALESSANDRO Francini Bruni and their darling son, Daniele. I sit at the table and watch their boy play with his toy train on the floor. I look at my bulging belly and ask myself what I'll be like as a mother. I won't be like my own, one who gives her child away and becomes a stranger. Or like Jim's, ruled by her man's fist as much as his tongue. I watch Clotilde jump up every time Daniele expresses a wish for biscotti or the privy. She displays such patience with her son and I wonder if I can be like that, always ready to put the little one before myself, before Jim.

My stomach is fit to burst after our dinner of ravioli and roasted veal, and the briny olives I keep popping into my mouth, and I wriggle in the chair to ease my fullness. We are quiet, wedged with good food and talked out. The only sound is Daniele's wooden train as he pulls it across the tiles. I think of my family at home in Galway and wonder if my mother ever brings me to mind, especially on days like this. I conjure the glow of a flame in every Galway window to welcome the Holy Family and the Child Jesus. I sigh.

Jim stands up. "Blow out the candles," he says.

Clotilde pulls Daniele onto her lap and Alessandro dances around the room and snuffs all but one flame.

"Oooh," I say for the sudden deep dark is enchanting.

Jim hops to the sideboard and I know that he's dousing the plum pudding that Stannie has so kindly sent us with grappa. I hear the strike of the match and slowly Jim turns, his face like a *púca*'s from the blue flames that waver all over the pudding he's holding aloft.

"*Fantastico*," Daniele says, breathing out the word, amazed, and we all laugh.

Jim places the dish before us then runs and gets a pot to cover it with, to extinguish the fire. He cuts fat wedges and, though I'm fit to explode from food and baby and all, I bite into the dark cake and the rich, wet, fruity taste of it propels me to Mammy's tiny house in Bowling Green.

"That, *amici miei*," Jim says, "is the taste of an Irish Christmas."

"*Buon Natale*," Alessandro says, holding up his tumbler of wine.

"*Nollaig shona*," I say, tipping my glass to Clotilde's and pushing away thoughts of Ireland as well as I can.

BIRTHDAY

❧

Brioni
FEBRUARY 2, 1905

JIM IS TWENTY-THREE TODAY. TRULY A MAN NOW. HE LOVES HIS birthday like no other day and I'm more than happy to make a fuss of him. Money is scarce, as we've been eating out every night—I don't like to share Clotilde's kitchen; I seem to bump against her every time I move, and the right pot or pan is always in use when I need it.

We've been dining in the Miramar, and nearby at the Osteria da Piero, where I like the fried fish and the men who sing, wave their wineglasses, and weep a little. But, despite the money that goes on those meals, I've hoarded coins in a stocking to put toward Jim's birthday and, with some of them, I bought a large bar of *torrone*. Even though his teeth are not the best, Jim cannot get enough of the almondy white toffee. And I have a plan for today that I hatched with Fräulein Globocnik, the Berlitz school's secretary, that I will unveil to Jim once I've had my fun.

"Tell me what we're doing, Nora," he mithers, pulling on his boots. "I've a right to know what my own celebration will be like."

"Don't be whining like a gossoon, Jim. You can wait." I whip up my hair and stab pins into it.

"Are the Francinis involved?"

"They're not. Little Daniele's snuffles are keeping them home." I settle the veil over the brim of the new hat Jim surprised me with, that we could ill afford, and put it on. More pins.

"My colleague Eyers then?"

"Yes, unfortunately, though I didn't really want that drip trailing us all day. Fräulein Globocnik invited him. I think he forced her."

"Ah, so we're going somewhere. And with Globocnik, the melancholy androgyne."

"I haven't a notion what that means, Jim, but keep it to yourself because it doesn't sound very complimentary."

"It means Globocnik looks sad and sexless."

"Stop!" I giggle. Though cruel, it's true. But she can speak English—always a relief to me here—and she was kind in the setting up of our day out. I pull on my jacket.

"So, an excursion then?"

"Yes, of course we're going somewhere, Jim, do you think I'd be in this rig-out to sit in?" I twirl for Jim in my dress that at least covers my ankles; with my growing stomach I was beginning to look like a scarecrow in the other one that rode up so unbecomingly at the front. "Will I pass?"

"More than that; you're very lovely, Nora," Jim says.

WE TAKE A STEAMBOAT OUT TO THE ISLAND OF BRIONI GRANDE and it chugs gracefully across the strait; Jim stands by the rail smoking and observing the glassy sea and I sit on a bench and do the same.

"Brioni Grande is famous for cheese," Fräulein Globocnik says and makes no other remark.

I take in her neat gray dress and the way that her skin almost matches it in color; she's a plain woman, to be sure, though she could be a little lovely if she tried. Eyers gawks at her, then resumes staring off into the distance in that brooding way of his. When the fräulein wanders to the rail to watch the water, Eyers slides up behind her and stands very close. I see him put his hand to her waist and she shrugs him off. He sneaks up beside her again and I smile to watch this awkward little pursuit. Then the fräulein turns her head and says something sharp to Eyers and he nods curtly and walks away. I wish he'd leave Fräulein Globocnik be and stop his pestering.

Once off the boat, Eyers, the fräulein, and Jim are determined to see the ruins of the Roman *villa rustica* up the coast but, after a while, I can't walk much farther. I spy a nice flat rock with a view of the bay and I sit.

"I'm going to stop here, Jim, and catch my breath."

"I will stay with you, Signora Joyce," Fräulein Globocnik says.

"No, no, I want to rest my toes. You go ahead with the others." Jim idles by me, too, though I can tell he's dying to walk on. "Off with you," I say, for he loves to look at old buildings and talk of their history with those who know about such things.

He kisses my hand and I watch him saunter on with the fräulein and Eyers and it occurs to me how very much at ease he looks on this white rock in the Adriatic Sea, in his pale suit and hat. He has grown a mustache of which he's very proud and he worries it will tiddle my nose and make me sneeze when we kiss, but I haven't the cruelty to tell him that the mustache is such a wisp of a thing that I can't feel it at all. Jim thinks himself a very pretty man, and so he is, and today there is a gleam of happiness about him.

The fräulein keeps step beside Jim and, in her utilitarian gray, she really does seem rather mannish and I wonder if she loves women as Jim has hinted to me and, if so, what happens when they lie together. Do they crawl over each other's bodies as Jim and I do? Are mouths and fingers enough? I'd miss the hard, sure strength of him and the closeness of the joining of two bodies. Jim's maneen up inside me, and me moving over it, is the nearest to uplifted I've ever felt. I unpin my hat and wave its brim in front of my face though it's a cool day. My thoughts alone often heat me now that I'm with child and I can't get enough of Jim. We tear at each other two and three times a night so that I can hardly walk in comfort, most days, until evening time.

Jim, the fräulein, and Eyers disappear through the spruce trees and I lift my face to the sun, so ever present in this part of the world, and wonder if I really miss Ireland at all. I don't miss the Galway rain and I don't feel any backward pull to Dublin's dirt and the constancy and drudge of the work I did in Finn's Hotel.

Jim told me that Stannie went to Finn's, at his request, to see if they were angry with me for leaving so abruptly, but all they said was, "Miss Barnacle is gone away," as if I had stepped off the face of the planet never to return. But, yes, I suppose that's right: Miss Barnacle *is* gone away and there is a new woman in her place now—I am a wife (of sorts) and a soon-to-be mother. I'm not Nora of Galway, or Miss Barnacle of Dublin. I'm Signora Joyce of Europe. And I find I'm happier than I've ever been to be just that.

JIM'S VOICE, AND A LITTLE LAUGHTER, CARRIES THROUGH THE trees that line the track and presently I see my three companions returning. Fräulein Globocnik sets down her bag and pulls out a square of mackintosh. On it she lays a picnic of cheese, bread, salami, and wine and we all exclaim when she removes yet more— tumblers, tomatoes, and chocolate—from her small bag, which, it seems, can hold a market's worth of produce. Jim sits on my rock beside me, and the fräulein occupies another opposite us; Eyers squeezes in beside her and she flinches but rights herself in a blink.

"Eyers has been teasing me about my competence in Italian, Nora," Jim says.

"Your version of the language is dead, Joyce," Eyers says. "Come into the twentieth century, old boy, and join the living."

I'm affronted on Jim's behalf. "If there's one thing Jim knows, Mr. Eyers, it's words and languages," I say.

"That is quite right, Signora Joyce," Fräulein Globocnik says, and she hands me a glass of white wine and a cut of focaccia. "Your husband learnt his Italian from Dante, he tells us, and a more mellifluous wordsmith a man could not hope to ape."

"Well, I know little of Signor Dante, but I know Jim can get by with his Italian and more." I bite into the bread and, thirsty now, sup from the tumbler of wine.

"Francini is teaching me his superior Tuscan Italian, Eyers," Jim says, "never fear."

"Joyce, you need to leave this backwater and go to Italy. You'll never thrive here. Go to Roma, to Firenze. I have no desire to travel farther for now, but you must go and improve your word hoard. *Presto!*"

"We do all right," I say. "I'm learning Italian, too, from Clotilde Francini. Though I may try French instead for we mean to go back to Paris altogether, don't we, Jim?"

Jim nods but Eyers shrugs and throws his eyes heavenward. He's a cheeky pup, to be sure, and my tongue itches to castigate him. *You may have scant ambition*, I want to say to Eyers, *but Jim and I have no intention of staying in Pola forevermore; it's far too dreary for us.* But I turn away because I don't want to cause a ruffle in Jim's special day.

I keep my gaze to the sea, which glimmers like a jeweled carpet and the sun does her work in heating us nicely. Fräulein Globocnik's tomatoes, soaked now in olive oil and sprinkled with salt, are more delicious than any I've ever had and I thank her over and over for her thoughtfulness with the food and the drink she has brought.

"How extraordinarily good it all tastes," I say.

"Dining *en plein air* vivifies the soul as much as the taste buds," Jim says.

The wine makes my tongue a little sour, but the salty salami softens that and the black chocolate we eat rounds out the whole lot perfectly. I'm getting a little used to the continental food, though there are days when Jim and I talk of nothing but floury potatoes, butter, corned beef and cabbage until we work ourselves into a state of hunger and distress.

The light on the sea sparks and jumps in a mesmerizing show and our silence is content and companionable.

Eyers leans forward and knocks his glass off Jim's. "*Buon compleanno*, Joyce," he says. "May your ink never run dry."

"*Grazie mille*," he answers.

"*Alles Gute zum Geburtstag*, Signor Joyce," the fräulein says.

"Many happy returns, Jim," I say and tip my glass to his.

He smiles and kisses the tip of my nose and I can tell that for Jim the birthday outing to Brioni Grande has been a big success and that makes me extraordinarily glad.

RETURN

Trieste

MARCH AND APRIL 1905

"NORA, NORA!"
        Jim's shout carries up the stairwell and I climb off the bed to see what's making him roar like a sailor. I get to the door and he rushes toward me.

"What? What is it, Jim? Is somebody dead?"

"No one's dead, my morbid Gooseen. Nora, we're going back to Trieste!" He giggles and twirls me around.

"Are you codding me, Jim? Why? What's happened?"

"Oh, we'll be out of this hole-in-the-map place at last." He waltzes me about the floor. "Away we'll go, my Nora, far from this naval Siberia."

I stay our dance. "Did you lose your job, Jim? Tell me now if you did."

"Nora, you faithless creature. I did not. I'm to teach at the Berlitz in Trieste."

My throat clenches—we're to move again and this time with a baby coming soon. Clotilde will be here and I will be there. Who will help me? "But why, Jim? Why now?"

He frowns. "I thought you'd be delighted, Nora."

"Of course I am, Jim, of course I am." I smile broadly, though the thought of getting used to another new place is a little wearying. "I suppose we've been hoping to get out of Pola. Isn't your writing all bogged down and maybe somewhere new will make that better?"

"It will, my darling."

"But what's changed?"

"Francini says there are rumblings about an espionage ring here in Pola and the Berlitz chaps think it safer to get all foreigners out tout de suite and that means us. And Eyers and the Francinis, too."

"Clotilde will be in Trieste, too? Oh, that's mighty." I fix my rumpled dress. "I declare to God, Jim, you couldn't be up with them, could you? Spies in Pola, no less."

"Ah, it's just an excuse for the damn Austrians to exert power."

My head is still a bit muddled, but Jim seems so buoyed up that I'm determined to think well of this change too. I smile, forcing myself to quash all worries about moving, about the baby, about spies. Clotilde will still be in my life—that will be a comfort in the new place.

"Jim, it will surely be better for us to be back in Trieste." I love novelty, don't I? Always new things excite me. "Won't it be an adventure more than anything else to try somewhere different?" I say. What little I saw of Trieste charmed me—the handsome Piazza Grande, the Miramare Castle. "It will all be grand, surely? The Francinis will be close and our little one-een will be born there, too, my love." I rub my belly and Jim nuzzles his face into it the way he likes to.

"He certainly will."

WE'RE LODGING WITH SIGNORA MOISE CANARUTTO, A LOVELY Jewess on Via San Nicolò, Trieste. And the Francinis are here, too, and it's good to have Clotilde nearby for she has promised to help with the baby when it comes. Questions bubble up in me, things I want to ask her—womanly things—but my Italian is not good enough yet, so they'll have to wait.

Things are the finest, save for the curse-of-God heat of the place. Even inside our room, the swelter crawls under my hair and into my armpits and wraps itself around me like the bindings of Lazarus. My ankles are fat as hams and my fingers so bloated that I can't bend them. Jim goes to work at the Scuola Berlitz next door and I lie all day on the bed, like the wreck of the *Hesperus*, moaning and groaning. If the vast, ungainly weight of my body doesn't kill me, the Trieste sun surely will.

"It's one hundred degrees outside," Jim says when he comes home to me at lunchtime. He mops at his face with his shirttail. It's unlike him to be so slovenly, but we're both upended. "And the bora is only making it worse."

The bora is what they call the mad-wind and it blows year-round, on unpredictable days; but it doesn't cool the sun's glare, like you'd expect. The Triestini love and respect their wind, which makes me think they're all as crazy as the bora itself and that soon I will be too.

"I'm going insane, Jim," I say. "This city and its heat is making an imbecile of me."

He sits on the side of the bed. "Might it not have something to do with the baby inside you, Nora? Don't women get turned about when carrying a child?"

"I don't know, Jim," I wail. "What do I know of women or womanhood or any of it? I have no one to talk to. No one to ask questions of."

"Oh my Gooseen, my pirate queen, my sleepy-eyed girl. It will all come right."

His sympathy only makes the tears drop from my eyes, cascades and waves of them that I don't even bother to brush away. My front is permanently wet from crying and my cheeks are scalded.

"If only," I sob, "I could escape from my body, for ten minutes even. I wish I could unhook the baby and set it down, so that I could walk in peace, and sleep, and feel light again. It's like living with an anvil strapped to me, Jim." I wipe the snot from my nose with the back of my hand. "I can't escape the heat or my body. Each way I turn, the great lump of myself is in the way."

Jim takes me in his arms and holds me and croons; I know he cares greatly, though he worries that my distress and sadness will bring forth a morose babe. And I fret that if I can't stop the waterfalls of tears, he will get fed up and leave me altogether and then who will I be?

WE GO OUT TO LIFKA'S BIOSCOPE TO CHEER US UP, WE'RE BOTH fond of moving pictures and it's cheaper than the theater. The oppressive heat has died down a bit as it's evening and I feel a little calm walking through the Città Vecchia to get to where the traveling cinema has set up. We can hear its huge pipe organ chirruping a tune from far off and the city feels festive around us, with other couples walking arm in arm and talking in low voices.

"Are you all right, Nora, my love, not too tired?"

"I'm grand, Jim."

Up to Lifka's we go and the usual dancing girls go about their movements outside before we're let in for the show. I watch their slender bodies dip and plunge, and I long for the time when I'll be like them again—able to bend any old way that's needed, instead of huffing around, slow and heavy, like a bloated crone.

The doors open, we take our seats, and the film starts at last. I'm amazed, as I always am, at how the people are up on the screen before us, moving about, and yet they're not here at all. This story is about a girl whose wretched man is fluting about the town with every Sally or Mary that comes along, embracing and kissing them. He thinks nothing of her, stuck at home with thoughts only of him. In a scene where they're out on a walk, the blackguard throws the poor lass into a river, no less, and runs off, followed by a crowd and an angry carabiniere.

"Oh, policeman, catch him," I roar out, rising from my seat. Jim pulls me back to sit and he's laughing but I'm indignant. "That horrible man will need to be put away, Jim, no mistake."

"He will, Nora," he says, "don't worry, the villain will get his comeuppance."

When the show is over we walk as far as the Caffè Pirona but since the Berlitz in Trieste pays less than the one in Pola, we can only have one little treat before heading home. For the moment, I'm content to sit and swallow my lemon gelato and thank the Lord that Jim sticks by me, in spite of all my griping. I try not to moan and groan, but I'm finding it lonely here and hard. I was just getting used to Pola and everything feels entirely different again.

After the Pirona, we walk back through Trieste, the sea lapping in the port, and I see the beggar boy who we often spy near the church. His dark currant eyes and his hair, all sticking up like feathers, always pull on my heart. I slip the fellow a coin.

"We have little enough, Nora," Jim grumbles.

"He's only a baby," I retort and the boy looks up at me and there's a blank sadness in his face that makes the well of tears start to gush again.

Jim steers me away. "What is it, my love?"

I gesture to the boy. "It's him and it's our own babe, it's the heat and the lack of money, and that I've no one to ask about the aches and pains of being pregnant, and oh, all of it, Jim." I use the back of my glove to soak up tears. "We have so little to live on. I thought we'd have a wee place of our own, somehow. I want a home, I don't like being up on top of other people all the time. And I don't want any child of mine to be so reduced as to have to beg on the street. That boy is somebody's son," I say, glancing back.

"No son of ours will have to be a beggar, Gooseen, I promise you that." He squeezes my waist and looks serious. "We are not, perhaps, living the easy life we hoped for, Nora, but when my book is published, we'll be high on the hog."

"Will we? I hope so, Jim." I want so much to trust him.

CLOTHES

❧

Trieste

JUNE 1905

THE WOMEN AT MARKET ARE MEAN-SPIRITED AND BAD. THEY bark at me if I touch their produce, and because my Italian is faulty, sometimes they won't serve me at all, unless Jim is there to snap back at them in their lousy Triestine dialect. I refuse to shop anymore, so Jim buys our bread and chocolate and cheese and, otherwise, we eat out, though it's costly. Some days, when Jim is too busy to come home, I take lunch with the Canaruttos and pay a few coins to the signora for it. Money worries are our constant companions.

It's not just the market sellers who are nasty to me—Mr. Eyers likes to upset my heart with his tittling tales of ladies that Jim is attentive to at the Berlitz school. I let on I'm not bothered but, alone all day, my mind turns in on itself. And when I go out walking, to distract myself, I see women on the street nudge each other and giggle about my clothes, which I know have little style. But what woman looks her best when she is low on coins and heavy as an ox besides? They look at my belly as if it's an obscenity and tut loudly. That only makes me stick my stomach out more and my lip with it. Still, I like to present myself well and I long for the baby to come so I can buy a pretty white lace frock, like all the ladies here wear, and a huge straw hat to match. Jim will surely have sold one of his books by then and we'll have plenty rattling in our pockets.

Jim is mortally upset with the Richards fellow in London who guaranteed he would publish Jim's book of poems then, just as promptly, decided he wouldn't. But the stories are coming along well, Jim feels, so with luck we'll have money soon that I can spend on making myself smarter. By our calculations the baby will come in August, so there's not too long to wait.

Today, for economy, I'm attempting to cut out and sew baby clothes; Jim's aunt Josephine—a second mother to him—sent me patterns. But the thin paper sticks to my sweaty fingers and rips when I try to pull it away and I prick myself with the pins so often that my blood stains the material and my howls would wake the divil himself. I'm not a natural dressmaker and bending over the table has me tired, stiff, and crabby. I'm hungry, too. Jim is to bring me a bit of lunch today and he's nearly an hour behind time and I'm very cross.

When he finally arrives, he finds a heap of patterns, material, and pins on the floor and me prostrate on the bed in frustrated anger.

"Where were you?" I growl.

"One of my students wanted to talk over some finer points. I didn't see the time going."

He sits on the bed and I lean in and sniff. "Were you drinking?"

"The young man took me for a glass or two. I couldn't refuse."

"No, no, never mind that your wife is starving to death," I sneer. "Have your wine!"

"Now, Nora, I need to keep friendly with these students."

"Friendly, is it? Like the way you were friendly with that young Anny, the banker's daughter?" He flinches. "Ah, you see, you think I know nothing, Jim Joyce, trapped here like a fat old milk-cow. Well, don't you forget that Eyers loves to talk out of turn and is only too happy to whisper to me in the Pirona about which signorina has lately been catching your eye."

He snorts. "And you'd believe that English bastard above me?"

"I know who you are, Jim Joyce, and what you are. Remember that." I fold my arms across my belly.

"How dare Eyers try to poison you. And in your delicate condition." Jim grabs my two hands and holds them tightly. "He's an ignorant clot, Nora. Why just yesterday he sidled up to me and in that horrible twitchy voice of his says, 'You know, Joyce, it amazes me the way eccentric people dress. If you have no taste, stick to gray, old fellow, it always looks gentlemanly.' Then he winked, the brat. Like all English, he has no manners."

"Well, the dirty skite. No taste, indeed. You're a finer-looking fellow than him by a long mark, Jim."

"Pay him no mind. He's a shit-stirrer of the lowest stamp."

"He is, Jim, that's all that can be said for him. And the less shit in the pot, the faster he'll stir."

He giggles. "Now, my dear, after that fine analogy, I will serve you your lunch."

"My stomach thinks my throat's been cut, Jim. I'm famished!"

I fall on the bread and mozzarella he has brought—the high temperature has me off hot food—and I munch a tomato like an apple, the juice washing down my chin. Jim fills a glass with beer for it's the only drink that doesn't give me gullet pains. When I'm sated, I sit up on the bed and sigh, a little sleepy now. Jim kisses my closed eyes, now one, now the other, and leaves me to go back to the school.

CLOTILDE SHOWS ME HOW TO MAKE MY SEWING BETTER AND I'M grateful for her help. She cut the patterns for me and we sit in a shaded spot in the Canaruttos' courtyard to fashion two smocks for the baby. A few birds keep up a lazy to and fro in the trees, but otherwise it's quiet. Clotilde examines my sewing, rips back a bockety line, and shows me again how to keep the stitches tight and small.

"*Piccoli e precisi*," she says, pointing to her fine work.

"Ah," I say, demonstrating that I understand with a few improved jabs of my needle.

She looks at the new line of stitches. "*Perfetto*, Nora." She rolls the *r* in my name so prettily that I try it myself.

"Norrrrra." It doesn't sound like her way of saying it. "Norrrrra."

Clotilde laughs and repeats my name, "Norrrrrrra," dragging out the *r* so much that she sounds a little crazed. We laugh together and I think it's lovely to have a friend to stave off the loneliness that some days threatens to smother me, even if we can't chatter and gossip properly as I did with my friends at home.

"*Grazie*, Clotilde," I say, holding up my half-finished baby smock.

"*Prego*, *bella* Nora," she answers and we smile at each other for a moment before bending our heads again to our work.

MELANCHOLY

⌒

Trieste

JULY 1905

JIM HATES HIS JOB. HE WANTS NOTHING MORE THAN TO LEAVE it. And, after the refusals from Richards, the publishers, and the other crowd, Lane, he was sure the one called Heinemann would bring out his book of poems, but he has heard now that they will not. Jim grows weary of waiting for the time when he'll actually have a book of his own; his poems are wonderful and he deserves that accolade like no other, it's what he dreams of.

Tonight we're both as morose as two ewes robbed of their lambs. Nothing cheers us. We don't even talk of home comforts, or of Irish food that we miss, or of any plan or scheme to move to Paris. Jim sits at the small table, his ink bottle and pen to hand but he writes not poem nor letter nor story. His *pince-nez* dangles on its chain and he stares ahead of him at nothing at all. The sweat rises on his forehead faster than he can dab it away and he has a second handkerchief tucked into his collar to protect it. I'm in chemise only, for the heat presses on me like a clothes iron, but even the lace neckline annoys my skin.

"It was an experiment to move here, Nora. Have we failed?"

I could give him a maudlin reply, but instead I say, "Of course not, Jim." I push out my belly. "Look what we've managed." He smiles but it's a wan attempt, made with effort. "And you've written those three new stories and all those pages on the novel. *And you teach eight classes a day.*"

"Also, let's not forget that I've swindled a tailor." He pulls at his lapels. "And acquired glasses and a watch." Jim pouts his lip. "Still, Nora, my salary is only fit for a stoker and I'm afraid this damnable heat will turn us both stark mad before long."

I rise from my misery bed and go to stand behind Jim; I put my hand to his shoulder and he covers it with his own and sighs from a place of deep melancholy. It's bad enough that I'm low in myself without Jim being dragged to the same place; it hurts my heart to see him so downside-up. One of his poems, that I've taken pains to memorize, comes to me and I recite a bit for him:

> *O' Sweetheart, hear you*
> *Your lover's tale;*
> *A man shall have sorrow*
> *When friends him fail.*
> *But one unto him*
> *Will softly move*
> *And softly woo him*
> *In ways of love.*
>
> *His hand is under*
> *Her smooth round breast;*
> *So he who has sorrow*
> *Shall have rest.*

The last words seem to hang in the air between us so I say them again: "He who has sorrow shall have rest." When I bend to look into Jim's face his eyes are wet.

"For the first time in a long time, I feel like a poet," he says. "Thank you, Nora."

"You're a beautiful writer, Jim," I say. And he is, though truly some of his stories baffle me as much as the Moore fellow's ones. But, it seems, some of my own stories live within Jim's writing. It's a queer feeling, but is he not entitled to take parts of me and mold them for his good use? Especially if it will get him a book published and move us along in this life.

Jim turns and lies his head on my belly. "Lovely babby-house," he says.

"It's like a big egg," I say.

"It is." He lifts my chemise and kisses my bare skin. The baby shifts inside as if in response. "Look, she knows it's you, her daddy."

"Hello, baby, this is your babbo," Jim coodles into my stomach. "We're waiting for you, little one. Will you be Lucy or will you be George?" Jim has chosen these names—Lucia for light and George after his poor dead baby brother and I'm happy to let him do the choosing. He sighs again.

"Is there a way, Jim, that you could leave the job at the Berlitz?" I ask.

He stands and leads me to the bed and we both sit up on it. "Not until I secure something else, Nora. Not until I get a publishing contract for either the poems, the stories, or the novel." He lies back and shuts his eyes; they've been bothering him more lately. "It's not the students I dislike, though some are stupid, it's the way we're supposed to teach them, the speed of it, the crudeness. I get bored and angry, enunciating daft sentences in English like some mad school cleric. All I'm missing is the twitchy stick. Even without it I'm afraid I'll clout one of the students someday out of pure boredom."

"But you're glad we're not in Dublin, Jim?"

He's silent for a few moments. "I am, I suppose, though sometimes I wonder. I left Ireland to get away from convention and here I am, a conventional teacher barely able to live on my conventional pay." His voice rises. "All I want, Nora, is to dip my pen and write tiny little sentences. All I want is for you to be happy and comfortable too."

"I'm a burden to you, Jim, with all my lamenting and moaning."

"No, no. It is I who complains the most. But would it suit you better to go home, Nora? Not west to Galway but to Dublin, maybe? I've been thinking that Stannie might share a little cottage with us, to defray costs. A little place in Chapelizod, perhaps, by the river."

"We could eat leg of mutton every night, Jim, with buttery carrots and turnips. And I'd put a black kettle over the fire and watch it boil. I'd love that—to watch a normal kettle at its work."

"And Stannie and myself would talk the way we used to, not in the irritating, circuitous way that letters afford."

"You lack good company, Jim, and I'm sorry for it."

"I do and I don't," he says, squeezing my hand.

"Oh, Jim, if we were in Dublin, I could walk about in comfort on my own, not like in Trieste where everyone gawks and gossips about one another."

"It's the Triestine way; in Dublin they pull you down behind your back."

"Well, they know we're not from here and I hate the way they stare and mutter."

"My lovely Gooseen, why did I bring you here? I don't think you're a plant that can be safely uprooted and moved; I fear I've damaged you." He throws his arm across me and nuzzles his face into my stomach. I push his chin upward so he can see me.

"Now, Jim. In truth, if we were to return to Dublin, how

would we fare?" I imagine us there, the Joyce family all around, sitting up on us and whatnot. My mother, too, perhaps, coming to Dublin to try to lure me home to Galway. "Just think, Jim, if one priest got an idea that we weren't married. Well!" I shake my head. "At least here no one knows us and we're free to be ourselves; there's a lot to be said for that, isn't there? We're getting used to it a little, aren't we?"

Jim nods. "Stannie told me that when Pappie learned your name was Barnacle he said 'Well, she'll cling to him anyway.'"

I snort. "Did he now? It's easy to see where you got your wit."

"Oh, but it's I who must cling to you, my darling Nora, for I know you'll be the making of me."

"Hush now, Jim. We'll get along together. What will be will be." I tuck my arm into his and we lie and doze and the great heat of the day begins to lessen in the twilight around us.

BABY

⁓

Trieste
JULY 27, 1905

TODAY I'M LUNCHING WITH THE CANARUTTOS; JIM HAS A half day at the Berlitz and he means to go to the baths for a swim after teaching. The signora knows that I can't stomach much these days and she gives me small portions of her bean stew or balls of mozzarella with bread; that way I can finish the food and she won't take offense at anything uneaten. This afternoon she serves a sweet sausage dish with thyme and I eat a little, but the indigestion that plagues me these days is worse than ever and I can manage no more than a few mouthfuls. The tight, full feeling in my neck has moved lower and I feel as if I were in the clasp of a huge snake that's determined to wring the life out of me. I push away my plate and stand up.

"*Grazie*, Signora Canarutto," I say, and I mime sleep by folding my hands under my cheek.

"*Prego*, Signora Joyce," she says and flaps her hands to let me know she understands that I'm tired and that I should go.

In our room, I pace the floor for when I sit pain rises up inside as if it means to choke me. I'm surprised when the door opens and Jim comes in, jacket slung over his shoulder.

"Are you not off for a swim with Eyers?"

"The damn man is nowhere to be found. Typical of that slithering Jaysus. I didn't want to go alone."

I stop pacing to grip the back of a chair. "My lunch is dancing like the fires of hell in my gullet, Jim."

"Sit awhile, Nora, take some rest."

"It's no use. When I sit down the pain runs right to here." I put my hand to the underside of my stomach.

"Oh," he says and frowns. "Might you take the weight off your feet anyway, for a moment, to see if it stops?"

Jim helps me onto the bed, lifting my poor swollen legs and putting two cushions behind my back. Another pain bands my body and reaches such a height that I grunt loudly.

"I'm all right," I tell Jim, for his face is creased with concern.

"Do you think it might be more than indigestion, Nora?"

"What else could it be?"

"I don't know. Something to do with the baby, perhaps?"

"Amn't I more than a month off my time, Jim?"

"I suppose."

Another spasm and I belch, but it brings no relief. I try to roll onto my side, groaning as I do so, for some instinct tells me that I will be more comfortable if I can only get onto my side. Jim now begins to walk the room, a thing he does in times of high agitation; I watch him worry his mustache with his fingers and clip back and forth.

"You'll wear a hole in the signora's floorboards," I say.

"I'm concerned about you, Gooseen. You seem very unwell."

"It'll pass, Jim. Doesn't it always?" Another cramp and I gasp, for it hurts in a way it hasn't before.

Jim grabs his jacket. "I'm going to get Signora Canarutto."

And, before I can stop him, he's gone. I must doze a few moments because the next thing I know the signora and her two grown daughters are in our room, clucking above me like poultry over a chick. They speak in Italian with Jim.

"The signora wishes to examine you, Gooseen."

I begin to nod my consent, but my skirt and petticoat are already being lifted and she puts her hands to my bare stomach. Just as she does, another of the burning cramps takes hold and I grind my teeth together until it is gone. Signora Canarutto covers me again.

"*Sì*," she says to Jim. "*Sì*," to me and waggles her fingers comically, smiling like a loon.

I look to Jim.

"The baby is on its way, Nora. Early, but definitely coming." He shrugs but looks frightened. "The signora is sending for a midwife she knows, a Signora Scaber. And I'll get Sinigaglia to come, the doctor, one of my students."

"All right so." I'm glad that Jim is taking charge for I can't budge an inch or make a decision. I'm not ready and not sure I'm able but, if the baby means to come now, so be it.

I watch the Canarutto women get the room cleared for the midwife by lifting our table and chairs out of the way and setting them along the walls in an efficient dance. They chatter quietly in Italian and, despite the coming and going pains, I seem to float above the scene like an angel peering down to earth.

JIM IS SENT AWAY FROM OUR ROOM TO HAVE DINNER WITH THE Canarutto men. The signora and the midwife stay with me. They talk a little, but I can only understand the odd word and, anyway, my mind and body are joined now in a vast downward thrust. It's as if I'm the only living thing and all I have to do is this great work of getting the baby through me and out. The task is mighty and I'm tired but, also, there's a great wedge of determination inside me, a great desire to work through the pain and come out the other side. My body seems to know its own way and I kneel up on the bed or lie on it with eyes closed letting each attack gather then retreat. The midwife has me breathe through my mouth—in and out—and she pants along with me to show me how.

"Hee-haw," I go, mimicking her like a donkey, but she's a firm and kind woman and I'm glad of her beside me, helping me along. "Heeee-haaaaaw."

Now my body tells me that I need to move off the bed and I grip the footboard and rock myself through pangs that threaten to keel me over. The spasms band the body like the hoops on a barrel; they press into me and down through me and, though they scorch my very core, I don't cry out. Low grunts seem to serve me better and so I huffle and snort like a sow and, by containing my noise, I seem somehow also to contain the worst of the thunders of pain.

"*Brava*, Signora Joyce," the midwife mutters and I catch her eye and nod. "Hee-haw, hee-haw."

Signora Canarutto comes behind me and rubs the small of my back with her fierce little hands. I'm grateful to her for it seems to ease me. I wade through what seems like hours, the crescendo of the pain and exhaustion finally getting me back onto the bed, the urge to push upon me. I hunker and hold the top of the headboard and I bear down with all my force and the midwife babbles in Italian and I think it's a little comical that she has so much to say, that she's trying to instruct me, but I can't understand her.

"Get Jim," I say, thinking he could translate but the signora shakes her head.

"No, no," she says and I realize the time for talking is over.

A knock to the door signals that Doctor Sinigaglia is here. He is a clean, crisp man despite his impossible name and he says little. He murmurs with the two women and I ride the crest of another cramp while the one behind it builds. They signal to me to turn my body and they begin to help to get me onto my back for, the midwife mimes, the doctor must look between my legs. I'm halfway into position when I feel an almighty rip and burn, I whimper and flop onto the bed, my back arched, and there comes a huge, searing tug. The next thing I know the doctor is holding high the baby and it's covered in lumps of lard over skin as purple as a plum.

"*Un bel maschio!*" Signora Canarutto cries out.

The baby bellows; I clap my hands and laugh. I have given Jim a son, a fine Irish gossoon.

BOY

❧

TWO TELEGRAMS GO WEST TO IRELAND, ONE TO DUBLIN, ONE
to Galway.

"Son born Jim."

"Son born Nora."

There is little else to say. Our Giorgio is here and his mamma
and babbo are very happy about it. I have plenty of milk and the
baby stays clamped to me most of the day—greedy, like all men.
He has a pretty little snout and slender, soft fingers, so tiny I'm
afraid to bend one but, then, his own grip is mighty when he grabs
a finger and holds on. Giorgio's face is pink like a boiled ham, but
the doctor said he will gain his natural color soon. His eyes are
dark blue like mine and it's odd and lovely to see my own eyes in
his darling little face.

Jim holds the baby and sings to him, the aria Sinico wrote
about San Giusto, "Viva San Giusto! Viva San Giusto!"

I join in on the "Viva, viva" and watch them, father and son,
face-to-face, the one serenading, the other focused and calm and
wise as an ancient one, and my chest expands with love. If only it
was always like this, if only Jim always stopped in with us in the
evenings, instead of traipsing from taverna to caffè.

Georgie doesn't cry much, for which I'm grateful; Jim says his poor dead baby brother, George—after whom we've named our son—cried a tornado, but he was sickly always and that might account for it.

"Giorgio listens so attentively," Jim says, "he's taking it all in."

"No doubt he'll be a singer like you, Jim."

"And like Pappie in Dublin too."

The doctor says I must rest a few days more before taking Georgie out in the pram that Clotilde has so kindly lent us. I will have to finish stitching his bonnet so that the sun will not broil his precious head.

I SIT PUSHING A NEEDLE THROUGH LINEN AND TAKING BITES OF A jammy hunk of bread, taking care not to make the material sticky, which involves frequent stops to lick my fingers. My appetite has returned and it's glorious to once again enjoy food. Jim's here, not out at some taverna, for which I'm grateful; he's at the table, answering a letter from his brother.

"What does Stannie say?" I'm keen for some good wishes about the baby from Ireland, for no doubt none will be forthcoming from my own family.

"Read it for yourself."

I take the pages and go through them fast. I'm disgusted. "But it's all about your novel, Jim. He barely mentions Georgie or me."

"Look there, Aunt Josephine sends her congratulations. She writes 'Brave Nora.' And doesn't half of Dublin know we're parents now? Cosgrave sends blessings and Skeffington, too. All my old pals know."

"Bloody Cosgrave and Skeffington. Who cares about them?" I lift the bonnet I'm making for Georgie again and poke my needle into it in anger. I'd been hoping for questions from Jim's sisters at least, as to the size of Georgie and his eye color and whether he takes his milk well, but it seems they have no interest in their nephew.

"Nora, you mustn't sulk over other people's lack of care. Didn't Curran send us a pound? Isn't that a more practical way of showing support?"

"And why does Curran need to send us a pound, Jim? Is it to cover the price of absinthe and wine and grappa in every caffè you pass in the Città Vecchia? Is it for you to lash around in the taverna with your sailor pals and pour drink down their necks, too?" I throw down my sewing. "That pound may have been sent for all of us, but it certainly won't benefit Georgie or me."

"Calm yourself, Gooseen. That money will cover some of our many expenses."

"Don't 'Gooseen' me, Jim Joyce. We wouldn't need Curran's pound if you stayed in of a night instead of gallivanting all over Trieste like some kind of prince."

"Prince, is it? I'm far from that, I tell you." He laughs.

My fury rages and pushes me out of my chair. "Don't dare laugh at me, you scut. How do you think it feels for me having to send word to Alessandro Francini to go out at night and find you to fetch you home? How do you think I get on, here by myself with a span-new baby, fretting and worrying over your safety while you get drunk with seamen and peddlers and probably whores for all I know? Do you think I enjoy it?"

He stands to face me. "Nora, keep your voice down, you'll disturb the Canaruttos."

"I don't care, Jim Joyce, if I rouse San Giusto from his tomb. You need to stop squandering *our* money in every caffè in this city and mind that you have a wife and a child, a *family* to look after now."

"I'm working ten hours a day, Nora, at that pit of a school, though teaching repulses me. When I'm not up to my neck in moronic students, I try to write." His voice rises. "There are only so many hours a man can apply himself. Perhaps you think I should stop writing and give all to commerce?"

"Well." I clamp shut my mouth because, even though he has little luck with the writing, I also know that it keeps him sane, somehow. Steady. I know that things would be worse if he gave it up.

"Jaysusin' God, Nora, I only have a little drink to ease me; my life is not uncomplicated, you know. I came here to be free, so that we'd *both* be free of Ireland's curses. My mother died because of Irish social virtues, strangled by church and state alike—I don't want that for you. But here I find I must work like a madman, teaching English at such a gallop that there can be no delays for elegance. It bores me and I despise it, but it must be done for us merely to survive. It's not exactly what I had in my mind when I made the plan to come away. I feel as if life has been interrupted and there is no chance of undoing that interruption."

He sits on the edge of the bed and I go to him; I thaw. "None of it's simple, Jim. Not the leaving nor the arriving nor the living. But we have each other and we have Georgie and that's a life too. We must get along. We have to get on with it."

"We do, I suppose."

I take his hand and kiss the knuckles, each one in turn. "I don't mind you having the odd jar, Jim. That's normal for a fellow. But you must remember always that we're straitened and, until you sell one of your fine books, we'll be low on funds. We're both of us given to spending, it's true, but the money has to be made, saved, and used for things we truly need."

He kisses my nose. "It does. I will stop home more, Nora. I promise you, my Gooseen, my love."

IN THE END, BECAUSE JIM DOES NOT STOP HOME MORE, AS PROMised, I have to take in washing to earn a few lire. Soiled rags, chemises, blouses, towels, trousers, pinafores, socks, vests, sheets, and petticoats. I keep Georgie by me in the pram in the courtyard and, in a dolly tub, I scrub away other people's sweat, blood, piss, cack, and grime with scalding, soapy water. Signora Canarutto shakes her head when she sees me, soaked to the armpits and sweaty, my hair unraveling from its pins. And I know it's not me she's impatient with, but Jim.

STANISLAUS

Trieste
OCTOBER 1905

S TANNIE AGREED TO COME AT LAST AND, THROUGH JIM, HAS
secured a job at the Berlitz, but when he arrives, he finds us
undone. He came yesterday, tired and a little silent after his long
journey. At the train sation, the first thing Jim says is, "Do you
have any money?" He can be an awful thoughtless yoke when he
wants to be. I pucked him in the side but, of course, he paid no
mind. I only kept my tongue because I didn't want a public row.

"You're so very welcome, Stanislaus," I said and gave him an
awkward hug. He dipped his head into the pram to admire Georgie.

"A bonny fellow, Nora," he said, smiling up at me with a brotherly pride.

We took Stannie directly to the Caffè Pirona, but still he didn't
talk much and Jim ended up with a puss on him feeling, no doubt,
that his brother should be lauding him for setting up this new life
for us and for bringing Stannie over to share it. To me, his brother
seemed wary. He looked from one to the other of us when we
spoke Italian, as if we'd lost our minds. Jim says the only way for
me to learn the language is to speak it, so I try very hard to do just
that. But I suppose it's rude in front of Stanislaus who doesn't yet
have a syllable.

They're out now, gone to the Berlitz already to introduce Stannie to Artifoni and to get his teaching schedule. He'll earn almost as much as Jim, which both pleases and displeases the same fella.

"Why should a single chap make as much as a married man with a child?" Jim complained to me. But, of course, he means for Stannie to hand over most of what he earns "for the good of the family." Us.

Signora Canarutto cleared out a small parlor that she doesn't use for Stannie to have as a bedroom and he will be comfortable, if cramped, in there. At least he'll have a bit of privacy, which is more than I have. Sometimes I crave a little time alone to just let my thoughts scatter.

I sit in my chair and nurse Georgie, watching the lovely slide of milk from his mouth when he stops suckling a moment to smile up at me. He fixes his blue eyes on mine and I sing to him, "Is it the laughing eye, Eileen aroon?" Georgie latches on, then lets go my nipple and smiles again; he lifts his darling head toward me as if asking for more songs. I sing a verse and tickle his fat belly and he squeals in delight, his funny little kitten noise.

"How your mamma loves you, wee Georgie. How your papà does too, your lovely babbo. And now Uncle Stannie's come to join us. Isn't it marvelous altogether?"

Things, of course, are not as marvelous as all that, but I daren't let the baby know. Jim and I are taking lumps out of each other. Every time he turns up, after going missing at night, I bawl and screech at him like a banshee. He fights back telling me of his artistic temperament, while flopping around drunk, drooling over the baby, and waking him out of good sleeps that give me rest.

"Artistic temperament, my rear end," is my usual roar back.

I sometimes wonder where's the Jim gone who accosted me on Nassau Street in Dublin, June more than twelve months ago. He was a confident, carefree fellow to be sure, but the man I'm with now is cranky and careworn. Of course he has more worries and concerns—we both have—but it's as if we left our best selves beyond in Ireland. We came here and slowly lost our spirit.

Jim had no idea, I suppose, how little he would relish the teaching. But he doesn't think of my anxieties or irritations. It's easier for him to ignore that I scrape the muck and pee off the undergarments of strange Austrians while trying to care for Georgie since he's never home to see it. I thought that Stannie's arrival would lighten Jim, but he had a face like thunder this morning when they left and there was no need for it. His poor brother may already be regretting his move to Trieste.

Some days, to rile Jim, I sit and write letters home to my mother. As I fashion the words, I say them aloud.

"Dear Mammy, I have no life here at all, I miss Galway. I would like my son to be an Irishman. Please may he and I come and live with you. We will have him baptized in Saint Augustine's and you can stand for him, Mammy, and Uncle Michael too . . ."

Then I seal the pages in envelopes, neatly addressed to Mammy's house in Bowling Green, and missing only a stamp. I prop them between the ashtray and the teapot and leave them there. But I never post them. Jim pretends to ignore the letters, but I see his eyes linger on them from time to time.

STANNIE VERY KINDLY BROUGHT ME A BOX OF INDIAN TEA—THE Russian stuff you get here is a rare kind of pisswater. As I make tea, Granny Healy floats across my vision like a revenant. She was particular about tea-making, as she was about most things. I wonder if she hadn't died when I was so young, and I hadn't gone to work in the convent, and if I hadn't ended up sparring with Uncle Tommy, would I have stayed in Galway and not run away to Dublin and then to here? Ah, I suppose there's no profit in that style of thinking whatsoever.

I let the tea draw then carry Georgie back to the room and prop him between pillows; I dash back to the kitchen to fetch my tray. The baby babbles to himself and I sit at the table by the window and dunk biscotti and enjoy the soggy sugariness on my tongue; I sip and savor the gunpowder heat of my drink. Georgie dozes and, though there's laundry to be seen to, I climb onto the bed beside him and close my eyes. A rapping sound wakens me and I'm surprised to find the room dark. I go, groggy, to open the door and find Stanislaus there.

"Where's Jim?" I ask, peering past him, a nip of irritation biting me.

"I don't know, Nora, is the God's honest truth."

I tut. "Didn't you both leave here together, Stanislaus?"

"We did, but Jim is as greasy as lard."

"Well, that's true." I gesture. "Come in, Stannie." We sit opposite each other. "Tell me."

"We were in a caffè and I told him it was time to go home. He spied a friend through the window, he said, and wanted to step outside to talk to him. When I looked out the caffè door, he was gone."

"Jim was moldy drunk, I suppose."

"He had a drop taken, all right."

"The dirty blackguard; he promised me this wouldn't go on. I thought it would be different with you here."

"Was I brought to Trieste to be his keeper?" The bitterness of this hovers in the air between us.

"Ah, Stannie," I say, after a moment, but we both know there's truth in what he said.

"It's all right, Nora." He pushes his hand through his hair and sighs. Stannie is stocky and muscular, smaller than Jim, and altogether more somber, but there's a steadiness to him that comforts me. He doesn't take a drink and, though he's three years Jim's junior, he has more of the man about him somehow. I watch his hand ruffle his hair and reach out to grab it.

"What's this?" I say; his knuckles are purple and bloodied.

He pulls away. "It's nothing."

"Don't, Stanislaus. It's bad enough that Jim lies to me, I won't take it from you, too." He looks at me, steady as a statue. "Now, tell me what really happened."

"When I went out of the caffè after him, I spotted him streeling off down the street in the distance and followed him, all through the Old Town." He glances at me. "I knew Jim was trying to give me the slip and I was annoyed. I'm not here a wet day and already he wants to be rid of me."

"That's not it at all. He gets maudlin when he's drunk—he probably wanted to sing songs with the sailors in one of the harbor taverns."

Stannie snorts. "Are you making excuses for him, Nora?"

I sit on the bed. "I'm not. I suppose I just know the pattern and I'm weary of it."

"Anyway, he slithered down a laneway and I almost lost him, but he was, ah, he was, relieving himself so . . ."

"We all piss, Stannie, don't be saving my presence."

He grimaces. "I called out to Jim and he told me to go home.

"'Home?' I said to him. 'What home have I now after coming here to help you?' Jim screamed, 'You're my brother. It's only right that you lend a hand. Didn't I get you a job? A place to live?' He continued to piss and then he shouted 'Pup!' at me. 'Ungrateful pup!' I got angry, Nora. I went up to him and told him he was just like our father, the seed and breed of him, and that he'd end up like him, too, old and sad and a drunken nuisance. Jim grabbed my collar and yanked me sideways." Stannie stops and looks straight at me. "I confess, Nora, that I punched him in the jaw."

"Oh, Stannie." Though Jim's antics when he drinks are a plague to me, my stomach contracts in pity for him—his poor jaw! But I feel for Stanislaus, too—he surely didn't know this is what lay ahead of him when he left his home.

"It gets worse, though, Nora. He reeled away and fell into the stream he'd left on the cobbles. But I just turned and walked off. I'd had my fill of him by then." He looks at me, wary. "My thoughts were this: I picked him up once too often back in Dublin; I didn't come here for that."

I hold out my hand and take his. "I'm sorry, Stanislaus." I close my eyes and shake my head. "I suppose he never told you in his letters that he's out every night of the week, slugging back absinthe like it's water."

"He shouldn't be spending his money like that. *Your* money." He pets my hand tenderly.

"Sure, don't I know it? My heart is in pieces with him. I have the care of Georgie and this place. And the laundry I take in, besides." Stannie pulls his hand away and pockets it. "I'm sure Jim has told you that the teaching makes him wretched."

"It's a living, isn't it?" he says.

"It is. Until one of the books gets published."

Stannie snorts. "Then you'll be wealthy, I suppose?" His tone is scornful.

"Maybe."

"I'll give Jim one thing—he has never, ever had a lack of self-belief. It's a scarce and profitable thing for an Irishman."

I nod. "Jim believes himself a true artist and, because of that, he believes teaching is well below him."

"He has a family now. A fine writer he may be, but you need

to eat. It's a rare author who earns money, though, Nora, you must realize that."

"If that's so, Jim has convinced himself he's one of those rare men." I get up. "I'll make us some tea, Stannie."

"Don't go to any bother on my account, Nora."

"What bother is it to make my brother-in-law a sup of tea, when he's been so kind as to bring me the good stuff? Watch Georgie there a minute."

The kitchen is empty and, while I wait for the water to boil, I go and quietly open the door to Stannie's room, as if it might tell me more about him. He has few possessions—a bundle of books by the bed and a clean shirt hung on a hook, a clothes brush and one for his hair; the bed is neat as a monk's. A room that reflects him well, Stannie is not a man for chaos. I close the door, make the tea, and return to him.

"Now, here we are." I pour our tea and take some biscotti from the tin and put them on a plate.

"It's not easy being related to someone like Jim. He's cleverer than us all and he knows it. He can outtalk anyone and do the worst of everything, but still he comes out all right." Stannie sighs. "I get no credit for anything."

"I appreciate you, Stannie. You'll be a great comfort to me, especially if he continues his gallivanting."

He nods. "Are you happy here, Nora?"

"If Jim would stop his trick-acting, things would be easier, I suppose."

We both hear a scuffle and then the screech of "*Viva San Giusto! Viva. Viva.*"

"Here he comes," Stannie says, "ready for his audience."

Jim bursts through the door; I can see a purple blossoming on his jaw where Stannie hit him. "John Stanislaus Joyce, where in the name of Jaysus did you skite off to?" He flaps a hand in our direction, then holds it aloft. "Curtain rises. A homely scene. Two Irish emigrants take tea in an Austrian . . . ." he looks around " . . . hovel."

"Shut up, Jim, you'll wake Georgie."

He waddles over to where the baby lies asleep on the bed. "Is he not a fine, long, fat boy, Stannie? A rare specimen of Erin, being a son of Connacht and Leinster, too?" Jim belches loudly and giggles; he loses his footing for a moment, stumbles, and holds on to the footboard.

Stannie pushes back his chair and rises. "Good night, Nora."

"Ah, stay and finish your tea," I say.

"Go, go, John Stanislaus, my boy. Yes, go now to your virtuous bed."

Stannie stands for a moment and stares at Jim, looking as if he has a century's worth of words he would like to spill, a hundred years of grievances, but he says naught. He nods to me and takes his leave.

"You're a thundering disgrace, James Joyce," I say. Pushing past him, I climb under the covers and pull them to my chin. He stands dabbing at his jaw with one finger, his sottish sway making my bile burn. "I'm supposed to feel sorry for you, I suppose, because your face is sore? May it be a lesson to you." I turn to the wall. I feel Jim flop onto the bed beside Georgie; he knows better than to reach for me.

HEARTSORE

❧

Trieste
NOVEMBER 1905

Tell me about Nora the girl."

"Ah, haven't I told you everything already? And who says I'm even talking to you?" I waggle my toes by his nose and Jim grabs them and bites gently. He was out late last night, again, and though I begged Stannie to go and uncover him and bring him home, Stannie wouldn't, and he went to his room and shut the door firmly against me.

Jim wipes his spit into the sole of my foot, tickling me. "Tell me about the priesteen again," he says. "Father Fumbly Fingers Flannery."

"I will not; Jim, will you stop?"

He groans; no doubt his head is alight with pain. "Go on, Nora, give me some auld story to ease me."

I sigh; Jim so loves to hear these tales, but does he deserve them when night after night he disappears and no cajoling of mine makes a whit of a difference? He pokes at my feet with one finger—jab jab jab—until I give in.

"I told you about Willie Mulvagh, I think?"

"You did. He was the Prod that got you on the train to Dublin after your uncle found out you'd been dallying with him, against orders. Mulvagh was the camel's back. Or the straw, I suppose."

Jim rubs my feet and I take one of his in my hand and do the same. "Willie worked in the mineral water factory and he'd bring some of the 'windy waters,' as we called them, with him when we met to walk out."

Jim sniggers. "Where did you walk, Nora, with the bold Willie?"

"Oh, along by the river Corrib—I always liked to watch the water frothing like porter toward the sea. We'd go along by the gaol wall, too, and down Nun's Island. There was a pair of swans who favored the underside of the bridge there. I liked to watch them swirl and twirl about each other."

Jim hoists himself up on one elbow and pushes down the sheet so he can see my face. "And was he respectful of you, the young Protestant?"

"He was of course."

Jim slides his hand up my leg. "Did he try to touch you, Nora?"

"Stop!" I laugh and swipe at his hand.

"Or was he fonder of making you touch him?"

"I was a deal younger than he, Jim. Far too young for that." I pause and remember Willie's urgent kisses, his guiding of my hands to his most heated place, his moist panting against my cheek when he was ready to burst. I toss my head and my words begin to tumble: "Willie often gave me little presents: the bottles of mineral water, as I said; a nice box of Cadbury's chocolate cremes, sometimes, that I'd share with my friends. He had a good job, doing the books in the factory."

"He had money so. You're sorry you left him, I think."

"Oh, shut up, Jim. How could I be?" I wave my hand over the hump of Georgie under the sheet. "And, anyway, no one would have allowed us to stay together. Uncle Tommy beat the tar out of me after catching sight of me with Willie. I told Uncle, night after night, I was going to devotions at the Abbey Church when I was meeting Willie. He was raging when he saw us together and marched me home, banging his stick to the ground and almost stepping on my heels in his haste. I thought Uncle might kill me that last time; I dropped to the floor and hung on to his knees, begging him to leave off me. 'I'll beat the lining out of you, you little bitch,' he screamed and that was it. I knew I had to get out of there."

"The blackguard. Did you not ask your mother to make him see reason?"

I snort. "Mammy always sided with Tommy. She thought me very bold." I sigh. "Anyway, Jim, here we are in Trieste, and Willie, no doubt, has found himself a decent girl of his own faith to be with and that's all there is to say about it."

"Did you love him, Nora?"

"I was fond of him. It was a long time ago now."

"You were wildly in love with Mulvagh, it seems to me." Jim drops my foot and I can feel the fester of his jealousy around us, it's a wound he likes to disturb and set oozing.

"Jim, I don't reprimand you for your youthful carry on; I say nothing when you ogle women in the street, or when word is passed to me of your classroom fancies. You've a lot more to be shamed by than I."

He grunts and rises, lifts up the woken Georgie, and kisses him on the forehead, then hands him to me. I put the baby to my breast and lie on.

OPERA

꙳

Trieste

DECEMBER 1905

J IM'S CHRISTMAS PRESENT TO ME IS A NIGHT AT THE OPERA.
Normally, he would go by himself but Stannie has offered to
keep an eye on Georgie so we can both go. I squeezed as much
milk as I could muster into a bottle and told Stannie how to heat it
and he shooed me off like a mother of twelve, telling me it wasn't
the first time he'd fed a child.

Jim has been to see the show a few times already and his face
softens when he talks of it. We walk toward the Teatro Verdi and
I'm excited for it'll be my first time in the door of the place. The
opera is about a love affair in Paris between a poor poet and his
girl. I love the sound of it because it reminds me of us and the way
we, too, will be in Paris someday, for that is where I hope we'll
go eventually.

"Tell me the story of the opera, Jim."

"Should I? Or would you not prefer to just witness it unfold?"

"Give me a little, remind me."

My hand is along his arm and he squeezes it. "All right, my
Gooseen. *La Bohème* is the sad tale of the lovers Rodolfo and
Mimì, he a poet, she a cold-handed seamstress."

"It's sad, Jim? Oh. What happens in the end?"

"Nora, my Nora. Let us just go and watch and see."

The night air is cold, but the great mill of people moving across the Piazza Grande toward the theater provides shelter. Tonight the Triestini are gay and light and they call out Christmas greetings to one another. We get to the Verdi and I halt, making Jim stop too.

"Is it very fine inside?" I ask, looking down at the shabby coat I've had since we left Ireland over a year ago.

"Don't worry, my pet. We are going up to the gallery. The grandees sit below and won't notice us."

"Is that supposed to put me at my ease, Jim Joyce?"

He pats my hand and moves us forward. "One day we'll occupy stall seats. Or a box, yes, we'll have a box. Until then, it's the high *loggione* for us, I'm afraid."

We pick our way up through the throng to the gallery and take our seats. I peer down to the stalls and the circle; the red and gold of the theater is lit up by electric lights and the stucco on the tiers of boxes makes them look like the fanciest of iced cakes. I wiggle my behind into my seat and take Jim's hand.

"We can see everything," I say, and I can hear the wonder in my own voice.

"With a telescope we'd see more," he says.

The man beside me is large and garlicky and he's talking loudly to his companion who says nothing but "*Sì, sì*" to every observation. In the seats in front of ours, two sailors are laughing like children as they pass cards to each other. There is a comingle of smells about us: garlic, sweat, syrupy eau de cologne, and the deep, creamy-sour smell of unwashed skin. I wave my gloves in front of my nose to tamp it all down.

At last the lights lower and the opera begins, and I'm thrilled to my core to see Paris before me once again.

"Look, Jim," I nudge him, "it's like they cut a lump out of a street in Paris and put it up on the stage."

"Hush, now, my love. Let us listen and watch."

And so we do. I'd been worried that I would understand nothing, but I can follow most of what they say and what happens and, when I'm lost, Jim guides me back. I fall in love with Rodolfo, then out of love with him when he seems to neglect his Mimì. I follow them through their time at the caffè when they visit with their friends, their lack of money, the little jealousies and misunderstandings, through the snowy winter and on to spring and poor, poor Mimì's death.

"No, no," I cry out when she's gone, and I weep for her cold little body and her Rodolfo who is left alone. I soak my own hanky and Jim gives me his, and, when the lights go up, it's hard to believe that we have left Paris and are back now in Trieste and we must carry on as if we haven't been moved to distraction by Mimì and Rodolfo and their sad, lovely life.

"There, there, Nora," Jim says, escorting me down the stairs.

"All I want to do is run back in there and gather Mimì up," I say.

"Me too," Jim says, and I take his arm and we make our way to the Caffè Pirona for I need a little Marsala after the wrenching sorrow of the opera. Who would've thought that a story told in Italian song could affect a body in such a deep way? Who would've thought that it could make your own lack of money and straitened life feel a little rich?

OUR SMALL ROOM IS A-PRICKLE. THE TWO MEN ARE LIKE A PAIR of stallions with no mare; they sit and toss their heads and bite snippy remarks back and forth at each other. I'm only waiting for a hoof to go out and a slap to be delivered. Stanislaus is sore be-

Now they're sitting opposite each other at our tiny table, drinking their coffee in cold silence. Jim lights a cigarette before Stanislaus has finished his fig pastry and I can see Stannie's dander is up, as can Jim. Still, he blows smoke at his brother in a long, thin stream and stares across the table with a grim face and I know there'll be an all-out row if I don't do something. I finish nursing Georgie and hand him to Stannie.

"The man will be here shortly, Jim, for this clean laundry. Give me a hand to get it into the sack."

Stannie holds Georgie up and coos at him. "*Ciao*, Giorgio. *Ciao, ciao*," and this seems to rile Jim.

"Stanislaus," he says, "would you rather be a tuppenny clerk in some clammy Dublin basement? You should thank your stars that I brought you here."

"What I'd rather, Jim, is a smidgen of acknowledgment that I came here to help you out and that you appreciate my efforts."

Jim leans across to Stannie. "You might want to think a bit harder about who has helped whom, brother. Don't you live under my roof, Stanislaus? Eat off my plates?"

"For the love of Mary in heaven, will you leave it go, Jim?" I say and grab his arm and drag him to the bed to help me fill the laundry sack.

Stannie stands and throws Georgie onto his hip, crossing the room to stand in front of me and Jim. "Watch your lip, Jim," he says.

Jim snorts and I take Georgie from Stannie, who shoves his hat onto his head and leaves. When he's gone, I lay Georgie down on the bed.

"Be careful," I say, "your brother will only take so much from you."

"He should be crawling at my feet in benediction, Nora, for delivering him from Pappie and the crowd in Dublin."

cause, instead of coming home to me and Georgie after work at the Berlitz last night, Jim went to see *La Bohème* again. I was a little jealous when he said it, but he explained that he needs to swallow stories many times in order to construct better ones himself. Stannie, though, is not as forgiving.

When Jim had come in, late of course, he'd complained about the high smells in the *loggione*.

"Nora," he said, "it was as if the armies of Greece had been called from the battlefield without notice and came to sit among us. The God-forgive-me stink off them! Onions and piss and mildew, and the drink seeping from their pores. I'll need to bring a vial of salts with me from now on."

Stanislaus, who was helping me fold my laundry, hissed, "Isn't it well for you, off in the Verdi while, to keep you in theater tickets, your wife picks shite off other men's drawers?"

Jim grunted. "What do you care?"

"I do care! I care very much when you act the man-about-town while Nora toils and I sweat through hours at the school, so's to hand up to you."

"Ah, Stannie." I glanced at Jim; who was plucking at his mustache with one finger and looking at his shoes.

"'Ah Stannie' what, Nora? Don't be defending him! What kind of a life is this?" He tossed a linen jacket to the floor and I picked it up, afraid it would get dusty or marked and I'd have to wash and dry it all over again.

"Go to the devil, Stannie," Jim said, in a low, mean voice.

"Hell might be better than being stuck here with the most viciously selfish man to have come out of Ireland." Stanislaus laughed, a flimsy, mirthless sound. "Good luck to you, Nora. May you survive the cruelty of this man you've chosen. Few others will." He got up and marched off to his room.

I shove my words from my mouth as hard as I shove the folded clothes into the sack. "You can be sure, James Joyce, that your brother doesn't quite see it the way you do. Watch yourself. Stannie's your greatest ally. If you keep up your provocations, he *will* go. Back to Pappie and the family, back to some Dublin basement." I knot the top of the bag and look at Jim. "Just to get away from you. Is that what you want for him? For us?"

COMMUNE

❧

Trieste
FEBRUARY 1906

C LOTILDE COMES TO SEE ME AND, BECAUSE WE'RE ALL IN OUR
room, there's nowhere for her to sit. Stannie, of course, jumps
up and offers her his seat.

"*Grazie mille*, Signor Joyce," she says, sitting down, and Stannie reddens to his hair-tips. I see Jim about to comment on the fact
and I shake my head sharply.

Clotilde takes Georgie and I go and make the tea. I'm delighted with the bit of womanly company for there's only so much
I can take of the two chaps toing and froing over the Russian army's surrender in China, and the writing abilities of Tolstoy as
opposed to Turgenev, and whether their pal Gogarty betrayed
Jim's friendship with his actions in Dublin, and the Lord knows
what else. They never want to talk about normal things. I'm like a
mute half the day and, sometimes, when I do butt in, they go quiet
for a few moments then carry on yapping together as if I'd said
nothing. I'd be better off talking to the windowpanes. I prepare
the tray, slicing up a bit of my leftover Christmas pudding, and go
back up. The two men are standing, jackets on and hats, walking
sticks in hand.

"You're going out?"

"We'll take ourselves away, Nora," Jim says. "We're obstructing you. And you, Clotilde. We are mere clutter and should let you ladies wag your chins as only ladies know how." He bows to us, Stannie does the same, and they go.

"Ah, isn't it nicer without them?" I say to Clotilde and we both giggle.

We eat the fruity, whiskey-rich pudding and drink our hot tea and Clotilde oohs and aahs over my baking and over dear Georgie.

"Baby is so big," she says, and I'm pleased as a duck who can whistle, for it's my own milk that has him good and round.

"The child is a little porker, Clotilde. A fine maneen, aren't you, Georgie?" The baby is propped up on the bed, chewing on his fist. "He'll soon be eating like a man, won't you, peteen?"

Clotilde startles me by lunging forward and grabbing my hand. "Nora, this place is too small for all of you. Look how you have no space." She waves and we both look around at the clutter of our things that fills the room. "Alessandro and I have secured a fine flat near the train station, on Via Giovanni Boccaccio. There are plenty of rooms and it is cheap. Please, Nora, you must come live with us."

"Oh, Clotilde." I feel the burn of tears in my throat, her constant kindness is a balm to me. But then I think of Stannie. "Do you mean all of us should come? Stanislaus too?"

"*Sì, sì*, Signor Joyce also, that is Stannie, too."

I clap my hands. "If the flat's near the station, it's near the sea. How pretty for Georgie to see the water every day, to breathe its cleanness. And little Daniele, too."

"Exactly; our boys will be healthy as fresh cabbage."

I giggle at this and imagine daily walks on the promenade with Georgie. I imagine him a year from now toddling, his lungs blessed with marine air.

"Oh, wait till I tell Jim, he'll be delighted. Signora Canarutto has been so good to us but, if we had proper space, we could buy some furniture of our own. And we'd be all together again, like in the old days in Pola." I pump her hand up and down. Just look what Clotilde can do that Jim can't—she has found us a home. "*Grazie*, Clotilde, thank you, my lovely friend."

"*Prego, ma bella* Nora."

WE ARE ALL TOGETHER NOW IN THE FLAT THE FRANCINIS FOUND on Via Giovanni Boccaccio and Jim is to have a book published in London and we've opened wine to celebrate. Grant Richards, who so sloppily treated him about his book of poems, is happy to bring out the stories set in Dublin. Jim is extraordinarily happy and sees our fortunes picking up wildly. Alessandro Francini has Georgie's bonnet on his head and he has, somehow, folded his long body into the pram, which Jim is zooming around the large salon. Clotilde laughs noisily at the daft getup of her husband, and I giggle alongside her. Alessandro has the baby's rattle in his hand and he shakes it then sucks the end of it noisily as if drinking milk from it.

"My son, my son, look at my beautiful new son," Jim calls out to Georgie who is staring hard from his high chair at all that's going on.

Stannie is at the piano, a cigarette dripping ash onto the keys as he bangs out polkas and mazurkas, and little Daniele is running behind Jim, laughing crazily.

"*Papà è un bambino*," the child screeches.

Jim, to entertain Daniele further, performs his spider dance, the one he does when he has drink galore onboard, flailing his arms and waggling his legs and the boy copies him and they wriggle and toss themselves about madly.

Clotilde and I stand by the sideboard with our glasses of wine, taking in the whole silly scene; my jaw throbs from laughing so much. Only Georgie is quiet; he watches the men and Daniele with a face as placid as a marble Jesus.

"Let us all eat together tonight," Clotilde says, "to further honor this book that is coming."

"Let's," I say.

Jim is out of breath from spider-dancing and from pushing Alessandro around and the two of them confer and laugh in the corner.

"Clotilde and I are going to make some food for everyone."

"We'll have a little party," she says.

"Ah, Nora, why don't we go out? Doesn't my news deserve a proper blessing?" Jim says. "Let's all go to the Bonavia and have fried eel. Or that fish broth you and Georgie are so fond of. We can have champagne!" Joyce looks at Alessandro and Stannie. "What say you, boys?"

I glance at Clotilde; she and Alessandro don't dine out as we do. She seems to have more energy for shopping and cooking than I have, and she collects her pennies in a way that I haven't learned. Often she tells me it's more economical to eat at home, but I prefer not to have to do housework when we knock elbows doing it. And especially not today when there's reason to be gay.

"All right, Joyce," Alessandro says and Clotilde nods, though I can see she's hesitant, calculating probably what she'll have to do without in the week ahead.

"Yes," she says, smiling at her husband, "why not?"

On the street, the three men walk ahead of us and the boys, and Jim and Alessandro must already be a little drunk for their voices are pitched very high. They're passing stories about the dog that lives at the Berlitz school.

"I pushed him along the corridor with my foot one day, Joyce, to make sure he took a shit outside your classroom," Alessandro shouts. "We all know how much you love dogs, our incontinent friend, especially."

It's hardly the right kind of story for the outdoors or in front of the children. Jim normally hates this sort of talk in public, but he and Stannie throw back their heads and laugh mightily in that way they have. Clotilde keeps her eyes fixed forward, but I want to go to Jim and the others and tell them to keep their voices down. I want to say to Jim that I'm not sure I like Alessandro's influence on him, the coarseness it brings on.

Stannie has told me, too, that Jim's classes are the talk of the school because he sees little reason to follow the curriculum that bores him. Instead, he speaks to the students of socialism and the faults of Ireland and he tells them to drink absinthe on an empty stomach to broaden their minds. Jim, it seems, is changing before me—acting the boor and forgetting his manners—and I've no idea how to stop it. All the lightness and fun of the afternoon slithers from me and I'm sobered. I link Clotilde's arm and pull her to my side in a firm, companionable way and she sends me a rueful smile.

"Men," she says, with a roll of her eyes.

"Yes, men," I agree and we walk on.

JIM IS IN A FURY OF WRITING, NIGHT AFTER NIGHT. HE SAYS HE must finish two more stories at least for Grant Richards for the *Dubliners* book.

"Now is the time to do it, before the blackguard changes his mind, Nora."

I keep out of his way and let him sit and scribble, the candle burning to a wick and him hunched over the table, rubbing at his eyes and mumbling to himself. I change the candle and he doesn't look up. Sometimes I go to Clotilde to talk and darn, or I lie on the bed and nurse Georgie and let Jim do what he needs to do. The writing is like a great want inside him, a hunger that can't be sated. He fiddles and faddles with it for hours and cries out in frustration when the words refuse to fall in the right way. But when the writing goes well for him, he's content as a pig in muck and builds up a vigor that always leads to one place. Tonight, his pen rages across the page and he smokes fewer cigarettes—some nights I can barely roll them fast enough to keep up with him—but now all goes well. And I know that soon he will leave his pages and come to me.

I get Georgie off to sleep and put him to the footboard. I wriggle out of my drawers and sponge myself below over the po. I put on my lovely Pim's nightgown; it is still good and unworn, for I keep it for special nights. I hop onto the bed, my pillow at Jim's end, beside his. If he notices me readying myself, he says nothing. He stretches his arms over his head and yawns, glances to me and smiles.

"What's the new story about, Jim?"

"It's about a pious nun and her saintly sister."

"Is it, Jim?" I hike up onto my elbows in surprise.

"No, Nora, not at all. It's about two dirty gallants."

I lie back. "That sounds more like a story of yours."

He skids across the room and hunches over me, taking me by the waist. "Does it now? Does it, indeed? Do you like the dirt I write?"

He lies up on top of me and I can feel the stiffness of him through his trousers and through the cotton of my nightgown. We kiss as we always do, in a wet-warm frenzy, and Jim pins my arms over my head and goes lower to suck at my breast, drawing Georgie's milk into his mouth. He groans and whispers my name, "Nora, Nora, Nora."

"I love you, Jim."

"I love you, too, my gorgeous Gooseen."

His hands fumble for his belt buckle and his trousers are down and gone, and he has my nightgown rucked up to my belly and his fingers tickle and caress me before he plunges them into me and digs briskly, just the way I like. My mouth streams across his neck, and his mouth is on my breastbone, his breath crashing hard and then he's inside me, the shocking stiff length of him and it's divine to hold him and be held and to be fucked and loved all in the one go.

CHINA

ᘏᕉ

Trieste
MARCH 1906

I'M LICKING THE WINDOWS OF THE SHOP THAT HOLDS THE CHINA I want. The dinner service, white and violet-sprigged, has been on display for weeks, and whenever I get a chance, I come and stare. The idea of that beautiful service has seized hold of me and I'm like a herring in a net when I think on it—desperate and gasping. I while away silly amounts of time imagining what it'd be like to have a huge dining table, in a home of my own, that could hold it all. I imagine spooning potato soup for Jim and Stannie from the violet-decorated tureen into the fine bowls. I see Georgie eating biscotti off one of the delicate dessert plates. I hold my fingers to the window as if I might call the china to my hand and spirit it away with me.

"It's a beautiful set," says a voice to my side and I whip my head around to see Stannie.

"Oh, you startled me." I smile in relief. "Yes, it's very lovely, Stanislaus, but stuff like that is not for the likes of me."

"Some day, Nora," Stannie says and offers me his arm. He takes on a mischievous look and flicks his head toward the shop. "Will we go in?"

"What?" I glance at my tatty coat. "We probably shouldn't."

"You can hold some of the pieces in your hands and see how it feels. Come on!" Before I can refuse, he steers me in and the bell over the door tinkles and the proprietor is upon us. "My wife would like to inspect the violet service," Stannie says, winking at me and I suppress a laugh.

With as much high-and-mighty as I can raise, I nod, and the man lays out the beautiful plates and cups and bowls on the counter before me. I lift a cup and run my finger over the violets that scatter inside the rim and down the bowl.

"So pretty," I whisper, shy all of a sudden to find the china in my grasp, as if I truly own it. I take up a cake plate and marvel at the bright flowers and the gleam of the gold rim; I hold up the plate, admiring its delicate nature and how gracefully it lets the light in.

"You may leave a deposit if you wish, signor," the man says to Stannie and he looks to me, wanting me to play along.

I put down the plate and smile at the shopkeeper. "Not today, sir, I thank you."

Stannie's grinning at me behind his back and he comes and links arms with me and we tumble from the shop onto the street. We keep our heads about us until we're a few paces from the door, then we giggle like children.

I sigh. "Just think, Stannie, there are those who can saunter in there and buy that service or anything they please."

Stannie tightens his elbow around my fingers. "You deserve a man who can give you everything, Nora."

I feel my face get warm. "Jim will be able to do that, by and by."

Stanislaus eases his grip. "Ah, yes. Good old Jim." He smiles. "He will, he will."

◦⁓◦

TWENTY-TWO TODAY AND I'M FEELING EVERY YEAR OF IT. I expect no palaver and no presents, but Jim brings home some *torta al
limone* and we eat it after our dinner, its bittersweet glory reducing
us all to silence the way fine cakes do.

"Well, now, that was lovely, wasn't it?" I say to Stannie and
Georgie who are still finishing theirs. I sip my tea and smile at my
three men. "This is a nice birthday."

"There's something else," Jim says, producing a flat package
from under his chair and laying it before me. He and Stannie share
a smile.

"Well, whatever is this?" I shake my head. "There was no need,
Jim. We have the dentist's bill to pay and Georgie needs boots."

"Oh, open it, Nora. You deserve a treat on your special day."
Jim lights a cigarette and watches me undo the wrappings, first
tissue paper and then paperboard. "I thought long and hard about
this one," Jim says.

I find another thick layer of yellow tissue inside the board and,
as I unfold, I see a glint of gold and, then, a bright sprig of violets.

"The dessert plate," I cry and look at Stannie, but he won't
catch my eye.

"One plate for now, Nora. Soon you'll have the whole set.
Who's a clever maneen?" Jim says and he puckers his lips for a
kiss. I go to him, kiss him, and hold his head to me. Stanislaus
glances up, a coy but pleased cast to his face.

Thank you, I mouth. He nods and looks away.

MIGRATION

~

Trieste and Rome
MAY TO JULY 1906

J IM SAYS IT'S TIME TO LEAVE TRIESTE. HE'S HAD A HANKERING
for Italy since we came away, not to mind Paris. Italy at least is
only across the border, so it's there we're going. The teaching is
not for Jim. He wouldn't mind having a few private pupils, but he
feels at check in the school, too bound by rules. And, anyway, the
Berlitz is in an uproar. Jim and Stannie come home with news of
it and it's all our talk over dinner.

"Our dear Signor Bertelli was a bounder, it transpires, Nora,"
Jim says. "He's filled his pockets with Berlitz money and scarpered." He laughs.

Stannie scratches his head. "The only complication is that
now Signor Artifoni says he can only afford to keep one English
teacher."

I whip my head up from my plate of *gemelli*. "Jim?"

"Worry not, Gooseen. Stannie and I have talked it through on
the way home. He should stay and I should go."

I toss down my fork in annoyance—three mouths Jim has to
feed! "Why?" I stare from one to the other. "I mean no badness
toward you, Stanislaus, but we have Georgie to think of. Jim, why
should it be that Stannie gets to keep his job, not you?"

Jim pokes the sauce around his pasta. "Because I brought Stannie here to work at the school and I mean for him to stay. Because I have had it up to my neck with the inelegant clods who populate my classes taking up my precious hours." He stares at me.

"But it's all right for your brother to put up with them?" I tut. "And what about me and your son, Jim? Are we to beg on the streets for bread?"

Stannie clears his throat. "You know, I really don't mind looking for something—"

"No!" Jim stuffs some pasta into his mouth and chews it slowly. The rest of us watch and wait. "Nora, you and I, and Giorgio, are going to Rome. In Trieste we are too much at the mercy of the Berlitz. And it's time for a change."

"But Rome, Jim? It's so far from here." I feel a little fear rise in me.

"I have been looking in the Roman paper, the *Tribuna*, and there are jobs. I have already seen one that's to my liking." He takes a scrap from his pocket and hands it to me.

"Nast, Kolb and Schumacher. That sounds horrible. Like a disease," I say. "What is it?"

Jim takes back the advertisement. "It's a bank, Nora, and they need a correspondence clerk, with fluent Italian and English, which I have. What things am I good at, my Gooseen?"

"Talking, Jim." I suck my lip. "Writing, I suppose."

"Exactly that, Nora. Writing. Misters Nast, Kolb, and Schumacher want someone to write all day and they are willing to pay twelve pounds a month for the work. A deal more than the Berlitz. So you see, for the likes of myself, the work will be as simple as scratching an itch on my behind. And it's lucrative besides."

I look around at our bits of furniture that we bought on

installment but are still not paid in full. "Will we be taking our bed and the new chairs?"

Jim sighs. "No, Nora, we can't. The furniture will, I suppose, be repossessed in a tick. So to speak."

I put my hands under the seat of my chair and squeeze it. Perhaps if I cling on, Jim will let me keep my blue chair and the lovely washstand with the marble top that we chose in a moment of high extravagance. Jim watches me and shakes his head; I put my hands into my lap.

"Will Rome be awfully different from Trieste?" I ask, looking from one to the other of the men.

Stannie gives a grim little smile. "It will be vastly different, I imagine, Nora. It's Italy not Austria, after all."

I nod and smile, make my heart stout as I so often am required to do when it comes to Jim. "Well," I say, "won't it be an adventure, all the same?"

"That's the way, Nora, my love," Jim says, petting my hair before striking a match for his cigarette.

I look at my brother-in-law; he'll be left behind, like the furniture. "Poor Georgie's going to miss his uncle Stan-stan terribly, won't you, pet?"

Stannie stands abruptly and shoves on his hat. "We won't worry about that now," he says. "Jim has to secure the job first, doesn't he?" He bows and is gone.

I pick up a cigarette and Jim leans in to light it for me. I watch the smoke roll from my lips and billow out over the table like a gray veil. Georgie will indeed miss Stannie. I will miss him too. And I'll be sad to leave Clotilde, my only friend. But who knows what pleasures Rome will hold for us? Jim has decided we must go and I, of course, will follow.

❧

ROME IS A-BOIL. THE AIR SHIMMERS LIKE WATER IN THE JULY heat above our heads. The sun blinds us outside the train station; pale buildings and golden statues blaze and I feel as if my eyes might melt. We take a carriage to our lodgings in Via Frattina and I feel disquieted and so very weary after our journey.

Our landlady, Signora Dufour, is grim—she does not even smile at the baby when she greets us and we're not used to that. She lets us into our room and we climb onto one of the beds in our clothes and sleep in a huddle for a few hours, trying to let the trip drain from us. When we wake, we're starving and we take ourselves out to the street to find a caffè. We eat a little pasta with cheese and I'm happy to see Georgie with a handful of spaghetti and a grin on his face.

"Ibsen came to Rome, Nora," Jim says.

"Is that why we've come, so you can follow where he went?" I say, wishing Ibsen had stopped at home.

"Perhaps."

Sometimes the things that move Jim through life mystify me; the man doesn't seem to have a plain thought or action and I, it seems, can only trot along in his wake. Ibsen came to Rome indeed. Well, Mister Ibsen, Nora did too.

ETERNAL

❧

Rome
AUTUMN 1906

T HE DAYS IN ROME SEEM TO CONTAIN MORE SECONDS AND minutes than those in Trieste and their monotony has me at cross-purposes with everyone and everything: Jim for bringing us here and for disappearing into the bank from Monday to Saturday, then into the caffè at night, and into his writing when he can. Georgie for being a small and simple one-year-old and no company at all for a grown woman. Rome itself for being hot and boring and rotten with ruins.

"This city is nothing but a mausoleum," Jim says. He jigs and jolts in his bed at night because he's having constant nightmares; I call across from my and Georgie's bed to try to wake him out of his terrors. Jim tells me that he dreams he kills people, hides their bodies, but knows that soon his secret will be unearthed and he will hang. "I play a horribly active part in these murders, Nora," he says this morning, though he doesn't say exactly what that means. We're sitting over our coffee and jammy rolls, before he heads to work.

"At least there're plenty of old boneyards around here to hide your victims in, Jim." I try to make him smile. He snorts—not quite a laugh. Our mutual melancholy passes back and over between us like the weight on a pulley rope, but I attempt to find happiness in the small things, such as our shared breakfast. Sometimes they're the only moments we spend together in a day.

"Do you know what it is, Nora?" Jim says. "Rome is like a man who makes his living by exhibiting his grandmother's corpse to tourists."

I laugh. "Oh, Jim." I stand, kiss his forehead, and he pulls me to him and speaks into my stomach.

"My lovely Gooseen, why have we come here?"

"Because Ibsen did." I sigh. "For the money I suppose, Jim. For a chance for you to do something other than teach. To be in a proper Italian city, not one run by Austrians."

Jim lifts his head to me. "But my fellow clerks are so damnably irritating, always complaining about their itchy holes and broken balls." I giggle. "Already I've had enough."

He stands to put on his jacket and, through the oft-repaired back of his trousers, I see his drawers.

"Jim, loveen, throw off them trousers quick, the seat has got worse."

He swivels his behind, and his head, too, to look. "For the love of Jaysusing God," he yelps, "I'm about to go!" I run for needle and thread. Jim slips out of the trousers and, as swift as I can, I resew the slipping patch. "This is why I have to bake all day in my tailcoat, Nora, while the other clerks are in shirtsleeves. My arse hanging out!"

When he's gone, I sit in the chair and flop my head into my hands and rub at my forehead. Georgie, who's playing with a toy horse on the floor, comes to me. He puts his fat wee hand onto one of mine and drags it away from my face.

"Lovely *Mamma*," he says, and this small loving gesture makes tears flood from my eyes. I grab Georgie onto my lap and hug him, and I sob and bawl until I'm spent.

TODAY WE'RE MEETING JIM FOR LUNCH. IF GEORGIE AND I DIDN'T sometimes go to Jim during his two-hour *pranzo*, we would barely see him. We have little money what with Stannie's earnings leaking back to Dublin and Jim's small advance from the bank already eaten up, but Georgie loves a good meal. I like to put him to my breast, his little face full of admiration for me, his belly full of my milk. But it's joyful, too, to see him in a high chair in a caffè, his tray loaded with presents of sliced apple and biscotti from a bustling *cameriere*. The Romans love children—our landlady is unique in her nose-turning from Georgie, it seems.

I park the pram outside the caffè, lift Georgie out, and let him toddle in to his darling babbo. I've collected our post and I'm excited to give Jim a parcel from Aunt Josephine. She sends him the Dublin newspapers and books he asks for and, often, a little note for myself.

Jim swings the baby high. "Giorgio, my sweet man," he says and puts him into the high chair that the *cameriere* already has waiting.

I hand Jim the package and he undoes the strings and paper with his accustomed haste; we divide up the newspapers and, while we wait for our food, share little extracts with each other. When Jim reads of a book that's been published, by some fellow he knew in college, it makes him gloomy.

"The man can't write a convincing sentence, Nora. But his family is wealthy, so I suppose that helped to get him his contract."

I reach over and squeeze his hand. "It's not fair, Jim."

"I am destined, it seems, to be ever the muzzled ox who threshes grain—I do the work, but I don't get to enjoy the fruits."

Jim is given to drama when it comes to the success of those he deems beneath him in ability; I get tired of it, but I know I have to keep his spirits high. "Now, now," I say, "let's not be too glum. Things will get better. Trust in me, trust in yourself."

He shakes the newspaper violently. "We can't read the future, Nora. And if some English printer refuses to publish *Dubliners* simply because old Queen Vicky is referred to as 'that bloody bitch,' well, I throw up my hands, that's all."

In truth, there are some innuendos and unpleasantries in Jim's stories that the printer for Grant Richards is also in terror of, but Jim loves to latch on to one grievance and mold and mash it into whatever he wants it to be.

"Your book will be published, dearest, be sure of that."

"Ach, how can I be? If I took out from the collection every small thing that gave offense to some jumped-up Englishman, there'd be nothing left but the title."

Our food is laid before us, three glorious mounds of *bucatini* pasta in butter sauce. Georgie pushes his hand into his and eats. Jim slurps at his second glass of wine though I have not so much as taken a sip from my first. He is down today and my coaxing is having little effect.

"Go easy on the wine, Jim," I say gently, "or you'll fall asleep over your desk this afternoon."

"Well, it'd be better than having to listen to Fat Bartoluzzi warble on about the best position for one's blotter." He forks pasta into his mouth.

I lift the note addressed to me from Jim's aunt and read it.

"Aunt Josephine says the pudding I made 'must have been a

great treat for the boys,' meaning you and Stannie, I suppose. She asks after Georgie, too, of course."

Jim leans over and squints at the page in my hand. "Not a full stop or a comma to be found, naturally."

"Only you care about full stops, Jim. The rest of us couldn't give a fiddler's fart."

He smiles and we both settle back with the papers to read all the news from home and I'm glad of the little bit of silence reading them affords.

OUSTED

～

Rome
DECEMBER 1906

I HAVE SOMETHING TO TELL JIM THAT I'VE BEEN HOLDING ON TO since Friday and I'm searching for the softest way to say it, the way that will anger him the least. We buy five slices of cooked roast beef, a few of the meatballs called *polpetti* in tomato sauce for Georgie, a couple of rice-stuffed tomatoes and some salad, and we carry it to a wine shop where they provide plates and cutlery. When we have our meal arranged, the man brings our wine, a warming red for this winter evening.

"Jim, there's something I need to say. To tell you."

He looks up from his beef. "I know what it is, my Gooseen. You want to say that there is not one decent caffè in Rome and damn Pope Pius to hell for it."

I laugh obligingly but go on. "No, my love, it's a lot more serious than that." I pause, unsure how to begin.

"Speak then." He forks rice into his mouth, but I lay down my cutlery.

"Jim, when you were at the bank on Friday, Signora Dufour came to our door."

"And what did she want? Less noise from Georgie? Less nighttime singing from me?"

"Well, yes, probably both those things. But, more than that, she's raising our rent and we can't afford it."

To my astonishment Jim's reaction is to break into a smile. He pours more wine for both of us, and he lifts his glass and nods for me to do the same. He clinks his wineglass to mine and swallows and I do likewise.

"Nora, I thought you were going to tell me that I was shortly to be a father again. Signora Dufour is a morose lady but she is not unkind. She won't put us out before Christmas. So let us relax, enjoy our meal, and think about this on a day when it will not harm our leisure."

Needles of annoyance shoot through me. "But, Jim—"

He raises his hand. "It will be all right, Gooseen, trust me."

I want to argue with him; I want to tell Jim that the signora has indeed complained to me several times about the din we cause. I want to remind him that Stannie is tormented by Jim's constant begging for money, that his brother is fed up surviving on bread and ham while we dine out, and he talks more and more of returning to Dublin in his letters to me. But I let it pass. Instead I help Georgie to stab a meatball onto his fork and lift it to his mouth. If Jim thinks things'll work out, perhaps they will. For today, I'll quiet my worry and hope that he's right.

I STAND IN THE DOORWAY OF OUR VIA FRATTINA ROOM AND AT-tempt to bar Signora Dufour's way. Jim's behind me, haranguing her, and she barks back; I throw in an argument where I see fit. The landlady goes suddenly silent, places two fingers into her mouth, and lets out a shrieking whistle that summons two broad men from belowstairs. We pack our trunk quickly and Jim lifts a sleeping Georgie from bed. It's half eleven at night and it's lashing rain.

Jim huddles Georgie and me into a restaurant on Via Frattina and runs to hire a car. With trunk and baby and rain it's impossible to traipse the streets to find a hotel. He returns with the car, and the driver suggests suitable places for us to try. All the time Jim calls Signora Dufour *"una strega"*—a witch—and we laugh when Giorgio says, in a serious voice, *"brutta strega"*—ugly witch.

Jim fixated on the idea that the signora would not evict us in December but here we are, wandering like the Holy Family looking for a bed. I'm cross with him for not heeding my warnings about Signora Dufour. I glance at him in the dim light; he has Georgie clutched to his chest and his chin is worrying the child's head. He's chastened, it's clear to me, and for that, at least, I'm thankful.

NATALE

❧

Rome
DECEMBER 24, 1906

OUR TOP-FLOOR ROOM, ON VIA MONTE BRIANZO, IS NEAR the Tiber and I can smell the river, a stinky, evil serpent. The room is bare: one bed, a chest of drawers, a tiny table, two slim chairs. The floor's made of stone and it's perishing cold underfoot. We share a kitchen. Georgie will only get a few marbles in his Christmas stocking.

Jim has two private students now, on top of the bank, so we see less of him than ever. Even tonight, Christmas Eve, he's with one of them and my only hope is they don't lead each other astray with drink, Jim is so easily seduced by grappa. I tidy our few belongings and wrap the small notebook and nibs I got for Jim in a clean hanky, tying it with some old ribbon from a hat. When I have it presentable, I hear his footfall on the stairs, and I conceal the parcel under the pillow. I run to open the door, so happy am I that he's come home to me.

"Shush," I say, holding a finger to my lips, "the maneen's asleep."

Jim kisses my forehead and we both go and stand over Georgie in the bed and watch the gentle pulse of his chest. Jim reaches into his pocket and takes out a paper bag.

"It's all I can offer, Nora," he says, "but I promise you better times, and better presents anon, my lovely goose."

I take the bag, delight rising up through me. "What is it, Jim?"

"Something small for you and something for Giorgio, too."

I fish out a tiny parcel of green tissue and and open it, careful to save the paper, and find a ceramic brooch. It has gilded edges and is painted with butterflies, pink roses and a trail of blue flowers. "Roma" is scrolled in navy lettering across the top.

"Oh Jim!" I collapse in tears because I expected nothing and to have something so sweetly pretty charms me. Jim pulls me to him.

"Happy Christmas, Gooseen. The blue flowers match your eyes, see?" He rocks me gently, takes the brooch, and pins it to my blouse.

"It's the loveliest thing, Jim."

He goes to the kitchen to brew some chocolate and I take the *cantuccini* I've been saving from the tin and arrange them on the violet-sprigged plate. I look again into the paper bag and there are two sugar mice for Georgie. I quickly wrap them in the green tissue paper and put them into his stocking with the marbles. When Jim comes back with the mugs, his Christmas present is on the table and he smiles to see it. Jim is a great man for celebrations, and though we've both mismanaged our money in every way, it feels good to give each other some token, no matter how miserable. He unwraps the notebook and pen nibs and says he's very happy.

"What did you eat tonight, my love?" Jim asks, dipping his head as if to avoid the poverty of my answer.

"I had rigatoni with oil and a good pinch of salt. Not so bad." I say. "I gave Georgie the bit of cheese we had; he ate enough pasta for two men."

"They belch out clouds of appetite boosters from Saint Peter's to make sure the faithful keep sated and dull, Nora."

"We certainly seem to be hungrier since we got here." I sip the warm chocolate and crunch through several *cantuccini*. "Isn't this grand, Jim, all the same?"

"Nora, Nora, Nora." He reaches across the table and clutches my hand. "Your optimistic good humor astounds me. I sit here thinking of all we lack and you see only what we have."

"Sure, we don't need much besides ourselves, do we?" I say, indicating him, myself, and Georgie in the bed.

"We really don't." He kisses my fingers. "I've been concocting a new story, Nora, for *Dubliners*. It strikes me that none of the stories have alluded yet to the great hospitality of Irish people. I think Grant Richards will like this one, it will soften the rest, maybe. And it might put a gallop on him to publish the book."

"Will this new story talk about hospitality then?"

"It will. I mean, it'll still be about paralyzed people, the difficulties they have in understanding one another, but it's set at a party."

"A Christmas party, Jim?"

"In a sense, yes. It's the feast of the Epiphany, the sixth of January."

"*Oíche Nollaig na mBan*; Women's Christmas. My granny Healy was very fond of that day. She always put her feet up and I served her tea."

"The women in my story don't rest at all for they are preparing a great celebration for friends, relatives, and neighbors. These are older women, like my great-aunts, but there's a capable niece who lives with them too. They're three wise women." He stops as if picturing the scene and murmurs, "The Three Graces, laying on a feast."

"A feast? What do they have, Jim, to feed people with?" My stomach jolts in anticipation.

"They are not unwealthy ladies, these hostesses, and they put on a great spread, Nora. They're generous people who believe in eating well."

"Oh, tell me, what kind of food they serve, Jim. Do they have a goose?" My spit spills around my mouth at the thought.

"They do. A fine roast goose—not a Barnacle goose, mind. They have a nice, plump Danubian." He grins. "And a big ham, dotted with crumbs."

"They'd have a spiced beef, Jim, I think. Can you imagine the smell of it?"

"Yes, oh yes." Jim goes to the chest and opens the top drawer, where he keeps his paper and pens. He sits again and writes on a clean sheet: *goose, ham, spiced beef.* "There's a long table, Nora, filled with plates. And a sideboard, also well stocked. They have those dishes, you know the ones, they look like cabbage leaves, only fancier."

"I do! They're green and veined and they have a big stalk at one end."

"That's the boys. And on those leaf-shaped dishes the good ladies will pile raisins and almonds; a lovely block of Smyrna figs."

He writes: *leaf dish x 2, figs, almonds et cetera.*

I groan. My belly is stuck to my back with the hunger; I put my hands to it. I look to the violet plate, but we have eaten all the *cantuccini.* There are six more in the tin, but I'm saving them for tomorrow. Jim is looking at me as if waiting for more suggestions.

"The ladies have bowls of custard, Jim, sprinkled with grated nutmeg. Granny Healy loved that, we had it on Sundays."

He lights two cigarettes to quell our gnawed-up innards, hands one to me, and goes on. "There are boiled sweets and chocolates in bright wrappers; a fruit stand with oranges and fat red apples."

"Decanters made of crystal, so they catch the light, with port and sherry, both. And a punch bowl, with tiny cups hanging off the side."

"Bottles of minerals and stout and ale. Whiskey for the older men." Jim smiles and jots it all down.

"Jellies of every color and jams—apricot and strawberry. A blancmange like a pink and white castle." I see all the food on the magnificent table as if it were before me. "And they have to have an enormous plum pudding, Jim, one big enough to feed all the guests."

"A mighty pudding. It sits in a yellow dish on top of the piano—these are musical ladies, Nora—waiting to be doused and lit up at the end of the meal."

Our knuckles meet in the ashtray where we both stub our cigarettes. I look at Georgie's stocking and Jim's eyes follow mine.

"We could share a sugar mouse," I say, conspiratorially. "The pair of mice might be too much for him."

"Two whole ones would surely sicken the boy; I should've thought of that. Quick, Nora." He grins.

I hop up and plunge my hand into the stocking. I unroll the two mice from the tissue paper, rewrap one, and take the other to the table. Jim already has the sharp knife. He slits the mouse from nose to rump and we stand looking at it.

"It's like some horrible experiment," Jim says.

But we both grab for a half and stuff the maimed, sugary creature into our mouths. We giggle as we relish the sweet melt of it on our tongues and against our teeth. We lick our fingertips like gossoons when all trace of the mouse has long disappeared into our bellies.

"Christ on the cross, I never tasted anything as good," Jim says, lighting another cigarette.

"Nor I." I glance at Georgie. "Are we terrible, Jim?"

"We're not, Nora. Giorgio knows no difference. He'll be delighted by his stocking anyway."

I bite my lip. "He will, no doubt. He's small, he knows little." I look at Jim, quiet now as he smokes and thinks. I put out my hand to him and he takes it. "We'll have better Christmases, Jim, I'm sure, plentiful ones. But here we are together, our little family, and isn't that a blessing in itself?"

He leans across the table and kisses me. "It is, Nora. It surely is."

RETURN

Trieste
MARCH 1907

ROME WAS A FAILURE AND NO AMOUNT OF IBSEN IN THE AIR could make Jim like it and he did what he always does when he finds things hard—he took to the drink. Last week he stayed out all of one night, soused out of his brain, dancing with other men on the Pincio hill, shouting, according to himself: "I'm the king of the castle, get down, you dirty rascal!" He was playing out his disappointment after another publisher rejected *Dubliners*—he had given up on Richards publishing the book. But I wish he had done that at home, quietly with me and Georgie. He managed to get himself robbed. Two hundred crowns, almost his whole month's wages, gone. I was furious. So much so I could barely speak to him when he came back to our room and confessed it. I only thanked Mary in heaven that I'd made him give me some money for safekeeping.

But today my fury is softened. Rome's behind us. Jim quit the bank. He tried to get a post in Marseilles—we wanted a port city, not a tourist spot like Rome—but no one needed him. So here we are, the three of us, chugging north back to Trieste, though it's not clear to me yet what Jim intends to do there. Still, we feel better for leaving Rome and Jim will surely find some teaching.

"It's like going home," I say.

A small smile. "It is, Nora. Home to our warm seaport."

He pops a rhubarb pill into his mouth and must swallow it dry for we have nothing with which to wash it down. Jim wonders why he gets such foul indigestion and makes no connection between it and the drink. I feel annoyance bubble again and I try to freeze my tongue, but I can't help myself, there are things I need to say, and one thing, in particular, he *must* hear.

"I know why you drink, Jim."

He brazens. "Indeed, Nora. Do you?"

"I do. You want to lose the sharp edge of yourself, to drop away from your own mind, your cares. The same way a baby lulls itself into sleep." He raises his eyebrows and folds his arms. "But you're no gossoon, Jim. You're a man. And all them edges you soften grow back twice as hard in the morning. Have you noticed that?" He nods slowly. "And it's me and Georgie who must knock against them. You're not right in yourself, then, until you've had the next softening grappa and the next bottle of wine and the next absinthe. Do you understand that about yourself?"

"I don't sound like much of a man, Nora, when you outline it so," he murmurs.

"Well, you have to *be* a man, Jim Joyce. You have to think about what it's like for me and for your son. Do you think we enjoy lying awake, waiting for your step night after night, just to know that you're safe?" He shakes his head. "Jim, I want no more drinking. And no more talk of 'decayed ambitions,' if you please. If you want to write, you must make the time to write. Boozing and carousing will get you nowhere." I glance at Georgie who has his face and one fat finger up to the window, the better to name off all he sees from the train. I look back at his father. "We'll soon be four, Jim."

He blinks, looks at my stomach. "Are you telling me you are *enceinte*, Gooseen?"

"I am. We should have kept to our separate beds as we planned, Jim," I say wearily but, in truth, I'm warmed by my growing body, by the idea of another child.

"Giorgio will soon have a brother to torment, as I do Stannie." Jim's voice rises with excitement.

"Well, you never know. Georgie may end up with a sister to bow to." I allow myself a laugh.

Jim drops to his knees and takes my hands. He kisses my belly through my skirt. "*Benvenuto*," he says. "Welcome, little one." I puck him with my toe and he sits back up. "When do we expect the happy event, Nora? How long have you known?"

"I've been suspicious since Christmastime because of the great hunger that overtook me like a tide. But I couldn't tell a sinner when it'll be born."

"I shall call to Doctor Sinigaglia the moment we reach Trieste. You must see him at once."

"No, Jim. The moment we reach Trieste you'll find us somewhere to live."

STANNIE HAS A FACE ON HIM LIKE A MIZZLY MONDAY WHEN HE meets us at the station. Jim sent him a telegram to tell him we were returning: "Arrive eight get room." We could only afford four words. No doubt Stanislaus is as surprised as ourselves that we're back in Trieste. It's been hard on him, I suppose, having to send bits of his wages down to Rome, while trying to support the crowd back in Dublin, too, as best he can. Stannie does without for the good of everyone else; he's a fine type of man in that way. And he looks well now, slimmer, yes, but he's taken a tan to his face and looks more European than Irish.

Georgie wriggles out of my arms and runs to his uncle. "Stannie, Stannie," he calls.

Stanislaus swoops up the boy and snugs his face into his neck. "You're huge, Giorgio. A monster." He kisses his nephew before setting him down, shakes Jim's hand, and then extends his hand to me.

"Will you come here, Stannie?" I say and embrace him. "You look like a true Triestino now."

"See, Stannie, the train!" Georgie shouts and they go to the side of the track to watch one puff away.

Stannie comes back to us. "So what now? Artifoni is adamant that there's no job for you at the Berlitz, Jim. Things are too tight. What do you mean to do?"

"I will give private lessons."

"It's March, Jim. Come summer, nobody will want English lessons."

Jim laughs and links his brother. "Well then, Stannie, I have you."

I can almost feel the blood rising in Stannie's veins. "Jim will get work," I say quickly, "don't fret."

"Of course I will. Won't I have one more gob to shove pasta into shortly?" Jim looks at Stannie who looks at me.

"Nora? Are you in the family way again?"

"I am."

"Lord God," he says, then, remembering his manners, he congratulates me. "You will need a quarter, a proper place to live with decent space."

"Where are we to go tonight, Stannie?" I ask, knowing it will sit better coming from me.

"You may take my bed and I'll have the floor."

Jim tuts. "You didn't find us a room?"

"With a few hours' notice? You're some blackguard, Jim." Stannie turns to stand chest to chest with his brother and I fear they're going to start thumping the lard out of each other, so I step closer.

"The Francinis will take us for a few days while Jim looks about for a room."

"Rooms, Nora," Stannie says. "And don't you owe Alessandro and Clotilde a deal of rent money from when you left?"

"We do, but the Francinis are kindness itself. They won't hold the debt against us." I bite my lip, realizing what I've said. "I don't mean to imply that you would, Stannie."

"Can you imagine me with my own quarter?" Jim says, as if he hasn't been listening to our talk. "A lovely set of rooms, complete with servant, nicely turned out childer, a saintly wife, and a small bank account. No, I don't think that's in my future somehow; it would frighten the shite out of me, brother. A decent-size room of any description will do us nicely."

I try to imagine having a maid, someone to make meals and wash clothes and take a broom to the floor, but I let the gorgeous vision dissolve. It will be a fluthering miracle if Nora Barnacle is ever waited upon by another woman.

We walk down the platform, Jim and Stannie dragging our luggage and Georgie trotting along beside, chattering to his uncle who smiles and answers him. I've missed Stannie; it warms me to run my eyes across him. We emerge out of the train station and into the Trieste evening, and when I see the city before me, I can't stop smiling, I'm so thrilled to be back.

WE'RE TAKING THE AFTERNOON AIR; AWAY FROM OUR ROOM ON Via Santa Catarina. Georgie clings to me so, which makes me feel I can't breathe, and I must get out and stretch myself.

Jim pouts sometimes. "Giorgio loves his mamma more than his babbo."

"He's spent most of his life in my lap, Jim. Now that he's weaned, you're free to spend as much time as you want with him."

But, you see, that's not what Jim wants at all. No, no, he wants to write and to read his newspapers and books in peace; he wants solitary walks and time to linger in a caffè and bouts of drinking with strangers. He doesn't want the care of Georgie, he just wants his admiration and love. And he has both, I tell him this frequently. We walk on, Georgie bouncing ahead, all a-chatter with some invisible friend.

Jim is moderately happy because Artifoni can give him a few days teaching at the Berlitz and his book of poems, *Chamber Music*, will be out soon. Jim says they're not good, calls them "auld love poems," but I think they're beautiful and tell him that often. So, despite all, things are looking brighter and our return to Trieste has been, if not triumphant, at least an improvement on lonely old Rome.

SETTLING

৵৹

Trieste
MARCH 1907

My belly grows by the day; Doctor Sinigaglia says the
baby will come in July, just like Georgie did. This had Stannie and Jim sniggering daily about "the annual copulation."

"Heed your stupid tongues around Georgie," I snapped.

That shut them up.

We've been relying on the goodness of Stannie, and the
Francinis say we can pay back later the rent we owe from last summer. I hate to live this way, but I have the care of our son and, soon,
the new baby, so it's up to Jim to get money from somewhere. The
only reason Artifoni gave him a few hours at the Berlitz is because
he's afraid Jim will poach the best students for private lessons, like
the count and the baron who make the school look so fine, but
who are awfully fond of Jim and would follow him out the door.
However, the pay from those classes at the school is not enough,
no matter what type of gentry saunters through the place.

Jim, of course, is the cat who keeps living, the nine-lifer, and
he scuttles into Santa Catarina to tell me his latest news. I'm bathing Georgie in a puddle of water in a basin and, being a child who
doesn't like to be washed, he's moaning his head off. Jim looms

over us and waits for me to notice that he has something particular to say.

"What?" I bark, trying to keep hold of Georgie's soapy arm while I scrub his bottom and legs. He wails like a man under torture. Jim remains silent, waiting for me to look up at him—he always requires a proper audience. "You're like the priest who stalls and stalls until his congregation is fully quiet," I say, sick of his dramatizing. I glance at him for I wound him sometimes without fully meaning to.

He frowns. "Nora, Signor Roberto Prezioso is giving me some work. Writing work."

"What kind?"

"I'm to pen articles for his paper, *Il Piccolo della Sera*."

"And what's the pay at a newspaper like?" I pick up the jug, test the water with my finger, and begin to rinse the suds off Georgie.

"Play bubbles, Mamma?" he asks.

I can blow them as big as footballs, but now is not the time. "No, darling," I say, and he puts on his sulkiest face.

"Well, Nora, the pay is the best thing. Prezioso took me aside after class and said he'd like me to write a piece on the Fenians. He sees the parallels between colonized Ireland and the Irredentist movement here."

"So?" I say, my impatience with Jim growing. I wrap Georgie in a towel and pat him dry.

"Let me finish, Nora, won't you? Can't you leave the boy for a moment while we talk?"

"And have him run naked through the building and make a disgrace of me? No, I can't. Everything doesn't stop because you walk in the door, Jim." I sit hard into the chair and drag Georgie's underclothes on over his damp skin. "Doesn't Alessandro Francini write for that paper, *Il Piccolo?*"

"He does." Jim makes a show of lighting a cigarette, which he'll slowly smoke until he has my full attention. When Georgie has at least trousers on, I let him down and he scampers away to his toys. "Nora, Roberto Prezioso said to me: 'Joyce, I will pay you at a higher rate than other contributors for two reasons. First, because you are writing in a foreign language and, second, because you so clearly need the money.' Isn't that marvelous, Gooseen?"

"That this Prezioso knows we're poor? Marvelous indeed." I scowl at Jim though, in truth, I'm as pleased as a dog with two pockets. But I'm also exhausted, and so moidered with the endless care of Georgie, that I don't feel like showing it. But Jim drags me from the chair and waltzes me around the table, around our son at play on the floor, and over to the window.

"Signor Roberto Prezioso is our savior, you see that, Nora, don't you? Prezioso by name and nature. From now on, I shall call him nothing but Mr. Bob Precious." He holds me by the waist and kisses my lips. "This is good news, Nora."

I allow myself to smile, take the cigarette from his fingers, and smoke the last of it. "It *is* welcome news, Jim. How many articles?"

"Who knows? Hundreds probably." He kisses me again. "I shall call the first one '*Il Fenianismo*' and I will tear down the church as much as the English in it."

"Oh, you and the church. Their religion is a great comfort to Irish people, to all people. The church is not as bad as you say, Jim."

"No, it's not. It's twenty times worse."

I think of the extra money and my heart burbles like a contented dove. Jim goes to the old chocolate box where he keeps his writing things, takes out a notebook, and scribbles something down. His eyes have the writing look in them, as if his mind has moved into some exalted place and the world about him no longer exists.

"Go to a caffè and get started," I say, waving at him.

"Are you sure, Nora?"

"Won't it put *papardelle* pasta on our plates? *Polpetti* too."

"*Polpetti*! *Papardelle*! *Polpetti*!" Georgie shouts and waggles his hands. We giggle.

"*Sì, sì*, Giorgio," Jim says, "and soon we'll dine on many more good things besides."

He dips to the floor and kisses Georgie on the head. He rushes to me, kisses both my cheeks, and is gone.

I FEEL AS IF WE'VE GONE BACKWARD IN TIME. I DRAG MYSELF around Trieste, my belly in my way, just as I did two years ago with Georgie. This go-around, though, I'm altogether tidier, not just in body but in attire. Though we haven't much to spare, Jim likes to buy me a nice ribbon for my hat if he sees it, or clean, bright gloves for, he says, he won't have me pottering around the city like a rag-bag. I have a new dress that can be let out as my front expands. At least the vast heat won't descend for another few months and, please God, it won't be as bad as it was in 1905; the sun almost did away with me back then.

What's different, too, is that we breakfast with Stannie every morning. Mostly, there's no hurry on Jim, for he gives lessons only two days a week, but we like to rise with his brother and eat together. Today they're spatting back and forth, as is their custom, and I consume my breakfast and listen idly.

"No one who has any self-respect stays in Ireland," Jim says. This is the subject he's writing on for the *Piccolo* and we must listen to him talk endlessly of it.

"Some people have no choice but to stay in Ireland," Stannie answers. "And what Irish person, home or abroad, has self-respect anyway? Isn't it the national disease, self-hatred tied up with timidity?"

I snort and both their heads swivel toward me. I have my bare feet up on the bed, the legs of my chair swinging, and I'm eating honey from the jar with our one good spoon.

"What?" I say to their stares.

"Some among us, of course," Jim says, "are the essence of what it means to be self-assured."

The two brothers look at each other, smile, and bend their heads to their bread and jam. They fancy, I suppose, that I don't take their meaning. But I understand them fine; Jim sees himself as the great thwarted intellectual and he's that, as sure as eggs, but he's also a father and a husband, in the true sense of that word, and that I *don't* let him forget.

"Go on, the pair of you," I say. "Less auld talk and more getting yourselves out the door, if you please. You have lire to earn and I have tidying to do."

Obedient as lambs they both rise and pull combs through their hair, Stannie at the looking glass to make sure he's neat. They put on their jackets, say their good-byes to Georgie and me, and I'm left once more in silence.

BOOK

✧

Trieste
MAY TO JULY 1907

IT'S A DARLING THING, JIM!" I'M HOLDING THE COPY OF *CHAM-ber Music* in wonder and passing my hands over the cover. He has collected a parcel of the books from the post office and brought them home so that, after him, I might be the first to see them. Elkin Mathews has done a fine job of the book. I lift it to my nose and sniff gently.

Jim laughs. "That was my first action, too, Nora."

"The smell is glorious. And isn't it wonderful that the book is green, like Ireland?" I say, running the tip of my finger gently across the moss linen, then over the golden letters of Jim's name. "Now, doesn't it look very fine indeed? Like something a prince would have."

Jim laughs. "Oh, Nora," he says, shaking his frayed shirt cuffs, "I'm not likely to be mistaken for royalty."

I hold up the volume. "This is an absolute credit to you, Jim. There'll be great praise of this book at home, wait till you see. The literary fellows will be punching each other out of the way to be the first to applaud it."

"Open it, Gooseen, go on."

My breath comes short as I turn the cover to find—though it

hardly seems possible—that the insides are even better than the front. "Oh, Jim, look." There's a drawing of a piano with columns around it that are draped in scrolls of sheet music. "The publishers thought of everything."

"I'm heartily glad you like the book, Nora," he says, his face lit up like summer.

I turn the pages reverently, afraid to soil them or bend even the smallest corner. I find one of the poems I really admire and read part of it now to Jim:

> *O, it is for my true love*
> *The woods their rich apparel wear*
> *O, it is for my own true love,*
> *That is so young and fair.*

My eyes clutter up with tears, so moved am I by the poem once more, but also by the fact that Jim now has a real book, a gorgeously made one. That he's a published author, as he's always wanted to be. Jim can hold his head high now—he's not just a teacher—and those scamps back in Dublin who scourge his heart with their tattling talk will have to sit up and take heed.

THE FIRST REVIEW WE GET TO SEE IS FROM ARTHUR SYMONS. Aunt Jo has promised to send a copy of *The Nation*, the magazine that it appears in. We're like sausages dancing in hot butter so jittery are we waiting for the post. The parcel comes at long last and Jim rips it open but then can't bring himself to read the review and hands the magazine over to Stannie. I take Giorgio onto my lap and we wait.

"Go through it first," Jim says, "and if it's terrible, don't read it out." He puts his *pince-nez* on and off, agitates the back of a chair with his fingers. "No, do. Call out the bloody thing, whatever it says. Go on!"

Stannie clears his throat and begins. "'I advise everyone who cares for poetry to buy *Chamber Music*, by James Joyce, who is in no Irish movement, literary or national and who has not even anything obviously Celtic in his manner.'"

"Hurrah for that," says Jim and I laugh.

Stannie, who cares more for nationalism than Jim does, looks at us sternly and I nod for him to go on. "'The poems are all so singularly good, so firm and delicate, and yet so full of music and suggestion . . . No one who has not tried can realize how difficult it is to do such tiny, evanescent things as that; for it is to evoke, not only roses in midwinter, but the very dew on the roses . . . There is almost no substance at all in these songs, which hardly hint at a story; but they are like a whispering clavichord that someone plays in the evening, when it is getting dark. They are so slight, as a drawing of Whistler is slight, that their entire beauty will not be discovered by those who go to poetry for anything but its perfume.'"

"Oh," I say, "now doesn't that sound grand?" I'm not sure what Mr. Symons means entirely, but it reads well, all the talk of roses, perfume, and music and catching people's fancy.

Jim frowns. "'No substance' Symons says. 'Slight.' You were skipping over parts, Stannie. Is there worse?"

Stannie shakes his head. "There's some more comment, but it's a very positive review, Jim. Symons says there's beauty and hidden depths." Stannie searches the page again with his eyes. "Look here, he pronounces that the poems are 'firm and delicate.' That's lofty praise, Jim."

Jim lights a cigarette and blows smoke out into the air. He nods sharply and holds his hand out for the magazine, which he then hands to me. "Put it away, Nora," he says.

JIM'S NOT HIMSELF AT ALL; HIS LOVELY VOICE HAS BEEN REDUCED to a whisper, he complains of aching knees and elbows, of being too hot then too cold, and he slobs around like a sack of spuds, not even interested in going to a caffè for one little drink. But he refuses to take to the bed and get rest, though he shivers and moans and can't get comfortable.

"Should we ask Doctor Sinigaglia to come?" I say to Stannie.

He looks over to the chair where Jim is slumped with a book on his lap, though he doesn't turn the pages. "Let's see what happens and how he progresses, Nora. Is he drinking the lemon water regularly?"

"He is but with no good grace. He seems worse to me, Stannie, since Sunday."

"I can hear the pair of you snoddering like two old sows." Jim's throat rasps like a rusty gate. "What are you saying about me?"

"I want Doctor Sinigaglia to have a look at you."

"I'm not dying," Jim whispers, lifting each leg with a long groan. "Though it feels a little as if I might be."

"He's wretched, Stannie. Would you see if the doctor can spare a few minutes?"

Stannie goes off and I coax Jim into the bed for, if the doctor sees him up and dressed, he surely won't take things seriously. The hours tick by and Jim dozes and I try to keep Georgie quiet, but he's not a lamblike child so, eventually, I shunt him out into the corridor to play. The baby in my belly kicks wildly and I have to stay still until the frenzy calms. I stand by the door, close my eyes, place both hands to my stomach, and wait for the kicking to stop. When I glance to Jim, he's watching me.

"She's a wild one," I say.

"Does it hurt?"

"It feels as if she's tumbling like an acrobat. Sometimes I think she means to kick a hole in me and climb out."

"Our little dancer. Do you think it *will* be a girl, Nora?"

"Only God knows that, Jim."

"And as *he* doesn't exist, even *he* doesn't know," Jim says and laughs, but the laughter hurts his throat and he begins to cough, a brittle sound. Jim beckons me over to the bed and I go to sit by him. "Thank you for looking after me, Gooseen. I'm not a patient patient. Pappie never let us be sick when we were children, so I don't know how to conduct myself."

"It's all right, Jim." I hold his tired head to my skirt. "I'll mind you."

A rap to the door and Stannie comes in with Doctor Sinigaglia who goes to Jim and throws back the sheet. He lifts Jim's shirt and we all peer in to see that his stomach is pocked with red spots. Sinigaglia asks in rapid Italian about other symptoms and Jim lists them off.

"*Febbre reumatica*," the doctor says, "for certain."

"Translate for me, Jim."

"Rheumatic fever."

I cross myself. There were many that died of the same thing back in Galway.

"He must go to the hospital, Mrs. Joyce, particularly as you are with child, and it's better to keep him from Giorgio, too."

"With luck it'll develop into Saint Vitus's dance, Nora, and I'll do a jig around the hospital ward to entertain my fellows." Jim cackles.

"Do *not* joke about it, James Joyce," I say, trying to quell tears. "Will it cost us?" I whisper, but the doctor hears and understands me.

"We provide care to all who need it, Mrs. Joyce."

Stannie puts his hand to my arm. "Don't be worrying, Nora, about anything. I'll get Jim over to the Ospedale Civico. Everything will be grand."

LIGHT

Trieste
JULY 1907

I LEFT THE SHUTTERS OPEN LAST NIGHT, HOPING FOR A BREEZE to come down from the Carso to stir the close air in our room. A fat cut of sunlight falls across the bed and I admire the lemony shine of it across the shadowed sheet. My mind idles and I find myself wondering why we're made at all, us people. Why did God put us on this earth, no better than beetles, when it comes to it, to run around and eat and drink and sleep? To push ourselves from here to there; to move, daily, our small piles of possessions from one spot to another.

I get up and let my thoughts wander on a while, as they do when this kind of melancholy descends, and for the thousandth morning in a row it feels, I do the same things: pee in the pot, wipe myself, dash water onto my face, dry it off, make coffee, sit at the table, slather jam onto bread, eat it. The only difference this last while is that Jim is away in the hospital, so I've no one to complain to about my endless nighttime fumbles for the pot, or the ache in my spine, the vast heaviness of my breasts, or the rude thrust of my belly. I talk to Stannie some mornings, of course, and Georgie, but not of such intimate things, and I miss Jim like the maimed soldier misses his absent limb.

Georgie sleeps on this morning and I let him; my thoughts are company enough. The baby inside me wriggles, woken, I like to think, by the jolt of sweetness from my apricot jam. Jim says he'll have to take on a private student so we can buy bigger and bigger pots of my favorite jam. Kind Jim. Darling Jim. Noble Jim. My greatest love, stricken by rheumatic fever. What if he's mortally ill and God takes him? I cross myself and pray to the Blessed Virgin, and her son, to spare Jim. I'd go into the grave after him if he died; I'd have no taste for this life without Jim. Tears plop onto the table and sobs racket through me. Now Georgie is out of the bed and over to me; standing in his nightshirt, he dabs at my face with his sleeve.

"Mamma, *per favore non piangere*. Please don't cry." And his wee faceen is so crumpled with worry that I shake the maudlin off myself and force a grin.

"It's all right, Georgie," I say, pulling him onto my lap. "Mamma's all right."

He wraps his little body around the egg of my belly and whispers, "*Bambino*."

"*Sì*, Georgie, *è un bambino*," I say, amazed at his knowing this for we haven't told him that there's a little one on the way. "But you're still my only one, my baby darling."

We sit and I rock my son, and along with him the tiny one within, and my worries shiver away into the morning.

I GO TO THE JACOB'S BISCUIT TIN WHERE WE KEEP OUR MONEY and it's empty save for a few sad coins. With Jim not working, there's nothing to put in it. What if he dies on me altogether? What on God's earth would I do then? I shake my head to remove the thought.

"I'll take in laundry again," I tell Stannie.

"No," he says, "you most certainly will not, Nora. I'm able to look after you and Giorgio until Jim is out of the hospital."

"Doctor Sinigaglia says Jim could be another month in there. It seems terrible to sit so squarely on you when you earn so little. What are we to do, Stannie?" He grimaces. I know Pappie and his sisters continue to beg him for money. It's not fair and I feel it keenly. "Let me take in a small bit of washing; it would please me to earn a few lire. It sits on my conscience terrible that we're a burden to you. I'll only take in ladies' things, undergarments and such."

"I'd rather you didn't, Nora. In fact, I forbid it and Jim would too. Your time is near and you should be at rest as much as possible, not bent over a tub of filthy garments."

"But I—"

Stannie holds up his hand. "No, I mean to be firm now. I'm covering Jim's teaching hours at the Berlitz, after all. We'll be grand."

But I know Stannie will borrow from the school to get us by and we'll all be up to our oxters in debt by the time Jim is well. I sit on the side of the bed and Stannie sits at the table, turning his cup but not drinking the coffee.

"You're a good man, Stanislaus Joyce."

He nods in that embarrassed, dismissive way of his. I throw my feet onto the bed and lean back.

"I'll leave you in peace, Nora."

"Stay awhile, Stannie, won't you?"

"I can't. I have to talk to Artifoni about Jim."

I nod, drowsy now. Stannie comes over and carefully arranges my shawl over me. He puts his hand to my shoulder and I pat it. "Thank you," I say and smile up at him. His eyes on me are tender and he looks like he wants to say something, but he pulls his hand away quickly and is gone. I wonder, sometimes, if I should be a bit more distant with Stannie, less softhearted. I love him and he loves me, but it's not the same as what I share with Jim. It's not *that* sort of love. But Stannie might mistake me, if we go on as we are. But I also know I couldn't spurn him, be cold toward him and pretend I don't care for him—he's lonely enough without that.

I lie on and doze while Georgie plays with his toy animals and chatters to himself. I have fleeting dreams; one where we're in a broiling, lion-filled South Africa—a place Jim recently thought he'd like to live—and then we're in Dublin, flying above the river Liffey on this very bed. I dream I'm being licked down below and it stirs me nicely; I prop on my elbows to watch, but it's Stannie's face that comes up from between my legs, wet from my juices and with a determined look to his face that I've never seen before. The surprise of it pulls me out of sleep and, when I'm properly awake, I have a feeling like a belt being tightened around my middle and I realize that it has started: the baby means to come today. I groan. With Stannie gone, I'll have to get to the hospital on my own.

I HAUL MYSELF TO SIGNORA CANARUTTO'S AND SHE TAKES GIORgio; the signora thinks I'm only going to visit Jim, and I don't want to alarm her. Neither do I want her to offer to pay for a cab for me, I'd be too embarrassed to accept. But halfway to the Ospedale Civico I regret my pride. The heat is vicious, it seethes around my face, and I'm finding it awkward to walk and breathe, and to carry my basket of things I've readied for the baby on top of dealing with the pains that threaten to floor me at every hand's turn. I keep having to stop, set down the basket, and push my palms into a wall to steady me. I try not to gasp aloud with the agony of the searing in my lower body; I don't want half of Trieste crowded around me to gape and comment. The baby is bearing down fast and I feel as if I'm going to give birth on the street. I push forward, my gait a labored waddle, and at last I see the long stretch of the hospital building. I force myself on, each step a torture, for it's now as if the baby's head is squashed down between my legs. I gain the foyer at last and drop my basket on the floor.

"*Aiutami!*" I call out. "Help me!"

A porter and a matron come running and they lift me, like circus strongmen, onto a bench. There I gasp and snort, my breath and sweat and the bouncing pains making a shivery rag doll of me. The man grabs a rolling chair, its seat flimsy and the wheels wobbly, and speeds back over to where I'm slumped, trying to stay alert and in control of myself, though I feel like a tormented animal.

"*Ecco, signora,*" the nurse says, taking me by the elbow.

"That thing will fall asunder if I sit in it!" I stare at the dainty wicker seat, but another pain grips me like a vise and, while I'm frozen inside the scorch of it, they take their opportunity and lift me into the chair. I'm crying out "Oh, oh" and scrambling up the ends of my skirts, for the baby's head is bulging in my drawers for sure.

The porter rushes the chair along the corridors and the nurse has her hand on my shoulder and it feels like the touch of an angel. I put my fingers over hers and she grabs mine, squeezes.

"You're safe, signora," she says.

Our daughter is delivered moments after my back meets the bed and the nurse squeals with delight, lifts the baby high and shows her to me, the long blue and blood-streaked body. I lie back, close my eyes, and send up thanks to God.

"Welcome, *a leana,*" I whisper, "little child, daughter of ours." I open my eyes. "Lucia Anna is here, our little Lucy," I say, hoping that Jim, over in the men's wing, will somehow hear me.

FAMILY

❧

Trieste
SEPTEMBER 1907

ONCE HE WAS WELL AGAIN, IT WAS STRAIGHT BACK TO HIS own little world for Jim. When he is pleased with himself, everything and everyone else is fecked out the window, as if Jim's the only thing that exists. It's like he's inside a soap bubble that no amount of pricking will pop and, in there, he smiles and chuckles, scribbles and nods, happy as a sow in mud. In his little kingdom of soap, he has satisfying conversations with himself that don't center on a bawling babe, or a bold little boy, or a brooding brother, or a man who blithely leaves his job to bring private students into an already up-on-its-arse home. He writes his notes and his stories and mulls over who-knows-what fresh idea like a man untouched by the world.

"I could box the head off you," I say, trying again to slip my nipple between Lucia's gaping gums while she bucks and squeals as if she's being trounced.

"What's that, Nora?" Jim says, dragging his gaze for half a second from his books and papers.

"I said you're annoying the shite out of me, James Joyce."

"How so?"

I tut and shake my head, get a waft of my own unclean hair.

When was the last time I had a chance to wash it? I stare hard at Jim. "We're up to our necks in debt. What do you mean by leaving your post at the Berlitz, now of all times?"

He looks startled. "I mean to earn a decent living, Gooseen. The Berlitz is belly up with Artifoni gone, I'm better off away from it. My articles bring in a few bob. And I can charge these private chaps ten crowns a lesson."

"And the private lassies. Don't forget to mention the lady students you're so fond of, Jim Joyce."

Just last night I had to watch him teach English verbs, at my table, to a bespectacled matron who fawned over him like a love-sick girl, touching her hand to his and bending her head close to whisper, as if I were not there at all. I clattered plates to remind her whose home she was sitting in on her well-padded backside.

"Ladies. Gents. Counts. Paupers. I will teach anyone who wants to pay me, Nora. And you must learn to be glad of it, my Goose."

"Perhaps, but I don't have to love it when some woman is dripping herself all over you like honey." I tut. "It shouldn't be up to me to let them know you're taken."

"And I am taken. Don't worry yourself."

"Don't let me have cause to! If you'd marry me, of course, I wouldn't have any need to worry."

"What difference would that make?" His look to me is startled. "We need no priest to keep us solid."

"Maybe *I* do," I say, properly irked with him for all he maddens me with. At last Lucia latches on and begins to feed; I never had such trouble with Georgie. Perhaps boys find it more natural to suckle a woman. "What has you so pleased with yourself, anyway?" I ask.

"When I was ensconced in the hospital, I thought of the right way to finish 'The Dead' and I just now wrote the ending." He smiles, such a warm, lit-up smile that I can't help but be buoyed a little by his pleasure.

"Ah, I'm happy for you, Jim. Go on, read it to me."

Georgie is out on the landing battering a pot lid with a stick and, with Lucia crooked along my arm, I go to the door and nudge it closed with my foot so that I can hear Jim properly. I sit up on the bed and nod, to tell him to begin. He coughs, holds up the page, and reads:

"'A few light taps upon the pane made him turn to the window. It had begun to snow again. He watched sleepily the flakes, silver and dark, falling obliquely against the lamplight. The time had come for him to set out on his journey westward. Yes, the newspapers were right: Snow was general all over Ireland. It was falling on every part of the dark central plain, on the treeless hills, falling softly upon the Bog of Allen and, farther westward, softly falling into the dark mutinous Shannon waves. It was falling, too, upon every part of the lonely churchyard on the hill where Michael Furey lay buried. It lay thickly drifted on the crooked crosses and headstones, on the spears of the little gate, on the barren thorns. His soul swooned softly as he heard the snow falling faintly through the universe and faintly falling, like the descent of their last end, upon all the living and the dead.'"

My ears vibrate with his words. *Snow was general all over Ireland.* Jim looks over and sees the tears that course down my cheeks. *Snow falling faintly through the universe and faintly falling.* How beautiful it is, how true to home. It astonishes me the way Jim can bend words and order them into something that makes a pulp of the heart.

"How do you like it, Nora?"

"You got it, Jim," I whisper. "You got Ireland."

He smiles broadly and nods. "I think I did, Gooseen. That's

it precisely." He shakes the page in the air. "I felt 'normal' writing this, Nora, if you see what I mean. My mind and my pen joined together and the words fell and it was as if I wasn't present at all. Ireland came to me—under snow, even in this sweltering heat—and I took her and I wrote her. I'm uncommonly pleased with myself."

"And so you should be, loveen," I say gently.

JIM ROCKS THE BABY AND SINGS TO HER TO STOP HER SQUAWLING. "Sleep now, Lucia of the light. Sleep, my slumberous-eyed Lucy," he croons.

Just like me the baby has a droop to her eye, but it's worse than mine, truth be told, and I hope it doesn't mar her appearance as she grows. Lucia looks like my own sister Peg who would never let any visitors to Mammy's house see her, so sensitive was she about the slouch of her eye. But I won't let that happen to my girleen—she will hold her head high wherever she goes.

Letters fly back and forth to Ireland. Jim's pappie asks if he was "quite mad" when he chose Lucia's name. His sister Eileen writes, "What on earth made you call her that?"

"Like proper shamefaced Irish citizens, they feel self-conscious pronouncing what's unusual," Jim says. "I'll write *Lucia* out phonetically for them. Loo-chee-ah."

"They'll learn how to say it quick enough," I snap. "Won't they have to if they ever plan to meet her?"

I feel insulted by their comments. We called her Lucia Anna because she was born on Saint Ann's day and I wanted to honor Mammy who is known as Annie but, when we got the birth certificate back, her name had been switched to Anna Lucia. But what matter? We know who she is. Jim says Lucia is the patroness of light and sight and that makes him happy. Stannie jokes that we have "a gentleman's family" now, with our boy and our girl.

"Some gentleman that brother of yours is," I say but, truly, I'm delighted with Georgie and Lucy and Jim, my three stars. And Stannie the moon, shining above us.

Though I'm consumed and exhausted with the care of the children, it's a satisfying kind of fatigue when they fall asleep in my arms, the soft, hot weight of them on me in the bed. Little one-eens, made of our love. Lucy fusses so at my nipple and I'm engorged like a cow and she roars as if half starved so, eventually, we get the banana bottle and teat and make up powdered milk or a runny pap for her. It quietens her and it means Jim can feed her, too, and leave me with my arms free, which is a nice feeling. He dotes on Lucia entirely and sometimes it's like I'm on the other side of the universe when he rocks her and croons; I'm not needed at all, by either of them.

Jim teaches his handful of aristocrats and businessmen and talks of importing Irish tweeds to Trieste—"Tweed? For this heat?" I say. And he dreams aloud of moving to Florence and of resuming his singing lessons so that he might give concerts for vast sums. I let him ramble away; he's not content unless he's brewing some scheme.

Aunt Jo sends "a thousand welcomes to the little lady"; Pappie threatens to go to hospital and leave "feet-foremost" in his coffin. He wonders if he'll ever get to meet his grandchildren.

"The auld wretch will outlive us all," Stannie says.

"Sure, what graveyard would take him when he can't pay for a plot?" Jim says and the two of them cackle like old maids.

"Won't he go in beside your mother?" I ask, and they stare at me as if I've said something mad.

THE YEAR TRICKLES ON. NEWS COMES THAT THE BOYS' YOUNG brother Charlie has gotten a girl in trouble, but he then agrees to marry her and they take off for Massachusetts in America, to who knows what life. Jim sneaks back to his drinking ways and Stannie tries to help by roaring at him when he rolls in, buckle-legged and garrulous, waking us up and the children, too.

"Do you want to go blind? Haven't the doctors told you that alcohol damages your eyes?" Stannie shouts, night after night, thumping Jim in an attempt to make him sensible. "Do you want to walk about guided by a little dog?"

I ask Stannie to stop—Georgie is frightened and Lucia wails—and then he's angry with me. "You always defend him, Nora. It's always his side you take."

"I just want peace, Stannie."

"You'll never have peace as long as you're with that fella," he says, jerking a hand at Jim who sways and smiles like any ordinary old sot. I look between the pair of them and wonder if he isn't right.

WANT

~❧~

Trieste
JANUARY AND FEBRUARY 1908

JIM'S SISTER POPPIE WRITES FROM DUBLIN. THEIR FATHER IS upset, despite the money both boys sent him for Christmas, affording him and the family a nice feed of turkey, ham, goose, bacon, plum pudding, and punch—so much more than we had. We couldn't even have New Year's Eve lentils, which, according to tradition here, bring wealth and luck for the year ahead. Two things we could certainly do with.

Today I go to our Jacob's biscuit tin—our money box—and it's empty, though I left enough there to pay the bootmaker, for I can't pass his shop without him throwing his fist in the air, and I want to pay him now before he comes out and thumps me. Jim is sleeping off his wine, so I take money from his pocket and leave him in his sore-headed heap.

When I get back, there's uproar. Jim and Stannie are chest to chest, hands to each other's shoulders as if they mean to tear the flesh from each other. Lucia sits shivering in her pram, snotty and red. Georgie's hands are over his ears and he's telling everyone to shut up.

"What on God's earth is going on?" I ask.

Stannie doesn't move his eyes from Jim. "This blackguard,"

he says, "is accusing me of taking money from his coat pocket, when the fish in the sea know that he pissed every last *centesimo* down some alley last night."

"Money that I *need*," Jim roars.

"As if we don't *all* need it." I turn to Stanislaus. "Was it your money, Stannie?" I ask, guilt nipping at me. The boys employ a messy back and over system of credit, exchange, and borrowing, that I don't always understand.

"It is, Nora."

I look at them, ready to bite the throats out of each other. "I took it," I say, a pop of fear in my throat.

Their arms drop and they swivel like puppets toward me. "You?" Jim says.

I proud my chest, for hadn't Jim taken my money from the tin? "That bootmaker was going to run across the piazza and wallop me one of these days and Giorgio's boots need patching. I had to pay him."

"The bloody cobbler." Stannie's face is creased with annoyance and he groans. "Nora, I wish you'd waited, at least until Friday. Jim's owed sixty crowns then and we would've been right as raindrops."

"Well, excuse me, Stannie, but most of the time I don't know who owns what coins or who owes who, or whose to be paid what, or when it's likely to happen. I'm the last to know any bloody thing!"

Lucia hiccups and begins to wail and Georgie goes to her and pats her head, his small hand moving down her back in brotherly comfort.

Jim, calm now, grabs his jacket and fixes his tie before the small square of mirror. "It can't be helped."

"You're going out? I haven't a penny for food."

Jim turns to look at us all, his voice cold. "Nora, you might have considered that before raiding my pockets. You will have to see if the landlady can provide something today for you and the children. Stannie, you're on your own."

I flump into a chair, gravely disappointed that at this moment Jim chooses to walk out the door and leaves me to beg from the woman we pay our rent to. I muster my lowest, sternest voice.

"It's time, I think, for me to write to my mother and tell her I'm living with a man who can't give us so much as a crust."

"Do that, if you wish," he says lightly. "I'm sure old Ma Barnacle would love to hear what's become of you. Meanwhile, I will go and get credit somewhere. For *all* of us."

I jump up, startling Lucia into a round of bawls. "Go! Go! I know the only place that will give you credit, the only kind you want. Go now and get drunk. That's all you're good for. Your old friend Vincent Cosgrave told me you were mad. He wondered what was I doing with you at all when I could have a nice young man who'd marry me and see me right." I begin to snatch up the morning's dishes and dash the crumbs off them onto the tablecloth. I toss the dishes onto the bed and shake the tablecloth out the window in big, violent waves. "Tomorrow I'm taking the children to the priest to be baptized. Faith, I tell you, those children will not grow up to be like you, James Joyce. They'll be good citizens. Proper people. They won't let other people starve!"

LOSS

Trieste
SUMMER 1908

JIM IS OFF THE DRINK. HE SLIPS UP, I SUPPOSE, ONCE A MONTH. A fortnight ago he broke his promise to me—and himself—spectacularly; he went onto an English battleship in the harbor one night, with Alessandro Francini, and drank so much that he passed out. Francini had to haul him off the boat and home to me by himself, not a finger lifted by one naval man. But Jim's eyes flared up terrible the next day and he had to get the leeches on them, and that frightened him so much that he's been saintlike since. Not so much as a sip of grappa has warmed his throat.

But we're all atop each other here and nasty-tongued with it. Stanislaus, especially, is like a pot ready to boil over. Jim, to be fair to him, found us a quarter on Via Vincenzo Scussa, and the boys' pupils were willing to help us raise the deposit, but our landlady here wanted our back rent before we'd leave and threatened to keep our furniture if we didn't pay. So now we are stuck here for we can't afford to pay what we owe, nor can we buy so much as a chair for the lovely quarter in Via Scussa.

And now it all blows up.

Jim stands behind Stannie's chair and talks to his back. "We could do it, you know, move to Via Scussa, if you wouldn't insist on paying back that four hundred crowns you owe that chap at the school you borrowed from."

Stannie's hands curl into claws. "And ruin my good name with him and every other pupil at the Berlitz who is willing to offer me credit? I think not, Jim." His face is rigid.

"Your good name," Jim grunts.

Out of the chair leaps Stannie, sending it toppling backward, just missing the wheels of Lucia's pram.

"Go easy!" I shout.

"Yes, Jim, *my* good name. Mine! Not yours, for you're known only in this town as *Il Ubriacone*, the drunkard. Not as a teacher, not as a writer. As an *ubriacone*."

"I haven't taken a drop in weeks."

"Well, we'll see how long that drought lasts." Stannie leans in. "You"—he pokes Jim in the chest—"won't tell me how to conduct my affairs any longer. You do not own me. You do not rule me. And I'm not here to pay your rent."

"I never said you were. But a brother helps a brother."

"I've saved you and your family from starvation too many times, Jim. I have to think of myself now."

He marches out of the room and comes straight back with an armful of clothes and his valise; he throws it up on the table and stuffs his things in.

"Ah, Stannie." I go to him and put my hand to his arm. "Don't be doing that. Stay, won't you?"'

"It's not you, Nora, or the children." He glances tenderly at me. "You know that."

"If you leave, I'm reliant on him for everything," I say, in a low voice.

Jim, sitting now with his nose in a book, coughs. "I can hear you, you know."

"I'm sorry, Nora," Stannie says. "I've had a bellyful." He squashes the valise shut and lifts it, puts on his hat. "I'll let you know where I fetch up."

Georgie watches Stannie open the door. "*Ciao!*" he calls. His uncle waves, blows him a kiss, and is gone.

I turn to Jim. "Now look what you've done. My heart is scalded with this poor way of living. Poor Stannie." I look at the door. "Poor us."

I'M WOKEN IN THE NIGHT BY A SCORCHING PAIN IN MY STOMACH that reaches around into my lower back. I turn over to try to ease it but let out a gasp for it seems to worsen. My innards have been a stew of pains and noises these past weeks and my poo either slides out like water or won't come at all. And food doesn't hold much interest for me. I get up, go to the pot, and try to push something out of me but naught comes. I feel uncommonly wet below, so I put my hand down and it meets with sticky heat. I yank up my drawers, totter to the window, and open the shutter. When I hold up my hand to the dawn light, it's covered in dark clots.

"Jesus, Mary, and Joseph," I hiss and run to the water basin to wash them away. I put my fingers down again and there's a large, warm lump there. I pull it out and examine it in the light; it looks for all the world like a cut of meat. I go over to the bed. "Jim," I whisper, poking him in the back. "Jim, something's amiss."

He wakes and shoves on his glasses. "What is it? Are the children all right?"

I nod swiftly. "I'm bleeding black things from down below, Jim. There's globs coming out of me, like bits of liver."

"Jesus Christ." He leaps like a goat from the bed and leads me to the chair. "Sit a moment, Nora." He looks down. "Oh, your nightgown is destroyed."

A pain rips through my lower half and I cry out. "I think I'm dying, Jim!"

"No, no, you're not, my love." Jim pulls down the covers and puts a folded towel on the bed. "Come, Nora, and lie up here."

I rise from the chair, take a step, and feel another blob passing into my drawers. "Jim, more has come out of me!" He swoops me up in his arms, places me on the bed, and lifts my nightgown. There is a steady mess of blood flowing from between my legs, and the pain is now an unvarying ache. "It feels like birthing, Jim."

"Lie still now, Gooseen." I lie still though the pressure and ache in my back makes me want to writhe. Down with my drawers and Jim picks up a bloody lump in his hands and picks at it. "Nora, it *is* a type of birthing. Look." He holds out his palm and on it is the tiniest of forms, like a baby bird broken too soon from its eggshell.

"Ugh, don't show me that, Jim, it doesn't look right." I turn my head away.

"Your courses have not been coming on lately, Nora, I'll wager."

I look at him, understanding now. "They haven't, but I'm not long after Lucia; I thought I was safe." I put my hands to my stomach to try to ease the pains that run through it.

"It can happen anyway." He studies the unformed baby with its fishy eyes. "So small," he says, kisses one finger, and places the kiss on its tiny body. He stretches out his hand again. "Do you want to say good-bye, Nora?"

I shake my head. "Take it out of my sight."

STANNIE BRINGS ME A POSY OF PINK CARNATIONS.

"What are they for?" I ask.

"For your loss, Nora."

"Ah, it doesn't matter, Stannie, it was barely formed." My voice is gruff, but I suppose that just smothers my guilt; I'm not sure that God approves of women who see the death of a baby, even a half-made one, as a blessing.

"It matters a bit," he says.

"But how would we have fed another child?" I take the flowers from him and stick my nose into them so that he can't see my shame at the relief I feel. "How did you hear of it, anyway?"

"Jim sent word to me at the school. And a kind of apology for before." He leans in. "I'm sorry, Nora."

"Look, it's no real sorrow to me, Stannie; I didn't even know it was there. And amn't I run off my feet with the other pair, anyway?"

"Still, a child is a child."

He's starting to annoy me now and I wish he'd let it go. "A child that never grew beyond a minnow. That's enough said about it." I push the flowers into a jar. "Where are you staying?"

"I got a room on Via Nuova."

"So you won't be coming back to us?"

"I won't, Nora."

I nod and go out to the kitchen to make some tea; I'm only beyond the door when Jim comes in and speaks to Stannie.

"I may be the only one to regret the little one's truncated existence."

I feel stung that he sees me as coarse and uncaring. "If you could feed us, we might have an army of childer," I mutter and continue on to the kitchen to wet the teapot. *Isn't it nice for men to want babies*, I think, *when it's not them who has to be weighted down by them for near ten months, or who have the care of them after for twenty years or more?* I clank and bash my way through the tea-making, irritated by Jim and his lofty words. Truncated existence, indeed. Of course it would be very grand to have a scatter of children, but that's a rich person's game. With little money we'd be mad to have a big family. I feel bad that the little baby died inside me; it's a sad end to an innocent life and it makes me wonder if I did something wrong. But, truly, the way things are, I think we're all better off. I need to be practical, the way my mother was, and I mean to be just that.

JIM IS ALL TALK AGAIN ABOUT IMPORTING DONEGAL TWEED, that's when he's not planning voice lessons we can ill afford.

"Can you not just settle?" I say. "Isn't that businessman Ettore Schmitz paying you all right to teach him? And those others?"

Stannie, who takes his dinners with us again, pipes up, "But don't you know my brother is the man of many futures, Nora?"

Jim, who's lying along the bed smoking a cigarette, like a concubine in a painting, smirks. "I am also considering, in case it's of any interest to you two biddies, my complete retirement from public life." Stannie snorts at this. "For now, I think I would be wise to devote my attention to getting rid of my rheumatism—to recuperating—as well as having my voice trained and getting fat."

"Of course, you're not the only one recuperating," Stannie says, glancing at me.

I shovel *gemelli* into my mouth and see to the children; I don't want to think about the miscarriage, that's over with entirely. Jim stays silent, which is what he does when he doesn't care for what's being said, or when the stars don't shine on him alone.

"Enough of tweed and singing classes and getting fat, Jim. Aren't you going to be a great writer?" I say. "Isn't that enough?"

"Nora, my dear, I have not written a sane or lovely word since last April."

I stack up the empty plates, lift them, and cross to the bed. I kiss Jim on the forehead. "It'll come back to you, Jim," I say, knowing how the absence of words pains him.

CARESS

❧

Trieste
SUMMER 1909

JIM OF THE MANY FUTURES MADE A NEW PLAN: STANNIE WAS TO take Georgie to Dublin to meet the Joyce family, to make reparations with Pappie who, it was hoped, would be charmed by his grandson; the boy would soften the old man, was the thought. Georgie hounded the landlady and the other tenants, asking them if they might lend him a valise for his trip to "Dubirino" with his uncle. In the end, Jim couldn't resist the idea of impressing Pappie himself and poor Stannie was ousted and Jim took his place on the triumphant trip home. But I miss them both terribly and I worry that Jim's sisters, who are never warm toward me in their letters, won't treat my son nicely. Stannie says they'll make an enormous fuss over him and comfort him if he misses me. I gather Lucia closer to me with Georgie so far away; I pet her head and she rewards me with her little monkey grin. I kiss her hair and she wriggles and fusses, for she is nothing if not a contrary child.

Stannie didn't celebrate the children's birthdays with us, just before Georgie and Jim left—sometimes I think he willfully avoids our flat. Us. Me. But he comes today to Via Scussa with a *caprese al limone*, Lucia's favorite lemon cake, and a bag of colored macarons for me.

"Such treats," I say, looking at him shyly.

He puffs his chest like a dove and smiles. "Well, Nora, I've been appointed acting director of the Berlitz now; my pockets are a little fuller." He pats his breast.

"Congratulations, Stannie, that's great news." I go to hug him and our arms clash and it's a little awkward. I make coffee and we sit, the shutters wide to the bright afternoon and a soft breeze lifting the edge of the lace tablecloth. Lucia puts her hands up to Stannie and he pulls her onto his lap and she makes him feed her tiny cuts of the cake, like a bird nourishing its baby.

"With Jim Joyce away from us, you seem to have relaxed, Stannie." He grunts in reply, but he seems to me more like a man in charge of himself, easier in his bones, when his brother is nowhere in sight. "And Lucia has you where she wants you."

He looks at me and there's a peculiar light in his eye. "Amn't I a slave," he says, "to the pair of you?"

I turn away for I feel heat rising from my neck to my cheeks. I take the macarons from the bag and pile them onto the good plate, a little tower of pink, yellow, and purple fancies.

"Look, Lucia. *Delizioso!*"

She puts out her paw for one and Stannie reaches across to get it for her and our fingers collide; I snatch my hand back as if bitten and then feel like an eejit. Stannie chooses a pink one for Lucia and I watch him feed it to her.

"Would you like one of your own? A child, I mean," I ask quietly, imagining him with a scatter of sweet-faced gossoons and girleens, all making him their willing drudge.

He lifts his eyes to me. "Sure, who'd have me, Nora?"

We stare at each other for a long moment. "Plenty would, Stannie." My words come out hoarsely. "A lot of nice women would be glad of a decent, steady man like you."

"Apart from the only one who matters to me," he says.

I turn my face away and lift my hair from my neck; it's sticking to my skin in the heat. Stannie is saying that it's me who matters to him, I suppose. I blush, unsure where to look. I prink at the wide satin ribbon that falls from my waist and run my fingers over its smoothness. I hear Stannie set Lucia down onto the floor and she toddles off to her toys that lie behind the sofa. He's suddenly before me, taking my hands and pulling me up to stand before him.

"Nora," he says and there is beseechment in his tone.

I swallow hard. "Stannie, we … I …"

One hand comes through my hair to the nape of my neck; it feels heavy there but cool. I lean back into it, enjoying its strength that seems to surge, in turn, through my entire body. Stannie groans, the brute, rooted sound of man, and his mouth is so close to mine that his breath steams my lips. I feel my own heat bulge through my sex and my stomach, and my breaths come short. Stannie's lips crush mine and he releases my head to caress my breast. I moan; this is all purely mad, but my body has taken over and responded. I know we should stop, but excitement and fear somehow keep me in the spell. I flicker open my eyelids to look at Stannie and see Lucia watching us; I step back and push Stanislaus away. Lucy rushes to me and plunges her face into my skirts.

Stannie drops his head and gasps, "Oh, Nora."

We stand still, my hands on Lucia's hair, and stare at each other. I shake my head, and though his look is tormented, he nods swiftly.

"Now, Lucia," I say in as normal and bright a voice as I can muster, "will we all three go for a walk by the harbor? Will we go walkies with Uncle Stannie and look at the boats?"

"*Sì, sì*, Mamma," she says and runs for her doll.

I look at my brother-in-law, my heart still babbling inside me. "It's all right, Stannie," I say. "It's all right." I look away. "No harm done."

LETTERS

⤳

Dublin and Trieste
AUGUST 1909

A LETTER COMES FROM JIM AND IT'S THE WORST THING I'VE ever read and I'm split open with sadness and confusion and I'm ripping with anger besides. How he denounces and mistrusts me! He says he won't go to Galway to see my people, as we had planned, nor will he go to Maunsel's and see about his book being published.

I know I had a small, indiscreet moment with Stannie, but that's as nothing compared to what Jim accuses me of. He writes these blame-filled words to me and how they sting, for they are all lies:

I have heard it from your lover's lips. I cannot even write my sorrow, my degradation. I sit here and cry, wrung out. The vision of you with your mouth on his, your body laid before him, dances before me. Pity, me, Nora, I am suffering mightily; my faith in you is smashed to smithereens. I will cry, I know it, for days. I cannot call you my love or my Gooseen or any other affectionate name because, like everyone else, you have betrayed me. You, you, who were my only faithful one. Is this the end, Nora?

*This I ask you: Is Giorgio mine? We lay together on
October 11th for the first time, in Zürich, and yet he came
on July 27th. That, by my sums, is 9 months and 16 days.
You bled little onto the sheet, Nora, I recall. Were you
fucked by another before me?*

He accuses me of having trysts with that eejit Vincent Cosgrave, a man I would not touch with a bargepole let alone a yard-
stick and, yet, here I sit charged with all sorts of indecency by the
one person who knows and loves me best. Accused of duping him
as to Georgie—I cannot stand it! I crumple up Jim's horrid letter,
toss it into my trunk, and resolve not to write to him at all, for why
should I reply to such vile things? I will send only silence across
the waves to Dublin. It's all Jim deserves.

STANNIE COMES TO VIA SCUSSA, WAVING A POSTCARD. "WHAT DO
you know of this?"

I take it from him; it's dated the eighth of August. Like the
letters to me, the tone is abrupt. Jim says his business in Dublin
is ended and he tells Stannie to send money for his passage home
immediately.

I flop onto the sofa. "So he means to come back soon."

"But why, Nora? Has Jim had a row with Pappie? The letter
I got from him the other day was full of the joys of his return to
Dublin, people were saying how well he looked: in splendid health,
mature."

"Mature, is it? The man's a child." I get up and go to the bedroom. From the trunk I take the letter I received and bring it to
Stannie. "Read this," I say.

He sits at one end of the sofa, I the other; Lucia puts herself
between us, her head twisting, all watchful, like a tiny owl. Stannie

reads Jim's hateful letter with his mouth open and his forehead a rack of creases.

"Mother of Divine God, such things to say to you!" Stannie reaches over and presses my hand. "Are you all right, Nora?"

"I don't know what to think, Stannie. I'm too shocked to even cry."

"What have you said to him in return?"

"Nothing. I won't write a line to the bastard until he apologizes to me."

Stannie gets up and pours me a glass of grappa. He gives it to me and puts his hand to my shoulder. "That Vincent Cosgrave was always a pup. I warned Jim about him; I told him he was two-faced." He winces.

"Cosgrave is a dirty liar. What did he hope to gain by saying those terrible lies to Jim? And after five years. Is he that jealous of him, that nasty in himself?"

"Sadly, Nora, I believe that he is. Cosgrave told me way back that he meant to steal you from Jim."

"Steal me? As if I were some sack of chattels?" I gulp back the grappa, let it scald my belly. "Fuck and shit and shite on it, Stannie, what am I to do?"

"Write to Jim, Nora, tell him the truth of the matter—that Cosgrave is a stirring brat. Tell him there's not a word of fact in what he's said."

I pinch my lips tightly. "I won't write a line to him. No, I won't." I hop up and begin to fold the clothes that I've been meaning to put away. "Jim Joyce won't tell me how badly he's wounded when I'm the one attacked. No, no, he certainly will not."

Stannie drops his head. "Jim's wretched, Nora. Only you can ease him."

"Well, he can find his ease up his arse. I'll not write a sentence to him, not a solitary word, until he takes back his accusations. Is Georgie his? Did you ever hear the like?" Stannie gets up and puts on his hat; I cease my folding. "Where are *you* going?"

"I'll write to Jim. He's in a bad way. I know what it is to pine and feel disconsolate." He glances at me. "I have to end his misery."

"Off you go, so. Do that. He'll not see an envelope with my handwriting on it for a long time."

Stannie lingers by the door. "Will I come back later on?"

I don't look at him. "Your name is in the pot, Stannie. You'll eat with me and Lucia, surely."

"I will."

ANOTHER LETTER FROM JIM. THIS TIME HE ASKS IF I'M UNWELL for he hasn't heard from me. He doesn't pause to think about the wounds he's inflicted on me, oh no. Now all is well with Jim, for his friend Byrne, and Stannie, too, have reassured him splendidly. He doesn't take my silence for what it is—deep hurt—he needs other men to tell him that I am without stain in this matter. Oh, Jim, Jim, Jim, though you ask to be forgiven, you injure me further.

Noble Nora, my sweet girleen, can you forgive my contemptible carry on? Byrne says that Cosgrave and Gogarty concocted the lies between them, to drive me mad. It worked. Stannie says Cosgrave meant to steal you, but you fought him off. They are blackguards, all of them but we will vanquish them together, will we not? My sweetheart, please forgive your boy. Send me one word of denial, dearest, to ease me and make me happy.

Still he suspects me! Perhaps I'm too simple a woman for him, too Galway, too lacking in education, too poor. Maybe I'm in his way and he wants freedom now, maybe that's why he writes things to me as to make me fret and cry for hours at a time, alone in our bed. It might suit Jim better if I was to leave him, place our children in a home—for I cannot support them—and leave him by himself with his paper and pen.

I've been reading *Chamber Music*, to try to get back to the Jim I know, to the man that is made of love, not the jiber that Dublin seems to be making of him. In the poems I find the Jim I believe in, the man of softness and fine sentiments. I hope he's the one who returns to me in September.

I write and tell him he's been brutal and unthinking toward me, but now he can do something for me, to make it up. I'm run ragged with the care of the children and the flat. Even with Georgie in Dublin, Lucia takes all my time and mind. I ask him to bring one of his sisters back to Trieste to act as helpmeet to me. Aunt Jo has often said that young Eva is a good seamstress, so she's probably capable at other things, too. She could share Georgie's room and, sure, what is she doing in Dublin, anyway, save being got at by Pappie for being idle? I tell Jim that if he does this for me now, we can go on in love and harmony.

He writes to say that he will do as I ask and to tell me that I never leave his mind.

My lonely bed is tortured with desire for you, my mind leaps to disturbed places, I see you over me posed and preening, chaste, grotesque, languid. I wish to be master of you, body and soul, you are musical, strange, perfumed. There are words that I want to write to you but

instead I fantasize you might write them to me. A
private letter, Nora. It might calm my bulging desire
for you.

I read this and I swell with lust and love for Jim; it's so hard to be without him. A private letter? I think I know what he means; I will have to think about that and concoct something. He tells me he has signed the contract with Maunsel's for *Dubliners*— I'm so proud—but doesn't say if he'll go to Galway. My heart lodges in my throat with longing when I think of him visiting Mammy in Bowling Green, for I'd love to be there, so that they could see how grand we look together. And another small part of me almost melts with nerves at the thought of reproaches from Mammy and Uncle Tommy and my sisters. What would they say, I wonder? But Jim they will welcome, I'm full sure of it. And our Georgie. Oh, how I would love to smell the sea around the Claddagh, with Jim by my side, and feel the cold Atlantic air pinch my cheeks.

I take some paper and a pen from the box and try my hand at a private note, something to bind Jim to me while we long for each other.

Jim, I am asleep, and the night is sweltering so I've
taken off every stitch and I lie on my belly under the sheet
in our Via Scussa bed. You come to me and are happy to
find me sleeping, you peel back the sheet to see my naked
flesh, the length of my back, the mound of my behind.
Your cock rises up, you have no control over it, and then
you lie atop me, your sweat mingling with my sweat, and
I drowse awake to find you pounding up into me from

behind and whispering words of lust into my ear: fuckbird,
my little hoyden, lovergirl, damned lustful angel. Your
hands reach under me to squeeze at my breasts which are
fat and round as you like and you cannot control yourself
and you release your seed into me on a hard stream of
pumps and you fall on my back and kiss my neck over and
again.

By return Jim writes,

My little runaway, imagine it, I am sitting at your
mother's table. I have sat all day with her, talking, while
Giorgio chases the ducks and hens on Bowling Green.
When I listen to Annie Healy Barnacle talk, it is clear to
me that she is my love's mother and I like her enormously.
She sang "The Lass of Aughrim" for me and I was so
very moved. Your mother said, "Jim, your eyes light up
like candles in your head when you speak of Nora." It is
true!

Your love-note was so welcome, Nora, and, oh my
darling, you surpassed my expectations. Let me just
say the page stayed in one fist while the other worked
over and again until I was limp. Thank you, ma bella
Nora.

Jim says he's had a necklace of ivory made for me with words
from one of his poems engraved on it: "Love is unhappy" on one
side and "when love is away" on the other. He says the necklace
is the story of our love. What a fine man Jim can be when he
tries.

44 FONTENOY STREET, DUBLIN
7 September 1909

*Only silence from you, dear, though I suppose you
thought we would be at sea by now. We leave here tomorrow, Eva, Giorgio, and I. Please read all my letters to you
again. And please don't quarrel with me anymore, Nora.
Only you can keep my love aflame. I wish I was asleep in
your arms now. I have been wretched in Dublin. Will you
mind me well when I am back?*

*Are the right parts of you plumping out, Nora? Do
you drink the cocoa I sent? I giggle to myself to think of
your girlish breasts. How ridiculous you are, dear! Your
son is four and you are a grown woman—you must begin
to act like that now, you cannot remain the curious girl
from Galway forever.*

*And yet my heart softens to think of that slender body
of yours, the small shoulders and slim arms. You're a
rogue! Did you snip the hair below to remain a girl? I want
you to wear black drawers for me. I want you to learn well
how to please me, to make me desire you. I know you will
and that we will be happy.*

*Don't cry, Nora, when we reunite, I want your eyes
to glow. Take me in your arms, feel tenderness for me,
and lead me right. Look well for me, dear—have your
hair clean and free of ashes, it's not right to look slovenly
at twenty-five young years! Have something warm to eat
ready for us, won't you? Let me feel happy from the moment I arrive, dearest. I shall want a good cup of coffee in
a nice little cup. Have a salad for me, but don't let onions*

or garlic into the house. And, Nora, don't, in your first words to me, mention money or debts, please.

I cannot wait to see Trieste, our beloved shelter, again and, from the train, the white glow of the castle at Miramare. Good night for now, my Gooseen. I have written to you much, I am bringing a present for you; I am not so bad, am I?

Jim

RETURN

༺ঞৎ༻

Trieste
SEPTEMBER 1909

H E IS BACK WITH ME, MY WANDERING, WILLFUL BOY.
Stannie meets them at the station and I wait here, in
my good gray dress with a fresh blue under-blouse and my hair
half up, half down, just as Jim likes it. I have *polpetti* in *ragu* and
fat *papardelle* ready for them after their long journey. I hear their
voices in the stairwell, Georgie's the highest, and I rush out onto
the landing to greet them. My son runs to me and jumps up into my
arms and I cover his face with kisses.

"Oh, my darling, I've missed you. Look how manly you are!"
I set him down and marvel that in a few short weeks he looks much
less like the baby of my imagination.

"We stayed with Pappie, Mamma, and his house was untidy
and stinky." Georgie pinches his nose and I laugh. "I went to the
church with my aunties; it was full of sweet smoke. And I took
the train to meet Granny in Galway."

"Doesn't that sound grand, Georgie? You've been busy."

Jim hangs back and I glance at him, shy as a new bride, but a
small cry of pleasure croaks from my throat at the sight of him. He
pushes his sister Eva forward and she holds out her hand. She has
the Joyce eyes and her mouth is flat and sad. I'm nervous of her—

I wonder what she'll think of me and if we'll get along—but I step closer and shake her hand warmly.

"Hello, Mrs. Joyce."

"Nora, of course," I say, "call me nothing but Nora. You're welcome here, Eva. You must be exhausted altogether. Come in, come in."

Lucia, who stayed back in the flat before the din of so many people, dashes to Stanislaus and puts up her arms. He lifts her, but hands her across to Jim who buries his face in her neck; it's my joy to see them reunited. Jim looks at me and I go to him and it's as if he's an apparition, so long have I wished for this moment. I put my hand in his and cannot stop smiling; Jim leans in and our lips meet and linger.

"*Basta*! Enough!" calls Stannie good-humoredly and we break apart.

They all sit to table while I serve. Eva doesn't eat much, but sighs, bites her lip, and stares around the room. She looks as if she might cry at any moment. I make coffee and Eva sits with her hands around the cup; she dips her nose to smell the coffee but doesn't taste it.

"Eva, would you like to put your head down for a spell?" I ask and she nods, so I lead her to Georgie's small room and the bed I have ready for her beside his cot. "It must be very strange for you, dear. You'll settle in time."

She nods, her face a picture of misery and I feel sorry for her. I wave at the bed and she lies on it, shoes and all, and I leave her to fret over her homesickness alone. When I return to table, my plate is missing and a brown box decorated with gold sits in its place.

"Is this my gift?" Jim nods. I open it and groan with pleasure; the necklace is such a delicate, unusual bauble that I can scarce believe it's mine. There are five cubes of ivory on a gold chain with an inscribed ivory pendant, a little smaller than a domino.

"Oh Jim! I'm afraid to handle it." I trail my finger over the inscription on the ivory tablet.

He leaps up and comes to me; he takes the pendant from its orange silk bed and unclips it. "Love is unhappy when love is away," Jim murmurs.

"So is love's brother," Stannie mutters and we both turn to him in surprise. He grimaces, folds his napkin. "I'll bid you adieu for today," he says.

"Ah, no, Stannie. Wait until Eva rises. Stay and hear all the news from Ireland," I say. I dip my face nearer to his. "Please."

He half smiles. "I will so, Nora."

Jim tells us of all he saw, all he did: how he had a card made up announcing himself as a journalist from the *Piccolo della Sera*, which meant he could get free train tickets and such. He describes a night at the Gresham Hotel with people who were so warm; a second night with his friend Byrne and how they got locked out of his Eccles Street house, but Byrne managed to climb through a window, open the door, and admit Jim like royalty.

"When the people I met at the Gresham heard *Dubliners* was coming at last, they said over and over that I was their great hope for Irish literature. How do you like that, Stannie boy?"

"Did nobody ask after me?" Stannie says, his voice low.

Jim flinches. "Everybody did, of course. I had half a dozen messages for you, but I've forgotten them, it appears."

Stannie seems to shrivel and I bristle on his behalf. Why can't Jim have a care for his brother's feelings? I refill Stannie's coffee cup, but he pushes it away. "I'll be off, Nora," he says.

"Will you come for your dinner tomorrow?" I ask.

He glances at Jim. "I'll see."

When he's gone, Jim pulls me into his lap and I can feel the bone of him through my petticoats and skirt. "Get those children to bed, Nora, so that we may go to ours."

"Wait in there for me, so," I say. "Keep yourself awake."

I rumble the children into their nightclothes and wash their faces with the bare slick of a rag. They're not sleeping when I run to look after myself, but both are tired and will drop off soon. I can't wait to feel Jim's hands all over me, to feel him up inside me; my whole being tingles with the thoughts of what we'll do. I strip to my skin in the water closet, dash a wet cloth under my arms and below, dab some citrusy eau du cologne on my neck and on the inners of my thighs. I pull a fresh chemise over my head. I've threaded blue ribbons to the sleeves and neckline to match my eyes; Jim likes these small touches. I swiftly unpin my hair and let it fall down my back, fluffing it out with my fingers. In I go to Jim. The shutters are open a crack and I can see that he is naked under the sheet. I slide in beside him and trail my fingers down his chest to the sweet tuft of hair where his cock nests.

His eyes flicker. "*Sono stanco,*" he whispers. "I'm so very weary."

My great errant lover, returned to me at last after all our travails, is too tired for his fuckbird.

FRIENDSHIPS

❧

Trieste
OCTOBER 1909

THERE'S A STRANGE LITTLE WOMAN WHO SITS IN THE PUBLIC
garden; she's always bareheaded, her white hair streels down
her back like seaweed, and her clothes are unkempt. Jim says she
sleeps outside. The old woman sits on a rock, throws scraps for
birds, and talks loudly to herself, but she's harmless. She and Lucia
always look at each other and smile when we pass by; maybe it's
because the woman doesn't demand a conversation from Lucia, the
way others do, that my daughter likes her so much. Lucia calls her
la Nonna.

"Can I bring *la Nonna* a biscuit today, Mamma?" Lucia asks.

"Yes, you may."

Eva is teaching Giorgio how to fashion stitches, for he wants
to make a waistcoat for his sailor doll, and Jim is meeting a student, so Lucia and I set off by ourselves to the gardens. Lucia has
wrapped two biscotti in a napkin and she holds it in her hand like a
religious relic while we walk up Via Scussa. It surprises me that a
child of just above two years can have the wit to want to be kind to
someone. That Lucia wants to make friends with a vagrant is less
extraordinary to me—there's something odd and wayward about
most things my daughter does.

La Nonna is on her perch, a scatter of hopping birds at her feet. Lucia lets go my hand and steps up to the woman as if she's expected. I hang behind and watch. *La Nonna* reminds me of the gaol women in Galway, the ones who roamed the lanes and were in and out of prison for stealing apples or trapping hares, and who seemed to belong to nowhere and no one.

"*Buongiorno, ragazzina,*" *la Nonna* says.

"*Buongiorno,*" Lucia says and holds up the napkin. She folds back the corners to reveal the biscotti. "One for you, one for me," she says, as she takes a piece and bites it.

The old woman claps her palms across her chest and laughs. She opens her mouth in a wide gawp to reveal that she is toothless, but she takes the biscotti anyway and sucks on it like a baby. The two eat their biscuits and eyeball each other and it seems to me some great communion is taking place. Lucia's so quiet and contained at home that often I feel that I don't understand her at all and yet, without words, she and this woman speak a common language.

When Lucia has swallowed the last of her biscotti, she dabs at her face with the napkin, waves to her friend, looks to me, and walks on. *La Nonna* and I nod to each other, but her gaze turns to fix on my daughter, trotting through the fallen leaves on the pathway like a tiny adult, a good deed done.

"A special girl," *la Nonna* says. "She will be a special woman, too."

And I'm suddenly astonished to realize that Lucia will grow to be a woman just as I once did, just as *la Nonna* did, and we don't know, nor will we for a long time, who she'll be or where she'll end up. The idea undoes me and I rush after Lucia, scoop her into my arms, and cover her head with kisses.

EVA IS HORRIBLY UNHAPPY; SHE WEEPS AT NIGHT AND EMERGES
from the room each morning with puffy eyes and a downturned
mouth.

"Her homesickness is making her unwell," I tell Jim.

"What is there to miss in Dublin?" he asks her, bewilderment
stronger in him than sympathy.

"Well," Eva says, "everything."

I wonder that she misses her drunken father, their cramped
house, and the constant threat of eviction. But, at the same time,
I know it can feel unsettling to be uprooted, to have to get used to
new food, a different atmosphere, and, most especially, the ways
of other people.

"The weather itself is strange to me," Eva whispered yesterday. "I would love to feel rain on me, Nora. Nice, cold rain."

I nodded for I understood what she meant. "You'll get used
to the climate, *a leana*. You'll grow accustomed to everything
before long, I promise," I said, but in my head I thought, *the poor
child*.

Stannie, who was here on one of his regular visits to Eva, gave
her money to go to the Cinematograph Americano and she took
me with her and, at least, it took Eva's mind off herself and her
woes for a while. We watched one picture that made fun of ladies'
big hats being in everyone's way, and another about a woman and
her daughters who are taken hostage by criminals, and we laughed
and felt fearful and were nicely diverted.

But it's morning again and Eva is slumped at the breakfast
table, not eating, with a Mother of Sorrows look about her. Jim is
losing patience.

"Did you enjoy the moving picture last night, Eva?" he asks, to remind her that she's looked after.

"I did," she says testily, for she knows what her brother is implying—that she's not grateful enough, that she needs to buck up. "It's a wonder, isn't it," Eva says, "that a city like Dublin doesn't have a single cinematograph. With all the people there, wouldn't you think there'd be great demand for it?"

Jim draws hard on his cigarette and stares at his sister. "You would indeed," he says, "extraordinary demand." He lunges forward and stabs his cigarette. "Get me a pen and paper, Nora." I can hear his brain begin to tick-tock over some scheme, as sure as eggs. He grabs the paper I bring without a word of thanks and begins to jot. "Who do I know in Trieste?" he says.

"The world and its mother from the caffès round the harbor," I say.

"No, no, not those fellows, Nora. Who are the rich men of my acquaintance? Those who might invest in something, a business venture?"

"Well, there's Signor Schmitz who has the paint factory."

"No, not Ettore, I need to go higher. Who are those chaps who run the Americano and the Edison? And don't they have another cinematograph in Bucharest?" It's clear Jim requires no answer; he's feverish in the concoction of his plan. "They do, I remember the name: the Volta. That's it!" He scribbles on his page then looks up at me over the top of his glasses. "Oh, Nora, this could be the making of us entirely. Think of it, Dublin's first cinema!"

I nod my head, remembering the plan to be a bank clerk in Rome, and the plan to import tweed, and the other one to bring skyrockets to Trieste, and the plan to work in the new university in Dublin, and the plan to move to Florence. I sip my tea and eat my shortbread and say no more.

ABSENCE

✦

Dublin and Trieste
WINTER 1909

JIM COMES HOME SCUTTERED FROM A CAFFÈ, LATE THE NIGHT before he leaves again for Ireland, though I've prepared a good farewell meal and Stannie's brought a *panettone*. We eat without him. I'm miserable and sit at table giving out long yards about Jim.

"See how he treats us, one and all? He has no manners that man, not for us, at least. Oh, he has plenty of high words for any guttersnipe about the town, but none that come home with him." I cross my arms over my chest. "He may stay in Dublin once he gets there, for all I care. Let him rot in Fontenoy Street with Pappie, let him die trying to build his cinematograph. What use is the blackguard to me?"

"You're very hard on Jim, Nora," Eva says. "Isn't he just out having a drink like any fellow does?" I glare at her, not daring to open my beak for fear of what squawky madness might fly out.

"Jim drinks a bit more than the average fellow, Eva," Stannie mumbles. "He's not an easy man; Nora puts up with a lot."

We eat on in silence, the children looking at us with big eyes.

Eva scrapes back her chair eventually. "I'll get the children down for the night," she says, scooping up Lucia like a baby and carrying her toward her bed. Eva makes goo-goo faces at Lucy and they both giggle and whisper, as if they share secrets.

Stannie is silent for a while then speaks up. "He'll be away for a long while, Nora. Don't be too hard on him. It's only yourself you'll injure."

"Hmm," I say, my gut knotted with annoyance.

"I'm off." I nod and Stannie leaves. I sit on and wait.

When Jim falls in the door, I leap up and roar "*Imbecille!*" His face takes on a wounded look, but I feel more like smacking the cheeks off him than anything else. Running to Ireland to set up a cinematograph, indeed, when we need him here. "You're nothing but a bloody imbecile, James Joyce," I hiss and stalk away from him to my bed.

ON THE TRAIN STATION PLATFORM, WHERE WE PART, THE FOUR cold beats of *imbecille* ring in my ears: *Im-be-cil-le!* I don't completely regret shouting the word at him, but he'll be gone for two months or more, it'll be our first Christmas apart, and my heart cracks a little to see him sad-eyed beside his trunk, off to Ireland and me left behind. We say good-bye brusquely.

"Mind yourself," I say, with a peck to his cheek.

He grabs my hand. "Good-bye, my love. Be good."

Jim stands in the train doorway to wave, but I have to lower my head so that he won't see my tears. I turn my back and gallop down the platform, my eyes spilling.

I'm left in Trieste with a mopey Eva and two small children and a large pain in my backside. And now he punishes me. No letter has come from Dublin, just a postcard to say he arrived. No pages full of love, nothing to say whether Pappie is well, or if Jim and his backers have secured premises for the cinematograph, or anything at all. I want only a morsel, to know Jim is not angry with me. I cry over the little framed picture of him by my bed and regret my mad temper, though he drove me to it. Who is the imbecile now? I hold Jim's photograph to my breast and sob like a woman in mourning. I worry that in Dublin the old haunts will become attractive to him again, those places around Tyrone Street, and the women there. Or that he'll reacquaint with the well-to-do ladies who were his friends before he met me. His silence cuts me.

At last he writes, but reprimands me for calling him an imbecile. He says the Volta Cinematograph will open on Mary Street in Dublin and that with profits from his venture, he'll buy me furs: a hat, a stole, a muff. His letter is strange and wayward. He writes,

I hate Ireland and Irish people. All I witness here are lecherous priests and false, cunning women. I thought tonight of that priest who fondled you in the presbytery in Galway and I wondered if you too are against me because, if you remember, we passed a priest in Trieste a fortnight ago and I said, "Aren't you repulsed by the sight of him?" and you said, in a short, dry way, "No, I'm not." These things silence and wound me. I am an envious, lonely, proud, discontented person. You should be nicer to me, more patient. Who is there but you? I weep as I write this, Nora. We have just this one life to love each other. Be kind to me, my darling. Bear with me though I am insensitive and awkward.

My odd, graceless Jim, he feels everything so deeply, most especially when we're apart. He nurses small ills like pets and hurts himself with them. I swell with pity for him for it can't be easy to be away. He tells me his sister Eileen wishes to join our Triestine tribe. Well, she'll be company for Eva and she'll earn a few useful pennies too. I'm happy to have her though it means I'll be sur-rounded by Joyces; perhaps I'll become one myself some fine day.

Jim sends me reindeer gloves to keep off the biting bora wind and a selection of others in soft leather. He promises, too, twelve yards of tweed to make a dress and coat.

"I'll be the belle of Trieste," I say to Eva when I open the parcel of gloves.

"But, Mamma, you have only two hands!" Lucia says.

I laugh. "See how kind your babbo is." I give Eva a pair of white kid gloves and she thanks me. "See, clever Lucia, I mean to share."

Eva and Lucia go about together like two little spinsters; it warms me to see them light in each other's company for they both need that. Today they are bringing soup that I've made to Stannie, who has taken to his bed with a bad cold. Between us we mean to make him well again.

STANNIE FIDGETS WITH HIS PASTA, PUSHING IT FROM ONE SIDE OF the plate to the other. Eva glances at me to see if I'm going to ask him what's the matter, or if he means to cough it out himself.

"Come on, Stannie, what ails you?" I ask.

He sets down his cutlery and faces me. "Herr Scholz came to see me."

"Our Herr Scholz? The landlord? What did he want?"

"He didn't like to come to you, with Jim away. He gave me this." Stannie hands me a folded page and I open it and try to read the words, but my Italian is not up to the task. "Tell me, Stannie."

"It's a writ, Nora. You owe four months' rent, and if you don't pay at least two, Scholz means to evict you."

I smack the table. "For the love of all that's holy! Jim told me we were all right before he left. He promised me." Georgie, Lucia, and Eva all cease eating and stare at me like strung puppets. I push back my chair and stand, thinking of the gloves and the tweed, the cost of them. "Oh God almighty, I'll have James Joyce's scalp for this. What am I to do now, Stannie?"

"I've already sent a telegram to Jim." Stannie was never happy with the Volta scheme and it's clear now he's boiling. "The man is his father's son, no doubt about it."

Eva tuts. "All Jim's furs and necklaces and fireworks and he doesn't pay the rent."

I glare at her. "Isn't he putting a roof over your head?"

I see a look pass between Stannie and Eva and I want to knock their two crowns together. I'm furious with Jim, to be sure, but I won't have a strapeen like Eva criticize him. I go to the box of paper and pull out a sheet. Jim will get the whole of my anger now, whether he likes it or not.

VIA VINCENZO SCUSSA 8, TRIESTE
15 November 1909

How could you do this to me, Jim, and to our children? I know you have expenses there, what with your father's hospitalization and the care of the girls left to you, but what about us? Are we not your greatest care, your largest responsibility?

Lucia and Georgie sit here now but tomorrow they may sit on the street with la Nonna and with the lost boy outside the church, because you have not done your duty, which is to make sure they're not cast out onto the streets like the beggar Bartimaeus in Jericho. Is that what you want for these children, to roam Trieste in rags, their hands out for coins?

*You disgust me, James Joyce. You make false prom-
ises to those whom you claim to love the most. You're not
a man. How can you be when you fail to protect us? How
can you be when you so clearly lie with prostitutes for that
itch that ails you is got no other way? I'm leaving you,
Jim. I'm going back to Galway to throw myself at the
mercy of my mother and my uncles. I can't stay another
moment here when I don't know from one day to the next
if you're faithful to me or if my children will be without a
place to live.*

Nora

His return letter to me is abject, wretched.

*I don't even dare to call you by your name. I feel like a
cur who has been thrashed across the eyes. I am degraded
before you.*

He says I should leave him and let him sink back into the mud.
His words stir me and I feel foolish and ignorant—where
would I go, truly? I don't want to go to Galway, I never want to
be without Jim. I look at the beautiful gloves he chose for me and
cry knowing that he bought them with a big heart and that all I do
is scold him and write angry words. I pick up my pen again and
write nothing but kindness and forgiveness to him. By return he
tells me he ate dinner in Finn's Hotel and begged to see the room I
once occupied there.

*I think of you in that room, Gooseen, burning quietly
with love, and I cry for you in your simple dress with your*

simple manners. I cry that you ended up with my ignoble
love, I cry with pity for myself who is unworthy.

This strange land, this strange hotel, the shadow of
a strange girl staring out over college park. A mysterious
beauty hangs every place she has lived! I sob. In her is the
beauty and mystery of life, of this world, the doomed race
we come from, the pure spirituality of my boyhood. Her
very soul and name and eyes that are blue, wildflowers in
a rain-drenched hedge. Her soul trembles beside my own, I
speak her name to the night, I weep because the beauty of
the world passes like a dream behind her eyes.

His words have such grace; I swallow them down and let them
settle inside me. I lie on our bed to read and reread and bask in
them. An idea occurs to me: I can't match Jim's words for beauty,
but I can rope him to me with certain words of my own. I take my
pen and scratch out another private note, one that will keep Jim in
my spell.

Via Vincenzo Scussa 8, Trieste
20 November 1909

Jim, the fact is that I will have to punish you for your
horrible ways and for your neglect of me when you return
to me from Ireland. You think I will not reprimand you,
no doubt. You think me too small and girlish, perhaps, to
discipline a man. But when you get here I will order you to
take off your clothes and, if you disobey me, I will sit on
you and pin your arms down until you howl for forgive-
ness, and until your prick quivers and begs for my mercy,

until I let it fuck me. Because I long for you to fuck me
again, Jim. I wait here, your little fuckbird, open and wet.
Now, there is something for you to think about!

Your Nora

44 FONTENOY STREET, DUBLIN
2 December 1909

Nora, you rogue! I hardly dare to be familiar with you
and you write me such a thing! I am agog when you write
what you will do to me if I disobey you.

Don't take offense at what I write, dear, you are
firstly and forever my blue rain-drenched flower. My
love for you allows me to honor the everlasting beauty
and tenderness mirrored in your eyes, but also it means I
want to force you onto your soft belly and fuck you from
behind, a hog riding his sow, rejoicing in the stench and
sweat that rises from your arse, glorying in your upturned
dress and girlish drawers and in the fluster of your blushed
cheeks and tangled-up hair. My love allows me to cry
tears of pity and regard at some small word, to tremble
with love for you at the sound of some note of music, or
to lie top to tail with you and feel you fondle and tickle
my balls, or sticking your fingers up the back of me and
your hot mouth sucking off my cock while my head is
lodged between your plump thighs, my hands clutching
the cushions of your bum and my tongue licking hungrily
at your red cunt. I have taught you almost to be overcome
by my voice singing or whispering to your soul the passion
and sorrow of life and at the same time have taught you

to make lewd signs to me with your lips, to rouse me with
filthy touches and sounds, and even to do in my presence
that most shameful and dirty act of the body. You recall
the evening you pulled up your clothes and let me lie on
the floor looking up while you did it? Then, love, you
could not even meet my eyes.

You are mine, Nora, mine! I love you. All I have
written above is only momentary madness. The last drop
of mine has hardly been spurted up your cunt before it ends
and my love, the love of my poetry, the love of my eyes for
your strange beguiling eyes, blows over my soul like a bora
of spices. My cock is still hot and hard and quivering from
the last brutal thrust inside you when a low, tender hymn
sounds in sorrowful worship of you from the dark cloisters
of my heart.

Nora, my darling, my blue-eyed blackguard girl,
my Gooseen, be my harlot, be my mistress (my frigging
mistress! my fucking whore!) you will always be my wild-
flower of the hedges, my beautiful rain-drenched flower.

Jim

He hopes the "coarse immodesty" of his letter doesn't offend
me. By God, it does not. It sends me, instead, into a frenzy of heat
and I can barely stand to be with other people for I need to be
alone on my bed to read his sinful words over and over and to ride
my own fingers on the pleasure and badness of them. Oh Jim, oh
my beautiful man, if I turn you to a beast as you say, you do the
same to me.

... Nora, you lead the way. It was you who slipped
your fingers into my trousers to tickle my prick; it was you

who frigged me until I spurted warmly onto your fingers,
all the time looking steadily at me with those saint's eyes
of yours. It was you who first told me to "fuck up," riding
my horn, you stuck my cock into your cunt, love, you did
that ...

PRESENCE

❧

Trieste
DECEMBER 1909

Eva is acting the dry auld duck though I'm the one who should be mopey and sad this Christmas Day, with Jim so far away and not due back until January. She sits at the table and snivels.

"I wonder what they're doing now," she says. "I wonder did Pappie hire a piano and are they singing. Eileen draws the neighbors to the door with her singing voice." Over and on she goes about how much she misses her sisters. She sniffs and whimpers, and Stannie's jaw clamps every time she sucks snot into her nose.

"Do you need a handkerchief, Eva?" he says and she shakes her head.

"You're probably missing the bit of goose, too, are you, Eva? And the roast potatoes?" I say and she nods miserably into her plate of pasta. "Well, at least we have plum pudding."

A tear slides down her nose and I give her my hanky. "Thank you," she whispers.

"Will we open our presents?" I say, pushing away the plate of *stracotto di maccheroni* I had worked so hard on but that ended up a lumpy mess. "We can have our pudding afterward."

Georgie and Lucia drop from their chairs and are across the

room like skyrockets to their stockings. We all sit on the rug; I hand parcels to Eva and Stannie—a blouse for her, a shirt for him. Eva holds up the blouse for all to admire the frilled collar and cuffs. She smiles for the first time in a week and I'm pleased to have made her happy. Stannie opens his present and takes out the shirt.

"It's the perfect shade of green, Nora," he says. "I thank you."

He gives me a box of Florentine writing paper, the envelopes lined and swirled with varicolored flowers and fruit. "Well, that paper's miles too good for my auld scrawl," I say.

"Not at all, Nora." He grins shyly.

"It's beautiful, Stannie. Many thanks to you." I reach over and press his hand.

Eva gives us both jars of marmalade that she recently made, tied prettily with orange ribbons, and she gifts spinning tops to the children. At last I can open the package from Jim. Though I know it's the bound edition of his handwritten *Chamber Music* manuscript that he promised me in a letter, still my heart skips and scatters with anticipation. We gather around the parcel and I'm grinning like a fool. I undo the wrappings and gasp: the book is covered in cream leather and our initials—JJ AND NB—are entwined in gold on the front, along with the Joyce coat of arms. The parchment pages are heavy and Jim's fine hand runs across them in India ink, the words startling, neat, and even more beautiful for their setting.

"Has anyone ever received such a gift as this?" I say. And with such love attached, I think. My fingers reach to fondle my ivory necklet and I think what vast luck that Jim chose me and that I, indeed, chose him.

Stannie lifts the book and examines it. "Very fine," he says.

I don't even know that I'm crying until Lucia comes and puts her small arms around me. "*Ti voglio bene*, Mamma," she says and blots my face with her sleeve.

"I love you too, my precious darling." I hold her and kiss her dear head, so like her father's. Georgie comes to me for caresses, his proud little face lifted to mine, and I kiss him over and over. But, once I realize that my tears won't cease, I lift *Chamber Music*, leave the company, and go to my room to compose myself. I sit on our bed and hold the book to my chest as if it were Jim himself; I rock myself and mourn that he's not with us; it's not right for a family to be ripped asunder at Christmas, business or no business.

A knock to the door and Stannie lets himself in. "Are you all right?"

"I am," I reply, but my flowing eyes betray me.

He comes and sits on the bedspread beside me and his arm snakes around my back; I lean into him, letting my head fall to his shoulder. Oh, the solid, comforting bulk of man, how can I live without it? His hand steals up into my hair and I let my sobs racket and he soothes me with small, gentle noises from his throat.

"There, Nora," he says softly, "there now."

He puts his hand inside his jacket pocket and pulls out a small wrapped slab of *mandorlato*, my favorite almondy treat.

"For me?"

Stannie nods. "I didn't want to give it to you in front of the others; they'd have it eaten before you could blink."

He unwraps the slab, breaks off a chunk, and feeds it into my mouth, his fingers lingering on my lips and his eyes locked to mine. I chew the *mandorlato*, though it's hard to swallow in my upset state, and the sugariness of it consoles me a little. I allow my head to drop into Stannie's lap and I curl my feet onto the bed cover. His other arm comes down over my waist and I can feel its heat even through my new tweed dress that I wear today for Jim, though he can't see me. Stannie's hand comes under my chin and he tilts my head so that we're looking full into each other's faces.

His mouth is close to mine; we look at each other as if daring the other to move first. Just when Stannie drops his lips onto mine, the door opens in a rush and we both startle; it's Eva, a face like murder on her when she sees us. I'm mortified and I pull myself upright and set my feet on the floor.

Eva agitates the doorknob and glares at us. "Georgie slapped Lucia and she's bawling and won't stop. She wants you, Nora."

"It seems we're all prone to tears today," I say brightly, not looking at her.

"All except, Stannie," Eva says. "He seems very happy with himself."

I brush past her, my heart jolting in my chest, and leave the pair of them to glower at each other. I go back to my children.

WORSHIP

❦

Trieste
JANUARY 1910

JIM IS BACK TO ME WITH TROUBLED EYES AND A BOUT OF SCIAT-
ica, both of which keep him abed until all hours. He can't work,
of course, because he's not able to see to write and, therefore, he
can't correct lessons, so his private pupils must wait patiently for
his recovery. As must we all. It puts the worst into you when someone in the house is sick, but not in a way that seems like *true* sick-
ness. Jim can walk and talk and be himself, as usual, and though
I worry about his health, I'm also annoyed by him and the whole
mix makes a terror of me. I bash about the place tidying and making food and whatever, while he takes his ease.

Eva is happier now that her sister's here and Eileen is an altogether livelier girl, of whom I grow fonder each day. This morning
they're pinning on their hats for Mass and I feel a pinch of envy at
their togetherness and their dance around the flat, readying themselves.

"Say a prayer for me, girls," I say, as they pull on their gloves.

"Would you not come with us altogether, Nora?" Eileen asks,
as she does every Sunday.

"Ah, I won't. I'm out of the habit, as you know." The truth of
it is, I think it might upset God, and Jim, too, if I went.

Eileen's mouth settles into a pucker, her way of letting me know she's unhappy with me. She wrangled from me that Jim and I are not, in fact, married and her head nearly fell off with the shock. She blessed herself over and over.

"Oh, what would Pappie say if he knew the truth? What would he think, Nora?" she moaned.

"Daddy is no saint," Eva said, and she got a pinched glare from Eileen for her trouble.

"And what about your own people, Nora? Do you not *want* to be joined in the sight of our Lord, for your conscience's sake? Or for the children's, surely?" Eileen asked.

"Well, I wouldn't mind, but Jim is against it, dead set. You know what he's like, Eileen."

She rolled her eyes and shook her head and I knew I'd have to prepare Jim for an onslaught.

Off the girls go to the church and Jim calls me to bring in his coffee and rolls. "Are the daughters of Erin gone to kneel before their idols?" he says.

"Ah, stop, Jim. You go often enough to the Greek church, what difference is in it?"

He snorts. "The difference is that I go for aesthetic reasons while my sisters go to hug the altar rails and beg their God for a soft hereafter. Enjoy life *now*, I say. There is nothing beyond this moment." I light the Virginia cheroot he holds up to me and look at him, idling under the covers like a little king.

"It might not be a bad thing for Georgie and Lucia to go to Mass with their aunties sometime. Do we really want to rear them as heathens? Maybe they should go to the Greek basilica you're so fond of loitering in; you could take them with you."

He puts his hand over mine. "Your children are too wild for a place of worship, my dear."

"They're mine when they act up and yours when they're good, is that it?" He nods and crosses himself, closes his eyes and pretends to pray, to rile me. "My granny Healy would've called you a 'black rabbit,' Jim."

"Black rabbit. Heretic. Dissenter. Man of good sense. Phil the Fluter. I don't mind what anyone calls me."

I tut. "What we need is a good, clever priest to convince you to rejoin the faith."

"And what of *your* faith, Gooseen?"

"How can I even think to approach a holy house when we live like this?" I wave my hand between the pair of us.

"Go away out of that, Nora Barnacle, you love being an auld sinner." He drops the butt of the Virginia into his coffee cup where it hisses and pulls me onto him.

"Stop it, Jim," I say but my body goes lax, all the same. He's right, of course; I wouldn't trade the life we have to be a slave to priest or church again. But marriage? Well, that might be a different day's conversation entirely.

ONWARD

❧

Trieste
1910 AND 1911

THE FRANCINIS HAVE TAKEN STANNIE'S SIDE IN DISPUTES with Jim over money, so I don't see Clotilde much anymore and, though I feel the want of her friendship, at least I have my sisters-in-law.

When Georgie and I meet Stannie on Via Scussa one day, he tells his uncle, "We had no dinner today, keep that in your head."

"Giorgio!" I bark. "Keep a civil tongue."

"He's Jim's son, all right, Nora," Stannie says, giving me a plaintive look.

"I wish you two brothers would stop ramming heads and just get on. Come and take your evening meal with us again, Stannie."

"What's the point, Nora? Half the time I turn up to an empty flat, everyone gone to the opera or the cinema and my belly growling. Every penny of mine is in your pocket and Jim's. Or, more accurately, spent in the Teatro Verdi. Your priorities differ to mine."

I'm a little stung but only because I know he's right. "We miss you, Stannie," I say after a moment, and he clamps his eyes to mine so that I turn away, in case Georgie notices, for he seems to see everything.

"Much good it does anyone to miss another." Stannie tips his cap and walks on down the street. I watch him go with a shaky mix of relief and regret.

JIM'S BOOK OF STORIES IS DELAYED AGAIN, THE DUBLIN PUB-lisher has some objections and they can't seem to sort them out between them. While that's held up, he can't get on with the novel. And the Volta Cinema on Mary Street collapses, sending Jim into a tirade about Ireland of the betrayers, the useless bog, the cheating swindlers with swill as blood et cetera. He waits for a share of the sale of the cinema, but none comes, and with Stannie keeping to himself, we're foxed entirely, for we seem to spend faster than Jim earns. And to top it off, he comes home to me one day with a silk scarf.

"I have six mouths to feed!" I scream. "What am I to do with that?" I throw the scarf at his feet. "Eileen, get me the box of writing paper."

She carries the box to me and I start a letter to Bowling Green to let Mammy and my sisters know they will soon have myself and the children to support, for James Aloysius Joyce refuses to take care of us. Jim peers over my shoulder.

"You haven't sent your mother a letter in six years and, yet, today you feel the need."

"What of it? And stop reading my words." I put my hand across the page.

Jim lifts my fingers and bends closer. "If you must write to Galway, Nora, at least capitalize your letters."

I toss down my pencil. "You'd be better served, Jim, taking that scarf back to the shop and getting *our* money back so that you can feed your starving family. And, while you're out, go and apologize to your brother for whatever collection of shite has ye not speaking. He's the only one who'll keep us alive!"

AFTER AN APOLOGY FROM JIM, STANNIE'S GOOD HEART BRINGS him back to dine with us at night and we're saved for another while as Jim can cadge off his brother with no conscience. I'm both sad and glad that Stannie stops at Via Nuova and won't move in with us again—sad because he seems to be removing himself from us, but glad for sometimes his looks to me are so doleful and lovesick that I'm sure Jim, bad eyes and all, will notice. It's better, for everyone, if Stannie and I aren't able to be alone together. I may have relied heavily on him when Jim was away, but I love him as a brother only, and his regard for me is stronger than that for a sister, it's clear.

WE RENT A PIANO WITH A SMALL LOAN FROM ETTORE SCHMITZ and all enjoy Eileen's beautiful soprano voice; she hopes to train in Milan one day. We belt out Irish songs and Italian songs and the children learn everything so fast that it gobsmacks me. Georgie sings and sings, Lucia sways and rocks and twirls.

The girls and I cook together: chicken stuffed with cinnamon-peppered potato; veal shanks and risotto; stewed eels and polenta; bacon and cabbage. We're a busy, noisy household and, for the first time, I feel properly part of a big family. Jim asks if I want my sister Delia to come to Trieste to live with us, too, but I'm not sure that I do.

"A shipload of Joyces is one thing…" I say.

"You see no profit in sticking another Barnacle onto it?"

"Exactly, Jim."

I take in ironing, Ettore and Livia Schmitz's among it. This wounds Jim for he considers Signor Schmitz a friend and equal and it pains him that, in truth, Schmitz is his employer and mine and, now, Eileen's, too. She's acting as governess to their daughter. Still, he won't call them snobs, though they're as bad as the rest of Trieste, and nor will I; they keep us in rice, pasta, hats, and drawers and I'm glad of it. Their money also pays for the skivvy girl, Mary, who comes to help with this and that. She minds Georgie and Lucia while I iron; she meets Jim's students at the door and escorts them up the stairs; she even learns how to boil a decent spud.

Signor Prezioso, or Roberto as he likes me to call him, has taken to visiting me some afternoons when the rest of the household is occupied. Jim encourages his visits—he likes to be seen among the rich of Trieste—and he has me relate our conversations to him at night. Roberto talks of giving Jim more articles to write for his newspaper and lectures to deliver; Jim urges me to keep him happy. Roberto is a handsome, well-groomed fellow and I enjoy our visits for he makes me feel like a lady, and our hours together are like no others I spend. We sit, we look at each other, we talk about everything and nothing, we smoke, we eat cake. It's proper and absolute relaxation.

"Do you remember when you first gave Jim pieces to write for the *Piccolo*?" I say to Roberto one afternoon over strong tea and *presnitz*.

"Yes, he wrote of the uprising in Ireland."

"He did." I sip my tea and admire the way Roberto sits full in the window light, but keeps himself erect and unblinking in his chair, always polite despite the glare in his eyes. I get up to close the shutter. Roberto is a man who likes women, genuinely *likes* them, and he listens well; he doesn't think what he has to say is more important than what I talk about. I fold over the shutter, blocking the stream of light. "Now," I say, "that's better."

"*Grazie mille*, Signora Joyce."

I sit again. "Well, I don't know if I should tell you this, Roberto, but back then, we came up with a nickname for you."

"A nickname, Signora Joyce? How charming. And what was it?"

"We put your name to English, we called you 'Mister Bob Precious.' How do you like that?" I giggle.

"Bob Precious sounds very fine to me. Bob! I can pretend to be an American, *sì*?" He leans forward and lays his fingers over my hand. "While we are talking of names, will you give me permission to call you Nora?"

"Of course, Roberto. You might have called me that any time before."

He draws his fingers back and I put my other hand over the heat where he touched me. It's nice, indeed, to spend time with a man who makes no demands on me.

"You know, Nora, I have a nickname for you, too. A private one, one that I hold to my heart."

"Oh, do tell me!" It tickles me that he has the same funny impulses as Jim, to call me little pet names.

Roberto smiles. "Well, Nora, my name for you is '*Irlandina*.' Is that to your liking?"

"*Irlandina*. Little Ireland," I say. "I like it very well, Roberto."'

TODAY OUR BOB PRECIOUS IS IN HIGH SPIRITS. HE HAS BROUGHT a silver flask of grappa and he sloshes it liberally into the coffee we're drinking. His cheeks are pink—normally he has the waxy skin of all aristocrats—and he moves from his usual chair to sit near me on the sofa.

"Your husband is much occupied, Nora, eh?"

"Somebody has to earn a few crowns," I say and laugh.

Though Roberto runs the newspaper, *he* seems to have a lot of time for going about.

"Does James Joyce neglect you, my dear?"

His face is so close to mine that I can smell the sweet coffee-grappa mixture on his tongue and see a glaze of sweat all over his skin. I shiver though it's warm.

"Jim is most attentive," I say, finally, moving my head a little, for the sudden intimacy crashes around my body like a warning bell, though I find I thrill to it a little also.

"I hope he is," Roberto says. He reaches out and, with one finger, begins to trace the skin of my wrist that's concealed behind the lace cuff of my dress. "My *Irlandina*."

I know I should lift his hand away, I know I should walk to the other side of the room, but he's such a sweet man, so quietly assured and kind to me. It feels nice, and a biteen wicked, to sit close with Roberto and talk idly, to allow him to look at me and touch me gently, and, yes, to admire me, as if I were a woman of enormous leisure and enormous beauty, both.

"You are so exquisite, Nora, with your copper hair. *Il sole s'è levato per Lei*. The sun has risen just for you, dear Nora."

His beautiful Italian voice and his way with words churns me up. The sun rises for me! Never has a man said such a thing to me, to my face. Oh, Jim talks to me of wet flowers and so forth, but the sun feels like another matter altogether.

In a flash, Roberto lunges forward and his mouth is on mine. His tongue shoots, small and flat as a lizard's, between my lips and though I'm shocked, I open my mouth wider to his. His kiss is dry and blunt, and I try to loosen his mouth with the wet of my own tongue, but it doesn't work and I pull back, brought to my senses by embarrassment. I hear Mary come up the stairs, in from a walk with Lucia and Georgie, and I stand up from the sofa and go to the window. The children slam into the room.

"We have the beach in our shoes," Georgie calls.

"Mamma, Mary let us play in the sandpit in the park," Lucia says.

Roberto stands and I turn to him quickly for fear of what he might say. But he's as composed as a bishop and he greets Mary and the children before looking at his pocket watch.

"I am late for a business meeting, my friends. I shall leave you."

I stay where I am as he heads for the door, Mary leading the way. He turns back and I see that there are clouds about his eyes and I don't know if this is a look of pity or worry or regard.

"*Arrivederci*, Signor Prezioso," I call.

"*Arrivederci*, Signora Joyce."

I TELL JIM. I TELL HIM THAT ROBERTO HAS ATTEMPTED TO MAKE love to me and that he mustn't call on me again. We're alone in the kitchen, he writing, me cooking. Jim nods and asks for details; he's surprisingly calm.

"It was nothing; he tried to embrace me, that's all."

"Did he kiss you?"

"Not really," I say, conjuring the hard dryness of Roberto's mouth. I don't want to have to kiss him again, so I must stop him from coming here.

"You are irresistible, Gooseen, to men of letters, it seems." Jim laughs, but it's a brittle eruption and now I'm worried that he might do something to Roberto. Hit him, maybe. Jim's not violent, but if he had a few drinks on him and met Roberto, who knows, he might lash out with his cane. He takes off his glasses and rubs his eyes, a sure sign that he's thinking hard on something that's causing him upset.

I stop stirring my pot of risotto. "Now, Jim, leave it be. Don't go after Roberto. Send him a note to say he shouldn't call on me again. Let that be all. Be sensible, we don't want you to lose the income for the articles you write for him."

Jim looks up at me. "The man insults you, Nora, and I'm supposed to let it go? I'm meant to send a cordial note, is that it? Worry about a few miserable coins?"

I put down my spoon. "Jim, you said to keep Signor Prezioso soft and sweet, so I did that. You want to publish more writing with the *Piccolo*, don't you?" He mutters something and I lean forward. "What was that?"

"I said I don't wish to write for a betrayer."

"Oh, for the love of the Madonna in heaven, Jim Joyce, you and your bloody betrayers." I take up my wooden spoon and stir the rice like a demon. "I said to leave it! Can you not do what I ask?"

EILEEN BARGES INTO MY BEDROOM WHERE I'M ABOUT TO GET into my dress; Jim and I are going to the opera and he loves to see me in his Donegal tweed. She shuts the door and stands with her back against it. I pluck the dress from the wardrobe and look over; her eyes are jigging in her head.

"Eileen, I'm in my smalls. What is it?"

"Oh, Nora, Signor Prezioso is crying buckets of tears below in the piazza."

"What? Roberto Prezioso?"

Eileen nods. "Jim's railing at him on the street. He looks like he might wallop him."

My brow goes clammy and cold in one flash. "Oh God."

I pull on my dress and snap at Eileen to help me. She gets my top buttons closed and we hammer down the stairs. We run up the street and, ahead of us on the piazza, I see Jim standing right up against Prezioso. As we come nearer, I hear Jim half screeching and he thumps his cane into the cobbles.

"How dare you! How dare you!" he's saying to Prezioso in a strangled voice; Jim is purple and livid. Prezioso is dabbing at his face with his sleeve; he's shaky and he sobs as quietly as a reprimanded child.

I grab Eileen's hand, afraid to go closer. "Poor Roberto," I whisper.

She tuts and I look at her; Eileen's eyes take on a sly glint. "I've never seen Jim like this. What's it all about, do you suppose, Nora?"

"Don't do the innocent, Eileen. You know well it's about Roberto's visits to me." I clench my jaw. "Which you also know that Jim encouraged."

"Maybe this will learn you not to meddle with other people's feelings." We watch Prezioso hang his head while Jim stands over him, looking down in silence. "And Eva told me about Stannie and you," Eileen says, "in case you think she didn't."

I whip around to face her, my cheeks burning. "Leave Stannie out of it," I say.

We stand and blaze at each other for moment, like two children fighting over a top. Eileen holds my stare then steps back. "You're some woman, Nora. I'll say that for you." She glances at Prezioso and Jim, glares hard at me, then flounces off.

I go forward a few steps but Prezioso has gathered himself and is walking away, his head low like a man truly beaten. Jim turns and looks to me; he shakes his head, then walks the opposite way, across the piazza, toward a caffè. I won't see him now till morning.

TERRIBLE NEWS COMES FROM DUBLIN. STANNIE BRINGS IT TO US and he and Jim wake the girls to tell them. Their sister Baby is dead, young Mabel.

"Only seventeen years old and taken by typhoid," Stannie says.

"God love her," I say. "It's a terrible loss to you all."

"That man," Stannie says, meaning Pappie, and I nod for I know Stanislaus blames his father for all the family's woes.

Pappie is, of course, broken by his daughter's death; Mabel was his loyal comrade, the one who loved him best, he said, most cherished for being the youngest, the shakings of her dear mother's bag. Eva is so upset she can't even cry. After breakfast, she sits on the sofa, clutching a handkerchief, stricken and silent. Eileen blames their father too.

"Oh, that fella," she rants, "with his high stories and his low company. He couldn't look after a flea, never mind a family. Thank Blessed Mary that my mother died and didn't have to put up with any more of him." She rants on, pacing the floor of the flat, and her tears and snot flow like a waterfall; she stops only to hug Lucia and Georgie who eventually escape to the landing, dragging Fido, their new dog, with them. "Bloody Pappie, the useless auld git," Eileen rails, "not content with driving our mother into an early grave, he goes and kills Baby, too. Oh, our poor darling Mabel." She sits with a thud beside Eva and puts her arm around her sister and sobs into her shoulder.

"Baby was the best of us, Eileen, wasn't she?" Eva says, breaking her cold silence.

"She was, the poor pet. The sweetest, most affectionate child, despite all she endured."

"It was the dream of her life to join us in Trieste, Nora," Eva says.

"Sure, I know it was," I say. "Aunt Jo always says so in her letters, that Baby will be coming here as soon as she can."

"I'd best go home to Pappie," Eva says. "He won't last long after this. I should be with him."

Eileen sits up, ramrod straight. "You will *not* go home. No way are you leaving here, Eva. For what? So he can kill you, too, with the damp and the neglect and the misery of that awful place he's staying in now?"

"Stop saying that Pappie killed her," Jim says. "It was Ireland itself that did it. Bloody miserable swill-pit. The country can't take care of its own, so it makes them grovel in poverty and pray to heaven for a sweet hereafter. Selling them lies. Basting them with guilt. What bloody use is prayer to anyone?"

I put my hand on his arm. "Jim, it's not the time."

Eileen looks at me. "The house in Fontenoy Street was bad, but Aunt Jo says that Hishon's Hotel, where Pappie and the others are putting up the last while, is desperate altogether."

Stannie frowns. "Aunt Jo says the sewage there got into the water and did for Baby."

"Well, then Florrie and May and Pappie himself will be next," Eva says. She worries her handkerchief and looks around at us all. "I want to go home, Eileen. I can help them. I'll take a wee job with a seamstress and get them somewhere decent to live."

Eileen stands up. "We can talk about that later. Come on, let's all go to San Giusto and light a candle for Mabel."

Eva rises. "Do you think she had a lot of pain, Eileen? I couldn't stand it if I thought Baby was hurting and I wasn't there to mind her. Would she have been in agony?"

Stannie puts his arm around his sister. "It would have been peaceful, Eva. Baby wouldn't have known a thing. She'd have been in a kind of trance. A sleep." He glances at me. Jim told me that Aunt Jo's letter says Baby went deaf and that, in the end, she was like an animal in distress.

"Nora, Jim," Eva says, "you'll come to the church with us now, won't you?" Her look is wretched and she still hasn't dropped a tear.

"We will, of course, Eva," I say.

"Pappie called Baby his 'dotie darlie,'" Eva says. "Who will he love now?"

"Hush now, peteen," I say and pin her hat to her hair.

We leave the flat and our small, sad procession takes us up and down streets, with Jim in the lead; he always prefers a curly route. Even the children are somber for they seem to understand fully that their aunt has died and how that brings everyone low. At the cathedral Jim stops outside and is reaching into his pocket for his cigarettes and matches, when Eileen comes and stands in front of him and stares into his eyes; he cannot say no to her, so in he comes, too. The church is cool and quiet; we take a pew and kneel together, heads bowed. I ask the Virgin to take Mabel safely to her mother and, while I'm here, to look after us all in this sorrowful time, especially the girls. Finally, beside me, poor Eva lets a little whimper, her shoulders shudder greatly, and tears fall. Eileen and I gather in close to her; Eva'll not stay in Trieste with us much longer, of that I'm sure as sure can be.

RESTORATION

◆

Dublin and Galway
JULY 1912

Mammy and I have begun to write letters to each other—she took to Jim and Georgie like a pigeon to seed when they visited, and wrote recently to tell me so—and now we're friendly again.

Baby Joyce's death spooked my mind. "I keep thinking one of mine might pass before I get to see them, Jim. I couldn't live with their ghosts after eight years apart. How would I know them if they appeared to me? And would their spirits be sore with me after my leaving and my silence?"

"Don't worry, Nora," he says. "We'll arrange for you to go to Galway."

I take my box of treasures from the bedroom chest of drawers and sit on the bed: in it I have Georgie's first tooth, the children's locks of baby hair, my ivory necklet, along with Jim's letters, wrapped in the gray ribbon I wore in my hair the day he and I first walked out. Underneath all of it, snug in a handkerchief, is the wedding band Jim bought me before we came away and that I stopped wearing when I took in washing after Georgie was born.

I slip it onto my finger; it's tighter than it was, which pleases me—
I'm fattening up at last.

"You're not to wear that," Jim says and I almost drop with fright.

"For the love of God, Jim, don't be sneaking up on me."

"You don't need that ring, Nora. We are who we are and people must accept that."

"Mammy presumes we're married, Jim. Or did you let her know we weren't when you sat in her kitchen three years ago?"

His mouth goes straight as a pin. "You know well I didn't."

"But you expect me to tell her. Do you remember the beating my uncle Tommy gave me just for walking out with a boy? And you want me to tell my mother that her grandchildren are bastards and her daughter is living in sin?" I hold my hand up to admire the ring. "She'd throw me out on my ear. And rightly so."

WHEN WE ARRIVE IN DUBLIN, JIM'S PAPPIE, EVA—SHE HAD RE-
turned after Baby's death to Ireland last year—young Charlie, and his sister Florrie meet Lucia and me at Westland Row train station; Georgie stayed home with Jim in Trieste. Eva squeezes my shoulder affectionately, but drops down to pull Lucia into her arms and the two squeal with joy to be reunited. The pair of them have missed each other terribly.

I glance at Pappie and feel a small bit queasy with nerves—
will he like me at all? He's as ruddy and imposing as I expected and the wings of his mustaches give him a roguish charm. He steps forward and takes my two hands.

"Nora, Nora, Nora," he says, "you're as welcome as the flowers of May."

I grin, glad of his warmth; there's no hint of the ogre his children complain so much about. "Thank you, sir," I say.

"I'm no sir, girl. Call me John or call me Pappie, as they all do."

"I will so."

Lucia and I shake hands with Charlie and Florrie who are slight like Jim and quiet in themselves.

"Pappie has a great outing planned, Nora," Eva says, linking arms with me. "We're going to take lunch in Finn's Hotel."

PAPPIE HAS RESERVED THE TABLE BY THE WINDOW THAT LOOKS onto Lincoln Place—"So that all of Dublin might see us"—and I'm delighted as a duck to be sitting where I once slaved, being waited upon. I'll stay here until I go to Galway and what glory it will be to lie in a guest bed and not the garret of old.

"Now, isn't this just marvelous?" Pappie says, looking around at all of us. When his gaze lands on Lucia, babbling in Italian to Eva, his eyes fill and he dabs away the tears with his fist. "Isn't she a picture? So like our Baby. You're my new dotie darlie, Lucy," he says.

"It's Lucia, Pappie, *loo-chee-aa*," Florrie says. "You have to say it right."

"We call her 'Lucy' sometimes, too, Florrie," I say. "It's all the one."

"I believe young Georgie is wearing spectacles now," Charlie says shyly.

"He is, faith." I take out the latest family picture, which I have brought for them to keep, and hand it to Charlie.

"Oh, look at Jim with his new glasses," Florrie says. "His eyes are as big as a cow's!" Everyone laughs, even Lucia though she may not understand.

"And do you not think Georgie's new eyeglasses spoil his looks, Nora?" Eva asks.

"Whether they do or not, Eva, he needs them. The schoolmaster said he couldn't see a thing. He was falling behind."

The girls live apart from Pappie now and Eva looks well on it. She's not the downhearted wretch who stayed with us in Trieste. Pappie is shabby, but amiable, and is the man-about-town I've been led to expect; Jim is like him, with all his talk and bluster. We ramble on, over this subject and that, and we eat a hearty meal of chicken and ham. And all the time John Joyce watches me and Lucia, with his face alight, and it heartens me to see his regard for us blossom before my eyes. It's strange to be in their company, to be sure, people I barely know, though they are family now, and it's strange to be in Dublin where I feel skewed, not quite myself. It's the damp air and the absence of Jim, I suppose.

"BEFORE OUR JOLLIFICATIONS IN HOWTH, WE'LL VISIT THE BOLD Mister Roberts at Maunsel's." This is Pappie's greeting to me and Lucia as we finish our breakfast at Finn's. Charlie tips his cap.

"Yes, let's do that," I say. We mean to lock the publisher to a date for *Dubliners* and Jim says this is best done in a posse, to exert pressure. "Better to get Jim's business out of the way as soon as we can."

Mr. Roberts is a slippery fellow—he dodged Jim like a fox the last time—but I mean to pin him today. We're delighted to find him in and we're admitted to his office; after introductions, I go straight to it.

"Mr. Roberts, my husband is vastly unhappy with his treatment by you. What we need now is a date of publication for *Dubliners*. There's been too much evasion."

"Well now, Mrs. Joyce, the thing is, you see, that Mr. Joyce himself needs to be present, for I am proposing cuts to the book that he will need to approve. I cannot publish the book in its current form, for every publican in Dublin will sue me and Mr. Joyce besides."

"Sue him? For what?"

"For naming their establishments in stories that have, well, a peculiar vein to them. The publicans are not happy with the, eh, the immoralities in the stories."

I put my hand to the desk. "Mr. Roberts, my husband is a very fine writer and the pubs named will be more than glad of the notoriety, if you ask me. They have no need to sue anyone."

Pappie raises his hand. "My son will engage the best solicitor, Mr. Roberts, to ensure that all is well. There will be nothing untoward, peculiar, or immoral in his book. Make no mistake of that."

"I am glad to hear it, Mr. Joyce. Once we're satisfied that it passes muster, we will arrange for it to go to the printer."

Charlie nods vigorously and I may as well be vapor now for the men form a huddle as tight as the three Graces and I'm left looking at their backs. I clear my throat, but they continue to talk of legal this and opposition that until Mr. Roberts stands suddenly and says he is ever so busy and can we call again tomorrow? We're back out on Abbey Street in a flash.

"Eva and Florrie will meet us at the train station with Lucia," Charlie says and grins. "We'll enjoy Howth."

UP ON HOWTH HEAD WE SIT AMONG THE PINK RHODODENDRONS and the scrubby heather and look down over the Irish Sea that holds stars of light on its waves. Florrie has made egg and cress sandwiches and Eva has brought bottles of lemonade, and my lovely Lucia looks at home and happy among her Joyce relations. Normally it's Georgie who loves to sing for others but, with gentle prodding from her grandfather, Lucia stands before us and sings. Her little voice is high but soft and she gives us the lullaby Jim made for her:

C'era una volta, una bella bambina
Che si chiamava Lucia
Dormiva durante il giorno
Dormiva durante il notte ...

In a low tone, Eva translates for the others: "Once upon a time, a beautiful girl called Lucia slept during the day, slept during the night." The sea shimmers behind Lucy and her sweet words carry over the hill and float on toward the harbor. Pappie looks enchanted and we all drowse away under the spell of my daughter's voice until Charlie leaps up, startling me.

"Come on," he says to Lucia, "there's an ice cream fellow below at the harbor. We can try a little pot of his wares and look at the seals bobbing in the water."

We all get up and wipe off the grasses that cling to us. "Ireland has everything now," I say, stunned that anyone would eat ice cream in the Irish climate. "They eat gelato by the bucket in Trieste," I tell Pappie, who has bid me take his arm.

We wend our way down to the harbor, where the *tok-tok* sound of the boats brings Trieste to mind and, therefore, Jim. I buy a postcard picturing Howth; all of us scribble a little message to Jim and Georgie and I stamp and send it off, kissing the corner of the card discreetly before popping it in the box. It will make Jim happy to know that Pappie has embraced Lucia and me, to be sure.

Was the air in Galway always so crisp and cool? I fancy it was, I just never knew warm Mediterranean air when I was a girl and the contrast now astonishes me. The seaweedy smell that *is* Galway fills my nose as soon as I step from the train station onto Eyre Square and I feel as if I shall cry. The sweet familiarity of home moves me, but with it returns all the ache of being young, the wanting to leave and explore the world outside County Galway, but not being able to see ahead to what would be.

Soon I see my uncle Michael Healy, who will put us up in his house on Dominick Street, coming at a trot across Eyre Square toward us. He looks through me, though I reach out my hand, and walks straight past us. When I turn my head back, my mother is standing before me.

"Oh, Nora," she whispers, and she falls on me and holds me tight to her chest. We break apart and stare at each other. Mammy looks older and a bit careworn, but she's neatly dressed and well-groomed and I'm glad to see it.

"This is Lucia," I say, pulling my daughter forward.

Uncle Michael is back, his face all astonishment. "Well, now, Nora Barnacle, aren't you the lady, *a leana*? I wouldn't have known you from the man in the moon." He looks to Mammy. "Isn't she a picture, Annie?"

"Most certainly," Mammy says. "But she's Mrs. Joyce now, Michael, you must call her that."

"Nora does nicely," I say, glancing for a second at the wink of my gold band.

Mammy passes her fingers affectionately across Lucia's cheek. "And look at this bonny girleen."

I look around, feeling a little self-conscious in my cream coat and blue toque, every woman in sight is in practical black, though it's July. But Mammy's and Uncle Michael's eyes are so wide with admiration that I choose to carry myself as I would in Trieste.

"Let's get you to Dominick Street," Uncle Michael says. "I'll have your trunk sent down." He waves for a cab.

"Will we walk, Mammy? Sure it's no distance at all."

My mother nods and we join arms, though it was never our custom before. Uncle Michael hoists Lucia up to carry her and on we go.

∽

Uncle Michael's house sleeps, all is quiet. Uncle's abed for he rises early and Lucia is tired from all the novelty of meeting a score of relatives in her granny's house on Bowling Green. Uncle Tommy was stiff with me and I with him. I was nervous about seeing him, but he didn't affect me in the end; he seemed wary of me, too. What matter? Years have passed. I take my paper and pencil from the trunk. My heart is unsettled. It's like I'm here but not here at the same time; there's a dreamy feeling about seeing familiar sights: Lynch's Castle, the edge of the Claddagh village, the fast wash of the Atlantic that has my nerves tumbled; even Mammy's tiny house. The air feels sharp and unforgiving, and the constant lid of cloud seems to push down on me. I miss the blanketing heat of Trieste, the ordinary comfort of it. I go downstairs and sit in the armchair by the empty grate and wonder why I'm weary of Ireland already and how I'll get through the weeks ahead.

Jim is here! A letter came before he appeared, lamenting my silence. How could I be so monstrous as to forget our love and to send only a postcard from Dublin after five days of silence? Did I not know that he had pains that kept him from sleep? How could I not have written of our special places, our beloved Dublin city haunts? I mumbled at his letter that I was too busy paying for his family's meals and inquiring about the printing of his book, but here we are now, and all that is behind us and we're happy again. I think that Jim's a wonder, truly, to have raised money to run across Europe after me. He's soft and silly, no doubt—he can't survive a month without me—but he always finds the way to make things happen and that's why he's wondrous. He appeared last night at Mammy's door and I thought I was seeing a specter. The others laughed at us when they saw us reunite like people who'd been apart for years.

"Give up that kissing and hugging and mugging," Mammy said, hooshing Jim and Georgie into her already stuffed kitchen. I was pleased to see the golden shine of a ring on his wedding finger and I touched it gently as a way of thanking him.

"To ward off blindness," he whispered and I giggled.

"You're like newlyweds," Mammy said, looking pleased.

"We hardly recognized Nora when she came, Jim," my sister Delia said, with a shrewd little look to her. "She's a state! She's got so fat."

"And I want her even fatter, as round as a Christmas goose," Jim said, pulling me to him, and we all laughed.

Jim wakes and I lean over and kiss his forehead. *"Buongiorno, marito mio."*

"Good morning to you, wife." He blinks sleep from his eyes. "Did you ever," he says, "ask your uncle Michael for the fare to bring me and Georgie across?"

"Is that the first thing you want to say to me this morning and we together now?" I tut. "Didn't Signor Schmitz advance you money for lessons? Aren't you here?"

He scratches his head. "I don't know that you want me here, Nora."

Oh, isn't he the fellow who needs cajoling and petting? Such a boy! I soften my voice. "Of course I want you here, Jim, I'm so glad you joined us; the month seemed to stretch long before me." I kiss his lips. "And I couldn't ask for the fare once Uncle Michael told me he'd spent a bucketful of money getting a spare bone taken from his nose."

Jim giggles. *"Os nasus sparicus.* A spare bone, is it?" He throws back the sheet to show me his hand around his stiff maneen. I laugh, too, and he slips his other hand between my thighs and works it until I groan a little and soften and grow wet. But our chatter has already woken Georgie, who's in a cot under the window, and reluctantly I pull Jim's fingers away.

"Hello, Georgie Porgie," I say. "Will we go down to the beach at Salthill today?"

I get up and look out the long window. It's decorated with raindrops. Georgie comes to stand beside me. Lucia, it was decided, will stay with Mammy by night, now that Jim and Georgie are here.

"I wonder if Lucy is up yet," Georgie says. "She'll chase Granny's ducks without me."

"Don't worry, *a leana*, you'll have plenty of time to run after ducks." I put my finger to the cool windowpane. "How did I ever live with such drizzle and mizzle and pouring water?" I murmur. "It's no wonder the people look moidered as they trudge through it." Though it seems Galwegians come alight when the rain stays away, as if on dry days, a new, stronger, happier population fills the city.

Jim comes out of the bed and puts his arms around me. "The rain will cease and we'll all four take a family excursion."

Georgie begins to pull on his clothes and stands before his papà. "Shall we go now, Babbo?"

"Let's have breakfast first, my darling."

Uncle Michael has gone to work but has left us huge duck eggs, the color of the Adriatic, to boil. There's soda bread, too, and salty butter and tea that stews to bogwater brown and Jim and I groan with joy at the strong, Irish taste of it all.

"For the love of the saints, them eggs are like bits of heaven," I say, full to bursting after eating two.

Jim nods and helps himself to more bread, on which he spreads an amber yolk. He always eats hearty in other people's houses, our own table being so often sparse, I suppose. Georgie eats enough bread and gooseberry jam for a man.

We gather ourselves into jackets and hats and trot up to Bowling Green to collect Lucia, then the four of us walk the coast road out to Salthill, the rain easing away over the sea toward Black Head and County Clare.

"The air is lovely," I say. "It's as if I have new lungs and they're filled with sweet freshness every time I draw breath."

Jim pulls the air through his nose. "So pure."

I let him walk ahead and I look at him, strolling happily behind the children who jump, squealing, onto rocks and grass patches as if they've never seen such things before. For all our little squabbles, Jim cannot live without me and that pleases me mightily. I'm his woman and he's my man, bold and childish as he can be; I catch up and slot my arm through his.

"You like Galway, Jim?"

"I do, Nora. I intend to see as much of it as possible while we're here."

"Uncle Michael said you can borrow his bike any day that you please."

"He's a gentleman."

"Faith, he is."

The weather has the children rosy and I'm rounder and a little more content. I walk with Jim and savor the warming feeling that being an Irish family in Ireland gives me.

TRUE TO HIMSELF, JIM GOES EXPLORING ON THE BIKE. OUT TO Oughterard to see the graveyard, of all things, and beyond to Maam Cross another day, to stand where his relatives were wronged, as he says, a pair of Joyces, hanged for murders they were innocent of. I sit in Mammy's small kitchen, talking to her and to whoever is about. My sisters tell me all the news of girls I was pals with in school, who they're married to, who got in trouble, who's away in a convent. For a time, I love the gossipy silliness of it all but, more and more, I'm tired of listening to stories of people from another lifetime and, more and more, I find myself a little bored by the endless round of discussing the neighbors and their hurts and their joys and their money, or lack of it.

"Do you ever go to the theater?" I ask.

Mammy cocks an eyebrow. "To a play, is it? Sure, why would I do that?"

My sisters Kathleen and Delia stifle laughter and I feel my irritation bloom. "We go to the opera all the time in Trieste. It's beautiful," I say. "I think you'd like it, Mammy. The finery, the spectacle of it. The singing is gorgeous."

"Oh, Jim is fond of the music right enough," Mammy says, lifting a basket of spuds into her lap to peel them.

"I'm fond of it myself," I say, a cut to my voice.

"I suppose you were always different, Nora," Kathleen says, slicing lumps out of a cabbage stalk and handing them to each of us to eat.

"Different? What's that supposed to mean?"

"Just that you didn't grow up here. With us. You were beyond with Granny Healy and then in the convent. That made you a biteen different, I suppose. Unlike the rest of us."

I chew on the bittersweet stalk and swallow. Kathleen's right, but I don't want her to be. I feel like a Barnacle, like a Healy; I feel like a Galwegian and I feel Irish. But, I suppose, if I'm truly, wholly honest with myself, I mostly feel like a Joyce now, one who belongs in Trieste.

❧

STANNIE TELEGRAMS TO SAY THAT THE LANDLORD WANTS US OUT. After saying good-bye to my own family, I'm sitting now at Aunt Jo's kitchen table in Dublin, piling up winkles and razor shells from the beaches of Galway with Lucia. I'm mortified that Jim has read Stannie's telegram aloud for Aunt Jo and all to hear and I heat to my spine.

"Panicky Stannie," Jim says.

"But Signor Picciola probably means it this time, Jim, you know that," I murmur.

"Have you been behind on your rent, Nora?" Aunt Jo says. She squeezes Jim's arm as she says it; she touches him every chance she gets. Why is she asking me? I'm not the one who earns it.

"We are a large family," Jim says. "It's not easy to pay every bill on time."

I shake my head. "Poor Eileen must be fit to be tied," I say. "Isn't it just like Picciola to go there when she's alone?" I think of the three previous eviction notices that the signor presented us with and that we ignored, sure that he'd come around because he likes us and plans to take English lessons from Jim. I feel bad now that Eileen is left to deal with the landlord. And I feel worse that we're exposed in front of Aunt Jo who, despite her kindnesses, seems to have little time for me. It's all Jim with her.

"The Italians are almost as sly as the Irish," Jim says. "Picciola waited until we were abroad, right enough." He balls up the telegram and tosses it into the empty grate. "He can wait."

"How many addresses have you had in Trieste?" Aunt Jo says to me, and my neck hairs stand like soldiers with irritation.

"A few," I answer. "It's different over there, people move a lot." I know I sound like I'm making excuses and I want to like

Aunt Jo, to love her, but her possessiveness over Jim, and her nit-picky ways with me, are a burr under my skin. "Are you off to Maunsel's this morning, Jim?" I say.

"I am." He swigs back his tea. "I'm going to see *Dubliners* published, for once and for all."

"I'll come with you," I say, rising to get my hat and coat.

"Stay here, Nora," he says. "Can't you help Josephine with the dinner?"

"That would be grand," says Aunt Jo. "The house is full to the slates. Off you go, Jim, and see to your business."

I tut and sit down again and think Jo's awful vigilant of Jim for someone who's not even related by blood. He's her husband's nephew, that's all. But, to be fairer to her, she was fond of Jim's mother, I suppose, and she extended that love to Jim. I bite my lip and wish Jim well at the publishers.

GOD ALMIGHTY, MAUNSEL'S RAN JIM AROUND LIKE A PIG MARKED for slaughter. They refuse to publish *Dubliners*, though it's printed and all, saying again that it's perverse and that there will surely be lawsuits. He's up in Aunt Jo's parlor now, picking out mournful tunes on the piano and the rest of us sit here looking at each other like goms.

"Go to him, Nora," Aunt Jo commands me. "Can't you see this show of sadness is all done for you?"

I don't like her telling me how to act toward Jim. "He needs a few minutes to stew," I say curtly, "though really I'd prefer if he came down and ate the chop and spuds we made for him, it would do him more good than fretting alone." But I go anyway and he's hung over the keys like a marionette with broken strings, low in himself for sure. He plays a few sad notes.

"They're going to burn it tomorrow, Nora. A thousand copies

of the book. The words and sentences and lines and stories I held inside me like womb-bound babes and broke my heart to bring out of me. All of it will be tossed to the flames."

I'm shocked. "But it's yours, Jim. How can they do that?"

He shakes his head. "They can and they will, the blackhearted bastards."

"That can't be the end of it surely, love?" I put my hand to his shoulder.

"I got one set of pages from Roberts. But damn Ireland to hell, I'll never publish here. I'm taking the book to London where literature is at least understood."

"Have courage, *angelo mio*." I hug him from behind. "Shall we go home now, to Trieste? I feel like I'll never get my heels out of Ireland."

He puts his hand over mine. "Yes, my Gooseen, let's go home."

PORTRAIT

❧

Trieste
1913

JIM TEACHES NOW AT THE COMMERCIAL SCHOOL AND ENTER-
tains private pupils in the afternoon in our new flat on Via
Donato Bramante. We bought some furniture in the Danish style,
and the family portraits that Pappie sent Jim—once again certain
sure he was dying—dot the walls. What's even better is that Grant
Richards will publish *Dubliners* and the American, Mr. Pound, has
arranged for the novel Jim's been writing for years and years, *A
Portrait of the Artist as a Young Man*, to be serialized in a magazine,
beginning on Jim's birthday. Our fortunes have soared for sure.

I'm trying to fix two rends in Lucia's best linen frock—Eileen
says that Livia Schmitz proclaimed herself appalled when she
mentioned that I discard the children's worn clothing, so I mean
Eileen to take word back to the lofty Signora Schmitz that I, too,
can be economical, even in good times. Wealthy people have a
way of behaving that's alien to me.

"I'll show Livia Longhair that I'm as good as her and she has
no right to pass comment," I mutter.

Jim is across from me, smoking slowly and gazing at the paintings of his grandparents that watch over us all. His grandfather,

after whom Jim was named, looks like Pappie—he has the same startled eyes and I always think it looks as if he might jump from the canvas and tell us a fanciful yarn in which he himself plays a clever, comical turn.

"Nora," Jim says, "we need a picture of you."

"Aren't there likenesses aplenty of me?" I say, waving with my sewing needle at the frames along the mantelpiece.

"No, not a photograph. We need a painting, a portrait. In honor of *Portrait*." He mumbles this, half to himself, then stubs his cigarette and leaps from his chair.

"Where're you going, Jim?"

"I know just the chap for this." He throws on coat and hat. "A Venetian I met in a *piccola bettola* near San Giusto."

"It would serve you better, my man, not to darken the doors of taverns little *or* big." I bite the thread and examine my work; there's a lumpy scar on the frock now but it will do. "Do you mean to go to that *bettola* to find this artist?"

"No, he told me where his studio is, in a clattery place near the Porto Vecchio."

"Jim, there's a student coming at four, mind you're back in time."

He comes and kisses my head. "Fret not, my darling seamstress."

Off he goes and I'm left with my stitching, the pleasurable ticktock of the clock, and the occasional bird announcing its awakening from winter sleep. Sometimes being alone is the best thing to happen in my day.

CLOTILDE COMES TO VIA BRAMANTE TO SIT WITH ME AND WE bend our heads to our sewing like two old *nonne* on a July balcony.

We're not as close as we once were, but there are years of affection between us that can't be erased by a silly row over money and
Stannie and what is between brothers, truly.

"Jim brought home more seats," I tell her, pointing at the two
tiny chairs he turned up with a few days ago, "one each for the
children."

She wrinkles her forehead. "They look costly, Nora." She
squints. "Of French design."

"Oh, he says he got them cheap. How I didn't break them
across his head when he swayed in with them is God's guess."
Clotilde sniggers and I look down the long room with its scatter of
chairs and the upright piano where a cone of incense sits in a saucer
and sends up its churchy smoke. "It looks like a concert hall more
than anything else," I say and we both laugh.

"And don't we love a good concert?"

I nod. "Jim came in with the chairs the other day, all grins
and laughs, thinking himself a grand fellow. Lucy and Georgie see
the neat size of the seats and immediately hop onto them." I snip
my thread and hold up Georgie's shirt. "Not perfect, but what is?
Anyway, I'd sent him out for flour and raisins—I meant to bake—
and he comes back with those bloody yokes, the children sitting
on them in pure delight. 'How can I pull the chairs out from under
their backsides now?' I roared at him. And he sort of swayed and
looked at me as if through wet glass, a soft and happy set to him,
though he's been like a briar for months." I lean in to Clotilde.
"And now he says he wants some artist chap to paint me. Even for
Jim, this is all a bit contrary."

Clotilde reaches over to me and puts her hand to my arm. "If
your Jim is acting contrary, perhaps there are reasons for that."

"He doesn't need much to act strangely," I say, smiling.

"Well, Alessandro told me something, Nora, and I don't wish to alarm you by telling you, but perhaps I should?"

"What is it, Clotilde?" I look at her, worried a little.

"Alessandro says that Jim was acting fondly toward one of his students and he reprimanded him about it. In deference to you, my dear."

A shiver runs to my stomach. "Acting fondly? In what way? Who is this person?"

"Really, Nora, it's of no consequence—he assures Alessandro nothing occurred between him and the girl—but I mention it because you say Jim has been acting oddly."

"God almighty, do I not put up with enough?" I toss aside my sewing, go to the sideboard and pour a tot of wine for each of us. I sip mine, let its lemon-buttery taste coat my tongue before swallowing. I sit again and speak slowly, forming my thoughts as the words themselves form; I don't want my friend to think ill of Jim. "This is the way it is, Clotilde: Jim needs stimulation in order to write. I've had to learn this over the years. And if he gets it by ogling and fantasizing about some pampered young Triestina, well, so be it."

"You are sanguine, Nora."

I sigh. "I'm not, Clotilde. I'm just used to him." I tip my glass to hers and we both swallow back our wine. Used to him and tormented by him and in love with him, all three.

SIGNOR TULLIO SILVESTRI IS A SWARTHY, HANDSOME FELLOW. Jim has told me that the pair of them have great debates in the *bettola* about politics and art and the meaning of life, the kind of stuff that makes my mind warp. He tells me that Silvestri says war will soon hit Europe like a giant wave because Germany and Britain are gathering huge armies, but Jim doesn't believe him and nor do I. With me Silvestri is more restrained, evidently, for he barely speaks save to ask me to cock my head this way, or fold my hands that way. It's no pain to me to direct my gaze at him for he has something of the gypsy about him and a mischief in his eye that any woman would find pleasing.

Lucia has come to the studio with me for Jim was not entirely sure he wanted me alone for hours with his friend; the old dog of jealousy nips at his heels always, despite his own pair of wanty eyes that wander over every woman he sees and some more than others. Lucia is a mannerly little person, mostly, and she's more than happy to sit while Silvestri paints me. She's clearly half in love with the signor herself, especially when he produces a wrapped cherry sweet from his pocket for her. She accepts the gift in silence and sucks it while gazing solidly at the poor man.

"Lucia, why don't you go over there and play with your doll?"

"No, Mamma," she says, not even looking at me.

"Your daughter's presence does not bother me, Signora Joyce," the artist says, and I nod to indicate Lucia may stay where she is, staring in adoration while Silvestri daubs.

My mind scuttles over this and that thing as he works: Jim's fondness for his student who can only be that Popper girl, the one who blushes when she sees me on the street and scuttles by. She's a girl well insulated by money and her papà would never let any harm come to her. It's passed now, anyway, Jim's little fancy, I can retire any small worries I had. I think, too, on Frank Schaurek, the bank clerk who's paying court to Eileen—a Czech, no less—and wonder if he's a good match for her. He has a steady job at least. And I consider Lucia, for I ponder her always. I've often thought—and said to Jim—that the skittery-scattery look in Lucia's eyes bothers me. She stares into nothing so often and stays so still, as unmoving as a bottle on a grocer's shelf, truly, that it seems unnatural for a girl of six. When I was her age my desire couldn't keep up with my legs—I ran and jumped and played like a boy and no one could stop me, not even Granny. I had to learn how to go easy and sit like a girl was supposed to in those times. For sure girls need to behave now, too, but Lucia, unless she's lost in the dance steps she likes so much, or has one of her arm-flailing tantrums, barely moves. She sits and stares ahead of herself as if she's looking into the joys of heaven; her face takes on a holy air, but there are jumps inside her eyes, the kind a person gets at a good play or opera. And while her gaze flits, the rest of her is like a plaster *putto*, frozen in the act of looking.

"You were in Ireland last summer, Signora Joyce." I startle at Silvestri's voice. "Does it please you to go home?"

"Oh, it does and it doesn't. Ireland is such a rain-bothered place, Signor, there's no letup from it at all. I wondered last July how I went about my day as a girl, harried by constant wet. It's a raw mystery to me."

"But here we have such sun. And the bora, of course to make us all *pazzo*." He winds the side of his head with one finger and smiles.

"The heat of Trieste can be bothersome, but in Ireland the seasons roll back and forward and stop by on a whim. You never know if you'll be baked alive or drowned like a rat. At least here summer is summer and winter is winter and that's that. There's a comfort in the knowledge of it."

Silvestri smiles again and continues his dab-dab at the canvas.

"I am not Irish." Lucia rises from her chair.

I snort. "You are, you know. I'm Irish and so is Babbo, so that makes you pure Irish."

She begins to flap her arms and mutter, "Not Irish, not Irish."

"Stop it, Lucia. Keep your hands down, I've told you not to do that."

She stares past me. "Babbo says I'm European. Georgie, too. That is not Irish, that is European."

I glance at Silvestri; I'm perturbed that Lucia's raising a nuisance like this now.

"Don't contradict me, Lucy, I've said you're Irish and that's all there is."

"But you wish me to contradict Babbo?" Her face, bold and brassy, is lifted to me, and it's all I can do to stop myself from trouncing her in front of Silvestri. For a small child Lucia has the brazen will of a bull. She wraps her arms around herself and begins to slap her sides.

I'm both angry and embarrassed and I grit my teeth. "Stop that at once." Silvestri will think I cannot control my own children. "Lucia, behave yourself." I pull her hands away from her sides and hold them hard. "Lucia, you're being horrid."

Signor Silvestri puts down his paintbrush. "Shall we have some coffee, Signora Joyce? Perhaps some hot chocolate for Lucia?"

My daughter drags her arms back and starts to hit herself again and she hums now, a string of strange noises that grow louder and louder. My alarm rises; this is the worst behavior I've had from her outside the flat. Silvestri will think we're bad parents. I go to her and grab her shoulders.

"Lucia, stop that now. Lucia! Lucy, *basta!*"

But she will not stop and now her eyes roll about as if she's possessed. Oh God, have we made her this way? Have we caused Lucy's riotous behavior with our way of living, now here, now there? Jim always out by night, our rows by day?

"How can I help, Nora?" The artist comes to stand by me and he's fuddled now, a pained stripe across his forehead as he looks from Lucia to me. I am vexed by Lucia and don't know what to do to calm her.

"Go quickly and get her father."

TULLIO SILVESTRI DELIVERS THE PORTRAIT TO JIM IN THEIR FAvorite tavern and he rushes home with it. We're both pleased with how the painting has turned out, despite the bother with Lucia on the first day I sat for it.

"There now, he has captured your luminosity, Gooseen. Didn't he do a good job?"

"Mighty, Jim." I look at my image shyly.

"Silvestri thinks you the most beautiful woman who has ever lived, he said so."

"Would you go away out of that?"

I blush, but I'm more than pleased when Jim hangs my likeness with his family paintings for all to see. When Stannie and Eileen come in, they both compliment the picture.

"You look well in it, Nora," Stannie says, "very handsome," glancing at me with that shy, cocky look of his.

"You look a picture," Eileen says and chortles.

We open a bottle of the grassy white wine that Jim is so fond of and stand around like viewers in a gallery. I light a cigarette, let the smoke clutch my lungs before blowing it out, and try to look at my portrait as a stranger might. I hardly recognize the calm signora in the painting. I feel raggy and mad inside most days, with the care of the children and with Jim's antics, but in the picture I look serene.

"Silvestri has caught your good nature, Nora," Eileen says and squeezes my elbow.

"How much did it set you back, Jim?" Stannie asks, pricking the air with bother because he can't help himself around Jim.

"Five hundred crowns and worth every last one," he answers.

What he doesn't say is that we've no such sum available, and if we did, it would be eaten up by food and clothes and rent; poor Silvestri may wait a long time for his money. Jim slips in behind the piano and begins to play and we go through our favorite songs, all the old ones from Ireland and the new ones that Jim brings home from sailors he meets. It's a treat to listen to Eileen sing Puccini, especially "Mio Babbino Caro," the song to the dead father that makes me cry a little, as it always does. We drink more wine and Stannie makes hot chocolate for himself and we all take a chair and relax into the company. The boys talk about the unease in Bosnia and what it might mean for Austria and, especially, Trieste. I tell Eileen about the day we had to half drag a bucking Lucia home from Silvestri's studio and that all along the way people stood to watch the spectacle and how my face was like a radish from embarrassment. Eileen murmurs her sympathy then leans in and whispers to me.

"I want to tell you something, Nora, a little secret." She smiles.

"Oh, go on, tell me, Eileen." I bow my head to hers.

"Frank Schaurek and I mean to marry; that is, he asked me."

"Your lovely Czech bank clerk?" I squeak.

"Well, what other Frank do I know, Nora?" She giggles and holds her finger to her lips. "Not a word to Jim or Stannie yet. I'll tell them by and by."

I put my arm around her waist and half giggle, half squeal, making the boys look over, but Eileen and I put on our blankest faces and they turn away.

WAR

❧

Trieste
1914 AND 1915

I'VE NOT DARED BELIEVE THAT SUCH A THING COULD HAPPEN, but it has. Trieste is like a place sliced in two. Half are for poor, dead Duke Ferdinand; half are for the Irredentists. The piazzas are rotten with soldiers marching about and it makes the city feel dark and broody, two things it has never been. Cries of *"Avanti, Savoia!"* go up at night from bands of nationalists who roam about trying to stir up their own side and the other. Airplanes thunder over us and Georgie is terrified they will crash through our windows; guns smash the night in long lines of fire and, in truth, I'm afraid to go out half the time. Jim's only worry is that the postal service to London might be disrupted.

"How will my chapters of *Portrait of the Artist* get published in the *Egoist* if this bloody war goes on and on?"

"Some ego you have," I say and he snorts a laugh. "I don't know how you can find things funny, Jim, when all around us is gone mad."

Stannie, of course, is firmly on the side of the Irredentists; he agitates with them and goes on marches. "Trieste is an Italian city, not an Austrian one—it rightfully belongs to Italy," he says.

"Just as Dublin belongs to Ireland," Jim says, blowing smoke rings. "We all love our country when we know which country it is, isn't that right, Stannie?"

His brother scowls into his coffee cup and looks at me. "What to do, Nora?"

"What do you mean, Stannie?"

"Do you intend to go to Galway and keep your children safe?"

"Ireland is as churned up as here," I answer, "with gunrunning, and Home Rule up in a heap, and the unionists at the nationalists' throats, and the Lord knows what all. We're better off in Trieste, surely?" I swig from my tea and look to Jim who has absolutely no desire to return home.

"You need to make a plan, the pair of you, for Giorgio and Lucia's sake, if not your own."

I light a cigarette and drag deep on it. "Please, Stannie, don't be spinning out acres of talk at me, I don't know what to make of it all, truly."

Jim stays silent.

"STANNIE HAS BEEN TAKEN!"

Jim's eyes are wild as a goat's when he runs in, and I jump up, pushing Lucia off my lap the quicker to get to him. "What? What are you saying?"

"He's arrested, Nora." His eyes bulge. "Oh, that gob of his, he couldn't keep it shut."

"Jesus have mercy. Arrested?" I beat my fist to my chest; oh poor Stannie, oh what will happen to him? "Lord God, what now, Jim? Where will they put him?"

"I don't know, a prison, some sort of internment camp, that's where they lock up dissenters."

"For how long?" I can hardly take in the truth of it; they surely won't keep him for long.

"I really can't say, Nora." Jim's face has the collapsed look he gets when he's deeply troubled. I bless myself and go to him, wipe the January mizzle from his shoulders.

"This is terrible, Jim. I can't bear to think of Stannie in some jail; he won't get on well in some awful place, he's too particular." I get a vision of a dark, windlowless cell. "Who brought the news?"

"One of his nationalist comrades. A whole scatter of them were lifted last night. I have to find out where he's been put." Jim takes off his glasses and rubs at his eyelids. "How in blazes will I tell Pappie?" He slaps the table, making me jink sideways and sit hard onto the sofa. "Bastarding Stannie and his waggy mouth. Could he not keep his beliefs safely to himself, like a normal person? Did he have to shout them all over the streets?"

I grunt; it's not as if Jim ever forms an opinion that's not aired widely. I look at him, the large stare, the lines in his brow; he's gutted with worry, as am I. "Is there nothing we can do?" I say softly. "Could one of your highborn students help, that count fellow or the baron?" I know, even before he cuts me with a look, it's a foolish suggestion.

"This is war, Nora. It's each man on his own. Stannie did himself no favors and now look at him: he's an enemy alien! Jaysusing God, I should have stopped him, warned him better."

"You were never done cautioning him, love. Stannie's his own person, so he is."

Georgie comes and huddles beside me on the sofa. "Will they take Babbo, too, Mamma?"

I look to Jim and he shakes his head sharply. "No, my darling boy, we're safe. Your father knows how to keep his counsel when it matters."

Lucia sidles up, takes her papà's hand in hers, and jiggles it. "Babbo, Uncle Stannie will be safe too. He told me so in a dream."

"A dream? When?"

"Last night, in my bed," she says and blinks up at him.

Jim kneels down before her. "And what Lucy dreams is always right, we know this, yes? I will not worry for your uncle now. *Grazie, mia cara ragazza.*"

Jim looks up at me, a pinch of relief about his eyes, though his face is raggy with concern. I hold out my hand and he takes it; he rattles out a short laugh. "I suppose everyone in Trieste can speak English now, thanks to me. I'm surely not needed here anymore." He kisses my fingers. "*Mia cara*, my love," he whispers and I know that, despite all, he's afraid.

CLOTILDE COMES TO WALK WITH US UP TO CATTEDRALE DI SAN Giusto with Eileen and Frank. The cool April air pulls at our skin, but we move at a clip up the steep streets, Clotilde and I linking arms to keep warm. Eileen is magnificent in a feathered hat and a coat of cream over her gown.

"Pappie would be proud of her, marrying her bank man, and looking so fine," I say to my friend.

"He can be proud of all his family," she says, and I know she means poor Stannie, still locked up in the camp at Katzenau and missing this sweet day. I wonder what it's really like for him and if he's horribly lonely; I wonder how long they'll detain him.

"Everything is altered, Clotilde." We stop in the square outside the church and look down over Trieste.

"Yes, Nora, it's all changed, but isn't that just life? No sooner do we settle on one thing than it reshapes and we are not where we thought we would be."

"I don't mind ordinary changes: the children growing or Jim's work being different. But people being gone hollows me out. I miss Stannie. I worry about him." I glance at the bride and groom.

"Now Frank and Eileen are going to Prague the minute they marry and I'll miss her terrible too; she's a proper sister to me, no question. Our numbers are fading."

Clotilde frowns and steps away to call to little Daniele who is whooping and dashing about the piazza like a circus ringmaster with Giorgio. "Boys, boys, not so much shouting."

When she looks at me again, she can't hold my gaze. I move closer and dip my head to look into her face. "Clotilde, don't tell me you're leaving Trieste too?"

She sighs. "Alessandro says we will be safer in Florence."

My guts bind then unfix; I take a small gulp to stop me from crying, and Clotilde clasps me to her side and shakes her head. "The world fluctuates, Nora. We are only tiny puppets." She pushes at a tear that slides down her cheek.

"Mary and all the saints protect us, I can't believe you're off too." We hug each other fast and rock this way and that. We break apart and mop our eyes with our handkerchiefs. "Come, my dear one," I say, "let's enjoy today."

"Today is all we have, *mia cara amica*."

Jim is standing in the doorway of San Giusto able, for Eileen, to put aside his dislike of the church and be best man to his new brother. He has smoothed out lately, inside himself—the success with *Portrait* has boosted him and he's well into the writing of something new, telling us all it will be like no other book ever written. I'd well believe it for, when he reads passages to me, they sound like nothing but codology, strings of baby babble.

The early sun glints down on Jim in his borrowed morning suit that hangs off his chest like a sail but, still, he looks manly as he waits for us. Trieste changes by the minute and the war raging in the not-so-far-away seems to affect us more each day: there is less food, fewer men, hardly any English students.

"Come, Nora, you surely want to be at one family wedding at least," Jim calls, and I grimace though he thinks this is funny.

Clotilde and I walk across the square to join him and, for now, for Eileen's sake and Jim's, I bury my fears for what lies ahead of us all.

EXPATRIATION

❧

Zürich
1915

I COME TO ON THE TRAIN, CHILLY AS A CORPSE AND HUNGRY BE-sides. Lucia is butted up against her father and Georgie is tucked under my armpit; both are asleep. I stretch my toes and lean to look out the window: trees, trees, trees; rock, rock, rock.

Jim grunts. "We'll go through the Arlberg Tunnel soon, Nora."

I nod and look out again, my shoulders tangled like briars.

Trieste was evacuated; Jim's well-to-do students, the count and the baron, rallied around and helped with our visas so we could leave. Jim says they may have saved our lives. I still feel we're running from the shadows at our backs and won't rest quiet until we gain Switzerland. I think of Stannie, far away now in Katzenau and, if he gets out, with no family to come home to. I think of our flat on Via Bramante, still paid for while we're away, the clatter of chairs empty now, Jim's books rammed up against one another on the shelves, unread; my china cups gathering a fur of dust; the piano silent as a coffin. I see the ghosts of us there, watched over from the wall by the long-dead Joyces, by myself in Silvestri's portrait.

ZÜRICH, WHEN WE EMERGE FROM THE STATION, IS AS UNPOL-luted and immaculate as I remember it from eleven years ago.

"Even in June the air is a little brisk," I say.

"As fresh as a nun's drawers," Jim replies.

"And you could eat stew off the footpath," I answer, looking down.

The children drag their feet and complain of having to carry bags. They look around at the fancy-roofed buildings and down to the river where barges snail by, taking their leisure about their business.

"That's the Limmat," Jim says, and sniggers at his own joke.

"The river Limmat," I explain to the children. "And down that way is the Confiserie Sprüngli where they make macarons light as clouds and bright as rainbows."

Lucy tugs at my sleeve. "Can we go, Mamma?"

"We will, but not today."

She puts on her little pig face, a snouty sulk of an expression that always riles me, but now, I'm too tired to tell her to stop. Let her pout.

"Ah-ah, Lucia," Jim wags a finger and she restores her features at once, shocked that her beloved Babbo, so lenient always, has reprimanded her. Tiredness has us all crabby.

We make our way to the Gasthaus Hoffnung—the first place Jim and I ever lay together—and it's comfortingly unchanged. Unlike ourselves. I sigh to remember the raw, young Nora, a match surely for the unspoilt nature of Zürich itself. The Hoffnung even smells the same—a whiff of burning cheese and long-smoked cigars—and not a table or flower vase has been moved, it seems. We're remembered by Herr Döblin—Jim hails him as "my Dublin friend"—and made welcome. Georgie and Lucia run up the stairs before us, keen to see the place. Jim, ahead of me on the return, reaches back and grabs my hand.

"Do you remember, Nora?" he whispers.

"*Tu es touchée*," I murmur and he startles. "I have a brain, Jim," I say, "despite what you may think."

He groans a little. "If only we didn't have to share a room with the children tonight."

"I know," I say, reaching to run my hand round to the place where his cock nests, already growing to attention.

"I heard what you said," Georgie calls down from the landing. "If we were rich, Babbo, we could have two rooms but, alas, we're not."

"Cheeky pup," Jim says. He runs up and swings for Georgie, but it's a good-natured swipe and we all giggle, half crazed from the strain of hours of travel and leaving Trieste behind.

Our room holds two large beds; I close the shutters and Lucia and I pile onto one bed and the boys onto the other. We sleep and sleep until hunger bubbles rise up to our throats and wake us. We drowse into our standing, unable to put up with our gurgling bellies another minute.

"I WOULD TAKE THE AUSTRO-HUNGARIANS, THE WHOLE JIMBANG of them, plus the Italians, over Switzerland's boring bourgeoisie any day." Jim sips at a green-stemmed glass of Fendant de Savoie then holds it to the light. "At least the Swiss do good wine," he murmurs.

"We've only just arrived, Jim, don't be criticizing everything already. The children don't know Zürich at all, they might like its peace. Let them make up their own minds."

The children are watching him, their eyes sooty, their mouths— for once—quiet. We are huddled into the corner of a café and Georgie and Lucia are clearly concerned about the whats and whys of this new place. We order fondue and the children liven up, liking the play of dipping their tiny cuts of bread into the broiling cheese on long forks. Georgie loses a piece and Jim bellows, "If a man loses his bread in the pot, he buys the drinks. Come, Giorgio, loosen your purse strings, my boy!"

"Shush, Jim, you're shocking loud."

He looks wounded. "I'm only trying to cheer you all—you're a sorry band."

His voice is still too rowdy. I lean in and speak quietly, hoping he will match me. "None of which is helped by you lamenting Trieste and the rule of the Habsburgs. We're here now. We need to push our chests out and get on with it." I flick my hand at our children. "They didn't ask for the pain of learning a new language." I thump my chest. "I don't want it either. But here we are. Safe. We're not enemy aliens, under threat of being dragged from our beds to rot in some prison, like poor Stannie. So, Jim Joyce, you can retire your sentiment for the old life." I poke the table with my finger three times. "We. Are. *Here*."

He sips his wine and eyes me. "Isn't your mother the most wonderful woman who lives, my darlings? *Tua madre è meravigliosa, ragazzi!*" He leans over and taps my nose with his finger. "To my Gooseen." Jim raises his glass and tosses the Fendant down his throat.

THE CHILDREN ARE PUT BACK TWO YEARS IN SCHOOL AND THIS has Jim hopping. Georgie, at ten, is very aware of how this makes him look to the youngers and he's ripping about it, too. I don't mind at all; they struggle with the German—it's the Swiss brand of it, all shushy on the *s*'s, which reminds me of the Galway way of speaking. Anyway, the children will have to make do, they can't move ahead until they master Schweizerdeutsch, for who knows how long this war will rattle on for, or when we'll return to Trieste.

I miss our old life, of course, but I won't let Jim undo whatever good is to be found here by grumbling about it all the time.

"I miss the marine smell of the Adriatic," he said last night, the look of a condemned man on his face.

I pointed out the window at the Zürichsee. "Isn't there a lake as good as any sea out there?"

He shrugged and looked at me as if I were responsible for his melancholy, as if we aren't all overturned by being here, far from the only home we've known. He's a consequence of a chap and no mistake and I told him so.

I'm lighter today. I got a telegram and I'm walking to the bank—Uncle Michael Healy has sent us some money and I'll retrieve it there and it'll help with warm flannels for the children and, perhaps, a winter hat for myself, a nice furry *ushanka*, maybe, and a good, heavy overcoat. Jim bought a discarded coat for eleven francs from the landlady, but he complains that the man who owned it had unnaturally short arms. Also, with the money, I mean to make up a package for Stannie and send it to him at Katzenau: a tin of biscuits, some dried milk, cigars that he can use to trade with the other prisoners, a nice book, if I can persuade Jim to part with one he finished this week.

Zürich is altogether colder than Trieste. The snow never quite leaves the Uetliberg and her sister mountains that soar behind the city—Jim calls them "great lumps of sugar" and pretends he's not moved by the majesty of them. I look to their white caps now and imagine sitting atop the Uetliberg and racing down it on a toboggan. Wouldn't that be a wonder?

Yes, Uncle Michael's gift of money will get us straight: there are a couple of drafty rooms available in a rackety house on Reinhardstrasse that will do for now and we can pay something down and the money coming in from Jim's new students will soon have us able to settle, feel like we belong a little. Jim says Zürich is full of people like us; people like him, he really means—smart types who object to the war. Already he's found a drinking spot, the Pfauen, though he calls it the Pee-Cock and finds himself mightily funny each time he says it, repeating it in case I don't understand. There he has met artists and the like and, for all his complaining, has found a niche for himself, a thing I'm still a-struggle to do. It's harder for women, for sure. We have to rely on other wives or girlfriends who are in need of a pal.

I gain the bank at last; the man at the counter is very official, not a smile, barely a hello. He hands me the money in an envelope and, when I get outside, I pull out the notes, toss the envelope to the ground, and walk on, smiling at the money in my hand. The clack of boots at my shoulder startles me, though I'm aware that someone has been calling out. I turn to see a policeman, his face aglow with rage, holding out the envelope I threw away.

"*Der Mülleimer!*" he says, pointing madly to a nearby rubbish bin like a man with a demon in his arm. "*Der Mülleimer, ja?*"

I feel my face pink up and I take the envelope from his hand and make a great show of walking, straight-backed and slowly, to the bin. I eye him and drop the envelope inside. I cock my eyebrow to ask if he's happy.

He throws up his hands, mutters, "*Ausländer!*" and marches off.

Ausländer is one of the only German words I understand. I know that he was barking "Foreigners!" and I flush with outrage. I've lived in Europe for more than a decade, I feel like no foreigner at all. Is it my fault that the Swiss need every surface in their city free of even the tiniest speck of dust and litter? If you ask me, it's not natural to want to be so tidy.

I stuff my money into my bag and trot back toward the Hoff-nung, stopping only to buy a box of macarons for the children at Confiserie Sprüngli. I pull out a pistachio one and eat it as I walk, not caring who sees me or what crumbs sully the sacred Swiss streets.

PLATE

❧

Zürich
1916

S TANNIE WRITES AND SAYS HE DREAMS OF ME, BY THE SEA-
shore in Galway.

> *You were a glimmer beside me all day after I saw you*
> *by the Atlantic, Nora, and I sat on my bed and took out*
> *your photograph that you so kindly sent. The camp corporal*
> *happened to be passing by.*
> *"Joyce, is that your wife?" he said, peering at you.*
> *"Yes, that is Mrs. Joyce," I said, looking grave to*
> *show I missed the fictional Mrs. J, and important, because*
> *I had a woman who missed me. Many here suspect me of a*
> *wife, but I have been coy on the matter until now; evidently,*
> *Nora, I'm not as foolish as I look. Anyway, my dear wife,*
> *the camp corporal proclaimed you "damned pretty" so I*
> *hope that pleases you and that my economy with facts has*
> *not shocked you. You'll see of course that the presumption*
> *was all the corporal's so, in truth, I am blameless.*

Stannie dreams of me and I dream of Eileen. I miss her like
I've never missed anyone, truly. She was so woven into our daily

life, I never noticed her properly and I feel sad about that now. In my dream I was lying on a hill and all around me were silver cows, eating the grass. A cow with big, friendly, navy eyes came to me and spoke loving words, as if he loved me. Next thing there was water gushing down the hill on all sides and Eileen appeared, in her wedding costume, smiling and happy, and then the cow died of his love.

I tell Jim the dream at the breakfast table and he laughs. "Cows are female, Gooseen. Was it bulls you saw?"

"No, Jim, they were cows—they had womanly faces."

He snorts and reaches for pencil and paper. "Womanly faces," he says, making a note.

"Are you writing down what I'm saying?"

His eyes fly to mine. "Of course I am, Nora." He scribbles again. "No bull, no cock," he says, glancing at me, "no pregnancy."

"Are you trying to pull a meaning from my dream, Jim?"

"Well, I don't believe one jot in all that analysis nonsense, but don't you think it's significant, or at least interesting, that your cow-lover died? Like Michael Feeney and Sonny Bodkin of old?"

"Ah, Jim." I splutter a small laugh. "How can you compare this with them? I'm only interested that Eileen was in my dream. It was a grand thing to see her. I worry about her." He holds up his hand to me, intent now on scratching down his thoughts while they're still fresh in his head.

JIM'S FAVORITE PLACES ARE NICE LITTLE SPOTS, I HAVE TO SAY. HE likes the Restaurant zum Weisses Kreuz and the Pfauen and the Café Odeon, and he doesn't come home blathered to us as much as he did in Trieste. Sure, more often than not, I'm along with him. Things are freer here—the men regularly bring their women to the cafés—and, of course, we have that little bit more money from his publications in magazines and so forth. I throw a few francs into the Jacob's biscuit tin whenever I get a chance, so that I have a little pile of money myself. It doesn't amount to much, but I like to see it build up; there's novelty in having a few coins to call my own.

I've met an English lady, a Mrs. Sykes, who goes out with her husband all the time; they're both actors. They're part of the group that calls itself the Club des Étrangers at the Weisses Kreuz—all are blow-ins to Zürich, like ourselves. Mrs. Sykes and I have taken to sitting together when we see each other. It's nice to talk to someone in English, other than Jim. I'm very glad of her company for it has been lonely here and my nerves are at me from the strain of everything being so very different and the seeping walls in our rooms and the children's endless complaining and Jim's lying about the place, under my feet, scratching away into his scribbledehobble little notebooks.

Tonight we're going to the Weisses Kreuz and Mrs. Sykes will be there and she always has the best of costumes, so I put on my green evening dress and it's very smart and spruce with its white collar and black velvet neck tie. Lucia sits on our bed to watch me and she is tossing her head about to make it very clear to me that she's in a sulk.

"Speak, Lucia, you know I don't like histrionics."

She frowns. "We go to school all day, Mamma, and then we must stay in this cold hell all night while you drink *Pflümli* and *Kirsch* with Babbo and your friends, and we sit here like dodos."

"I like neither *Pflümli* nor *Kirsch*, Lucia. I might have some red wine to warm me, that's all."

Lucia slaps her hand on the bedspread. "I don't care what

you drink, Mamma! I care about being left here. Giorgio pinches me and punches me; he won't let me alone when you're not here to see."

"That's not true, *cara*. Georgie is the nicest of brothers."

"Take me out with you, Mamma. I should like to meet everyone. I'd be ever so quiet and still."

I tut, fix a comb into my hair, and check myself in the mirror. "Lucia, that's enough. Nine-year-old girls and eleven-year-old boys don't go about at night. Adults do." She crumples her face, trying to force tears but they won't come.

Jim comes in. "Lucia, pick a tie for me, I need to look as fine as your mamma or people will think I'm a tramp she found on Reinhardstrasse."

I grunt to acknowledge the truth of Jim's slovenliness but Lucia laughs, as he knew she would, and hops to the basket where he keeps his ties. She pulls out a red bow tie and swings it out for her father to see.

"By herrings, a pillar-box dicky. Excellent choice, daughter dear! A seasonal bauble for my collar."

Jim hands the bow to me, tosses his chin heavenward, and I tie it for him.

Lucy sidles up and puts her hand in his. "Can't I come with you tonight, Babbo? I'll bring a book and read quietly, you won't even know that I'm there."

"Tonight is for us to meet our friends, Lucia. All day Mamma stays at home and your papà teaches and writes while you go to school. We need to unbend a little. Another day we will go out *en famille*, eh?"

Lucy pulls her hand away, but doesn't pout as she does with me; she wanders the room, looking forlorn.

"I've left some *pasticcini* on the good plate for you and Georgie; it's in the press," I tell her. Lucia's face bursts into smiles, which she tries to smother—I mustn't think she's happy—but the thought of the sweet cakes is too much and she scampers off, shrieking for Georgie. "See that you share them evenly with your brother," I call.

We step out and the cold air makes me shiver and my teeth take up a clacking dance; the window above us swings open and Georgie and Lucy are there, staring down to make sure we feel bad for leaving them. I feel no guilt at all and neither, I'll wager, does Jim; it's he who insists that I go with him, and neither of us believe in mollycoddling children or bending to their will.

"Mamma, Giorgio took my lemon cake," Lucia calls.

"Well, then, you must be without it," I say.

Jim sniggers and this enrages the children. "You lock us up like pigs in a sty," Georgie roars, "while you go out and be merry. It's damned unfair!"

"Damned unfair!" Lucia echoes and slams the window shut.

We look at each other, shrug, and trot on; I slip my arm through Jim's and cuddle in closer to try to steal some of his warmth.

"This frigid, frozen Zürich. Have you ever felt such bitter cold in all of your days?" he says, shuddering inside his coat.

"Never. I'm perished."

Once inside the Weisses we forget about our angry children, our damp rooms, and the icy December air and begin to warm up in the gaslight glow of the café.

TODAY MRS. SYKES IS COMING TO TAKE TEA WITH ME AND I'M searching everywhere for my violet-sprigged plate, one of the only things I brought with me from Trieste. I mean to pile it with gingerbread and cherry tarts for us to share over good strong tea. The English like tea almost as much as the Irish. I rustle through the kitchen presses, swiping mouse pellets to the floor; the mice are as plentiful here as the hairs on my head and they're that noisy I almost don't hear them anymore. I end up removing every pot and pan from every press for the plate is not to be found, and I can't understand what's become of it. Jim's out meeting with people—he has a notion to set up a troupe and put on plays—and the children are at school, so I must hunt down the plate myself. It occurs to me that I haven't seen it since the night we went to the Weisses Kreuz last week, when I left *dolci* for Georgie and Lucy on it.

"That plate is not in this kitchen and that's for certain sure," I mutter, while rearranging the shelves with all I've removed.

I go to the scullery and rummage through the linens in case it got trapped under them, then take myself into the children's bedroom. Perhaps they ate their cakes in here and forgot to return the plate. I check the bedside tables, I lie down and look under the beds. Nothing. I rise, catching my hair on the bedclothes as I do, and slump down onto Lucia's bed, realizing I will have to abandon my search as Mrs. Sykes will soon be here. I stand and smooth down the counterpane and my hand meets with a hard lump near the footboard. I fold back the cover, the blankets, the sheet, and there—in five sorry pieces—is my violet-sprigged plate.

"Oh," I whimper. "Lucia, you bad, bold child." I gather up the bits of china, think of dear Stannie, and feel that my heart is now a small bit broken too.

I HEAR MRS. SYKES RAP AT THE DOOR AND OPEN IT. "COME IN, come in, Mrs. Sykes, don't mind the cut of me, I've been foothering around." I pat at my hair, which is skew-ways from my antics under the bed and all about the place.

"You look lovely. But won't you call me Daisy?"

I blush for, though she's in her early thirties like me, there's something of the wider world about Mrs. Sykes. She's someone who holds herself perfectly and only speaks when she has something important or funny to say, whereas I blab out anything that occurs to me whether it's wise or foolish. I would feel strange using her Christian name.

"Let me just call you Mrs. Sykes for now," I say.

"As you wish."

I give her the only comfortable seat and I think longingly of our lovely Danish chairs in Trieste, the whole army of them, and our nice Via Bramante flat, and I'm a little embarrassed now to have dragged this elegant woman to our rooms.

"We hope to move soon," I say, feeling a little stiff because the place neither feels like a home nor looks like one.

She glances around. "You've made it very pleasant, dear." I wet the tea and we chatter about this and that, and she tells me about a third-floor flat on Kreuzstrasse that may come free soon as people she knows are vacating it. "It's larger than here," she says. "Perhaps it may be more suitable?" She reaches for another cherry tart. "Really, I ought to watch my figure," she says, but eats it anyway.

"Oh, Jim wants me fat," I say, and Mrs. Sykes splutters a laugh that sends pastry crumbs all over the floor and onto her fine brown frock. I laugh, too, and the air between us gentles and I'm glad for I sorely miss natural company.

"Whyever does he want you fat?"

I make a womanly shape in the air. "He likes a bit of meat to clutch on to. He feeds me cocoa." We both giggle again.

She picks the crumbs from her lap and eats them. "So, Nora, what of these plays our husbands are conspiring to put on?"

"Well, it surprises me entirely that Jim wants any part of it. He's the laziest man in Europe, to be honest. He thinks there should be a bed in every room so that he can lie back and read or write. He only teaches students because we'd starve otherwise."

"Well, my Claud says your James is very keen to get this acting troupe off the ground."

"Well, for a man who finds it a chore to shave his face and put on a clean shirt, it's a good one right enough." I sip my tea. "But I suppose it's to do with literature and that's all that excites Jim anyhow. They'll need money to do it, I suppose. The one thing we lack."

"Well, if they manage to get the funds," Mrs. Sykes says, "I hope they mean to choose plays with women in them, Nora, and I hope that we shall both have large parts." She tips her cup to mine as if we're supping wine and I smile at the idea of me being on the stage and at Mrs. Sykes's bright energy that seems to light up the air around her.

THE CHILDREN EACH HAVE A PUSS ON THEM LIKE A WET DAY IN January. Both sit with chins tucked low and arms across their chests. Georgie looks as if he might cry—he hates when I'm out with him—but Lucia has stiffened her jaw to let me know she doesn't mean to bend under my questioning.

"Just you wait until your father gets in, he'll give you a clout each for being so stubborn to your mamma." They know that's not true and I know it also—Jim would never raise a hand to his children; after years of his father's rage, he hates violence. We all turn our heads at the sound of the door; Jim is back. "Now, here's Babbo, wait until we see what he has to say to you pair of scuts."

Jim comes toward us and sees the five shards that are now the violet-sprigged plate. "*Mio Dio*! What happened here?" He looks at me, then the children. "Giorgio? Lucia?"

Lucy leaps to her feet and points at her brother. "It was him! He grabbed the plate from me and broke it."

Georgie stays sitting and in a calm voice says, "You dropped it, Lucia, so I think you'll find that it was *you*, in fact, who smashed the plate."

"But you were pulling it from me! You're a greedy pig, Giorgio. You wanted my last bit of cake and you yanked the plate to get it, so Mamma's plate was in *your* hands when it fell and broke."

"It's not just that ye smashed it," I say, quietly, "it's that ye hid it and then lied about it for days and days. That's what has me angry. Georgie, you're nearly twelve, you should know better."

"But it was *her*, Mamma, not me."

Lucy gawps at her brother and screeches, "It was not!"

"*Basta!*" Jim calls. "Enough, enough." He holds up his hands. "The world is at war, my dears, let's not infect our own home with it." Jim bows to me. "Mamma, I will get you a new plate."

"It won't be the same," I mutter. "I loved that plate, it was special to me."

Jim nods. "Children of mine, apologize to your mother." They are silent. "Now! Say you're sorry this instant."

Jim's raised voice startles us all and the children murmur apologies. But they're not my concern now for I can see that something has Jim rattled. I dismiss Georgie and Lucy to their room, pull him to the stove, and bid him sit.

"What is it, love?"

He lights two cigarettes and hands me one. "My old friend Francis Sheehy-Skeffington has been executed in Dublin."

"For the love of God. Why?" I bless myself rapidly. "He wasn't a warring man, was he? What happened?"

"It's gone entirely to hell in Ireland, they're blowing each other up in Sackville Street. All in the name of nationalism." Jim snorts. "War-mad, blood-mad fools. What use did it ever do anyone to shoot another man?"

"I'm sorry about your friend, Jim. But wouldn't you like to see England's rule gone from Ireland after eight hundred years of it? Would that not be better for the country?"

"Oh yes, let them declare Ireland an independent state. Only so that I can declare myself its first enemy!" He stubs out his cigarette, takes off his glasses, and rubs at his eyes. "We're better off out of it all, Nora. Switzerland may be a bourgeois Hades, but at least we're not going to get a bullet in the arse if we need to buy a loaf of bread."

"Poor Skeffington. His poor wife. We've no idea, truly, what it's like at home now."

"Nor will we ever. Nora, if I once more in my life threaten to go back to that snot-green island, you have my full permission to cut off my legs below the knees."

"Ah, Jim. It's all torn asunder, everything is upside down and inside out and here's me worrying about my auld plate." I scoop up the pieces and toss them into the bin.

He takes my hand and kisses it. "We can only concern ourselves with what's in our orbit, my love. The wars will fester on. But you, my darling, will have a new plate and we, and the children, will learn to like Switzerland."

CONVALESCENCE

❧

Zürich and Locarno
1917

IF I CRANE MY NECK A CERTAIN WAY, I CAN SEE THE GLIMMER OF
the lake out before me. Sometimes I squinch up my eyes and
pretend that I'm looking over the Gulf of Trieste and that Miramare is just up the way, pale and perfect under the sun. We are five
now—Jim brought home a black cat last week, for luck, because it
was following him. Jim's friend in England, Miss Harriet Weaver,
sent advance royalties for *Portrait*, which she'll publish soon, and
that has helped us with rent and so forth. Thank goodness for
ladies of letters.

Mammy writes—her heart scalded—because Uncle Michael
has had to move to Dublin for work and she's missing him fiercely
and young Tom, too, who is soldiering in France; she's lonely with
just Delia and Kathleen for company. She sends Tom parcels the
way I do to Stannie; milk and butter she sends him, and tea, biscuits, and cocoa, and I want to tell her not to spend all her pennies
on Tom for who knows if the things even reach him in France.
"This war is terrible," she writes, and it surely is, and she asks
me to get the children to pray for their uncle Tom—he's only a
child himself, if you ask me—and how can I tell her that Georgie

and Lucia wouldn't know an Our Father or an Amen from a bull's foot? She says her neighbor's husband died on a battlefield and the woman has seven wee ones and not the price of a candle and they took up a collection for her and I will send her something myself for, God knows, these are crooked, strange times.

JIM'S RHEUMATISM HAS RETURNED AND HE BLAMES THE WESTerly wind and is all up in a heap with swellings and cramps and bad humor. Uncle Michael writes to tell him to carry a potato in each pocket to ward off the pain.

"Swiss spuds are probably too smug altogether to provide relief to the likes of me," Jim says, but carries them anyway.

His eyes have been bad since we moved here, too, always weeping and bulgy, and he's feeling mightily sorry for himself. Some days the eyelids are so gummy he can't go and meet a student, so he's under my feet and I must write all his letters and he shouts at me about full stops and commas and capital letters when I forget to add them.

Early in March Jim gets some astonishing news—a benefactor in England wishes to give him two hundred pounds, in four installments, so he has time to write; we are ecstatic for it means we can stop fretting about every penny.

"Who in blazes has such riches to give away?" he says to me, waving the letter from a London solicitor and grinning like a lunatic.

I take the page, excited to see it for myself. "Slack, Monro and Saw," I read out—the name of the firm. "Might the money be from Mr. Yeats? Or Mr. Pound, the American?"

"Maybe, maybe." He takes the letter back and squints at it. "Well, God bless whoever he is. Here's a man of pure vision and I don't intend to let him down."

I lean in. "Look, it says 'the arrangement will continue while the war lasts.'"

"By herrings, Nora, let them shoot the shite out of each other forever, in that case."

He giggles with pure joy and, for the first time in weeks, goes to the table, takes out his pages and pen, and works on *Ulysses*, the story he's trying to get in order as his next book. We go to the Kronenhalle to dine and Herr Zumsteg welcomes us heartily, saying he's honored to have Herr Joyce at his table.

IT'S FOUR WEEKS NOW SINCE JIM HAD A BAD EYE ATTACK. GLAU-coma, the doctor says, and complications of it and it will make him blind if he doesn't have an operation. Jim won't hear of surgery for the moment because he's afraid, he says, and because the eyes to be operated on are not some theoretical eyes, but his very eyes, and that's what makes the difference. We live in near darkness to ease his discomfort—all shutters closed, all curtains drawn against the dazzle. Jim wears shaded glasses and the children tease him, call him *il cieco* and *der Blinde* Blindman. He takes it in good part and I read to him by candlelight and write his letters and he lies on the bed or sits in a chair and, for Jim Joyce, he's extraordinarily quiet and still. The doctor says that perhaps the climate in Zürich is not helping Jim's illnesses or humor and we should consider spending some weeks in the Italian part of Switzerland. Locarno, he suggests. I like the sound of that very much.

MY HAIRBRUSH IN MY HAND LOOKS LIKE IT HOLDS THE INNARDS of a horsehair mattress and, every time I brush, more hair gets matted into the bristles. Even when I wash my hair—a seldom thing, for it's such a production—I notice that my hands come away from my head with not just lather, but clumps of strands. I bring the hairbrush to Jim this morning to show him; he lays down his book, pushes his dark glasses atop his head, and opens the shutter a crack to examine it.

"I'm going blind, Nora, and you're going bald. What a smashing, dashing pair we'll make in the lofty Kronenhalle."

I snatch back my brush. "Don't make a laugh of me, Jim. My nerves are gone over this."

"I try for levity, Gooseen, only because we seem to be in such a sorry state and if I think too much on it, I'll bawl like an infant."

I pull the nest of hair off the brush. "Mrs. Sykes gave me Danderine tonic to use but what if it makes it worse?"

"Try the tonic, my love, it might help. Daisy Sykes is an actress, used to wigs and so forth that damage the hair terribly. I have faith in her, you must too. Dose yourself up with Danderine." He smiles.

I nod and we both go to the sofa and sit side by side. "It's more than just my hair, though, Jim. It's your poor eyes, and Lucia misplacing everything from my best gloves to your letter to Miss Weaver, and Georgie being so brazen and cheeky these days, and it's the oddness of Zürich and, oh, just everything. Being here has us all at odds and I think it's coming out in bad streaks in Georgie and Lucy."

Jim folds his hands around one of my own. "I know, my love."

"My nerves are pulled as tight as violin strings with just getting from day to day. I can't send Lucia on even the simplest errand anymore because she keeps losing things and I'm starting to wonder if she's not giving things away or destroying them on purpose."

"Surely not?" Jim's face creases; he doesn't like to hear his Lucy criticized, but she has become so forgetful and vague in herself that I fear to let her out on the street some days.

"And as for Georgie, sulking around the place, all grunts, like a bear roused from hibernation."

Jim sighs. "He's becoming a man, I suppose, and growing out of himself. Or into himself, whichever."

"We're too contained here, Jim. Every time I move, I trip over one of Georgie's legs, or that mee-anging cat, or some pile of papers that Lucia is sorting through for her scrapbook. There isn't an inch of space where I can breathe." I put my head to his shoulder. "Might we, Jim, might we go to Locarno as the doctor suggested, just for a few weeks, to feel some warmer air?"

"Dear Nora, with my eyes a little better, I would prefer to stay here and write more of *Ulysses*. It calls to me every moment of the day and I can see it spooling out before me, all I need to do is catch the words and get them down. It's there, I can feel the story in me, alive and throbbing, I just need some peace in which to harness it."

I'm heartsore but I nod. I know how keen he is to get back to the novel and that when he's settled into it, he doesn't like to move. "All right, Jim, all right." The cat slinks in from the bedroom and jumps into my lap, I rub his stomach to feel the thrum of his purring. Jim scratches the cat's head and he leans back in ecstasy. "You're the happiest one among us, Pusheen," I say.

Jim straightens up. "Nora, take the children to Locarno. The money from the benefactor can be used for it. Isn't there more to come anyway?"

I clap my hands with joy and the cat leaps off me to the floor. "Really, Jim? Can we go?"

He turns, puts his palms to my cheeks, and kisses my nose. "Yes, my Gooseen. I *insist* that you go."

"But weren't we to go there for your eyes, Jim?" Even in my pleasure I know that the trip was truly meant for Jim not us.

"The best cure for me is writing, my love. Take the children south. Speak Italian. Soak up the sun."

I kiss him long and hard, thrilling to the thought of heat and leisure in Locarno.

WE'RE PUTTING UP AT THE PENSION DAHEIM. IT'S COSTLY—a week here pays two weeks' rent in Zürich—but it has the cushioned edges of its Italian owners, the place is filthy with light and warmth, and it's comfortable. We have a small balcony and there's a vegetable market this morning and I sit in a chair with the windows wide, listening to the sellers call out their wares—*"Fiori!* *Fagioli freschi! Melanzane fresche!"*—and I close my eyes, picture their flowers and beans and aubergines, and pretend that I'm home in Trieste. And I conjure Jim, too, at work on his book back in Seefeldstrasse, without us to bother him, and I hope he doesn't get up to any mischief with his friends in the Club des Étrangers, for they're all artists and actors and seem to view life as one unending party. Not that there's any terrible harm in that, it's just that Jim never wants to leave a party and he may end up sick again if he overdoes the drinking. But I know, too, that he wants to please Miss Harriet Weaver by completing more chapters of *Ulysses* because he knows she'll be a good help to him in finding a publisher. She's proving to be his most loyal friend and makes heroic efforts on his behalf and she has loose purse strings, too, which is a blessing to us. I hope she's not as handsome as she is kind for, if Jim ever meets Miss Weaver, he might well run off with her!

The children and I walk up the incline to Orselina to see the Madonna del Sasso church and I expect at every moment that they will complain, but they don't, so I can take my time up the steep steps and stay inside my own thoughts while I look around. The weather is cool for August and, among the trees that line the way, it's damply green and inviting. The church, when we gain it, is yellow and white like an iced cake, and I enjoy studying its painted innards, so like the churches in Trieste. The cloisters have a pleasant view over Lake Maggiore and the hills beyond and I stand with Lucy and Georgie, each tucked under one wing, just appreciating the beauty before us. I'm quiet inside and, though Jim is not with us, I feel calm and content.

"Shall we lunch up here in Orselina, Mamma?" Georgie asks, always thinking of his stomach.

"We've paid for lunch at the pension, my pet, we'll go back there."

"I'd rather eat here," Lucia says.

Immediately Georgie leans across and pinches her. "Mamma says not."

"But I want to!" she shouts, rubbing her arm.

"Babbo has paid a lot of money for us to stay at the Daheim and we must eat there for that is part of the payment," Georgie says; he can never resist bossing his sister about. He's loud and people have begun to glance at us. "Do you think money can be picked from trees, Lucia, like leaves?"

"Now, now, Georgie, let's just go," I say, steering them away.

"But she's so bold, Mamma. She acts up horribly when she doesn't get her way."

Lucy wails like a banshee at this insult and the more I try to comfort her with hugs and soft noises, the more agitated she becomes, throwing her head back and squeezing the tears from her eyes in a most dramatic display. I drag her from Madonna del Sasso eventually, sit on a bench, scoop her onto my lap, and hold her tight until her tears and hiccups subside. We're a muted party descending to Locarno. It seems to me that Lucia deliberately disrupts all happy moments with her loutish behavior and that only Jim can keep her in check. I shall write to him about it after lunch.

But after lunch, in the pension, there is dancing and I forget, for a while, about Lucy's outburst.

PENSION DAHEIM, LOCARNO
6 August 1917

Dear Cuckold,

Yes, I will call you that, Jim, for today I was swept into another man's arms and transported. He's a handsome Parisian but he speaks very good Italian and it was my pleasure to hear his soft words about my ears. Before you jump on a train to Locarno, let me tell you that the only place he transported me was around the floor of the Daheim's dining room. All the tables and chairs were pushed back after lunch and we had dancing, with Georgie and Lucia in charge of the gramophone and choosing the music.

"What a pity one can't dance well to Wagner," I said to my Parisian partner and his smile dropped like an icicle under the sun and he didn't dance with me after that. So there's someone who agrees with you, Jim, about the German maestro, clearly he's widely misunderstood. (Though you say Wagner stinks of sex, as if that'd be something to put you off!!) Or maybe my Parisian thought I was German? Whatever, he disappeared and then Georgie got in a great bake with Lucy because she was winding the gramophone too often and he wasn't getting as many turns as he liked and in the end I had to march the pair of them upstairs. Your children are blackguards, Mr. Joyce, with not an ounce of manners between them. Well, I was tired after

our walk up to the Church of the Madonna and all that
dancing anyway, so we passed the afternoon on our beds.

When the children were asleep, I read a little of that
naughty book by Sacher-Masoch that you sent me. Am I
your Venus in furs, Jim? I think you want me to be. And
you know that I can be as seductive as that Wanda if I'm
treated well. Do you wish me to make you my slave, as
she does to her man? And how is your own naughty book
coming along, for I've no doubt that it's as untoward as
Portrait *and probably steamier knowing you. I'm sure*
that the writing eats you up and I hope that means you're
getting plenty of it done.

My hair is still coming out in handfuls but, other than
that, and the children behaving like harridans, I'm enjoying
my time here.

Best love from children,
Nora

I get back from a walk by the Maggiore, my hair full of watery wind and my eyes full of sleep; I'm hoping for a rest while the children are out entertaining themselves, but the signora is running at me, waving a telegram, and I know at once that there's bad news from Zürich. I snatch it from her hand and rip it open right there in the vestibule. It's from Mrs. Sykes. Jim has had another attack of the eyes and will be operated on today.

"The children!" I say, made frantic now by their absence because it means delay.

"Where are they, Signora Joyce?"

"I don't know," I wail, "they could be on a boat in the middle of the lake. Their father is not well, we have to get back to Zürich."

The woman sends one son to look for Georgie and Lucy, and

the other to buy our train tickets, while she helps me pack up our room. My heart fizzes in my chest for I know how much Jim fears the knife and what will we do if he goes blind?

"Is your husband seriously ill, Signora? I will pray for him."

"It's his eyes, he gets the glaucoma. He's had a terrible attack, he's having surgery today." I flop onto the bed and weep. "Oh, why am I not with him?"

The signora sits by me and puts her arm gently around my shoulder. "*Starà bene*. He will be fine." We hear a clatter in the stairwell and the children burst through the door. "*Bambini, bambini*, your papà's eyes have weakened. You must return to Zürich and you must be kind to your mamma on the journey and behave impeccably. Understand?"

The children nod solemnly and their serious little faces make my tears fall harder.

"LISTEN PROPERLY, NORA," JIM SAYS, "IT'S 'MRKGRNAO.'" He sits up in our bed, his eyes bandaged and his head tilted, a bona fide invalid, listening to the cat who obliges again with her odd little whine.

"I hear 'mee-ang,' Jim, not whatever it is you're saying."

"*Mrkgrnao*," Jim mewls, sounding remarkably like the cat, I have to own, and pawing at me like the animal himself does.

"Get away out of that," I say. "And you, too, Pusheen." I nudge the cat with my foot. "I don't like you petting him, Jim. What if his fur got under your fingernails and then got into your eyes?"

"I'm wrapped like a dead Egyptian, Nora, there's no danger of that."

I sit by him and hold his hand. For three days after we got back, I wasn't allowed to see him save through a hospital door; Jim had a nervous collapse and I almost had one myself from anxiety.

Professor Sidler told me the operation had been difficult and he forbade me to go in, in case it should excite Jim. I wasn't even allowed to call my love through the open doorway, but the professor assured me that he had told Jim I was there. I trust him, because he's a medical man with years of schooling, but I'm afraid of him, too, for he has power and abilities that I'll never understand. All I know is that in his hands lies Jim's fate as a seeing person and—more important to Jim—as a writer.

PLAY

❧

Zürich
1918

FEBRUARY IS UPON US AND JIM'S ALL SWEETNESS FOR HE ENjoyed his birthday and *Ulysses* is to be serialized in America, mad, bad language and all. Today he's gone off in a black suit borrowed from Claud Sykes. He got a letter from the Eidgenössische Bank of Zürich asking him to come and we're at a loss to know what it's about. I sit twisting my fingers in the flat and finally I hear Jim come in. I drop my risotto spoon and wipe my hands on my apron. He saunters in, his face as blank as a sheep's.

"Well?" I ask.

"Well, what?" says he, fingering a letter he has produced from his pocket. "Oh, is it this, Nora? Are you interested in knowing what's inside it?"

"Come on, Jim," I say. "My nosy bone is about to break." Jim laughs and I go to him and he hands me the letter; I read it aloud: "'A client of the bank who takes an interest in your work wishes to give you a type of "fellowship." We have 12,000 francs deposited to your credit.'" I squeal. "'You will receive 1000 francs per month from the 1st March.'" I look up at Jim whose eyes are twinkling like a girl's. "Mother of God, Jim. We're made."

"And high time, too," he says, grabbing my waist to waltz me around the kitchen. "We will strut like peacocks—and peahens, indeed—in the Pee-Cock Café and no one can stop us!"

JIM SUMMONS CLAUD AND DAISY SYKES TO THE PFAUEN, EVEN inviting Georgie and Lucy along with us, and we form a merry crowd. He orders white wine, the lovely chewy bread the children like so well, a variety of meats, and hunks of pockled Emmental.

"We had nothing as children," Jim says. I'm surprised to hear him admit it. "But my parents' motto was 'Share the wealth' so that's what our people always did. They divided everything up with their friends, with their family, with their neighbors." He tips his glass of Fendant to all our glasses. "By the holy farmer, my friends, we will put some of this blessed money to good use." Jim holds up his wine to the light and grins. "What does this remind you of, Sykes?"

Claud giggles. "Piss."

"*Genau, genau.* But it's the bright, sweet shade of an archduchess's piss, don't you agree?"

"Jim, the children are here. That's enough." I tap his arm lightly.

"Oh, saving your presence, ladies." He nods to Mrs. Sykes, to Lucia, and to me in turn. "But you see, my friend Sykes agrees with me."

Georgie snorts and Mr. Sykes laughs and raises his wineglass. "Henceforth, this Fendant de Sion, from the impeccable region of the Valais, will be known only as the Archduchess." They tip glasses again and each drains their wine in a single gulp.

Jim sighs. "May our dear Archduchess piss long and often."

"Jim, the children. *Please.*"

"We know very well what piss is, Mamma," Lucia says in a

flat, serious tone, making Mrs. Sykes bursts into giggles, and her laugh is so catching, we all end up in flitters.

JIM AND CLAUD SYKES HAVE THE MONEY NOW TO FORM A TROUPE and they style themselves the English Players and they go at it with great enthusiasm. They agree the first play will be by Oscar Wilde. Jim rather grandly says that "an Irish safety pin is more important than an English epic," never mind that Claud himself is English, but he's an easy chap and takes no offense. *The Importance of Being Earnest* is their first production and, with approval from the consul—though grumpily given—the Players are off. Jim being Jim the enterprise cannot be without strife and the man chosen to play Algernon, Henry Carr, proves to be a hothead. Two hotheads mean one cold row, and that's exactly what happens. Carr wants more pay, Jim says he agreed ten francs and that's that. Carr says he bought a suit to wear onstage. Jim says, "What of it?" Carr calls him cad and swindler. Oh, and I've to listen to all this at home afterward and what a buggering eejit Carr is, and Jim knows who the swindler is all right, and if high and mighty Carr wants a suit he'll give him a suit in court and how will *that* suit him?

"Jim, Jim, don't get so caught up in all of this that you forget about *Ulysses*," I say. "I want butter on my bread when the fellowship money has been eaten up by theatrics and lawmen."

He glares at me. "No man will stand between me and my work."

I don't remind him that it's been weeks since he sat scratching letters on pages.

JIM HAS A FRESH DISTRACTION BECAUSE HE'S A FINE MAN FOR novelty. An English painter called Frank Budgen and a Swissman called Paul Suter are his new, firm friends. I hardly see Mrs. Sykes and her husband now because Jim and this other pair are constantly going around together and, I fear, he's getting into his old ways with them. He can disappear in the afternoon and not return until the wee hours, leaving me with the full care of the children who are so often sulky and scrappy with each other.

He's gone today and I go to his desk to see if he's written much on the novel lately, but it's hard to tell for his pages are tossed and his notebooks leave me no clues. I sit on his chair and run my fingers over a bronzed statue of a woman with a cat; I glance up at the picture of kindly Ettore Schmitz that looks down on me and wonder how he and Livia and all their family fare during this long war. I lean in to study the drawing of Penelope that Jim keeps, as a talisman, pinned to the wall. Faithful Penelope who waits at home for her gadabout man. Jim Joyce most likely thinks more of her than he does of me. I pull out the tack that holds Penelope in Jim's sightline and repin her, face to the wall.

JIM BRINGS HIS NEW FRIENDS TO OUR FLAT AND I'VE HAD TO serve them coffee and fancies as if they weren't the ones helping him to spend all our money.

"Have you ever seen your husband's spider dance, Mrs. Joyce?" Frank Budgen asks me, as if this is some great trick like a dog that can walk a mile backward.

"I have, Mr. Budgen. It comes on him when he's too much drink taken, as you well know, for my husband gets drunk in the legs." I glare at Jim. "If certain people didn't lead him astray, he'd be home here with his family, where he belongs, and not gallivanting around Zürich like a man with no responsibilities."

Budgen bows. "I beg your pardon, Mrs. Joyce, I only meant it for fun."

I feel a little guilty for being sharp with him for he's a decent fellow. And Herr Suter is, too, but all I see are our francs dwindling when Jim's about the town with this pair.

Frank Budgen is a striking man, I must say; he's stocky, like Stannie, and has a strong, bearded jaw and a good thatch of hair that he keeps neat. Jim took me to see the nude statue of him on the Uraniabrücke, made by Suter's brother who is a sculptor.

"How do you like that, Nora?" Jim asked, as I gazed up. "Budgen comes here daily to remind himself what a handsome fellow he is."

"He's certainly well made."

"Oh indeed, in every way." Jim looked at me slyly. "He's altogether better put together then this scrawny fellow you're with." He plucked at his waistcoat, then linked his arm in mine. "Wouldn't you love to feel the brawn of a man like Budgen on top of you, Nora?"

I whipped my head around. "What kind of talk is that, Jim?"

He whispered in my ear. "You know, you could have a little dalliance with him and tell me about it afterward. It might help me to move *Ulysses* along. I need fresh things to write about."

My stomach lurched and dropped. If we weren't standing in broad daylight, by the river Limmat, I'd have pucked the head off him. As it was I hissed back, "How can you ask me to do such things, Jim?" I felt sick with anger and embarrassment. "You're a low pig and you should be thoroughly ashamed of yourself."

"But you told me about the priesteen, Nora. And the dead Galway boys."

Tears hurried to my eyes. "How is that even nearly the same? It's entirely different! Those were things that happened to me, I didn't go after them. I wasn't handed them and told to react. Oh, you disgust me!" I dashed away home, my ears burning with the upset of what he'd suggested.

I look at Frank Budgen now and heat to my scalp. Why can't the two of us alone be enough for Jim? Why does he have to gawk at other women and lust after them? Why must he suggest to me that I might lie with someone else, when I've no desire to do any such thing? The Lord knows, anyway, even if I did the low thing he'd asked, I'd be blamed for it forever. He thinks he needs this kind of nonsense to write but I know he doesn't. Jim Joyce is my love, but he's also a bother to my heart and a sore conundrum to my mind. I don't think the day will come when he'll grow to be the man he should be.

He's talking now about Irish wit and humor in novels and Budgen and Suter are nodding along as if they know what he means.

"What's all this about Irish wit?" I ask. "Show me a book in this flat that has it and that's one I'll read for sure, Jim."

His look to me is shocked. I suppose he thinks *Ulysses* is some great fountain of larking that spouts out of him, when all I find in it is harshness and palaver.

"My wife is out of humor, gentlemen. Nora, perhaps you should leave us men alone to talk and find one of your *Perl-Romane* magazines to read. That might lighten you." He glares at me as if instructing me to leave, but I'll do no such thing.

"I suppose you know my husband is writing a book?" I say to the men. They both nod.

"Yes, he talks of it often," Herr Suter says.

"Bores you with it, more like."

"No, no, we love to hear how he unknots the plot and the characters," Budgen says. "The other arts are always fascinating to me."

"You seem well-read, Budgen," Jim says, lighting a cigarette. "Who is the completest of characters ever written?"

Budgen sips his coffee and frowns. "Why, our Lord Jesus Christ, I suppose."

Jim snorts. "Nonsense! Christ was a bachelor, he never shared a bed and a home with a woman. That's what a man needs in order to live and be whole, difficult and all as it is." He glances at me.

"Well," Suter says, "Faust, perhaps?"

"Not at all, no, no. Faust is no man."

"Hamlet?" Budgen asks.

"Never! He's a son only." Jim is beaming now, happy, as always, that he's steering the conversation, talking of what lights him up.

"Your complete man in literature is Odysseus, I suppose. Your Ulysses."

"But of course, Budgen." Jim gentle-thumps his friend on the shoulder. "Ulysses is son to Laertes, father to Telemachus, husband to Penelope, lover to Calypso, fellow warrior at Troy and King of all Ithaca. Don't you see? He is man not god: a gentleman, an inventor, a complete fellow, for sure."

"It depends what you mean by 'complete.' When a sculptor forms the body of a man, he is rounded, three-dimensional, but not necessarily complete or ideal. All humans are imperfect and limited."

"But I see Ulysses from all sides, so he *is* all-round, like your sculpture—and we all now visualize the demigod on the Urani-abrücke, you know." Budgen smiles. "Ulysses is a complete man and a good man. And my Herr Bloom is decent, too; when he does something ignoble, he admits it, he'll say, 'I've been a perfect pig.'" Jim looks straight at me; is he trying to soften me, offer an apology?

"Do you know, gentlemen," I say, "Jim reads me bits of *Ulysses* on occasion and, let me tell you, what you'd hear in it is no better than what you'd hear in a swine pen." I get up. "More coffee, Mr. Budgen? Mr. Suter? Jim?" I go toward the kitchen without waiting for any of them to answer. At the door I linger to listen and they laugh quietly, like conspirators. Jim speaks.

"Do you see, my friends, what I've been telling you all along? My wife is entirely un-influence-able; she is resolutely her own woman with all her own ideas and ways. She takes absolutely no instruction from her lord and master."

Lord and master, indeed, Jim Joyce! I think we know who's master around here.

CHANGES

~~✦~~

Zürich
1918 AND 1919

THE WAR IS OVER! THE FIRST I KNOW OF IT IS THE SOUND OF church bells ringing and I put down my little butter churn and go out onto the street to see what's going on. Jim follows me—it's near impossible to drag him away from his pages these days—and he accosts a passerby who tells us that Germany has surrendered.

"The guns are down, no more blood will bleed."

"Oh, Jim, Stannie will be released! Young Tom will be able to go home to Mammy." I bless myself over and over. "Thank God in heaven for his mercy."

We hold each other close on the street then go back indoors, out of the November damp and cold. Jim pours some wine, though it's early in the day, and we raise our glasses.

"To peace everlasting," Jim says.

"This means we can go home now too, doesn't it? Back to Trieste where we belong."

"Let us see how things stand with Stannie, first, Nora. And Eileen and her family. Then we can begin to make plans."

I put down my glass, the relief and gaiety of the good news draining from me. "You do mean for us to go back, don't you, Jim?"

He squints at me. "I have important work in hand, Nora. I don't relish the disruption of a move right now."

My heart fizzles then tightens; I was full sure Jim would want to run away from Zürich and back to Trieste, as eagerly as I do, and I'm disappointed to learn that he doesn't.

THE FELLOWSHIP FROM THE EIDGENÖSSISCHE BANK DRIES UP overnight and, having found out who'd been gifting it, Jim asked for a meeting with the woman. She is Mrs. Edith Rockefeller McCormick, a wealthy American lady who likes to help artists.

I greet Jim at the door where I've been waiting for him to return. "Well, what did she say?"

Jim sighs and rubs at his eyes. "The bold Edith said that now that the war is over, I will be able to teach again and so she feels no need to support me." He grimaces and I divine that there's more to the story.

I peer at him. "Was that it?"

"No."

"What else?"

"She was also upset because I refused to be analyzed by her dear friend Herr Jung."

I squint at him. "Were you polite to the lady, Jim?"

"Of course, Gooseen."

"Might you not have gone along with her? Spoken to Jung? It might've softened her."

Georgie and Lucia have come to listen, too, for they know their comfort depends on that money, and they stand gawking like two nosy statues. Jim steers me into our bedroom and closes the door. We sit on the bed.

"Someone told Mrs. McCormick—a friend of mine,

apparently—that I am fond of the drink. That alarmed her, being a sober, upright Yank."

"I see."

"She wants to make a project of me, Nora. Cash in my bank in exchange for scrutiny of my mind, or some such." He shakes his head. "She was intractable, truly."

"And you refused. So that's it, then?"

"It would appear so, Gooseen."

"Who told her, do you think, about your drinking?"

He looks at me and there is sorrow in his eyes. "I'm at a loss."

RE-ENTRY

∿

Trieste
1919

WE'RE HOME IN TRIESTE—JIM AGREED IT WAS BEST ONCE the fellowship was gone—and though I longed to be here, I feel as alien as I did in Switzerland at first. It's as if the war peeled off the old times and ways of the city like dead skin and tossed them to the waves of the Adriatic. Oh, it still has its peculiar clamor with gulls and motorcars, and the air smells the same; the light is golden and the sea remains that beautiful steely blue, but the people seem different, drunk almost on their ownership of the city and they don't wear it well. In my deepest insides I thought an Italian Trieste would be the best thing in the world, but I see now that with the Habsburgs' days ended, the place has banjaxed itself and let the worst of its traits come to the top: the dirt, the unruliness, the indolence. Even the port, which once bustled with ships and boats from all over, is quiet as a boneyard. And our Via Bramante flat is gone—Jim neglected to pay the rent after Mrs. McCormick's money ran out and Stannie cleared our furniture for us—always to the rescue! But Stannie is no doubt heartsore from mopping up Jim's mess. He says the dust was ankle deep in the rooms and it's not hard to imagine when the place lay untouched for years.

So here we are, "in another momentous October," as Jim said, surrounded once more by Eileen and Frank, now with their two delightful daughters, Bozena and Eleanora, and Stannie, too, back from the internment camp and looking as fine as fish, and we're all holed up in Via Sanità, on top of one another in a way that's not welcome to any of us. How have we changed so much during our years apart?

Jim is most unhappy; he finds Trieste provincial now, after Zürich, and keeps repeating, "It's dead on its feet, just another ailing Italian town."

Stannie met us at the station when we got back and his face took on a shocked aspect on seeing Lucia and Georgie.

"Look at you both," he said, his face agog, "tall as church spires."

Lucy was shy with her uncle—she is contained at the best of times around strangers—but Georgie has clear and sharp memories of Stannie and the two hugged warmly. Lucia offered a sullen handshake and Stannie did not press her for more, being the kind, sensible fellow he is.

Jim stood back, watching, as is his way. Stannie came along to where I stood and embraced me, the warm block of him feeling good to me; he stepped back and grabbed both my hands.

"You've become a lady, Nora. You're looking very handsome indeed."

"I thank you, Stannie. You're looking remarkably well yourself."

Jim's eyes ticked between us like a metronome. He came forward and stood in beside me, causing Stannie to step back. "Of course she has the look of a lady, isn't she a gentleman's wife?" he said.

Stannie half smiled and kept his counsel and he was probably wise for I didn't want fisticuffs right there on the platform. Jim is not a subtle man, but it surprised even me that he'd flaunt our relative good fortune when his brother has been interred for years with who knows what hardships, for his letters didn't detail the strain of it all. I linked Stannie's arm for the walk back to Via Sanità but, even in those first few moments under the Triestine sky, I could feel that everything had shifted and we'd neither live nor love here as we once had.

JIM STAYS MOSTLY SILENT SINCE WE GOT BACK. HE SPRAWLS HIM-self across two beds by day, writing his chapters. The rest of us are like skittles bashing into one another, and we're all frayed and fighty. Stannie is broody. His silence is not like Jim's, though, for his mind seems to be casting back and he looks faraway and angry most of the time. He and Jim snipe at each other constantly, over the most trivial things.

Jim eyes Stannie, who is splayed out on one of our Danish chairs. "You look extraordinarily at ease on *my* furniture," he says.

Stannie keeps his voice low. "I've just emerged from four years of hunger and squalor and all you care about is my arse on your precious chair."

"Jim, Jim," I say, "remind yourself that they're the same chairs the landlord threatened to burn and that Stannie saved for us. You should be thanking your brother, not squabbling with him."

Stannie leaps up and both Jim and I flinch, but he goes to his room and slams the door.

"What gets into you, Jim? Why can't you just leave your brother alone?"

He shrugs and goes back to his newspaper.

We don't eat with Eileen and Frank, or Stannie. There are too many of us, so we conduct separate lives here, as much as that's possible. Jim grumbles constantly, annoying everyone. Even the Triestine weather, so fondly lamented by Jim in Zürich, is now all wrong. He wants to go back in time but, of course, we can't.

For myself, I miss the friends we had in Switzerland: Frank Budgen and the Sykeses and so on. I miss Mr. Budgen despite the vile portrait he managed of me. I thought, of all people, he would've captured me well, but I look snobby in the picture and old and dead around the eyes. It's not a good likeness at all; Silvestri's portrait is much better. Still, Budgen was a worldly man and easy to converse with and I feel the lack of him and the others powerfully, as does Jim. It's hard to get over the loss of good company. And, though I love Eileen's girls, I'd forgotten how entirely *present* babies are, how they suck on the hours until the day evaporates. Eileen is always running after two-year-old Bozena, little Eleanora on her hip, with a rag in her hand or a biscuit, or she's walking them out or putting them down to sleep, and my whole being is fagged from just watching her tend to them. And, oh, the noise of those girls! Did Georgie and Lucy ever create such a high racket? It's like living with a herd of blaring cows. And with our children bedding down in the living area of the flat, though they're big and long, and with the wojus heat that gathers in the rooms, it's all a bit too much. So, in our sweltering bed, when Jim begins to talk of leaving Trieste, I give him my ear.

"The American, Ezra Pound, has written to me again," he says, taking a letter from the nightstand.

"And what news does he have?"

"He says I need to go to Paris. He wants to show me around to the literary set there. All the writers are in Paris, Pound says and, therefore, I should be too."

Paris, finally! But we're so recently returned to Trieste, I wonder whether I really and truly want to move again. I think of the children a moment, so content to be back in the Italian world. "We'll get our own flat here soon, though, Jim. Mightn't it be better for Georgie and Lucia to stay put?"

"Nora, the children are adaptable, this we know." He shrugs. "And there are publishers in Paris, men of influence. If those philistines in America keep burning copies of the *Little Review* because they can't cope with an onanist, *Ulysses* will never appear in one volume. Mr. Pound insists that there are good people in Paris, ones who may help."

"Can't you just write to these people? I'm just not sure I want to upend us all again."

Jim kicks off the sheet that has wrapped itself around his feet. "At one stage, Nora, all you could think of was Paris. Don't you remember you started to learn French?"

"Of course I remember. *Aimez-vous les fruits?* is all I learned and all I can say still."

"*Aimez-vous les fruits?*" Jim grabs at my bubbies. "*Oui, j'aime les fruits, surtout les petites prunes.*"

I laugh while he pretends to devour me, then I kiss his crown and push him off. "It's too hot for any auld shenanigans." But I swiftly gather him back into my arms; maybe a move to Paris is just what we need. We're so cramped here and Trieste is not the way it used to be, maybe France would cheer us. "Would we be staying in Paris for good, love? It's not that I don't like the idea, but would it be fair to uproot the children so soon?"

He plays with my hair, pushing it gently back off my face. "Why don't we go for a few months, Gooseen? I'll finish the Circe episode of the book there. In fact, let's just have a fortnight in Paris and then I'll finish the book in England or somewhere. Wales, maybe."

"Or Ireland?"

"Why not? You and the children can take a long holiday and I'll write."

He smiles and I wonder if he's codding me, softening me with talk of holidays, just so I'll go along with him. I lie back and imagine myself back on our island home, the Atlantic on one side and the Irish Sea on the other, and I drift off to sleep washed in the green and blue cool of Galway.

EXEUNT

꧁

Paris
JULY 1920

PARIS IS ONE OF THOSE CITIES THAT SEEMS LIKE IT'S ALWAYS
existed. The ground of it is firm underfoot, it's a place content
in itself, sure-hearted. The people and the town are wound together and each enhances the charms of the other; both are at once
heavy and light, which is a rare trick to pull off. I feel sure that
Paris is where we were always meant to be and yet, also, I seem
to float above it, as if I'll never quite manage to worm down into
the earth here and be firmly attached. The last time I was here I
was but a girl, truly; I had no idea what life was about, or love. No
clue of the troubles and tongue-holdings of a marriage, the heavy
weight of the love for your own child.

I want a home now. Yes, I love the novelty of the wander
about, the giddy feeling of everything being new and fresh. But,
also, I'm dog-tired of existing as a temporary guest, of not owning
the bones of anything except the ones that live inside me. My very
guts yearn for a resting place, a spot that I can relax into and where
I can call down a real calm onto myself. I'm beginning to wonder
if mine isn't a blighted wifehood. Is Jim's need to roam and, now,
to be where the literary men are, an enormously selfish thing? Do

the children suffer because of their father's obsessions and, also, because I blithely go along with whatever he suggests?

Mr. Pound has found us a place—a servants' flat—in Passy. Our *rue*, rue de l'Assomption, is between the river and the Bois du Boulogne and, for position, you couldn't fault it, but the place is hardly fit to wash a rat in. It's cramped as a matchbox, there's no electric light, few plates, and it's on the fifth floor of the building. Lucia says the furniture is held together with spit and, true for her, there's nothing but a crude collection of flimsy items that hardly hold our weight. We have the flat for three months and, then, who knows where we'll fetch up.

"It's like living in medieval times," Georgie says, for it bothers him to use candles and oil lamps to read by.

"We will find a better place in the city, by and by," his father tells him and I wonder ruefully what happened to our holiday in Britain or Ireland.

Mr. Pound, who cannot do enough—he says Jim's a genius, no less—organizes a welcome party for us at the home of a Monsieur Spire, a poet. I put on my green silk dress, the ivory necklace, and a short satin coat that always makes me feel good and strong.

"Mamma, you look glorious," Georgie says and his compliment buffs me to gold.

Lucia comes and runs her hand over the satin; she keeps stroking me, as if I were her pet, and she's unwilling to let me go. I move toward the door where Jim is putting on his jacket and hat and she pursues me, her hand moving faster over me now, in little slaps that I know I'm meant to feel.

"Babbo's waiting for me, Lucy," I say.

She pulls her fingers away sharply and turns her back. This is Lucia—she often doesn't protest in words, it's all sullen looks and long stares, where it concerns me at least. With Jim she's more forgiving, and he with her. He dotes on Lucia, forgiving her pet-tishness; I prefer to use a firmer hand.

"Good-bye, children," Jim says. "Don't stay up to ungodly hours."

"We won't. *Bonne soirée*," Georgie replies.

Lucia keeps her back to us. "Good night, Babbo."

I pause, my hand on the door and I can't help myself. "And do you want to wish your mamma a pleasant evening, too, Lucia?" I wish she was as warm with me as she is with Jim; I can never figure out why she's so cold with me when I've really done nothing to deserve it. "Lucia?" I say again.

"Leave her be, Nora," Jim says, "she's just tired."

"Bold as brass is what she is," I snap, tugging open the lock and stepping out.

MONSIEUR SPIRE'S PLACE IS RATHER GRAND; THE ROOMS FLOW into each other and the walls have gold stucco such as you'd see in a church or palace. There's a big crowd of people gathered to meet Jim, but they huddle in groups and we stay back by the fire-place, clutching glasses of sherry and staring about us like a pair of gombeens. Jim doesn't want to drink in case his tongue rattles too much and he says something amiss. Mr. Pound heckles him to have wine, which embarrasses Jim, but, luckily, he notices Jim's discomfort and moves away. Around me I can hear conversations in French and I might as well be in the Tower of Babel for all I can understand. Pound comes over again to try to parade Jim around the room but, until a drink warms his gut, Jim'll remain still and silent, this I know.

"Come back in a while, Mr. Pound," I say, and he bows and joins a group nearby. I turn to Jim. "They're all here for you, love."

"And I'd rather be anywhere else."

"Remember you came for this, Jim, to meet with influential people. It'll be good for the book, so you'll have to dive in." He grunts and sips from his glass. "Look, go to the library that Pound showed us on the way in. Sit by yourself and have a good gulp of that sherry. When you've gained your courage, come back."

He squinches his eyes and one hand tugs at his beardeen. "I will so."

I watch him totter away, cane tapping the floor, and I see many eyes follow him. He makes a fine, if unsure, figure stepping down the room. When I turn back, there is a woman at my elbow; she's dressed in a man's velvet blazer and white shirt, with a flowing tie.

"Mrs. Joyce." American. She extends her hand. "Sylvia Beach." She grabs more glasses from a passing waiter and hands one to me. "Your husband writes dazzlingly, Mrs. Joyce."

"Well, yes he does."

"He has disappeared, it seems."

"Jim can be a little shy of company, he's gone to gather himself."

She looks alarmed. "Gone outside? Gone away?"

"No, no, he's skulking in Monsieur Spire's library, afraid of his life he might have to talk to someone." I smile. "If you'll go easy on him, I'll take you to him, Mrs. Beach."

"Miss Beach."

I nod. "And you can call me Nora."

She walks ahead of me, talking back over her shoulder. "You have children, Mrs. Joyce?"

"Yes, a boy of fifteen and a girl of thirteen. They're a harlequin pair, I have to say, Miss Beach, as opposite as night and day. Jim says Jane Austen named them—he calls them Sense and Sensibility."

Miss Beach laughs and whirls around to face me. "How charming! And which is which?"

"Giorgio is Sense. Lucia is the other."

She walks beside me now. "Do you enjoy Miss Austen's novels, aren't they a hoot?"

"Well now, I'm more for penny dreadfuls and romances, myself. Them or the *Daily Mail*."

She spurts a laugh, then says, "Quite right."

We get to the library door and Jim is within, examining a book. Miss Beach launches into the room.

"Is this the great James Joyce?" she asks.

Jim holds out his hand and says, "James Joyce."

"Miss Sylvia Beach, sir. A great admirer of *Chamber Music* and *A Portrait of the Artist* and the extracts I now read in the *Little Review*. They're extraordinary, you know." She drinks some sherry and examines Jim. "You're a modern man, Monsieur Joyce, and your art reflects that well."

Jim gives her a little smile, warming to her; he's a great fellow for praise. "And what do you do in Paris, Miss Beach?"

"I have a bookshop on rue Dupuytren."

"Booksellers do mighty work," he says. "What's the name of your establishment?"

"Shakespeare and Company."

Again Jim smiles. "A fine name for what, no doubt, is a fine establishment." He takes out his tiny notebook and writes in it, the name of the shop and its location, presumably.

"Please come by and see me there. Don't feel you need to buy anything. I lend books to writer friends as long as they can keep them clean."

I step fully into the room. "Oh, Miss Beach, he's very respectful of books. You wouldn't know Jim had read a book at all, he's that careful of them."

A dog barks somewhere in the Spire flat and Jim leaps like a chivvied cat. I go and put my hand to his arm. "It's all right, love."

"Is that dog here?" Jim says to Miss Beach. "Is it fierce?"

She looks bewildered. "I think it is here; Spire has a dog, for sure. Let me go and tell him to keep it locked up. You're not fond of our canine friends, Mr. Joyce?"

Jim strokes his goatee. "I was bitten on the face by a dog as a child, Miss Beach. I wear these whiskers to cover the scar."

The pair of them stand gawping at each other, awkward as strangers at a wake. Miss Beach swivels toward the door then turns back. "You can receive your mail at Shakespeare and Company, Mr. Joyce, if you like. Others do."

"That would be convenient."

Miss Beach smiles and studies Jim as if he were the rarest of specimens and he peers back at her and smiles, too. They shake hands then, like two businessmen concluding a deal, and Miss Beach looks between the pair of us and says, "Shall we rejoin the party?"

"Yes, let's," Jim says, eager as a girl, a grin wreathing his face.

I think Miss Beach already likes Jim enormously, and I can tell by his manner toward her that he likes her, too. Perhaps we'll make some friends and settle in Paris after all.

It's the morning after the party at Monsieur Spire's and Jim puts on his blue serge suit and black hat to go to Shakespeare and Company and those hideous plimsolls he insists on wearing, despite Georgie having given up his boots to him.

"Put on the boots," I say.

"I feel like a Dutch boy in his daddy's clogs in them, they're huge on me."

I sigh. "But them dirty auld canvas shoes, Jim. They're a fright."

"Nobody cares a whittle-whottle what I wear, Nora. They

care only for what I write, and what I might say about other writers, which will be very little."

"Oh, go on." I kiss his cheek and wish him well and off he goes, doing a Charlie Chaplin walk—toes up, arms and cane swinging—to make me laugh.

He's back within a few hours and I'm surprised to see him return so soon.

"Well?" I say. "How did you get on?"

"Grand." He holds up a book. "I borrowed this."

I take it out of his hand. "*Riders to the Sea*? Sure we know this one, Jim. What did you take this for? You might've got a new one."

"I was confused. Miss Beach is very, I don't know, very American, all fuss and bonhomie. My mind got addled and I just picked the first thing I saw."

"You like her, Jim?"

"Yes. She's openhearted, kind too, I think. She introduced me to her friend, a Mademoiselle Monnier, another book shop proprietor. I think, Nora, that they might be sapphists."

"Well, Miss Beach's outfit the other night was very masculine, all right." We look at each other and giggle.

"She says she will help us find a better flat. And she'll keep an ear out for English language students for me, too. What luck to have met her so soon. Miss Beach is one of those born to help others, it seems."

I put my arm around him and kiss his neck. "And you, my love, have a gift for finding just such helpers."

INDULGENCE

❧

Paris
1921

WHAT HAPPENS TO OUR BABIES? WE BIRTH THEM, FEED them, rear them up, guide them along as best we know and then, swift as swallows, they're gone from us. Oh, they may be under our care still, but they become, suddenly, as unknowable as the saints, as distant and strange as the moon, though we see them daily.

Georgie, being a boy is, naturally and without question, odd to me. What woman has ever fully understood a man? The men are like creatures from the deeps of the sea, so alien are they. But Lucia, female like myself, I always expected to have a great affinity with, a natural connection. But we're as cheese is to chalk— there's little common ground between us and, as the years go on and she races toward womanhood, our bonds loosen even more. It perplexes me. I thought she and I would be great with each other as she grew, but instead we seem to clang and clash. She looks at me some days as if I were some filth clinging to her sole, and she talks over me like I'm invisible at times, as if what I have to say is of no use to her or to anyone. Oh, she's clever like her father right enough, but so is Georgie and he retains his manners. Lucia says I pick on her, but it's she who starts fights and riles me almost daily.

Every morning she has some new complaint about her bed, her lack of fine clothes, or the complications of the French language, though she is very fluent. Every day she dances and dawdles about the flat and I have to hurtle her out to school so that I might have peace. She's a bold ringer and no mistake, a scold to my heart, but her father will hear nothing against her.

"You're too hard on her, Nora," Jim says, when I complain about Lucy's behavior.

"And you're *entirely* too soft."

I look at my daughter and I see the perfect splice of Jim and me: she has his inquiring mind and tendency to brood, and she has my looks, though she's slighter than me. When she is with her friends, I try to see if she's like them or if she is, as I suspect, a creature out on her own. Jim calls her a "flower of the rarest" and it makes me snort that he, of all people, uses the words of a hymn to praise her. I see Lucia more as a wildflower: she is not fully able for this world and she grows despite all uprooting but, mostly, I see her this way because she's beautiful and untamable and quare.

My Georgie is so easy compared to her. He takes his lessons, plays the piano, sings beautifully (when not too nervous to perform), and conducts himself like a man, though he's only sixteen. He's serious and polite and steady. Lucia flits about like a dervish, dancing and squawking one day, quiet and still as the tomb the next. I hardly know what to make of my own girl and that pains me. I snap at her and try to control her and, the more I do, the further she runs from me.

"Let her alone," Jim says, watching her twirl around the flat with a scarf through her hands. "She's like Isadora Duncan," he says. He calls to her, "You're an Isadorable now, Lucy. Dance, dance!" and she gallops on, tossing her head for her father.

"And what happens when she knocks over the breakfast table again and everything on it?"

Jim sends me a long stare. "What of it? Lucia is young and giddy. She's just expressing herself, finding freedom in her own body."

"That's exactly what I'm afraid of," I snap. "And don't forget that it's me who has to clean up when there's hot chocolate and coffee in rivers all over the floor. When there's glops of pastry mashed into the rug." Lucia slows her dance and turns to us. "Get your jacket on, Lucy. It's schooltime," I say. She mutters something. "What was that? I didn't hear you."

"I said 'I don't see why I must go to school.' Giorgio has a tutor. Why can't I?"

I take up the hairbrush and go at her head. "Because you're a girl and it's better for you to mix with other girls. It's just healthier that way. Ladies need company."

She snatches the brush out of my hand and drags it through her hair. "You left school at twelve. I'm fully fourteen. It makes no sense."

"Those were different days; I went straight into a job. Remember, too, I had no mother to guide me." Lucia goes to say something but bites down on her lip to stop the words. "Go on. What did you want to say? Something about my grandmother? About me?"

She drops her head. "It was nothing, Mamma."

I know that it was something—an unkindness meant to bring me down—but, to avoid a row, for I'm heartsick of bickering with this girl, I let it go.

THE IMPORTANT WRITER MONSIEUR LARBAUD HAS TAKEN A KEEN interest in Jim and *Ulysses*. It was Miss Beach who introduced them, of course; she's been a great friend to us.

"Larbaud claims he's 'raving mad' over the novel, Nora," Jim tells me.

"Well, of course he is. They're all amazed by your writing, aren't they?"

We're walking in the Bois, for Lucia likes to row on the lake and none of her friends are available to play today. The air is cold, but we're well wrapped up and it's nice to walk with my arm in Jim's, his rings flashing and his cane tap-tapping; I'm beginning to feel that we're part of something in Paris now, that we matter.

"Larbaud is using words like 'great' and 'immortal.' Obviously, *I* know I'm writing a good thing, but it lifts me when others concur."

I breathe deep on the green, fresh park air and watch Lucia row in lazy circles, her face a contortion of concentration. I peer closer. She's muttering to herself, a habit plucked straight from her father. Her head dips, the oars plunge, and Lucia's lips move in frantic conversation with no one.

"People will think she's mad," I say, nodding toward her.

"But mind, Nora, that 'a little madness now and then, is relished by the wisest men.' As the lunatic said to his oppressor. Or didn't say, more accurately."

"And what meaning am I to take from that, Jim?"

"Lucia is not mad, she's flexible-minded. There's a vast difference."

I look out over the lake, the black reflections of the surrounding oaks reach across the water to our daughter. She continues her circling and chatting.

"Is she happy, do you suppose?" I ask.

Jim sits me on a bench and huddles close. "People were not made to be happy, Gooseen, they were made to attempt things."

"I'd prefer to be happy above all else."

"But we can't be that all day, every day. We'd die of boredom." He takes my hand and slips one cold finger inside my glove to feel my skin. "Larbaud plans to have a small *conférence* about *Ulysses*. Adrienne Monnier will host it at La Maison des Amis des Livres. Miss Beach is beside herself with joy."

"They're good eggs, the pair of them."

"Miss Beach says it will raise interest in my work to the stars."

"Maybe then Miss Weaver's English publishers will change *their* minds and publish it?"

Jim sighs and rubs at his nose. "Unlikely, dear one. But people here will listen if Larbaud praises it, which can only help." He sits back and pokes at the ground with his cane. "All this censorship nonsense in America is making my teeth ache. What is wrong with those people that they can't take a little bloody realism? At this rate no one outside of Africa will print the damn thing as a book." He wriggles on the seat. "Obscenity, my hairy arse. And as for corrupting the minds of young girls. Give me strength!"

I gaze at Lucia and try to imagine her as young Gerty in Jim's novel. If Lucy was alone here on the bank of the lake and she raised her skirts, to titillate a man old enough to be her father, would I be alarmed? Indeed and I would. Why Jim has to put such sleazy little scenes in his novel I don't know. He says they're necessary and important, that he's showing up Ireland for what she really is—a contradictory place with contrary people—but will the public understand that? Ah, what's the difference? For Jim, *Ulysses* is the most significant thing in the world and, because of that, it's the same to me. And things are moving along, as slow as grass grows, it's true, but we're in a better flat at rue de l'Université now—the twentieth address at which Jim has been writing *Ulysses*, he tells me. And the Misses Beach and Monnier cluck around Jim like mother hens, making sure his nest is comfortable and he has all he needs to write. They call him Melancholy Jesus since he styled himself that one day and he enjoys their gentle teasing. And, anyway, amn't I here with Jim always, besides? How could he *not* thrive?

"The *conférence* in Miss Monnier's shop will be a good thing," I murmur, my eyes still on Lucy.

"I have to finish the book now, I suppose, scratch it down as quickly as I can. I'm itching to get to the last bit, the Penelope episode. The Ithaca part is chemical and geometric and mathematical, but Penelope will be soft and curvaceous and wide. It will be eight rambling sentences in total. I can see it, feel it, hear it scripted out before me. All I need is to get to it."

I grab his hand. "And you will, Jim. Stay in more, my love. Stick yourself to the chair and it'll be done."

Lucia appears before us. "May we go for chocolate, Papà?" She grins. "Say yes, Babbo!"

"Before lunch?" I ask, but seeing her rapid scowl, I correct myself. "Why not? Chocolate will warm our bellies."

When we stand Lucia slots her arm into Jim's and they walk ahead of me, their heads bent together. I trail behind them, a bind of jealousy twining with a knot of pleasure.

IT'S NOT IDEAL TO LIVE IN A HOTEL, THOUGH WE'VE SURVIVED worse spots, and it's not as damp as the flat in Passy. I would like to have my own little kitchen to cook in and entertain; my hands twitch with idleness. When Jim puts on his little white coat and the green valise comes out, with the thump-click of its locks, I know I'm dismissed. If he's to get *Ulysses* finished, he must haul the valise onto his lap, take out his scraps and notes, and set to. I leave him to get on with it and go to the phonograph shop where, for a few sous, I whittle away the afternoons listening to Herr Wagner.

"Go and commune with the obscene German," Jim says.

"So says the man writing a book ripe with obscenities."

"It's not all filth, Nora. It's a perfectly ordinary and funny waltz through Dublin, which you'd know if you could be bothered to read it all."

"Ah, hold your whisht, Jim. Haven't I read bits? And don't I hear enough of the rest of it from you to know what's in it? And as for Wagner, I like what I like. Let you like what you like."

Hat on, I go, and wonder, as I walk along, if husbands and wives have the same conversations ever and forever until one of them drops into the grave.

Unlike anywhere else we've lived, we're surrounded by English speakers here, many of them American. Like us they live in hotels or small flats; the wealthier ones in finer places. I have a new friend, Mrs. Nutting, who is a writer, too. She's not all caught up in herself, though, and I can tell her my small cares and woes without judgment. Some of the other wives, all clever and educated, think I'm useless to Jim. They ask if I write his letters and run his other bookish errands in a way that indicates that I should, that I ought to be a kind of slave to him, typing his words as he calls them out. The idea of it, to be permanently at his side and doing things for him! But my Mrs. Nutting knows what I am to Jim, she says it to me.

"That man would crumble to dust without you, Nora Joyce."

"Oh, I know it, Mrs. Nutting. I'm mother and rock to him. It can't be helped." I smile, thinking how Jim would fare without me. He'd barely eat a scrap and he'd drink himself to death, surely; I'm the only one who can tell him he's had enough.

Yes, the other wives and the literary women, who so love to scurry around the great James Joyce, find me a vast disappointment. But, hand on heart, I don't give a sailor's snot what they think. Jim is Jim, and Nora is Nora, and we know that despite any upsets and troubles we've had, we're strong as steel together.

And I have Mrs. Nutting, who helps with Lucia, too. She sees how bored and restless the girl is, how she struggles to keep friends, and she arranges for her to go to a holiday camp in Brittany with her niece.

SUMMER IN PARIS AND WE'RE ON THE MOVE AGAIN. WILL I EVER get used to packing up my little bag of belongings and the children's and wandering to yet another address? Monsieur Larbaud, who will be away for several months, kindly lends us his quiet flat on rue du Cardinal Lemoine, a place of polished parquet and burled antique furniture and an army of soldiers who live in a glass case, always on the edge of war.

The June morning we move in, I peer in on the soldiers. "If women ran the world, there'd be nobody shooting each other's heads off."

"Probably," Jim says, his tone dead.

"What's the matter with you?"

"Nothing."

"Are you missing Georgie?" He's gone to Zürich to visit friends and Jim never likes when we're not all four together in the one place; I don't relish it much myself.

"No, no. I'm glad Giorgio is off on his own; he needs it, I suppose, the company of men."

He walks away, beckons, and I follow him through the flat to the room that Monsieur Larbaud has suggested Jim use to finish *Ulysses* in. It's a tranquil spot, with a low, domed ceiling; I look at Jim again.

"What?" I say. "Isn't this beyond perfect? You can call down your fat Penelope, Molly Bloom as you style her, and be at your leisure with her here all day." I laugh but Jim is not smiling.

"It's like a tomb, Nora."

I tut. "You're giving me the pip now, Jim. Isn't this all you've ever wanted? A silent room where you can close the door on the world, on us, and get on with your novel?"

He rubs his forehead. "It is, I suppose."

"Sweet suffering Jesus and all the saints, Jim, just let yourself enjoy it then."

He sits into a chair. "I've had a note from Miss Weaver, Gooseen."

"Oh?"

"Someone has intimated to her that I'm 'a dipsomaniac,' of all things. And now she's alarmed."

I put my hand on his arm. "Isn't this just what happened with Mrs. McCormick in Zürich? Oh, Jim, people are unkind to you."

"Who are these betraying blackguards who want to cut the legs from under me, just when I'm getting somewhere?" The notion of Miss Weaver thinking ill of him is hurtful, clearly, but still he must find a way to make it her fault. She is just worried about her investment, it seems to me. "Harriet Shaw Weaver is obviously very sober in her habits indeed. She lectures me roundly on the evils of alcohol in her note."

I look at him and measure out my words. "Well, does a night go by when you don't take a drink, Jim?" He starts to protest and I stop him. "Well? Be honest with yourself. You might listen to the woman; you certainly refuse to hear me on the subject. The drink hurts your eyes and that hurts your writing, you know this is true. And every bottle of wine costs money, Jim, money we might better put in store for leaner days." He looks stricken and I soften; he needs to remain in Miss Weaver's good graces or we might starve altogether. I can't go back to the old days of living on the clippings of tin and scrapping for every crust. I put my arm around his shoulder and pull his head to my breast. "Now, Jim, who can have been telling tales to Miss Weaver?"

He shakes his head. "I'm confounded." He bites his lip. "I suppose it could be anyone. Plenty of the crowd around here resent me, though they smile winningly into my face. But I'll have to set our Miss Weaver straight or Protestant propriety will win the day and we'll never see another sou from the good lady."

"Write to her immediately, love."

"Oh, I intend to and I will tell her about every myth that circulates around my head and that she should not believe the gossip that reaches her. I'll tell her how it's said I'm in New York and dying; how they say I'm a cocaine addict, and that I own a chain of cinemas."

I tut. "Is that a bit far-fetched? She's a serious person."

"A serious person who—like all serious people—makes a difference in this world. In *our* world." He leaps up and grabs paper and pen. "I will fix this."

COMPLETION

✎

Paris
1921

J IM HAS HIS CHOICE OF DRINKING BUTTIES IN PARIS. MOST OF
the literary men, whether single or wed, seem as fond of the
drink as Jim is. The doctors tell him he's hurting his sight with his
carry on and he nods gravely and vows to give up, but once on the
town, his tongue wants to lap up every drop of Saint Patrice wine
in the city.

"You'll go blind, Jim," I tell him, just as Stannie used to long
ago in Trieste. "One eye is as good as finished already. Do you
mean to kill the other one off? How, then, will you write your
great masterpieces?" I snatch the hat from his head and he grabs
it back. Tonight he's determined to go and meet Mr. McAlmon, a
man who, as far as I can tell, was a teetotaler before Jim took him
on spree after spree. He bats me away and pulls on his coat.

"Don't nag me, Nora."

"We're only back from our dinner, why do you have to go out
again? Aren't we in for the night?"

"McAlmon wants to discuss something."

"Can't it wait? You have that poor fellow led astray with your
capers."

"You can lead a horse to water, Nora, but a pencil must be lead." He snorts.

"I'm in no mood for jokes, Jim. Stop at home with your family where you belong." I barricade the doorway. He stares at me, wobbles a bit; he's half cut already from the wine he had with dinner.

"Let me out, Nora. I'll abstain after tonight. I promised McAlmon I'd look over some poems for him. And he wants to talk of marriage, too; I gather he and his wife, the bold Bryher, are not having much success together."

I lean my face in until our noses meet. "Tell Mr. McAlmon if he wants to be a success with his wife, he should stay at home and not be gallivanting around the town, full to the knocker with booze." I step aside and out Jim goes; I thought, this once, he would listen to me. My heart is coddled with trying to keep that man well enough to do what he's meant to be doing. I hear Lucia humming to herself in her bedroom and think how fortunate the young are with their lack of life burdens. I go to my own room, undress, and slide into bed, exhausted from the push-me-pull-you with Jim over his drinking. These tussles have me worn to a thread.

I'M WOKEN BY LUCIA POKING ME IN THE BACK. "SOMEONE'S AT the door. They're banging, Mamma. I'm frightened." Her forehead is rucked with fear. I get up and push her behind me and, in our dressing gowns, we go together to the front door.

"Who's there?" I call.

"It's Robert McAlmon, Mrs. Joyce. Your husband has collapsed."

I unlock the door in a fury. Jim is upright, held by McAlmon, and there's a sheepish set to his face, but still I roar at him.

"Buckled drunk as usual, Jim Joyce. Get in here!" I grab at his jacket and drag him in.

"We saw a rat," he says, in a choked-off voice.

McAlmon nods. "Joyce took one look at the rat and fainted away."

"For God's sake." I know Jim hates rats as much as he fears dogs and despite myself, I mellow. "Help him to sit, Mr. McAlmon."

Lucia takes her father's arm on the other side and the three shuffle across the salon. Jim is a hardship to me but, at least, tonight it's not drink he's collapsing from.

In the morning, Jim's side of the bed is empty and I'm happy for that means he got up early to be with his horrible Molly Bloom and, therefore, the book will be finished sometime soon. I lie on, content to have the mattress to myself, but I hear a noise from the salon that disturbs me, a mewling sound, like a distressed cat. Up I get to see what's what and Jim's writhing on the floor by the sofa, his hands over his eyes, yipping with pain.

"Jim, Jim!" I dash to him and Lucia comes, too. "Run for Miss Beach, Lucy, bring her here."

"He needs a doctor, Mamma."

"Do as I say, Lucia, Miss Beach will know the right doctor to fetch. Go!"

Jim's in such agony that he can't speak, so I leave him on the floor with his head on a cushion. I get cold water to dab his eyes and sit by him and hold his hand until help comes.

THE DOCTOR MISS BEACH BRINGS WITH HER INJECTS COCAINE into Jim's eyes. Jim says it's the worst, most painful attack of iritis he's ever had, and I'd believe it, for his face is hollow as a spirit's.

"You must write less, Monsieur Joyce, and you must drink

less," the doctor scolds. "Both things put deadly pressure on your sight. Do you hear me?"

When the doctor and Miss Beach have left, I put Jim to bed. "How will I finish the book, Gooseen?" he groans.

"By following orders. You must swear off drink to begin, that will ease your eyesight."

He plucks at the sheet. "That's no life, to be stuck at home night after night, when half of Paris is lining up to greet me."

"Would you rather be blind?" I snap.

"Jaysusing God, just when I'm getting a foothold, just when I have a chance! Everyone wants to meet me." He holds up his bare hands. "The papers say I wear black gloves to bed. They say that I swim daily in the Seine having dived off the Pont Neuf. They say I write in a hall of mirrors." He grunts. "I'll write nothing now."

I feel sad for him, but I also know he needs to listen to the doctor's advice. "Paris will wait for you, Jim. And the gombeen newspapermen with their fancies, too. But you'll be a corpse if you continue the way you're going. Would that suit you? Or do you want, above all else, to be a man-about-town? Stumbling around, rotten with drink?" I'm so determined to keep him right that I become feverish in my speech. "Because if you'd prefer that, if you'd rather be a sickly bachelor, the dipsomaniac that poor Miss Weaver has been told that you are, then I can take Lucy and Georgie and go home to Galway. If you want to put wine and your writer friends and larking about in the Bal Bullier before your family and work, so be it." I point into his face. "But, Jim, mark me, you'll neither see nor hear from us again. Do you understand?" He pulls a grimace like a child parted from his lollipop. "I'm nearly twenty years putting up with your nonsense, Jim Joyce. No more. Do you hear me?"

He drops his head. "I hear you, Gooseen."

JIM COMES OUT OF HIS WRITING ROOM AND SLIDES UP BEHIND ME at the table where I'm dipping rosy wedges of Turkish delight into my tea. He kisses my neck. Jim is my good boy now. He has listened to me, listened to the doctor, listened to the concern of his dear Misses Beach and Weaver. He writes, he stops at home, he remains sober.

"Isn't October the best month, Nora?" he says, grabbing a sweet and biting it. "Always we achieve big things in October."

I know now that *Ulysses* is finished.

ULYSSES

❧

Paris
FEBRUARY 1922

IT'S THE FIRST OF FEBRUARY, THE DAY THAT THE SUN TAKES A cock's step forward, the feast of Saint Brigid. Tomorrow, on Jim's fortieth birthday, *Ulysses* will be published. Miss Beach, Jim's great savior, is bringing the novel out. She sees it as an honor, she says. We're taking the air with Djuna Barnes, a young American writer who's one of the Shakespeare and Company crowd, and I'm telling her all about the canny Saint Brigid who tricked a king out of land so she could build her convent.

"Brigid had a cloak just like yours, Miss Barnes, and she said to the king, 'Give me as much land as this cloak will cover,' and didn't she spread it out and it grew and grew, grabbing up field after field for the convent. Now, wasn't that very smart altogether?"

Miss Barnes flourishes her cape. "I ought to try that on the Champs-Élysées, what say you, Joyce?"

We both turn around to Jim, but he has lagged behind and is talking to some man; I look closer and see that Jim's face is very strange and I think his eyes might be burning and I run to him, followed by our friend.

"Jim, what is it?"

The man scurries off and Miss Barnes puts her hand to Jim's elbow. "Are you quite all right, Joyce?"

Jim glances over his shoulder with fear at the man. "That fellow hissed at me, Nora. He said, in Latin, 'You're an abominable writer.' Right into my face!" He grips my hand. "Gooseen, it's a bad omen for tomorrow."

I don't dare contradict him for I know the weight Jim gives to signs and portents; if he sees a fork askew, he thinks there'll be a fire at the printers; if a crow lands on a fence in front of him, the reviews will be bad; if there are thirteen people at the table, he'll ask one to leave. Sometimes I think he waits for things to go wrong so he can say "See, what did I tell you?"

"Oh, it's bad." He's begun to shake.

"Tosh! That fellow's no ill omen, Joyce," Miss Barnes says. "Don't give the Latin-spewing fool another thought. He's just some crank let loose from a *maison de santé* for the day."

But Jim looks as if he's been sucked of every drop of blood and his mouth hangs awkwardly. Miss Barnes and I take his arms on either side and guide him out of the park, toward home. His walk is slow and a deep gloom has settled on him.

As we're crossing the bridge, he peers into the river. "Perhaps I should rope Leopold Bloom and his cohorts to an anvil and toss them all into the Seine. Perhaps I should give up the whole writing enterprise."

"It's a bit late for that," I say. "But throw that auld Molly in, if you please."

Jim smiles wanly.

"Besides," Miss Barnes says, "who would Miss Beach run around after if her Melancholy Jesus stopped writing? No, Joyce, that simply won't do at all."

❧

EIGHT O'CLOCK IN THE MORNING AND THERE'S A RAP AT THE DOOR
and Miss Beach carries in the package like the priest carries his
chalice to the altar. Jim is battling tears as he unwraps the book
and lifts it out, the blue jacket shining as bright as the Mediterranean in summer. He sets down *Ulysses*.

"There it is," he says. "Here at last."

Lucia and Giorgio swoop in, but, instead of squabbling as they
usually might, they take it in respectful turns to hold the novel and
marvel at its size and weight and loveliness.

"See, it's the color of the Greek flag," Jim says. "The white
lettering represents the islands."

I stand by Jim, my hand on his shoulder, staring at the book
with what feels like a mother's pride—this is Jim's years of work,
all bound together and ready for its readers. He put great effort
into it; even when his eyes were at their sorest, he composed the
novel in his head. I may not love the innards of it, I may object
to bawdy Molly, but I'm proud of him, yes, and honored to know
him and impressed by his labor. And I'm made quiet by those feelings. For all his faults, Jim's an extraordinary fellow, truly, a great
writer.

"Congratulations, Joyce," Miss Beach murmurs. "The other
copy will go in the window of Shakespeare and Company and people will throng to see it. And then, when the rest of the copies arrive, they'll go like those proverbial cakes, I assure you."

"How can I thank you, Miss Beach?" Jim says. "Your courage
is phenomenal."

She reddens, shakes her head, and slips away, telling us she
will see us soon.

IN FERRARI'S WE ORDER OUR FAVORITE PASTA AND *POLPETTE* AND Jim keeps *Ulysses* under his chair, and Mr. and Mrs. Nutting and their niece Helen, and our friends the Wallaces, and even the waiters, are only dying to see the book but, no, Jim won't let them look until the meal is over.

"This man spent sixteen years concocting *Ulysses* and seven years writing it," I say with true warmth. "Ye can wait a few more minutes to admire it."

They all laugh and we eat our *torta al limone*, though Jim doesn't take a mouthful, nor did he eat so much as a scrap of his dinner, which means his nerves are jangling for sure. At last he reaches under his chair and takes out the book and proudly unwraps it to delighted murmurs. It's passed from hand to hand at our table and beyond; the waiters show it to the other patrons and we raise a toast to *Ulysses* with our glasses of Saint Patrice and it's all uncommonly jolly. Then Jim hands the book to me.

"The first one is always for you, Nora."

I take it with care and then hold it up and bounce it. "How much will any of you give me for this?" Everyone laughs and I clutch the book to my breast and shake my head. "No one will lay hands on it," I tell them.

The Wallaces and the Nuttings want to go to Café Weber and I let the children go with them, but I decide to take Jim home for, without an ounce of grub in his stomach, the wine has made him groggy.

"You've had more than enough," I say, pushing him into a taxi.

"Someone save me from these scenes," Jim calls out ruefully to Mr. Nutting, but we both know he's glad to go home to bed after his most exciting birthday yet.

"Shouldn't we have gone to the Weber with the others, Nora?" he says, his eyes closing and his head tilting backward.

"No, Jim."

He leans into my side and yawns. "A good day, Gooseen."

"Yes, my darling. A very good day."

IRREGULARS

❧

Ireland
1922

SMOKE RISES OVER QUEENSTOWN AS THE BOAT APPROACHES
and a peculiar ache catches my belly and doesn't leave me until
my feet touch Irish soil. With my father dead, it's clear my mother
won't be long after, and I've wanted nothing more than to see her
again. So here I am, the children, too, and Jim left behind in Paris,
a shivering wreck without us. We passed a week in London and I
got telegram after telegram from him, bleating about Ireland being
on the verge of civil war and pleading with me to turn around and
come back to Paris. I'll do no such thing, of course, having come
this far. I've had it up to my oxters with drink-laden parties and
soirées and highfalutin conversations that exclude me entirely, and
the Lord knows what else.

Ten years gone and, though Ireland has been a place of unrest
and killing, it feels the same. The buildings are filthy and the people look a biteen downtrodden and the air is heavy with smoke.
My uncle Michael takes us to lunch in Dublin with John Joyce and
they talk of nothing but raids and murders.

"What use is partition?" Pappie roars, belting the table with
his fist. "We're a country divided after those English blackguards
have squatted upon us for eight hundred years."

"The English aren't all bad," Uncle Michael says, and my father-in-law turns the color of turnip skin.

"Perhaps we should leave this subject for now," I say, nodding to Lucia and Georgie who, being youngsters, are enjoying the prospect of a row.

"They've pitted Irishman against Irishman, the dirty skites," Pappie says. "There's men dragging each other from their beds and shooting one another like dogs. It's a pitiful state of affairs altogether."

I shake my head and widen my eyes; Pappie takes my meaning, nods, and closes his mouth. The children are disappointed.

IN GALWAY STATION, THE PORTER TELLS US THAT THE RAILWAY hotel is being held by the Regulars as their headquarters and the Irregulars have taken somewhere else as theirs.

"They shoot at each other and upend us all half the night and half the day. The whole town is in a heap," he says. "Be careful, missus. Be careful of your boy."

Jim was worried that at sixteen Georgie would be pressed into service as a soldier, right enough, but I'd thought he was only panicking.

"Stay close to me at all times, Georgie," I urge.

We take rooms in Mrs. O'Casey's boardinghouse on Nun's Island, Mammy's place being too small. I spend my days sitting at my mother's table listening to her lament her children gone abroad and the dead husband she didn't love, but nursed to his end because that was the Christian thing to do. My sisters Delia and Kathleen roll their eyes and tell me all the gossip. After the first day, the children refuse to step into Mammy's house.

"Must we?" Lucia whines, when we get to the door at Bowling Green.

"It stinks of cabbage," Georgie says.

Their rudeness embarrasses me, but it's clear that they're very different people to my family and to the neighbors about. On the first day they refused, too, to eat Mammy's food and she was offended. How can Jim and I have reared such thoughtless raps? I'm mortified that everyone will think I've done a terrible job with them.

"There's nothing wrong with a plate of spuds and a cup of buttermilk," Mammy said that day, in a subdued voice. "A nice cut of bacon."

"Indeed and there isn't," I agreed loudly. "Isn't it the best of stuff?"

It's strange to me that though I'm still the same Nora Barnacle, I've raised children who don't fit into Ireland. Lucia and Georgie couldn't be more different from my family, and their poor manners shine like oil lamps in Galway. I regret not taking more care with their conduct and I wonder if it's too late. For now, I end up taking Georgie and Lucy to a café for their meals and I eat with Mammy and the girls myself, while the children sit outside on the windowsill like two crows and sulk. My heart is especially moidered with Georgie who usually prides himself on his fine manners. But I ignore the pair of them as best I can and sit inside, for I like to hear Delia and Kathleen pick apart the neighbors.

"That Mrs. Walsh is a ringer and no mistake. I swear she'd steal the sod from the fire when you're not looking," Kathleen says.

"Whisht, girl," Mammy says, but I can see the cast of a smile about her mouth.

"Oh, and as for Mr. Fahy from down the lane, Nora, he beats his wife to jam and screams every kind of scuttery nonsense at her behind that door, but the tie goes on for Mass and off he trots every morning."

"With his priesty face," Delia adds, nodding.

The girls rib each other about this chap or that. In truth, though, they're aging spinsters, stuck here now with Mammy, and it's a curious little household they make, the three of them, when all is said.

I WRITE TO JIM TO TRY TO EASE HIS MIND ABOUT THE TROUBLES IN Ireland, for he has himself on pins and needles with the idea of us being shot dead. The Regulars and Irregulars are visible, there's no doubt of that, and Georgie was accosted on the street and asked what it was like to be a gentleman's son; our clothes make us stand out. I was afraid for a little while, but I tell Jim not to fret, we're quite safe. Mammy and the girls are very casual about the whole thing and it doesn't cost them a moment's worry and so it mustn't concern me either.

I tell Jim that when Mr. de Valera, who refuses to accept the Treaty, came to Galway to give a speech he got a cold reception. Uncle Michael says there will be flare-ups on Easter Sunday to remember the killings of 1916. We'll stay inside, in case. It's indeed peculiar that Mr. de Valera was the only one left alive after 1916. His American passport saved him, they say.

Jim writes back to say he fainted in Miss Beach's shop and that his eyes are paining him with anxiety. I tell him to eat nourishing food, rest more, and not to drink, and that McAlmon and Hemingway will have me to answer to if they lead him astray.

I go to the convent to see my old nuns, and the children behave, and I'm proud of how nicely groomed they look and of their good manners to the sisters. There's no sign of the bold Father Flannery and it makes me smile to think how put out Jim will be to hear of his absence.

On Good Friday I go to the church and it lifts me to be there with Mammy and my sisters, there is something powerful in God, all the same. We pray hard for our brother Tom and sister Peg; not a word's been had from either of them since they went to England.

"I'm killed wondering where they are and why they don't write," Mammy says, clutching on to me in the pew.

"It's a sad thing and no mistake, Mam," I whisper, no comfort to her, for wasn't I silent myself for a long time? "They'll write to you, surely, by and by."

I buy a fur on tick as the air is more bracing in Galway than I'd expected and I'm cold—I ask Jim to send me the money for it and I also tell him, though I know he'll be hurt by it, that I'd like to stay away from Paris for a few months and I ask him for £12 a month to live on. I feel like myself a little, with Mammy and the girls, and it's nice to talk and be understood with ease, and to speak of familiar things besides, homely things. I might not stop in Ireland, though—London was very fine and I can see myself enjoying it for the summer or longer. I ask Jim if he might not consider moving to England. We know people there: Miss Weaver and Frank Budgen and Mr. Pound, and many more besides. We might be happy there. I would truly like a small home of my own and maybe in London we could get a little house and be comfortable, speaking English daily, and having a better understanding of the customs and ways. I fear Jim will say no.

I'M POKING A WODGE OF SODA BREAD INTO AN EGG WHEN MRS. O'Casey comes and stands beside our breakfast table.

"Another telegram for you, ma'am."

I take it and lay it by my plate. "Thank you."

"I hope it's not bad news you're getting all the time?"

I sigh. "No, Mrs. O'Casey, it's just that my husband relies on me terrible. He wants me home in Paris."

"Home, is it? In Paris?" She widens her eyes and rubs her hands down her apron. "Ah, the men are useless without us, missus." She glances at Georgie. "Saving your presence, young sir."

Giorgio shrugs.

I open the telegram and it's from Jim begging us to come home soon, just as I knew it would be. No London for me, so. I pass it to the children and sigh.

"Mamma," Lucia says, "has Saint Harriet provided enough for us to change our tickets and leave sooner? Babbo needs you. He needs *us*."

"Be more respectful about Miss Weaver, Lucia. Saint Harriet, indeed." But I giggle, for often I see Miss Weaver in my mind's eye with a sharp little halo around her head.

We all jump when there's an unmerciful banging at Mrs. O'Casey's front door.

"Bloody IRA men," Mrs. O'Casey mutters, "they think they own the place."

She goes to answer it. I leap up and beckon the children and shove Georgie behind the dining room door where he won't be seen; Lucia cowers behind him. We hear the crash-bang of men's boots on the stairs and doors being flung against walls, the fellows shout and curse and then there's the hard pop of gunfire, which nearly turns our skins inside out. I bless myself over and over I'm so afraid, and go to Lucia and pull her to my breast; Giorgio takes my hand.

"It will be all right, Mamma," he whispers.

"How will it be? They're all in a frenzy, shooting at each other like madmen."

We stay behind the door until the sniping stops and the men troop down again, barking swear words and ignoring Mrs. O'Casey who shouts "That's right, get out, ye pups"; she slams the door behind them. She comes to me, rife with apologies, but my heart is galloping and I've had enough of Ireland now. Jim was right, we shouldn't have come to this God-deserted country at all. Let them shoot each other as much as they want, I won't stay to let my children be murdered.

"I'm so sorry about this upset, Mrs. Joyce." Mrs. O'Casey is all bluster. "I can't stop them, they come in like that from time to time. They're bold brats, the lot of them."

"It's all right," I whisper, though of course it isn't, not one bit. I'm sick with nerves after the intrusion, the fright of it.

"The whole place has gone to pot, Mrs. Joyce, is all I can say to you. The Regulars and the Irregulars just do whatever they please."

My skeleton shivers inside my skin and I have to try hard to speak. "Mrs. O'Casey," I say, "we'll be leaving you today."

She nods and looks sorrowful thinking, I suppose, of the money she'll lose. "I understand, *a leana*, I understand."

"I'll pay you until the end of this week."

She smiles. "Let me help you to pack, dear. You've a long tramp ahead to Paris and your husband." She grunts. "Paris, bedad."

THE TRAIN SLIDES OUT OF THE STATION AND I SIT BACK AND SIGH. I watch the blue of Galway Bay retreat and feel nothing but relief. Mammy was sorry to see us go, but she understood that I didn't want to keep the children in a place where guns were being flung around as easy as toys. At Renmore the train slows then halts.

"Why are we stopping?" I ask the man opposite me.

"Ah, the Free Staters on the train will want to have a go at the Irregulars beyond in the barracks, missus. It's always the same." His look is cheerful, but I'm alarmed.

"Have a go? You don't mean—?" But before I can finish there's the firecracker sound of gunfire and I dive to the floor pulling Lucia with me. "The place is a bloody tinderbox," I whisper, sorry that we ever bothered to come at all. "Giorgio," I hiss, "get down. Get down where they won't see you."

"Stay where you are, young fella," the man says to Georgie and my son does what he's told, despite me gesturing to him madly to at least duck his head. Either he thinks he's being stoic or he's paralyzed by fear.

In Dublin, Uncle Michael takes us to a hotel for a cup of tea before our boat. I'm still shaky after all that happened in Galway and on the train but, when I relate the tale to him, Michael laughs so long and so hard he nearly falls off his chair.

"How is that funny, Uncle?" I ask, irritated by his laughter. "I was terrified. We all were. We might've been killed!"

"Oh, Nora," he says, wiping tears from his eyes, "you were perfectly safe. They only want to kill each other." He shakes his head as if I'm a class of simpleton and I'm furious with him. "So you won't be seeing Jim's aunt Josephine then?" he asks. "You're determined to take off early?"

"I just want to be gone," I say.

"She'll be disappointed not to see the children."

"Well, she may live with it," I bark. "We're getting out of this country for once and for all. I won't stay another second."

FAME

❧

Paris
1922 TO 1924

JIM LOVES ME WITHOUT QUESTION, WITHOUT CONDITION. AT the start—so long ago it's nearly hard to remember—he tried to make something of me, with books and advice and so on, but he failed. And that's good for us all. Doesn't he say himself that he hates women who know things? I know little. Well, that's not true, of course, for I know plenty about ordinary things, just not bookish ones.

"The devil's grandmother doesn't know as much as you," Jim says to me when I argue with him, but he knows I'm right on most things that matter, family things. Women have more sense than men, for sure. So I give a sensible answer to Mr. McAlmon, who visits us regularly, when he asks what it feels like to be the wife of a famous man.

"Your husband is now the most well-known writer on earth, you know. How does that sit with you, Mrs. Joyce? How does it feel?"

"I'll tell you what, Mr. McAlmon, it feels like living with a phonograph that can't be shut off. It's *Ulysses* this, *Ulysses* that, *Ulysses* the other. It's Miss Beach this, Miss Beach that, Miss Beach the other." I point at Jim who's half lying across two chairs, smoking. "That man can barely visit the privy without consulting Miss Sylvia Beach."

Jim laughs, but Mr. McAlmon looks taken aback. "Oh," is all he says, an embarrassed set to him.

"The children run out the door as soon as they're able for fear of having to return books to Shakespeare and Company or write out letters when Jim's eyes are at him."

"I see," McAlmon says, sorry I suppose that he asked the question.

"You're celebrated now, Jim, just as you always wanted," I say. "You're like a monkey getting peanuts flung at you morning, noon, and night, isn't that right?" Jim smiles his crooked little smile and nods; he loves me to rib him, really. "Mr. McAlmon, the problem is, you see, that we can't eat our dinner in peace in a restaurant anymore. People send notes over asking to meet him. They send wine that he doesn't need to drink. We're not even safe here: they ring our doorbell. They send flowers. They send requests for interviews."

"I do so hate interviewers," Jim pipes.

"But there are perks, surely, Mrs. Joyce?" McAlmon says, scratching his ear and looking like he wants to be elsewhere.

"If there are, I've yet to experience them." I lift the plate of éclairs. "More cake, Mr. McAlmon?"

PARIS IS TOO HOT FOR US, SO WE LEAVE FOR NICE—GIORGIO left behind to take his singing lessons. Oh, but Nice is a big fat yawn of a place; there's the sun and there's the bright Mediterranean and there's little else. And Jim, God help us, is laid low with eye trouble, so it's just Lucia and me, walking, eating fancy cakes by the half dozen, and staring at the water all day.

Today, while we stroll the promenade, the sea a mirrored glare beside us, Lucia says to me, "Do I look very strange, Mamma? You know, because of my droopy eye?"

I turn and tell her firmly, "No, Lucia dear. You're a beautiful girl."

"People stare at me sometimes, as if they want to penetrate me."

I shudder. "But everyone looks at everyone else, don't they, loveen?" I say brightly. "But what do you mean by 'penetrate'?"

"Oh, you know, get inside me. Inhabit me."

What a turnabout way the child thinks. "Try not to maunder over such things, Lucy, you're only upsetting yourself." I wish, somehow, she could stop her mind churning; she seems to come at things so oddly and she worries at them, until she makes them true.

Lucy holds up her hands against the sky. "My fingernails are satisfyingly dirty today, Mamma, see?" I look at the little moons of dirt under her nails. "People will see that and think I'm industrious. That I'm worth something."

My heart flutters. Why would she think she has no value, when we treasure her? "You're worth plenty, Lucia," I say, with firm sincerity.

"Thank you, Mamma," she says, her voice low and serious, and I wonder what makes her thoughts collide so and why she says such things. Have Jim and I made her strange by holding her so close to us? Are her solitary ways caused by us and is that aloneness what keeps her peculiar? We continue our walk, but my mind is upturned now; Lucia is not an unclean girl normally and I can't understand the crescents of dirt she's so proud of.

"How *did* your nails get so dirty, Lucy, what were you doing?"

"Ah well, you mustn't ask me that, Mamma, for then I shall have to tell you where I buried the gold." She lifts her hands, wriggles her fingers, and laughs, a maniac's sound, not the laugh of a youngster in her right mind.

"You mustn't say silly things, loveen. Remember we've spoken about that before?"

Lucy lowers her head, chaste as a novice. "Yes, Mamma."

I look at her, docile and quiet now, and I think that she nurses these strange thoughts of hers like a pet, a little bird that she feeds and coddles, keeping it alive. Someday that bird will spread its wings, open its beak, and rise up against her. Someday. Until then, I must try to stand between her and this foolishness, break them apart from each other, for what will happen if I don't?

Lucia lunges to the railing overlooking the sea and throws her chin upward. "Can you hear the clouds, Mamma?"

"What do you mean, Lucy?" Oh Lord, she has such curious notions and she must express them for all to hear. "No, of course I can't hear the clouds."

She points to the sky and grins. "I can," she says.

AVENUE FLOQUET IS A SUCCESS. IT FEELS LIKE A HOME AND WE can entertain in it. I take joy in polishing the sideboard and filling vases with pink camellias and stems of mimosa to make every corner bright.

For Saint Patrick's Day we invite our friends—Monsieur Larbaud, Miss Beach and her Miss Monnier, Mr. and Mrs. Nutting, and a few more. I cook a roast chicken and a nice side of ham and serve them with heaps of mashed spud, carrots, asparagus, and a rich gravy. After the meal, Lucia plays a jaunty piece by Schubert, and Giorgio sings some Handel, though his face reddens like a hot coal to feel all eyes upon him and I sweat, too, just watching him. Still, he sings like God's messenger and his eyelashes, deep as hammocks, curl dark and beautiful against his cheek when he closes his violet eyes; my applause for him is the loudest and longest. Jim and I sing some music hall songs and a few of the old Irish ones. We raise glasses of Saint Patrice to Saint Patrick and to the company. I allow Lucia a taste of the wine though Georgie, being against drinking, refuses the smallest sip.

The evening floats on and everyone looks so fine in their good clothes and my heart feels fat and full. Soon the wine goes to Jim's legs and he starts his spider dance, but his eyes are so bad, he doesn't see my footstool and over he goes onto his back, the eejit.

"Jim!" I call out, handing the tray of cakes I'm carrying to Mrs. Nutting. I run to him. He looks up at me from the floor and hoots a laugh.

"Help me, Gooseen." I shake my head, but offer him my hand and up he whooshes. "Now, where was I?" he calls out and everyone laughs.

Later, when there are only ourselves and the Nuttings left, and Jim is stretched out on the sofa, singing "The Brown and Yellow Ale" to himself while waving a wineglass, I speak to Mrs. Nutting.

"Look at him leeching there, drunk as a lord. He's good-for-nothing half the time. I sometimes wish I'd married a farmer or a ragpicker. Anyone but a writer."

"I think you're dreaming, Mrs. Joyce. Do you think those men, farmers and so forth, wouldn't drink? Or wouldn't be utterly wrapped up in their work, the way your husband is?"

"Ah, maybe they would drink and work all the hours, but they wouldn't be celebrated for it."

WE HAVE A NEW PLACE TO GO, THE CAFÉ FRANCIS ON THE PLACE de l'Alma, and we cross the river to get to it. We all love the Francis because from the *terrasse*, and inside the front salon, there's a splendid view of the Eiffel Tower, rising like a big brown hat pin from the *quai*. Sometimes we walk over to the café and other times, if

Jim's eyes are bad, we take the bus. I love the place for its comfortable banquettes and the way the red walls make me feel like I'm sitting inside a great red heart, warm and protected. And the food is delicate and delicious.

Tonight it's just ourselves. Lucia is with her new friend, Miss Kitten Neel, and Giorgio is gone to the opera with his teacher from the Scuola Cantorum. I love when it's only the two of us; I slip my arm into Jim's and we walk in sweet silence over the bridge to the restaurant, the warm September air beating about us nicely. Every so often we glance at each other and smile, glad it's just ourselves. I'm planning what to eat, maybe a nice slab of steamed salmon and a swirl of the mashed potato they do so well in the Francis.

"What will you eat, Jim?" I ask, my mouth a surge of spit in anticipation of the tasty fish I'll have.

"Anything I please, Gooseen," he says and it's true—we can have any dish that takes our fancy for Miss Weaver has passed her latest good fortune straight to Jim: an inheritance she got of twelve thousand pounds. I could scarce believe when it happened but, there you are, the woman is indeed a saint.

The maître d'hôtel greets us and gives us the table we like and we pass a companionable, mostly silent, hour over our food, though, as usual, Jim eats little. I look out at the tower, dark against the duskening sky, and the trail of traffic that passes. From the corner of my eye I see a couple approach our table and Jim sees them, too, for he stiffens like a heron; he doesn't relish entertaining strangers. The woman is thirty-odd and not pretty but she's superbly attractive—her dangling diamond earrings flash and catch the candlelight and her orange-and-yellow blouse is so very *à la mode*. Her husband is tall, blond, and open-faced.

"Americans," Jim hisses.

"Shush," I say, in case they hear.

"Mr. Joyce," the man says, holding out his hand. "Leon Fleischman of Boni and Liveright, New York."

Jim straightens himself. "You publish Ezra Pound."

"We certainly do."

"I know Pound, a fine fellow."

Mr. Fleischman gestures to his companion. "This is my wife, Helen Kastor Fleischman."

Jim introduces me and asks them to sit with us for it seems they mean to stay, whether invited or not. The men immediately begin to talk of Pound and Hemingway and George Moore. I turn to the wife.

"I'm mortally envious of the way you wear those earrings, Mrs. Fleischman. You look beautiful. If I wore them, I'd be mistaken for a streetwalker."

She giggles and pulls at her ear. "Why, thank you, Mrs. Joyce. They were a gift from my *Vati*; they do rather dazzle." She glances at Jim and lowers her voice. "I can hardly believe we are seated with *the* James Joyce, the most acclaimed writer in the world." She lets out a peculiar little squeak then calms herself. "Leon and I subscribed to the first edition of *Ulysses*, you know."

"That's lovely to hear," I reply, "but don't think Jim's anything special at all, Mrs. Fleischman. He's a man the same as any other, with all a man's frauds and faults."

Again she laughs and I find myself warming to her, though she's a different class of woman to me. She's of wealthy stock, surely, the kind of American who fetches up in Paris and has little to do but throw money around like snuff at a wake.

"Where do you live, Mrs. Joyce?"

"In the seventh. It's so hard to find a decent flat."

"It truly is. We're having a bad time locating an acceptable place."

"Oh, the want of a real home, somewhere to really settle, wears me to my marrow sometimes. I want it for the children as much as ourselves. Do you know what I'm telling you, Mrs. Fleischman?"

"I certainly do." She grimaces. "How old are your children, Mrs. Joyce?"

"Giorgio is eighteen and Lucia is sixteen."

"My David is four years old, nearly five. He's my tiny treasure."

"Mothers and their sons, Mrs. Fleischman." I smile, thinking of darling Georgie. "Boys are wonderful, to be sure."

The Fleischmans walk with us back across the Seine. Jim and Mr. Fleischman seem to get on grand and I comb his wife's knowledge of Lanvin and Lelong and Chanel. She recommends a hairdresser to me and I'll be only too happy to squander a little of Saint Harriet's pot of money to spruce myself, seeing that I'm the other half of the most acclaimed writer in the world. Jim invites them in and we smoke and drink white wine. When Lucia and Georgie return from their outings, they join us, both of them silent as a morgue, watching dazzling Mrs. Fleischman who reeks of the kind of ease and polished glamour that surely has an effect on everyone who meets her.

JIM CALLS MRS. FLEISCHMAN "THAT BUTCHER WOMAN" BECAUSE *Fleisch* means "meat" and her father made his money in cutlery.

"Stop that, Jim," I say. "Call her by her name. You wouldn't say those things to her face."

He snorts and grins. "I'm just glad you have a new friend, Gooseen," he says.

"You're only glad because she keeps me out from under your feet."

He's on another book. Which means he's gathering bits and taking things in and watching and scribbling and noting and muttering and we may as well not exist at all. He says it's a flowing river of a novel and that it'll be more Irish than Ireland and he's terrifically excited by, and eaten up with, it. The sight is bad with him, of course, so sometimes he nabs the children to take notes and other times he uses large sheets of paper and crayons so that he can see what he's about. It's like we all live inside this new book, which, to everyone else he calls *Work in Progress* but, to me, he has confided the true title, which is *Finnegans Wake*.

"Like the song," I say and sing a few lines:

> *Tim revives, now see how he rises*
> *Tim Finnegan risin' in the bed*
> *Sayin' "Whirl your whiskey 'round like blazes*
> *Be the thunderin' Jaysus, did you think I was dead?"*

"Well, the novel will be like the song only not like it," he says.

"Jim, it wouldn't be yours if it wasn't some kind of word soup, some insensible chop suey."

He laughs. "Now you're talking, Nora."

He may laugh, but he's worried, too—neither Stannie nor Larbaud, Pound nor Miss Weaver can make head nor tail of the extracts they've read. Stannie accuses Jim of wasting his talent. But Jim is sure of himself, sure of his path, and what can I do but hold his hand and trot along with him?

MRS. FLEISCHMAN AND I GO SHOPPING TOGETHER AND SHE HELPS me choose some flattering styles: a *devoré* coat in silver and black, with fur collar and cuffs, and some smart patent leather shoes. For my hair she recommends that I bob it and part it to one side and, with my newly fixed teeth, too, Jim says I look so youthful that Lucia and I could pass for sisters.

Mrs. Fleischman invites Lucy and me to her flat and we are delighted to go. We're not there ten minutes when she leads us to her wardrobe, which is almost the size of Mammy's whole house, and begins to hold up things against Lucia: a pretty lace-trimmed blouse in cream and a short navy skirt. Lucia is quiet and blushing but pleased, I can tell.

"Try them on," Mrs. Fleischman says. Lucy looks to me and I nod. She goes toward the bathroom but Mrs. F yells, "Oh come, Lucia, we have seen it all, dear. Strip here."

I'm used to the open ways of these young Americans by now. My ears scorch when they casually talk of their own bodies and their men's bodies and venereal diseases and pregnancies aborted. I say prayers for them in the church and light candles, too, though I never let on; I've started to visit any church I pass since I found such comfort in the one in Galway. Lucia, like the Americans, is also comfortable in her skin and immediately slips out of her clothes and, in turn, tries on everything that Mrs. Fleischman suggests to her. We sit on the bed and Lucy sashays up and down the bedroom like a mannequin and, in a beaded pink gown, she begins to dance. The slip and flow of the beads and the silk over her long, lean frame reminds me of what it feels like to be young and unsullied, to have a sure energy and power. Mrs. Fleischman must feel it, too, for she grabs my hand across the bed and we sit mesmerized by my daughter, who is as light and delicate as a fawn in her motions, all long legs and curved back and arms aloft. She stretches her limbs, lifting and holding her leg stock-still for impossible moments, then she moves suddenly again, in fluid falls and twirls. When she dances like this, our little troubled Lucia disappears and my daughter becomes her best, fullest self; all her awkward pieces fall away and she flows and glides, easy as a river. I watch her and wish she could be like this all the time. Lucy finishes her dance in an Egyptian pose and we applaud her loudly. I let a wild "Yahoo!," which makes Mrs. Fleischman laugh, but I see, too, that there are tears in her eyes.

"Oh, you're crying, my dear."

She blots her tears away with her sleeve. "It's nothing. I find dance so emotional, don't you? I could hear the music in my head. And Lucia is so fresh, so beautiful; the whole of life lies before her." She hops up. "You must keep this pink dress, Lucia." Mrs. Fleischman hugs Lucy. "You must take all of these things with you."

And she calls her maid who fills a bag with the clothes Lucia has tried on. I don't protest, but thank my friend because I can see that Lucy is thrilled with the idea of owning some new finery, especially that belonging to the impeccable Mrs. Fleischman.

SLUMBER

❧

Paris
1925

At last I have a home to call my own and furniture besides. The flat is near the Tour Eiffel, on Square de Robiac, and it's on the third floor, quiet and comfortable, and I feel settled to see Biscuit the cat mooching about beneath the sofa, and I couldn't be happier with my soup tureen and my champagne glasses and my walnut wardrobe and the rented piano and all the space we need. The only small annoyances are that Lucia claims she cannot sleep here—it is *too* quiet, apparently—and Giorgio goes missing so regularly we've taken to calling him the Lodger. He's not drinking, of that I'm sure, but something other than singing, and his little accountancy job, keeps him away at peculiar hours. Jim says it's the prerogative of the young to be stealthy and secretive and that I mustn't hound either of the children about their lives or they'll turn away from us.

"I care about them, that's all," I say.

"Naturally, Nora, but we mustn't stifle them either." Says he who can't survive ten minutes without me, even making me stay with him overnight in hospital when his eyes are operated on, the pair of us cooped up like two old hens for days on end, him with those horrible leech creatures on his eyes, me looking out the window at nothing.

Some nights, when Lucia can't sleep, Jim sits with her in the salon and sometimes she cries from weariness and says that her mind will not calm down enough for her to relax into slumber.

"All I want is for my brain to be silent," she wails.

Jim sings to her and rubs her feet but, often, even that doesn't soothe her and then they're both crabby and worn-out and I have to sidle around the pair of them in the daytime. I say we need to take her to a doctor, but her father says "It will pass" and that's that, as far as he's concerned. I worry that it won't pass, that she'll wander the flat like a wraith forever and that it will play havoc with her already fragile thinking and ways.

I go into her bedroom one night to check on her and she's propped up in the bed, still as a statue, staring into the dark.

"Lucia," I whisper. She doesn't move and I'm frightened; I go to her and touch her shoulder. "Lucy," I say.

She turns to me calmly, as if she's known I'm there all along. "Does your mind converse with you, Mamma?" she asks.

I sit on the bed. "What do you mean, Lucia?"

"Are there voices in there"—she taps my forehead—"that vie with each other? That insist on being heard?"

"No, there aren't." I push her gently to the pillow. "Lie down, my darling. Close your eyes."

"Yes, Mamma," she says, a tiny girl again and my heart ruptures with worry.

THE MORE WELL KNOWN JIM GETS, THE LESS HE WANTS TO TALK to people. Not all people, just those kinds of strangers who like to gawp at him and want him to sign their copies of his books and hope that he'll utter untoward or droll things. He won't give those sorts of people the satisfaction. No, Jim prefers to talk to porters and postmen, to waiters and washerwomen.

"They have better things to say," Jim pronounces, and when I'm wedged between poets and booksellers in the Bal Bullier or Le Trianon, I'm inclined to agree. It's all right if the women are there—we can compare dressmakers and bakers—but the men just want to outshout each other about who is superior, Eliot or Apollinaire, and outdrink each other until they're insensible. Continuous late nights are no joy to me.

Anyway, Jim is crotchety from eye tests and operations, and the endless lies from that Doctor Bausch about how his sight will improve by and by. He can't abide unasked-for attention from eager strangers, thrusting books for signing—their faces are a blur and he's in pain besides. Jim likes a small set, people he knows and trusts, McAlmon and young Arthur Power and the like. With them he can drink and talk in a way that pleases him. And Miss Beach, of course, she's his rock. Sometimes he refuses to go out with certain company at all.

Today Lucia picks up our letters from Shakespeare and Company in the new rue de l'Odéon shop—we set her these small tasks to keep her occupied, for she complains of ennui so often.

"Who could be bored who has all of Paris at their feet?" I say to her, genuinely confused at her talk of boredom.

"Or all of literature at their fingers," Jim chimes, waving at our bookcases. Lucy rewards us with arms across the chest and deep frowns.

But on her return from rue de l'Odéon this morning, Lucia is lit up and excited, and it does me good to see her so.

"What is it, Lucy?" I call when she storms into the salon, waggling a letter she has already opened.

"It was addressed to all of us," she says.

"And who is it from, loveen?" I take the gilded envelope from her and examine it.

"The Guggenheims, Peggy and Hazel."

"*Oh là là!*" Jim says. "The millionaire Jewesses writing to the poverty-stricken Irish Catholics. What can it mean?"

I slip a card out of the envelope and read it. "They've invited us to a party, Jim, all four of us, at Peggy and her husband's place near Notre Dame."

Lucia crouches beside my chair, rocking on her hunkers. "We have to go, Mamma," she says, her voice urgent. "*Everyone* will be there."

I look over at Jim. "Of course, Nora. Let you go and ogle the bohemian set and they shall stare in return."

"Sure, why would they want to look at me?" I pat my hair. "But do you not mean to come, too, Jim?" I ask, though I know he wouldn't relish such a party and my mind is already leaping ahead to what dress I'll wear and what outfit I can buy for Lucia, to cheer her and make her look fine.

"Nora, I fear the chitter-chatter of several Guggenheims along with Herr Kastor's girl, the divine Djuna, et cetera, would only addle this old brain." He taps his skull.

"They'll expect you, Jim. I'm sure it's you they want at their party, not me."

He shakes his head. "Nora, just let you and the children trip down to the Quartier Latin to drink champagne and admire Miss Peggy's paintings and let me sit here in peace with Biscuit the cat."

"And *Finnegans Wake*."

"*Exactement*."

MISS GUGGENHEIM'S FLAT IS GLORIOUS. I WOULDN'T LIKE TO live in it, there are too many geegaws about—nude African statues and garishly colored vases—and some of the artworks on the walls are a little grotesque, but there's a panache to the place, just as there is to Peggy herself. She's one of those women—like Helen Fleischman—who creates a feeling. It's because they've always been wealthy, I suppose, and they wear their riches, and glamour, tidily. Peggy's aura leaches into her surroundings, and her flat, even with all the furniture pushed back and the rugs taken up for dancing, is elegant and like a part of the woman herself.

Lucia hangs back by the salon wall, her mouth agape at the finery on the women.

"I thought we looked gorgeous leaving Robiac," she whispers to me.

I finesse the collar of her green satin dress. "You look beautiful, Lucy. Hold your head high." She bites her lip and stares at Hazel Guggenheim who's in a silver cap and white velvet sheath that clings to every bump and bone.

"Hazel has the body of a dancer," Lucia says. "Isn't she shockingly striking, Mamma?"

I gaze at Hazel; she looks to me like a mermaid got free of the waves. "Well, she's something all right." I place my hand to my daughter's back. "Come on, let's take a turn about the room, instead of standing here like mushrooms." We move around the walls, to look at Peggy's art collection. We peer at a painting that might be a leering mouth or could be the opening to a volcano. Our hostess joins us.

"Hullo, ladies," she says, putting her hands on our shoulders and we all three look at the painting.

"Is it a flower?" Lucy asks Peggy.

She laughs. "No, dear girl, it's a woman's sex." She puts her finger on the central pink oval in the painting and slides it up and down. "Don't you see?"

I blush and glance away—such a thing to have on the wall!—
but Lucia looks her full in the face and smiles. "Why, yes, I do see
it now."

Peggy stares at the picture. "I mean to buy one painting a day
for the rest of my life," she murmurs.

Isn't it well for you?, I think, but my eye is caught by Giorgio
arriving through the door with a gaggle of other young men,
Peggy's husband, Laurence, and Leon Fleischman among them;
I see Mrs. Fleischman straggling behind the group and cross the
floor to greet her.

"Mrs. Joyce," she says, shaking my hand and looking over my
shoulder. "Your husband is not with you?"

"Jim prefers to keep his own company tonight."

Mrs. Fleischman waves to our hostess, then takes my arm.
"Let's get some drinks." She steers me to the sideboard where she
helps herself, and me, to punch. "I'm surprised you came," she says,
waving her hand at the company, "so many young things."

I blush and wonder if I wasn't meant to accept the invitation,
if it was only a politeness to ask us. "Oh," I mutter, "Lucia wanted
very much to come. I, em, I want her to mix more, I suppose."

I feel foolish now, like a hag among nymphs. I startle when
Mrs. Fleischman shouts, "Hemingway!" and beckons the writer
toward us. His wife trots behind, looking as out of place as I now
feel; we smile at each other.

"No Joyce?" Ernest Hemingway says to me.

"Not tonight."

"Pity."

I sip my punch and look at my shoes, wishing that I was home
with Jim and Biscuit and the ticking clock, not facing hours as a
very square peg in a very round hole.

Hadley Hemingway slips in beside me. "Shall we commandeer that small sofa, Mrs. Joyce?" she says. I nod and follow her, relieved. We sit and Mrs. Hemingway tells me about her little boy, Bumby, and his fondness for bread dipped in sweetened milk. "I'm worried. He won't eat anything else just now."

"We used to call that 'goody' at home," I say and she smiles.

"Oh, how charming, I shall tell Bumby that. We'll call it goody from here on, too. Perhaps it's all right, as long as he eats something?"

"Don't worry, Mrs. Hemingway, their appetites change as they grow." I glance over at Georgie who is dancing cheek to cheek with Peggy. "Little boys are wonderful. And they love their mammas, don't they?"

"They sure do," she says, "and I'm mightily glad of it."

She's a big, healthy woman who looks like she'd be more at home up a mountain or chopping logs than sitting on Peggy's dainty purple sofa. I watch the lurching earnestness of the couples dancing; Lucia among them, clinging to one of the Irish boys who is part of this set; I narrow my eyes, wonder if he looks well-heeled or is just another hungry artist. Djuna Barnes holds Hazel Guggenheim like she'll never let her go and Ernest Hemingway is twirling a small dark woman like a top, though there's a waltz playing. I see Mrs. Fleischman let go of her husband and swing sideways into Georgie's arms, while Peggy goes to Leon; Laurence Vail is dancing alone, holding a *coupe* aloft as if expecting someone to fill it with champagne. They all look so natural and free; I watch them and wonder if I didn't squander my young years by hooking up so early with Jim. Might I not have had a little more fun before having babies and keeping a home and minding Jim and so on?

I turn to Mrs. Hemingway. "Ah, what are the pair of us doing here at all?"

She sighs. "Honestly, Mrs. Joyce, I'd rather be at home in bed with baby tucked beside me."

We clink glasses, listen to the burr of the gramophone, and watch the dancers swivel and sway around the floor in the warm candlelight.

UNIONS

❦

Paris
1925 AND 1926

M RS. FLEISCHMAN IS NOT AVAILABLE FOR OUTINGS SO MUCH
since her husband returned to New York; she's occupied
with little David no doubt, but Mrs. Nutting and I meet some afternoons and, in that way, I have womanly company. Today we meet
in Angelina's for tea and I'm brimful of contentment; Lucia slept
well—there was no wandering the floor or crying or fretting—
so we all got a good night.

"And where are the rest of the Irish tribe this fine day?" Mrs.
Nutting asks.

"Jim is writing his beloved book."

"Of course."

"And Lucy says she's bored and is sulking in her room." I
toss my eyes heavenward. "Georgie is out and about, probably at
the Scola Cantorum to take his lessons. Or running an errand for
Jim at Stratford-on-Odéon, as he calls Miss Beach's bookshop." I
frown; I think, now, that I didn't see Giorgio at all this morning.

"You mustn't treat Giorgio and Lucia like children, Mrs.
Joyce. They're adults, truly, and they need occupations, things to
keep them happily busy all day."

"But they *are* children," I say. "They're *my* children."

"All I mean is you need to find them something to do that will both occupy them well *and* keep them out of your hair." She plops a sugar lump into her cup. "At twenty and eighteen they need to do more than cling to their mamma and papà." She stirs her tea and arches an eyebrow. "You know this, dear."

"But Georgie sings, he takes classes, he has his wee job. And Lucia dances with her friend Kitten Neel and her troupe. That keeps them away for hours at a time. The children are not stuck to us, Mrs. Nutting, in spite of what you think." I bite into an éclair and let its sweetness fill my mouth before continuing. "My children are artists, like their father, they do things oddly."

Mrs. Nutting frowns and sips from her cup. "Mrs. Joyce, as you know, even artists must eat." I roll my eyes to indicate that I know that only too well. She leans toward me, her gossip face in full livery. "Have you heard who Peggy Guggenheim has taken up with?"

"Oh, tell me," I say, and she names some man I've never heard of.

"He's a painter," Mrs. Nutting says. "And you know Peggy was romancing Leon Fleischman, too, before he and Helen were together?"

I gasp. "Really? No, I never knew that." Mrs. Nutting always seems to know the deepest doings of everyone and she's never shy of passing them on.

"And Peggy was with Leon *while* he and Helen were together, too, it seems."

"Are you being serious?" These people's lives crisscross in such complicated ways, it makes mine and Jim's seem very old-fashioned altogether. "But Peggy's married to Laurence, what about him?"

"It all went on with Helen's and Laurence's approval, apparently."

"No!" I try to imagine having to share Jim with some other woman, with a friend. I try to imagine myself giving permission for such a thing. "I can't see how any of that would work, can you?" I grimace.

Mrs. Nutting shakes her head. "Oh, these young folk, they live differently from us." I nod.

"They certainly do." I relish hearing about the silliness of their lives, but feel relief that I'm too old and too ordinary to be caught up in any such madness.

"And you've heard all about poor Hadley Hemingway, I guess?" Mrs. Nutting says, creasing her brow.

"No, what's wrong with her? Is she all right?" I set down my cup the better to listen; I like Mrs. Hemingway, she always seems on the edge of things and a small bit bewildered.

"Well, that husband of hers has only gone and run off with Pauline Pfeiffer. Hadley's been left quite alone with her baby boy, while Ernest hares around Paris with that Pfeiffer woman. They have no shame!"

I sigh, thinking of poor Hadley Hemingway and her little Bumby, trying to get by alone. "I'm so sorry for Mrs. Hemingway, she's a decent woman, I've always been fond of her. Life will be harder for her now." I shake my head. "Wouldn't the men cripple your heart, Mrs. Nutting?" I tut.

Mrs. Nutting forks clafouti into her mouth and squeaks in appreciation. "Truly, the pastry chefs at Angelina's came down from the clouds." Mrs. Nutting talks on, musing over what Mrs. Hemingway will do now, whether she'll go home to Missouri or not; then she wonders about the effect the death of their father on the *Titanic* must have had on the Guggenheim girls—did it injure them, make them devil-may-care?—and I nod and half listen and just let her ramble on.

But the things Mrs. Nutting has said about Georgie and Lucy jink around inside my mind, distracting me: *Have* Jim and I prepared the children well enough to get on in life? Lucia, I suppose, will marry and if she does attach herself to a man, hopefully he'll be someone with money; that will make things softer for her and she needs that ease. But mightn't Georgie earn a living, wholly and properly? He hasn't warmed to clerking, much like his father. And perhaps his nerves are too jittery to make it on the stage as a tenor, as he hopes—he gets so addled before even the smallest of performances.

Well, no matter. They're our children and the four of us being together is the most important thing. When one of us is away, it always feels to me as if a side of the box is missing, or that there's a spillage that can't be mopped up—there's an out-of-placeness, an emptiness. We're better together, and jobs and occupations, and whatnot, only mean we'd be parted more. The children do enough, I'm sure, and we do our bit to help them and usher them along, the best we can.

Mrs. Nutting's voice comes as if from far way. "Mrs. Joyce. I say, Mrs. Joyce?"

"I'm sorry, my mind was maundering over this and that. What did you say, dear?"

"I asked if Giorgio is at home much these days." She sips her tea and raises her eyebrows. "And by these days you'll understand that I mean these *nights*."

I'm surprised by her question, but she's looking at me with eyes like a traveling rat's and I feel I must answer.

"Well, truly, Mrs. Nutting, I have to say that Georgie is being a bit mysterious lately. We barely see him. I think he's giving his all to his music, he very much wants to be a professional, it seems." I falter and Mrs. Nutting tortoises her mouth and pulls her head back. "What is it?" I reach out my hand, but she shakes her head.

"Do you see much of Helen Fleischman these days, Mrs. Joyce?"

"Mrs. Fleischman? No. I saw her at Peggy's party and she waved at me in Le Trianon the other evening, but we didn't speak. Why do you ask?"

"Would you consider her a woman with a steady life?"

I scratch my ear and frown. "Well, until you told me that about Peggy and Leon, I did think that, yes. Mrs. Fleischman always seems steady, with her husband and little David. She has plenty of money, of course. She comes across as settled, maybe a bit jumpy betimes, overly emotional perhaps." I recall her grabbing my hand when we watched Lucy dance, her tear-filled eyes.

Mrs. Nutting frowns. "Leon Fleischman is peculiarly absent though, yes? Returned to America recently. And for what?"

I stare at her. "How would I know, Mrs. Nutting? For work, I suppose. He has a job, unlike so many of that set."

"Mrs. Fleischman has a certain kind of ambition, Mrs. Joyce. She's a climber, a piggybacker, you know? Helen sits on people if she thinks it might get her ahead, do you see what I mean?" It's my turn to shake my head; this doesn't sound like the Mrs. F I know, the generous, laughing friend, the glamorous mother.

"Well, I wouldn't style her that way; she's been a lovely companion to me when I see her and she's so kind to Lucia."

"Hmmm," Mrs. Nutting says. She glances around and dips her head. "Mrs. Joyce, we are friends and I feel you should know what is going on." She sighs. "And what everyone from Montparnasse to Montmartre is whispering about."

"What?" A glut of panic makes a stew of my innards. "What are people whispering about?"

She sits up straighter and beads her eyes. "About Giorgio Joyce and Helen Fleischman."

MY HEART IS IN A HEAP AND I'VE TAKEN TO THE BED. TO THINK I had to be told by someone outside this house. Oh, my lovely son. I have Biscuit the cat with me for comfort and I try to hug and pet her, but she wriggles away and even that makes me forlorn. I make a last grab for puss and she hops to the floor, showing me the button of her behind as she saunters off.

"Away with you so, you scut," I shout. "Get me the hand mirror," I say to Jim, who's perched on the bed, and he fetches it for me. "Why oh why would Georgie not come and tell me himself? Why didn't he speak to us, Jim, instead of making himself fodder for the gossips?" I peer into the mirror and poke at my red, dried-out cheeks and my eyes that are puffed and slitty from weeping.

"They're like two pink macarons stuck to your face," Jim says.

I let out a sorry little laugh and tap at my eyelids with my cold fingers to try to reduce the swelling. My head is full of snot and I can hardly breathe from that and the heart-jerk of Mrs. Fleischman's betrayal.

"It's too deep a grief, Jim," I say, starting to cry again. "She's stolen him away from us."

"Now, now, Nora, let's talk to Giorgio and see what he has to say for himself."

"What can be said? She's thirty-one years of age and he's a lad not yet twenty. There's nothing right about that. It was a seduction. That's the word Mrs. Nutting used. She called Fleischman 'gusty' too. She told me all sorts." I moan. "Do you think we're to blame somehow, Jim? Is it something we did wrong in the rearing of Georgie?"

Jim shakes his head. "No, no, Gooseen. He's a grown man, responsible for himself." He pulls at his goatee. "If Giorgio was a heavy drinker, you might understand it better, you know, a drunken fall into her arms, for whatever reason. But it's clearly going on some time, unbeknownst to us. And to carry it on like this, to draw and stretch it out, as if it's important. As if it's *something*." He scratches his nose. "Nora, I always knew there were things afoot with Fleischman; I watched her, but I couldn't get to the nub of it. She's an ingratiator and you know I dislike them." He runs his hand through his hair. "But, somehow, I took to her anyway. A gusty girl, indeed."

"Girl?" I slap the bedspread. "She's a woman, Jim, an adult woman. A married woman. A *mother*."

"Yes, a mother to a son. Ah, has she no sense?"

"Has Giorgio none?" I fumble with Jim's fingers. "Mrs. Nutting told me that people are saying she realized she couldn't have *you*, so she took Georgie instead."

Jim snorts. "Well, that's a bear of a different color, is it not?"

"So you believe it?" I ask.

He fiddles with his dickie bow and pulls at his glasses. "No, Nora, I don't think I do. Helen Fleischman may be flighty and so forth, but I don't think she's casually cruel. I don't think she would befriend you and woo Georgie to try to get near me."

"But look at the Hemingways! That Pfeiffer woman set out to have Hadley's husband, apparently, and nothing was going to stop her. She was a friend to both Hadley and Mr. Hemingway beforehand. These Americans are like that, Jim. They're selfish beyond reason. They think of no one but themselves, of nothing but their own needs."

"Maybe Mrs. Nutting exaggerates, maybe she's just high on gossip. You said yourself she'd go up a hen's hole for news, the same woman."

I snort. "I did say that and I was certainly not happy to find out about Giorgio's antics from her, but isn't it better we *know* that we're being talked about all over Paris? Oh God." I agitate the sheet with my hands.

Jim kisses my forehead. "You're exciting yourself needlessly. Rest, Gooseen, and when Giorgio's home, let us see what he has to say."

I lie back. "Well, he'll be getting a clip around the ear from me, for starters."

"He will not, Nora," Jim says sternly. "He's a man with a man's rights. Remember that." I pout and put my head to the pillow and think I'll do what I please to my own son. Jim pets my head. "Does it matter so much, Gooseen? You and I are not married after all and plenty would consider that shameful."

"But no one *knows* about that, Jim! And we're as good as married after all these years, at least as far as other people are concerned. She lured him!" I struggle not to cry again. "I thought Giorgio had more sense. I thought Mrs. Fleischman had. I'm let down by them."

"I know you are, Nora, I know." He pulls the blanket up to my shoulder. "Sleep now, my pet." And he leaves me to rest as much as I'm able.

GEORGIE'S SKIN STRAINS ACROSS HIS CHEEKS AND HIS EYES ARE lit with an unfamiliar glow. He's fiddly, lighting a cigarette and stabbing it out after two puffs; his hands and legs jiggle though he's seated. Jim and I are on the sofa, opposite him.

"Did she force you into it?" I say.

Georgie grunts. "Don't be absurd, Mamma."

"She seduced you, though, didn't she?"

"Do you really believe that to be true?" Georgie laughs and I balk at the casual way he's treating me.

"Be civil now, son," Jim says.

I stare at Giorgio. "Helen Fleischman was *my* friend. And she's nearer my age than yours."

"Mother, I'm perfectly aware of Helen's age."

I pluck at my sleeve, enraged by his calm tone; I try to keep my head. "You'll have to give it up, Georgie. Everyone's talking about you. About us. It's not right or proper. Think of the cruelty you're doing. Not only is Mrs. Fleischman married, she's a mother."

"What does that matter? Helen is a woman in her own right. And she and Leon are free to do what they like. That's their arrangement, they believe in freedom."

I bristle. "I know all about their *arrangement*; it's no way for people to treat each other. It's a nonsense, in fact. They have a child, Giorgio. Where does all their *freedom* leave little David?" I light a cigarette and pull deep on it.

"The child has a nurse and is well cared for."

"A nurse?" I can't keep the jeer from my tone. "A child belongs with his mother."

"I was with you and we moved from place to place like tramps. David is loved and well looked after and has a home of his own. Don't worry your *bourgeoise* little head about him, Mamma."

"You cocky brat." I poke Jim in the arm. "Do you hear how he talks to me?" Jim holds up his hands as if to calm us, but it only angers me more. "Helen Fleischman is a bloodsucker and she'll spit you out before long, Georgie, mark me. Mrs. Nutting has told me about the carry on of her with Leon and the Guggenheims and the Lord knows who else. Do you think she won't do the same to you, Georgie? The woman will parade you about until she's tired of you and then she'll turn her back on you. She doesn't know the meaning of love. Or loyalty."

"You liked Helen well enough to spend hours and hours in

her company, Mamma, to eat with her and shop with her and take her advice." He leans toward me, his eyes like a mad dog's. "Helen and I are in love."

My heart bunches. "Says who?"

"What do you mean 'says who'?" Georgie rises and stands over me. "Say I! We both say it. We both mean it, Helen and I."

"But you're only a gossoon, Giorgio, a lad," I wail. "What would you know of love?"

"I know enough. And I'm the same age you were when you left Ireland with Babbo, am I not?"

I stand to face him. "You might be, but you haven't half the sense I had at twenty."

"Whatever you may think, Mamma, I'm a man and I can make my own choices."

I point at him. "She's not welcome here."

Georgie grimaces. "So be it."

Jim stands, too, and holds out his hands again. "Now, now, let's keep cool heads. We'll take our holiday in Normandy, as planned, and we can talk this through more rationally there. Away from Paris and its, eh, distractions."

Georgie steps back. "I'm not coming to Normandy, Papà. I'm staying here with Helen."

"To flaunt around with a married woman?" I cry. "To have every tittle-tattle in Paris gossiping about us?" I put my hands over my face. "God almighty, that Helen Fleischman is a disgrace."

"How dare you!" Georgie shouts, turns away, and marches out of the flat.

IT'S A TIME OF UNIONS AND DEPARTURES. GIORGIO SLIPS MORE and more away from us and into the arms of Mrs. Fleischman and there's nothing we can do about it. And Stannie writes to say he's engaged to be married to a girl of eighteen called Nelly, a student of his.

"More than twice her age," Jim says. "Lucky Stannie."

"Lucky Nelly," I say, making sure to drip bitterness into my voice. "She gets to wear a veil and trip up the aisle before God and man. More than I ever did."

Mammy writes to say my sister Annie has died and I'm not surprised for she was half-cadaver when I saw her last, worn out by life. She's buried and all by the time Mammy writes and I weep over her though, in truth, I barely knew her. Uncle Tommy is gone, too, and I feel a twist of sadness, but it passes swiftly; his blackthorn stick left a mark deeper than skin could ever show. Worst of all, though, is the news of Aunt Jo; Jim is devastated by her loss. Even though she said *Ulysses* was unfit to read—a wound to Jim—and though she was hurt by me not coming to see her in 1922 and was frosty with us since, at least we were *told* she was unwell and Jim wrote her a lovely letter that her family say she was truly grateful for. Why does God take people with such haste? And why is it always a shock to us here on earth when it lies before us all, the only sure thing?

Our woes are added to by a Mr. Samuel Roth in America who is serializing *Ulysses* in his magazine without permission from Jim or anyone, and Jim is gnawing his bones with anxiety over it.

"Roth is taking the bread from our mouths," he says, over and over.

"Or the wine from your glass," Lucia says and is met with a cool stare from her father.

But there is also joy. Eileen and her children come to us from Trieste and what luck to see them again. We put them up in a hotel near Square de Robiac and we eat and chatter and walk and laugh until our heads near fall off.

And Stannie comes, too, cheerful and healthy in appearance compared to Jim, it must be said. I meet him off the train, for Jim's glaucoma is flaring and his eye patch hinders his walking.

"Stannie, time is kind to you," I say, pulling him into my arms. He is a solid wedge to hold—I've always liked the bulky, strong feel of Stannie.

"As it is to you, Nora," he says, stepping back to smile at me. "Your hair," he says, touching the end of my bob, "very fetching."

"And you're to marry, Stannie."

He dips his head shyly. "I am and about time. To a lovely woman."

My heart jolts when he says "woman" for his Nelly is the same age as Lucia and I think of her only as a girl.

"Well, bless you both," I say. "Perhaps Jim will make an honest woman of *me* someday." I tuck my arm through his.

"How is he?" Stannie asks as we walk the platform.

"The eyes are murder; ten operations later and it's worse they get."

"But how is he in himself?"

"He's lord and master, Stannie, as always. Has everyone running about after him, organizing his life and minding him, Miss Beach and Miss Weaver included. You know how he is, the rest of us were only put here for Jim's use. If God himself came down from the sky, Jim would find something for him to do."

Stannie laughs. "It does me good to see you, Nora."

I pat his arm. "And it'll do Jim good to see *you*."

WE TAKE STANNIE TO LES TRIANONS AND CAFÉ FRANCIS AND the Closerie des Lilas, with Jim lashing the money around so Stannie can see. Jim is still a boy, with a boy's instincts, when all is said. McAlmon, Miss Beach, Miss Monnier, and the Nuttings are all in attendance and others come and go off the edges of the group, to greet Jim and me, and to meet the famous man's brother. Jim sits like a regent, rings flashing, cane by his knee, and receives them all, much more cordially than he normally would. But all the time his one good eye is locked onto Stannie, wanting him to admire, to be impressed; his brother, of course, will not rise to it, refuses to satisfy Jim. Stannie sits with his glass of Perrier and he chats quietly with me of young Nelly and of our old friends and neighbors in Trieste and of his teaching position. Night after night Jim gets drunk and flappy tongued; he talks fondly of Pappie; he reminisces about raucous nights in Trieste; he sings ballads, even in the cafés. By the end of each evening, Stannie can't smother his disdain.

"*Plus ça change*," Stannie says, with a theatrical sigh, one night in the taxi on the way back to Square de Robiac.

"Meaning what exactly, brother?"

"You always did love lackeys, Jim. What a wolf-pack of sycophants you've gathered around you."

"What do you want me to say? People flock to greatness, Stanislaus."

Stannie snorts. "They flock to cash. To Miss Weaver's horde."

Tension flurries between them as sure as if an electrical storm is gathering.

Jim turns to Stannie. "My cash has benefited you, brother."

Stannie snorts. "You have a selective memory, Jim."

"Right," I say, "that's enough from the pair of you. I won't have you vying and squabbling like a pair of gossoons. It's rare enough you see each other. Behave like men!"

And like two bold children they turn their faces away from each other and don't speak again.

CIRCLES

❧

Paris

1927 AND 1928

I ORDER TINY *TARTES TATIN* AND SOME SWIRLY MONT BLANCS from Angelina's and their apple and chestnutty smells fill my nose when I transfer them from the boxes to my silver-rimmed serving plates. Our young Irish friend, Tom McGreevy from Kerry, is coming to tea; he's an English teacher and he and Jim love to talk about the classroom, and, in some ways, Tom slips into the space left by Giorgio who's so rarely home—it's pleasant for me to have a young man to feed and fuss over. And it's lovely, indeed, to be able to keep a good table for guests; we're a long way from Jim and I sharing Georgie's sugar mouse in Rome and it makes me grateful for the money that's coming in now, for the ease it brings.

Tom McGreevy is able to discuss the extracts of *Work in Progress* that he's read in the Jolases' *transition* magazine and that pleases Jim. Jim talks of it as a river-book, a night-book, a square wheel, indeed, and Tom nods along and offers his own thoughts. For me *Work in Progress* is a word-stew and, though Jim explains it to me in detail, I have a job following along, though the whole thing has a sweet, melodious sound.

I said to Miss Beach in her shop yesterday, "Is Jim making things hard for himself with this curious fiction he's writing?"

She took my hands. "Don't fret, Mrs. Joyce." She winked. "Don't ever fret about the work."

I can fathom bits of *Work in Progress*, despite its difficult nature, and I detect a shining beauty in the mad soup of its words and its lovely Anna Livia and, yes, at least there's that.

Our circle moves and changes and now we see less of McAlmon, Power, and Miss Beach, and more of Tom, Maria and Eugene Jolas, and Stuart Gilbert and his lovely wife, Moune. Square de Robiac has settled us and my heart lies gentle in my chest most days for I know I won't be packing my little bag to scuttle off to some new digs. There are only two flies in the amber of my happiness: that Georgie persists in gadding about with Mrs. Fleischman who is still married, and that Lucia, to my mind, grows queerer in her ways by the day. Some mornings she's prinked and neat in her appearance and present, others she refuses to get out of bed and spends her day in a slovenly heap in her room. Today, thankfully, she's gone to rehearse with her friend Kitten and the dance troupe.

The business with Georgie presses deep into me: Mrs. Fleischman is not welcome at Robiac, and when I see her on the street, I turn my head away. It's not right for a married woman to cavort freely with another man, particularly one so young and particularly the son of her friend. My gut catches when I think too much on what they might be doing together, in her rue Huysmans flat, in bed, and so forth; the idea of her hands, and that prissy mouth, all over Georgie's skin makes me want to be sick. Oh, how can he do this to us? How can *she*? Helen Fleischman is a thistle, rooted into the middle of my family, and I want her cut down and gone.

I OFFER A PLATE PILED WITH CAKES TO TOM MCGREEVY.

"Eat up now," I say, "you could do with meat on your frame, dear."

He takes a Mont Blanc and balances his plate on his knee. "My mother says the same thing, Mrs. Joyce."

"There now, I'm your Paris mammy." I smile with satisfaction.

"Watch she doesn't follow you home to rue d'Ulm, McGreevy, and start ironing your collars and washing your socks," Jim says.

I hand Tom a linen napkin and roll my eyes. "That's enough from you, James Joyce."

Tom brings fresh news of Ireland and Jim makes little notes when he speaks, which Tom doesn't seem to mind. They talk of the League of Nations and Yeats's Nobel Prize and the Constitution of the Free State; they go over the deaths of Arthur Griffith and Michael Collins, heroes now that they died for Ireland.

"Did you ever know a Vincent Cosgrave in Dublin?" Jim asks.

"No," Tom says.

"Ah, it's a sorry business about Cosgrave. He was an old pal of mine; I styled him as Lynch in *Portrait* and *Ulysses*."

"Wasn't Lynch the one who wrote his name on the backside of a statue of Venus?" Tom turns to me. "Saving your presence, Mrs. Joyce."

"No need to save me, Tom. Do you think I haven't heard all sorts from himself?"

"That's Lynch all right, penciling his moniker on Venus's arse." Jim smiles. "Well, the chap he's based on, this Cosgrave, he came to a bad end."

"I'm sad to hear it."

Jim lights a cigarette and my stomach clenches for I know what's coming next. "Cosgrave tried to steal Nora away from me, you see."

"Oh?" Tom glances at me.

I shake my head. "It wasn't quite like that."

Jim ignores me. "Cosgrave drowned in London last year.

Never made anything of himself. I predicted his death in *Ulysses*, you know." Jim pulls long on his cigarette. "Maybe that's what happens to those who betray others—they meet a bad end."

Jim and his band of betrayers; he never tires of trotting them out, no matter the truth or not of their misdeeds. And poor Cosgrave, besides; drowning is a sorry death for anyone.

Tom, being a polite young man and sensing my discomfort, steers the conversation elsewhere. He asks if he might bring an Irish friend, new to Paris, to meet us.

"Of course you may, Tom," I say.

Jim asks who it is.

"A fellow by the name of Samuel Beckett."

"A Protestant name."

"A Protestant man. Interested in literature. Quiet but capable. I think you'll like him."

I pour more tea for them. "Bring your Mr. Beckett here any time you please, Tom."

JIM'S EYES WEEP AND WATER, THEY BURN AND ITCH. SOME DAYS they're so bad he can't get up. He finds the hours in the darkened room a severe trial for he can neither read nor scratch down words. I find them a trial myself for he wants me beside him and it means I can go nowhere and do nothing, save dance around himself with teapot and ashtray and newspaper. Because of that, it's a joy always to see young Mr. Beckett at my door. He has the patience of four saints and he sits with Jim and takes notes for him earnestly and they've become very fond of each other. Beckett is very willing to help Jim out with his papers and any other small tasks that come up.

However, once too often, I've noticed Lucia stare at Mr. Beckett as if she'd like to swallow him whole. She lets him into the flat when he calls—always seeming to know when it's him at the door—and she all but takes him by the paw to Jim, though he knows the way. I've seen Lucia hover her hand at Beckett's back, keen it seems, to touch him, to feel the heat off him. And the odd time he joins me for a cup of tea after being with Jim, Lucia sits with us and is either deathly quiet or foolishly raucous. Beckett's not an unattractive young man with his thatch of good hair and those plump lips; he's a little like a young Jim, truth be told, with his roundy glasses and serious face. Today Lucy pleads with Beckett to attend her next dance spectacle in the Bal Bullier.

"Oh, do come, Sam," she says. "I'm to wear a dazzling silver fish costume." She shimmers her hands over her body. "It clings."

"I will try to attend," Beckett says, his bright eyes sliding to the floor.

"Don't just try," Lucy cajoles, "come see me dance. I'm really rather good, you know."

Young Beckett smiles shyly. "Well then, if you're rather good, I shall have to come."

Lucia laughs and claps her hands. "There, I knew I could tempt you, Sam, I *knew* it."

Beckett's teacup rattles on its saucer and he looks as if he'd like the window to open and a great hand to come and pluck him out of our salon. I'm irritated with Lucia for her pushy spirits today and for calling him Sam when he's only ever been Mr. Beckett in our home but, I suppose, they're near in age and the young people now all act with deep familiarity toward everyone they meet.

"Let me pour more tea for you, Mr. Beckett," I say.

Lucy leaps up. "I'll do it."

She flirts like an American while she fills his cup, all wide eyes and silly grins, and it's all I can do to stop myself from pinching her. Mr. Beckett smiles in her direction, but he won't look at her;

it's clear he knows what's afoot and is simply not interested. Lucy is a girl who fixates on things and isn't content until she's exhausted all her energy on them. But Mr. Beckett is no man to get caught in her fanciful net—he hasn't the temperament to keep up with her and, besides, he's penniless. If Lucia is to attach herself to someone, let him at least have a healthy pot of cash, that's what Jim and I think. She won't be able to navigate the world as we have; she's too moody and unsettled in herself, too like a girl. And, for her own sake, I don't want her nursing fancies for men who have no interest in her—she'll be crushed when nothing comes of it and I'll have to mind her and cosset her back to good humor.

"And how's your work with my husband going along, Mr. Beckett?" I ask.

Lucia groans. "Sam doesn't want to talk about Babbo and writing now, Mamma. Let him alone."

Beckett shifts his long body in the chair. "It goes well, Mrs. Joyce; I enjoy his company immensely. Your husband has a startling mind."

Lucy writhes and flings up her arms. "And his daughter has a startling body! Isn't that so, Sam?"

"Lucia!" The impudence! "Have manners." Lucy grimaces and burrows back into her seat. I sip my tea and glance at Beckett. "And Jim tells me you write too?"

He blushes. "Oh, just this and that. I'm trying. I'm waiting, more than anything."

"Waiting?" I ask. "For what?"

He pauses for a long moment. "To be inspired, I suppose."

Lucia coughs to remind us of her presence and both Beckett and I ignore her, preferring to drink our tea until it's gone and Mr. Beckett can be released to his day.

C

Paris
1928 AND 1929

I'M DOWN WITH THE ANTS. JIM TRIES TO COAX ME BACK TO GOOD form and energy with little bags of buttery toffees and cream sweets, but none of them tempt me. He gets a brain-ache when I'm the one lying in bed, unavailable to him; he becomes a useless clod, mithering about like a dog who can't remember where he's buried his best bone.

"Won't you get up and sit on the sofa in the salon, Nora? I have a box of Turkish delight on the side table. You could settle yourself there and all you'd have to do is dip your hand into the box and eat."

"Ah, Jim, I'm useless as a worn rag. I'm neither able nor willing to lift my hand to anything." I wave across the bed. "I don't even want to go from here to the salon."

He nods miserably. "You'll be back on your feet soon, I suppose."

"I will, faith."

But I can't truly say what's the matter with me, it's a bit of tenderness and pain down below, but also a general feeling of sorrow. We had such terrible news from Stannie—Eileen's husband, Frank, killed himself when it was uncovered that he was embezzling from the bank he worked at, leaving her and the three children alone with only Stannie to help them. God love them all.

And the report of Stannie's wedding day knocked me, too, I suppose, though I feel sorry that he's had to be patient, waiting ages longer than he intended to be wed, for his money has been eaten up with the support of Eileen and her family. In truth I should be nothing but happy for him and his Nelly but, I don't know, their bridal picture leaves an ache in my jaw and makes my eyes tired besides; I feel bleak from top to toe to know that they enjoyed a blissful day and it looks like I never will. And right at the same time as the wedding photograph came, I began to get this weariness all over, I feel like a big auld slug lying in my bed, one that can't move an inch. Jim must've complained about my idleness and absenteeism to Miss Weaver in a letter, for she telephones the flat and testily tells him to take care of me properly.

"Saint Harriet nearly took my head off, Nora," he says forlornly. "She insists that we fetch a doctor or take you to the hospital."

"Well, maybe she's right," I say, stretching my aching body under the sheet. I'm not one for doctors, they scare me a little and I prefer to just muddle through, but after weeks of lying around like a sack of spuds, resisting the idea that I'm sick, if Miss Weaver thinks I *should* see someone, then maybe I will. Jim dispatches Lucia to ask Miss Beach to whom I should go.

THE AMERICAN HOSPITAL IN NEUILLY-SUR-SEINE IS A CLEAN and comfortable place and, though the operation on the tumor they found on my womb has made me sore, and the radium treatment is unpleasant, I like it here. I'd like it better, though, if Jim would go back to the flat and let me alone. He insists on sleeping on a cot in the room with me and his jig-jig and sigh-sigh all through the night drive me mad.

"Jim, will you go home out of that? I can't get a moment's rest with you. Let me recover in peace, why won't you?" He startles every time I say it as if he doesn't know well that his presence is more of a disturbance than a help to me.

"No, no," he says, "I have to stay, I have to keep an eye on you. Make sure you're being treated properly."

"But what about Lucia? She shouldn't be left alone, the Lord only knows what she's getting up to. She could have callers, you know, I wouldn't put it past her. Men. She might try to seduce Samuel Beckett while she has the place to herself." Jim begins to examine his fingers and turn his rings and he won't look at me. I stare hard at the top of his head. "Jim? What are you hiding? Lucia is at Robiac, isn't she?"

"Well…"

"Where is Lucia, Jim Joyce?"

"It's just that it all happened so fast, Gooseen, you being dragged in here and the operation and everything. I couldn't leave her alone."

I lean down to him. "Where is Lucy, Jim?"

"She's with her brother."

"At Square de Robiac?"

He grimaces. "No, at rue Huysmans."

I'm stung. "With Helen Fleischman?" I throw my hands up. "For God's sake, Jim, that's the last place I want her to be! What good can come of Lucia looking at the pair of them together, acting like man and wife?" I smack the coverlet with my palm. "Oh, what were you thinking?"

"I wasn't really thinking, Nora, I was reacting. And anyway,

Lucia already knows that Giorgio and Helen are together. What harm?"

"What harm? It's a bad example to her, Jim, that's the harm. And seeing them living like that will give her ideas about what's acceptable and what's not."

"But *we're* not married, Nora, not in any conventional way, at least, and that doesn't give her ideas."

I grit my teeth. "That's because she doesn't *know*, Jim. Neither of the children know." Again he refuses to raise his head to me. "James Joyce, why won't you meet my eye?" I clamp my hand over my mouth. "For the love of God, you haven't told Lucia, have you?" He winces. "Oh, sweet suffering Jesus, you have told her. I'll strangle you! But tell me that you haven't told Georgie? Please, tell me that."

He spreads his hands and glances at me. "It sort of emerged, in the palaver of trying to organize you to hospital and organize Lucia, too."

I groan. "How? How? Things don't just emerge, Jim. Just tell me *now* that Mrs. Fleischman doesn't know." He hangs his head and I have to lock my hands together for fear I'll trounce the head off him. "I'm bloody well furious with you, James Joyce. Furious!"

"I'm sorry, Nora, I was agitated and babbling. I didn't mean to say it at all." He holds his hand to his mouth. "It popped out."

"I'll give you popped out! I'll swing for you!" I lie back and clamp my hands across my chest. "God almighty, give me strength." Jim is silent. "We keep it quiet all these years and now we'll be laughed at all over Paris. The children will tell people; Lucia will, she's a blabberer. We'll be shamed. We'll be seen as hypocrites, because we are!" I moan, and my thoughts clatter and churn. The priest won't let me across the threshold of the church when I want to light a candle or just sit in peace. What if word gets back to Mammy? I'm raging with Jim, I can't believe he'd release our private life to the children like that, without even asking me if it was all right. And to Helen Fleischman, too! "Have you nothing more to say to me, James Joyce? Oh, that woman will be sniggering up her sleeve at me. The whole city will be nattering about us again. How could you, Jim? Oh God, oh God, I feel sick, call the doctor for me."

Jim scrambles out of his cot, but I pull the call bell before he can reach the door because I don't want that man doing a thing for me after this.

I'M BACK IN THE HOSPITAL AFTER A FEW MONTHS' GRACE AND THE doctor now says the whole lot has to come out, the precious bag that grew my darling children.

"It's the only way you'll get rid of the cancer completely," Doctor Fontaine says.

I trust in her; she's more than straight with me, woman to woman. I'm glad now that Jim is by me to hold my hand, for I'm afraid of the knife, but glad, too, it's not some decrepit old sawbones who'll perform the operation, but lovely young Doctor Fontaine.

Georgie has been around more—worried, I suppose, that his mamma is near her end. And with Mrs. Fleischman's—Helen's—French divorce now final, we've had to accept her help with Lucia with some grace. When I observe them, it seems to me that Helen and Georgie have something solid after all, there seems to be real affection between them, a sort of closed-in guarding of each other that I recognize from Jim and me. She touches him at odd moments; he holds her hand in company. And that they are still together after all this time says something; there has been no waning of their regard for each other. So, it seems, we must accept them and carry on.

Jim takes a separate room in the hospital this time and there he receives young Beckett and other friends and they talk books and smoke and I'm left in peace, mostly. Sometimes, Jim tells me, he's so inflamed with worry about me and my recovery that he walks to the chapel down the street and sits there in the silent dark and talks to God. I tease him, but I know he's ragged with concern when he resorts to such things for comfort and it pleases me to imagine him in a pew, smelling the sweet smoke from the thurible, and bowing his head before our Lord.

THE FLAT SPARKLES—EVEN THE WINDOWS SHINE—AND THE homely reek of beeswax hangs in the air; narcissi stand in every jug and vase around the salon, brightening the place like the sun. There's a new tea set with a deep pink rose pattern and cakes from Richaud's on the plates. Giorgio, Lucia, and Helen Fleischman stand in a little line to welcome me, as formally as if I were a queen returning from a world tour. Jim guides me into the room and a beautiful calm descends on me to be home at last; even Helen being here doesn't disturb my happiness in any way. I look around at the freshness of the scene before me, the color of it, after the plain white walls of the hospital, and my eyes fill.

"Thank you," I whisper.

Georgie steps forward. "Helen's doing, Mamma. She picked the tea set, too."

Helen flaps her hand. "It was nothing, my pleasure."

"I chose the flowers," Lucia says.

I kiss them each in turn, squeezing Helen's hand; if she must be here, I will be kind, and at least she's making large efforts to please me. Her attention to my comfort and happiness honors Georgie and I certainly can't and won't argue with that.

LUCIA DANCES IN A COMPETITION AT THE BAL BULLIER AND WE'RE all in attendance, McGreevy and Beckett, too, and I'm peppering, worried she'll make a wrong move, or decide not to dance at all. She's been muttering about not wanting to take part, saying she's not good enough. But onstage she comes, in her scaly cap and the costume that shimmers and slides across her body like a silver skin and, under the lights, she's a mesmerizing sight.

"Oh," I say, "oh!" when her arms contort and she's a strip of lightning moving across the stage, bending and leaping.

"I'm disgracefully proud of her," I whisper to Jim.

He nods furiously. "As am I."

Every time Lucia's leg rises high or she bends backward, easy as elastic, our little group leans forward as if we're all on strings that are attached to my daughter, to her magical, curving body, to her grace. On she goes around the stage, now a trout, quicksilvering through water, now a bird, flitting through the air. To watch her is to be lifted outside of your own body and to become the light, animal beam that is Lucia streaking across the stage.

"*Brava!*" we call when she takes her bow, and my stomach grips into a nervy knot waiting for the results.

"Lucia will surely take the prize," Mr. Beckett says and he's smiling, which is something he doesn't do much, and it pleases me that he's as charmed by Lucy's dancing as we are.

Lucia doesn't win.

The crowd murmurs then chants, "*L'Irlandaise! L'Irlandaise!*"

Jim stands and holds his hand to his ear and shrugs at the row of judges. They shrug in return. "Do you hear what they chant?" he calls, rousing the hecklers to call louder.

"The result is final," the head judge shouts and Jim turns his back on him.

Lucia joins us at our table, stripped now of her silver shift and cap. Her face is a portrait of misery and I'm worried she might cry and rage.

I clutch her hand. "I'm sorry, my darling, you deserved to win, you astonish us all with your gracefulness."

"Hush, Mamma," she whispers, glancing at Samuel Beckett with a disturbed set to her face.

Beckett doesn't raise his eyes to her and she gazes at him mournfully. He lowers the dregs of his wine in one draft and stands in a hurry, almost knocking over his chair.

"Good night to you all," he says, bowing first to me, then to Jim and the wider company, and leaving Lucy with her mouth hung open and no good-bye at all. I want to go after the man and box his ears.

Bloomsday

❧

Paris
1929

THE SIXTEENTH OF JUNE AND WE'RE ON A HIRED OMNIBUS TO Les Vaux-de-Cernay, a village near Versailles, with family, friends, and journalists, headed for the Hôtel Léopold to celebrate the French translation of *Ulysses* and the twenty-fifth anniversary of the novel's events. Miss Beach and Miss Monnier have taken it upon themselves to organize the outing, which they've christened *Déjeuner Ulysse*, and they may well regret the whole caper for Beckett and McGreevy, normally rather serene and usually very mannerly, have decided today to jabber wildly and sing endless old songs like a pair of escaped lunatics.

As soon as we're seated at the table in the Léopold, they begin to funnel wine down their throats and I poke Jim so that he sees what they're doing and will castigate them.

"*Way hay and up she rises*," sings Beckett, knocking his glass to McGreevy's, "*early in the morning.*"

McGreevy points at Beckett, trying to focus on his face, which is hard because he's laughing so much. "*Shave his belly with a rusty razor*," he roars and snorts, slapping Beckett on the shoulder.

Jim sits dumb as an oyster.

"Say something, Jim," I hiss. "Scold them."

He shakes his head and I'm too aware of the journalists sitting nearby to say anything myself, though I stare at the pair continually to show my disapproval. Lucia laughs like an imbecile when Beckett slides off his chair, and she runs to help him up, whispering something into his ear while she settles him in his seat once again.

"Lucy, Lucille, Lucinda, Lucia Anna," he says. "Little ray of light." He leers at her and blinks and she all but swoons for she finds it so hard to catch Beckett's eye when he's sober. I wish he wouldn't come after her now, drunk, for Lucia will think he's being sincere and it'll raise her hopes.

"You're in rare form today, Sam," she says.

"Indeed and he is," I say and Lucy reluctantly comes back to sit beside me.

"Beckett is drunk as a lord and McGreevy is no better," I whisper to Jim. "They're making bloody eejits of themselves; they must have been drinking all morning in Paris."

"Lucky them," Jim says. He stares ahead and eats nothing. He refuses to speechify when asked by Miss Monnier and drinks wine until it nearly pours out of his eyes. I grimace an apology to Miss Beach and her friend and try to keep one eye on Beckett, in case he upsets Lucia.

"You've had enough," I hiss at Jim, but he waves me away and lowers more.

"It's my day, Nora. It is, in fact, Mister Bloom's day." He holds up his glass. "To Bloomsday." He hiccups.

"Well, Jim, from now on, you can go to these literary events alone if this waste of hours is all I can expect." I slug my wine, which tastes like unripe peaches and push away the glass.

In the bus on the way home, Beckett and McGreevy continue to sing songs designed to aggravate such as "The Sash My Father Wore" and "Erin Go Bragh." I make sure that Lucy sits nowhere near them, but they upset everyone's peace with their high old time and we have to stop at a café to let them use the WC. The omnibus idles outside for ten minutes or more.

Miss Monnier shouts, "Let's leave them behind."

"Driver, go on," Monsieur Valéry calls. "We're all in agreement here. Leave them!"

I look around and, catching Georgie's eye, I toss my head toward the café. He and Helen get off the bus in search of the missing Irishmen and find them in the café, a bottle of wine open between them. Stern words are exchanged and Georgie and Helen return to the bus, shaking their heads.

"Drive on," Helen says.

The driver looks at my son. "Do what she says, man," he says.

Jim starts to giggle and he waves at the retreating café. "Farewell, Beckett! Farewell, McGreevy, ingloriously abandoned by our wagonette in a wayside café. Oh, to be young and free!" He stands up, waving vigorously, and encourages all around him to do the same. I pull him down.

"For shame, Jim."

"Happy Bloomsday, Nora," he says and settles his head on my shoulder.

WE SPEND THE REST OF THE SUMMER IN LONDON AND TORQUAY, with the children and Helen, and the Gilberts, too. Mr. Gilbert is writing a book about *Ulysses* and he and Jim confer daily, and Helen helps them out, too, note-taking and so forth. Giorgio disappears for hours on end while Helen works with his father. On his return this morning, he joins me in the glass room of the hotel that overlooks the sea, sitting heavily into the wicker seat beside mine. He closes his eyes, throws his head back, and sighs. The sweet, oily smell of cognac hangs between us.

"Have you been drinking, Georgie?" I ask.

"I'm a man, Mamma."

I turn my face away, disappointed in him, and surprised, for he's disdained drink up to now. I've noticed, too, that he eats less and less every time we dine.

"Are you turning into your father?" I ask.

Giorgio lights a cigarette. "What if I am?"

"I thought you'd more sense than that."

Georgie shrugs, but I can see a pinch of pain around his eyes; I'm sorry to hurt him but one drinker is enough in any family.

WE ALL GO TO THE RUSSIAN BALLET AND LUCIA IS SAD AND downhearted afterward.

"It's so enormous, so serious, so vast," she says. "It makes what I do with Kitten and the troupe seem juvenile. I'll never dance like those Russians."

"But that's classical work, Lucia," her father says. "You're a modernist. Like me." This cheers her and she smiles at Jim, the only one she has time for anymore it seems; I can barely raise a civil word from her and her monkeyish grin is like a memory only.

I like England enormously; it doesn't have the false friend feeling of Ireland or the snootiness of Paris.

"Can we try London out, Jim, as our home?" I ask often. "Come for a while and see how we get on?"

"Soon, soon," he says.

Which really means that he wants to get *Finnegans* done in Paris, before he'll go anywhere else and I have to bide my time, as always.

LUCIA SITS IN THE SALON AT SQUARE DE ROBIAC, LOOKING LIKE the kind of woman you'd see under a bridge. Yesterday, against my advice, she took Samuel Beckett to lunch at Le Perraudin and went straight to her room on her return, slamming the door mightily behind her and going to bed, though it was barely four o'clock. I got up from where I was reading the newspaper and tried to talk to her through her door, but she refused to answer.

Today I'm minding Helen's son, David, for his nurse has a day off, and Helen is taking dictation from Jim, whose eyes are weeping so badly that he can't write. Little David is solemn but sweet-natured and he stays in the corner by the window, reading through some old children's books from when our own were small. I sit opposite Lucia, taking in her mussed hair and disheveled appearance and the general unease that reeks from her.

"Well, what happened with Beckett? Tell me."

She clenches her fists. "He turned up to our lunch with a friend. Can you credit it, Mamma?"

"And you were vastly disappointed because you wanted him alone."

"Naturally, Mamma. Why else did I ask him? Why else did he agree to meet me?" She tuts and knots a strand of hair around her finger. "Immediately I couldn't eat. The fish I'd ordered wouldn't move out of my mouth and down my throat. After fifteen minutes of not eating, and horrid silence between us all, I jumped up and left the two of them there. I walked through the Jardin du Luxembourg and all the way home. Sam didn't even call out my name as I left the restaurant, never mind come after me."

"Beckett should have told you he meant to bring a friend to lunch, that would've been mannerly."

"He's cruel to me."

"Well, unless there's some understanding between you, Beckett can do as he pleases, I suppose."

"Mamma, you're meant to be for me, not him!" Her voice is

sharp and little David stops reading and glances over at us; I smile to reassure him.

I speak in a whisper. "I'm not *for* Beckett, Lucy, I just don't want you wasting your time if he's not interested in forming an attachment and, so far, I don't see that he has shown an interest." She lies down on the sofa and I bristle. "You needn't think you're going to loll around here all day like the queen of the Nile. Wash yourself, Lucy, for starters," I say.

She shrugs. "For what? For whom?"

"For yourself. For me. For little David over there." Her hair is poking about her head like a wire brush. "Fix your hair."

"Nobody cares if my hair is neat or not."

"I care. Babbo cares."

"Samuel Beckett clearly cares not at all."

I ignore this. "Your friend Kitten, no doubt, cares. Your dance teacher surely cares."

Lucia scowls. "Kitten, Kitten, Kitten. Look how lovely she is. See how well she moves. Don't all the men love pretty little Kitty. That's all anyone ever says to me. See how Kitten's eyes are straight and perfect. Unlike mine."

"Stop being such a raspeen, Lucia; I've never compared you to your friend before."

"It's not just you," Lucy says, scowling.

"Put a brush through your hair, that's all I'm saying. Or do you want to look like an urchin and shame yourself and all of us?"

"Shame? You know a lot about that, Mamma," she spits.

"How dare you!"

She hops up, marches to her room, and comes back with her brush, which she tears through her hair as if she means to drag every blade out of her head. David comes to sit by me and he stares at Lucia who begins to glare back in a wild, devilish way.

"What do you want, child?" Lucia says. "Speak!"

"Why," David asks, "if you're talking to me, are you looking over there?" He points to the corner of the room.

Lucia gasps. "You see, Mamma! Even a ten-year-old can see that my stupid eye is wayward and *wrong*!" She jumps up and storms into her bedroom.

David pouts. "Lucia never looks straight at me, that's all I mean."

"I know, pet," I say, "that's because she has a turn in her eye. She was born with it." I sigh. "And she doesn't like it much."

"Does it hurt?"

"No, loveen, it doesn't. Don't worry about it. Don't worry about Lucia at all," I say, but meanwhile my own heart is cross-hatched with distress. I hardly know what to do with Lucy, or what to say to her, most days.

LUCIA WANTS AN OPERATION TO FIX HER EYE.

"I'll never find a husband with this stupid squint." She glares into her hand mirror, begins to examine the scar on her chin—a tiny comma—and says it mars her looks even more. "Was I dropped as a baby?" she asks.

"No, you were not," I tell her.

"Did a dog attack me?"

"Never."

"Who will want me?" she says, poking her chin and lifting her eyelid with one finger.

"You are beautiful, Lucia," Jim says.

"Am I as beautiful as Napoleon's Joséphine, Babbo? As pretty as Mrs. Lita Chaplin?" She lifts her mirror again and stares into it.

"You are Mademoiselle Lucia Joyce, a rare beauty in her

own right," Jim says. "Why are you comparing yourself to those women?"

"I want to be as fetching as the wives of my heroes. What's wrong with that?" she shouts.

Jim looks over Lucia's head at me and raises his eyebrows.

Lucia feels left out when Giorgio sings at a concert.

Lucia has an eye operation that makes little difference to how she looks.

Lucia says she no longer wants to be part of her dance troupe.

Lucia says she doesn't want to dance.

Lucia gives up dancing.

Lucia cries for a month.

"Who is there for me?" is her constant wail. "Who in the world is there just for *me*?"

WEDDINGS

༄

Paris and London
1930 AND 1931

THE CHURCH WALLS TWINKLE WITH GOLD AND BLUE MOSAICS; I admire their pleasing pattern and allow my thoughts to unravel. I come here to pray and let my mind boil over one thing and another and it helps me to be out of the flat, to light a candle for the people I love, and to sit in the cool quiet for an hour. Today my mind is a broth of thoughts. I think about Samuel Beckett whom we've banned from visiting our home, for his slighting of Lucia. I think about how Jim misses his help. I think about Pappie, who writes to plead with Jim to come home and see him one last time; Pappie says he's leaving all he owns to Jim, a fact that makes us both laugh as the man has nothing. I think about the Irish tenor Frank Sullivan who Jim is determined to make a star of and how this harms our own dear Georgie. If Jim wasn't so busy lauding and boosting Sullivan, maybe Georgie's singing career might rise?

But mostly I think of Lucia and whether she's normal or not. I believe, more than ever, that there's something not quite right with her. It's not just the slovenliness and the bad humor and the obsessing over her looks, or over the slippery Mr. Beckett, it's as if there's something missing inside her. She's vacant when she should be present and shouty when she should be silent; she can't seem to stick to anything or discover what makes her happy. And, lately, we've had to scold her for launching herself at any man who glances her way—there was ugliness with an American sculptor she attached herself to who was not only married, he was unkind and, naturally, he dropped her with no explanation. A repeat of the Beckett incident in many ways. My poor Lucia, she will pick the wrong men to go about with, then she collapses when they don't want her. She gives herself freely, then can't understand her own pain. My daughter neither knows who she is nor cares to find out.

I haul myself out of the pew, go to the votive stand, and light a candle for my lovely, lost Lucy, my little star. I watch the flame bend and flicker, and I wonder if it's the rearing we gave Lucia that has made her so contrary, or if it's something that was already in her when she grew inside me. We're born with a soul, maybe we're born with all our faults, too? I hold my fingers to the candle's heat, feel its warm glow. Whatever way it is, all I want for her is happiness and that she'll find the love that she's seeking. I hope, of course, that she does but I know, too, that it will take a special fellow, some extraordinary man, to be able to handle our dear Lucia. And so, I say a small prayer that just such a man might find the path to our door.

JIM AND GIORGIO AND HELEN ARE IN A HUDDLE IN THE SALON when I get home.

"What are you lot conspiring about?" I ask, unpinning my hat and setting it on the sideboard.

Helen's look to me is sheepish. "Tell your mother, Giorgio," she says.

All three turn their gazes to me, something like fear in their eyes.

"Tell me what?" I'm alarmed now. "Is it Lucia? Has something happened?"

Jim rises and comes to me. "No, no. Sit, Nora. We have things to discuss."

Giorgio, flicking his cigarette nervously, blurts it. "Helen and I are to be married."

I flump into my chair. "Oh." I know I must congratulate them, but the words refuse to come. "When?"

Helen speaks. "In December, Nora."

I nod and push a smile across my mouth. "Well, isn't that grand?" Jim, like a pirate with his eye patch, glances at Helen and I look hard at him. "What else did you want to talk about? There's something else, isn't there? You said, 'We have things to discuss.'"

Jim shifts in his seat. "Well, Nora, Helen feels that if she's to marry Giorgio, she would like him to be, well, I suppose, she'd like him to be legitimate. I mean, for him to … if he should father a child … then, well—"

"What?" I turn from Jim to the other two. "What? What do you mean?"

Helen leans across and takes my hand. "Giorgio and I mean to have a baby together, Nora, once we're married, and wouldn't it be better if Giorgio had a true claim to the name Joyce, a legal claim? For inheritance and so forth? That way any child of his—of ours—would also be secure. For the future."

My thoughts reel, I can't grasp what she's getting at; I mean, I think I know, but I'm not sure. Is this to do with her money? Her father's? With *our* money? Georgie has no money to call his own, so it can't be that.

"I don't know what you mean by 'legal claim.' Joyce is his name, isn't it? I don't understand this stuff, I don't know anything about the law and things like that. Jim, what does it all mean?"

He smiles. "It's simple, Gooseen. If Georgie and Helen marry, you and I should marry too."

"WHY IS GIORGIO HITCHING HIMSELF TO THAT GIGOLO?" LUCIA stares at me from her bed, her hair a mad nest atop her head.

"Such a word to use, Lucy!" I say. "It's unkind to call her that and, anyway, women can't be gigolos." I bite my lip for, in truth, I find it a little funny. Helen is too old for Georgie, too rich, too nerve-ridden somehow, but they're determined and we must go along with it, it seems. And because of them, I'm to be married, too, though I'd like to have chosen my own time, not for my marriage date to be forced by Helen and Giorgio. Jim says now that he always meant us to wed at some point, but I treat that with the great lump of skepticism it deserves.

Lucy pouts. "I don't see any reason for them to marry. None at all. You and Babbo have gone along nicely without a marriage certificate." She frowns. "Though you've undoubtedly made fools of Georgie and me."

And fools of ourselves, I think. "They want to have a child, Lucia," I say. "Helen wants another baby."

Her mouth drops. "What? But the gigolo is as old as Methuselah. Can she even do that?" She makes the shape of a bulging stomach with her hands.

"Women can have babies beyond forty and they do. Helen has time." I sit on the bed. "Wouldn't you like to be an aunt, Lucy?"

"Certainly not."

I smooth her hair down with my fingers. "Lucia, the fact is, Babbo and I are to marry too."

Lucia pulls my hand from her head. "For goodness' sake, Mamma, you're wearing me out completely with all this talk of weddings." She lies down abruptly and pulls the sheet over her head; I sit for a few moments, hoping she'll look at me and say something kind, about my marriage. Despite how it's come about, I'm happy at last to be marrying Jim, more than happy, the thought of it has me giddy as a goat. I cup Lucia's cheek through the bedsheet.

"Don't you want to congratulate me, Lucy dear?"

"You can go now," she says.

THE HONEYMOONERS ARE BACK FROM GERMANY AND THEY TAKE us to Les Trianons for Jim's forty-ninth birthday. It's a quiet evening but, later, we raise a toast with the Jolases, Paul and Lucie Léon, Lucie's brother Alec Ponisovsky, who's teaching Jim Russian, and Padraic and Molly Colum, and it strikes me that, once more, our circle has shifted without me even noticing much. The Nuttings went home to America and Jim spends less time at Shakespeare and Company now and is convinced Miss Beach has diddled him out of royalties, which seems a little far-fetched to me, but Jim loves to make villains of people, so there it is. He's thinking now of letting the Jolases publish *Work in Progress*, not Miss Beach and Shakespeare and Company, and Giorgio agrees that he should.

"You're a world-famous author, Papà. You need a better outfit than Sylvia's dusty bookshop now. Think how it looks." He waves at the company. "Mr. and Mrs. Jolas will do a fine job. Don't you agree, Mrs. Colum?"

"Well, yes, no doubt they would do a splendid job," Molly Colum says. "But I feel your father has pulled enough legs. He's indebted to Freud and Jung, with all this interior monologue stuff, but will only credit some obscure old French chap. Isn't that right, Joyce?" She shouts at Jim as if he's half deaf instead of half blind.

Jim puckers his lips. "I do so hate women who know any-thing," he says, not looking at Mrs. Colum.

"Huh. You don't, Joyce. You like them hugely. Look at Weaver and Beach. They know plenty and where would you be without them?" She leans toward him. "And where, sir, would you be without your wife? A woman who knows more than every man at this table put together, if you ask me."

Jim turns to her and smiles. "*Touché*," he says and a tiny laugh erupts from him. "What, dear Mollycoddle, did you think of the last section of *Work in Progress* that I showed you?"

"Joyce," Mrs. Colum says, in her strident way, "it's outside literature."

Jim sips his wine. "Molly," he says, "it may be outside litera-ture now but, in time, it will be firmly *inside* literature."

JIM SAYS THAT FOR GIORGIO AND LUCIA TO BE HIS LEGAL HEIRS, we must marry in London, but it must look like we live in London to do that, so we pack up Square de Robiac and remove ourselves to Campden Hill, Kensington. Lucia will not call the flat in Camp-den Grove anything other than Campden Grave. Jim chooses the fourth of July—Pappie's birthday—for our big day. We do every-thing quietly, but still the newspapermen snuffle their way into our business and, not satisfied with announcing the date of our mar-riage on the front of their papers, they're outside the registrar's office, too, like dogs after hares, shouting, "But aren't you married already, Mr. Joyce?" We shove past them and, when I see the drab room within, a flash of Eileen's wedding in the beautiful church of San Giusto in Trieste lights up my inner eye and I clench my teeth. The world will realize that we've been unwed until now, no matter what yarns Jim spins, and the thought of it makes me shiver. Still, we're here now and that's enough.

Lucia sticks to my elbow, muttering to herself, and I swing around to her. "What is it, girl?"

"This is the worst day of my life." She flicks her hand toward her brother. "Everyone knows now that Giorgio and I are bastards and always have been."

I could slap her face, but I clutch my handbag with both hands to stop me. "Control your tongue," I growl.

THE PARTY IS LACKLUSTER. JIM IS GETTING MOROSELY DRUNK BE-side me and I feel I'd rather be alone in a dark room, with my mind emptied of every single thought, rather than here. The children are sullen and our few guests are as much fun as the departed at a wake. When I imagined this day, I always saw bright sunshine and myself in layers of Alençon lace and circles of happy faces around me; I saw a priest and a marble altar. I didn't see myself in my old fox fur and coat in a drab Kensington office and, after the ceremony, pull-ing my cloche hat low over my face to stop those horrible men with their cameras taking my picture.

Now Jim sits, a silent, crooked bird and Lucia is his double on my other side, a sulky little pullet, thinking of no one but herself. Giorgio would hop on the boat to France today, if I'd let him, to get back to Helen who's suffering through her pregnancy with queasi-ness and general unease. I sip a glass of brandy and look around at everyone. Nobody cares that I got no bouquet, no church, no iced fruitcake. It bothers no one but me that I didn't even get a wedding picture.

SANTÉ

୬ ୬

Paris
1932

AND NOW PAPPIE IS DEAD AND JIM IS A SORROWFUL WRECK.
He can barely dress himself and has disappeared into his sadness, it seems, never to come out. And with Jim down, we're all
down and our flat is a storm-tossed boat that I must try very hard
to steer. Jim's guilt and sorrow are wrapped around him. He talks
of Pappie constantly and can't seem to get over his death or do
anything but think of his departed father.

"I should have gone to him in Dublin, Nora. Oh, why didn't
I go?"

"Don't be shaming yourself, Jim, please."

"Poor Pappie. He was without doubt the silliest, yet shrewd-
est, man I ever met," he says. "I was always fond of him, Nora,
excessively fond. You know that?"

"I know, peteen."

"He knew too?"

"Your father knew where he stood with you, dearest."

"And Pappie loved me well."

"He did."

Jim shifts in his chair. "I can hear his voice in my ears, in the
base of my brain, isn't that strange, Gooseen? It's like an echo, a

call from far off." He puts his hand to the back of his head. "I wonder where he's gone to."

I would like to say heaven, but purgatory seems a more likely place for John Stanislaus Joyce, in fairness. "He's all around us, I suppose. In the air. And Pappie's in our hearts, too, like all our dead."

"Pappie was the same as me, or I'm the same as him—a sinner. That bound us to each other."

"Well," I say, "perhaps."

"I'm profoundly sorry I didn't go to see him when he asked, Nora. I think it was callous of me." He lifts his dark glasses. "He was an old man, I should have bowed to him."

"You didn't want to go back, Jim. It wasn't for lack of love for Pappie. Ireland itself repelled you."

He nods, pulls the shawl he's taken to wearing tighter around his shoulders. "What is life for at all, Nora?"

"Who knows, Jim? Who knows?"

Lucia marches out of her bedroom. "Life is for living," she flashes, pulling on her coat. "Though how anyone is supposed to live *here* is beyond me."

"Where are you going, Lucy?" I ask, my voice sharp; her lack of care for her father's grief annoys me.

"Away from this gloom-pit."

"Clearly," I say, "but who are you meeting?"

"A girlfriend. You don't know her." She pulls on her gloves. "Men are so disappointing, Mamma, I find." Lucia glares at her father. "I'm trying women for a while."

Before I can say anything in reply, she has swung out the door.

MARIA AND EUGENE JOLAS THROW A FIFTIETH JUBILEE FOR JIM, hoping to lift him out of his sorrow. Their flat is gaily decorated with colored bunting and pots of blue hyacinths and Mrs. Jolas has had a cake made with the cover of *Ulysses* on it. Samuel Beckett is invited, on Jim's insistence, and I'm pleased that he's had the good manners to come and it's nice to see the pair of them, heads bent in the corner of the Jolases' kitchen, unpicking some puzzle together. Jim is withdrawn and solitary these days, so I leave him and Beckett to their chat for he seems content.

Lucia arrives with Giorgio and some friends and she sashays into the Jolas salon as if she owns it; there are days when, true to her name, she lights up the space around her. Close by her side as she moves around the room is Alec Ponisovsky, brother of Lucie Léon. I watch him pour punch into cocktail glasses and hand one to Lucia, which she swigs in two gulps, easy as lemonade. She watches Alec, birdy-eyed, when he goes to get her some food.

"Go easy, Lucy," I say, sidling up to her; the last thing we need is for her to get a taste for drink, she's bad enough.

She wiggles her empty glass. "It's a party, Mamma."

"I see you're keeping close company with Mr. Ponisovsky."

She stares across at him. "Russian men are so elegant, don't you think?" She sways and balances herself, putting one hand on the back of a chair; she inclines her head toward me. "Alec is in love with Hazel Guggenheim and I'm in love with you-know-who." She dips her head to mine. "Monsieur B. Shush, don't tell." She hiccups and waves her glass. "But we won't talk about that." She looks around. "Where's my babbo? I want him to say those new names he has given the days of the week. What are they? Moansday, Tearsday, Wailsday, Something-day ..."

I hear Jim's voice from the kitchen, getting closer. "Here's your father now. We can sing Happy Birthday to him."

Her face brightens, and she looks toward the salon entrance. Jim comes through, Samuel Beckett close on his heels, and Lucia drops her glass; it smashes on the parquet. I bend quickly and pick up the broken pieces.

"What the fuck is *he* doing here?" I look up at Lucy who has flushed deeply and is pointing across the salon. "Who on fucking earth let *him* come?"

I stand and push her hand down. "Hush, now. That's enough, Lucy. It's your father's birthday and he wanted Beckett here. They're friends."

She whips her head around; her face is ablaze. "After what he did to me? After he made an absolute fool of me by bringing a chaperone to our *rendezvous*? After his humiliation of me?" Her voice is rising. "You let him back into our lives, just like that?"

"Quiet yourself," I whisper, stepping away from her to go to Jim.

Lucia picks up the chair she's been steadying herself on, lifts it high, and hurls it toward me; I leap sideways, shocked out of my brains, and the chair lands hard and loud on the floor, missing me by an inch.

"Lucy!" I roar, staring at her, my heart clattering behind my ribs with fright.

Georgie appears at my side. "Are you all right, Mamma?" I nod and glance around to find everyone silent and staring. Giorgio grabs his sister above the elbow and drags her toward the door. "How dare you, Lucia!"

THREE DAYS LUCIA SPENDS IN THE *MAISON DE SANTÉ* THAT GEORgie took her to the night of Jim's birthday. Three days I spend in my bed, a tossy-turny mess, both missing Lucy and feeling glad she's not here. My sorrow and my fear and my anger writhe together in a confused ball. If I let her home, will she attack me again? But she has to come home, really, this is where she belongs. Oh, my Lucia.

Jim and Georgie go to visit Lucy in the *santé*, but I can't stand the idea of the place, the sanitary smell of it, the lunatics wandering around with strange, vacant eyes; the ones, who like my daughter, prefer to screech and scrap. I don't want Lucia's eyes bearing down on me. She needs help, it's clear, but I can't help wondering if she really belongs in a *maison de santé*, it seems too hard on her. Lucia should be home with us where we can try to sort through the things that are making her act so crazily. It's time we took her in hand.

MOLLY COLUM COMES TO SEE ME AND I'M EMBARRASSED TO BE SO undone when she arrives; I've neither washed nor put on clothes for days and I look a state. I pull my dressing gown tighter.

"I'm sorry I'm so untidy, Mrs. Colum. Let me dress myself."

She dismisses me with a regal wave of her fingers. "Nora, I'm a frank person, as you know, and I've come to tell you that, as I see it, you need to get Lucia married tout de suite."

I nod, for Jim and I feel the same. "That would be a grand thing, but who'll have her now?" I ask. "No doubt everyone's talking about the scene at the Jolases' party for Jim."

She grimaces. "You have one hope: Alec Ponisovsky. I've been speaking to Lucie and Paul Léon and they're happy for Alec to propose to Lucia, in spite of her little outburst. He's a decent young man, you know this, and he's fond of Lucia. She won't do better. Offer a dowry with her, Nora. That will sweeten things."

I feel doubtful; will Jim be able to raise the money for a dowry? Perhaps Miss Weaver might help. It seems such an outdated thing to do—like paying someone to take Lucy off our hands and our consciences. But if the Léons and Alec are game, I won't argue with them. I feel my misgivings crumble a little and I let the idea root and hope sprout. This could be Lucia's best chance.

"I'll have to talk to Jim," I tell Molly Colum.

"You do that, Nora," she says. "And be firm. Get Lucia settled somewhere with someone, and all will be well. The girl needs a life of her own, a purpose."

HELEN GIVES BIRTH TO A COMELY BABY BOY, STEPHEN JAMES Joyce. *Deo gratias.*

Lucia is to marry Alec Ponisovsky.

Perhaps things have turned.

WE HOLD LUCIA AND ALEC'S ENGAGEMENT PARTY AT RESTAU-rant Drouant on Place Gaillon. We sit at a round table, Jim to my left, Georgie to my right, and the betrothed pair across from us. Lucy is dour all evening and I watch her pick at her eel and mushrooms and drink more wine than is wise. She turns suddenly to Alec.

"I like how you look," she proclaims, then turns away just as fast.

"I thank you," he says, staring ahead, and my heart drifts to my boots. How will these two make a marriage?

Georgie brings his mouth to my ear. "A girl with Lucia's condition should *not* be engaged, Mamma."

"Condition?" I say.

"Temperament. Tendencies. Look at her, she's like a child. A very sad and spoilt one."

"At almost twenty-five she's a woman, Georgie, and it's time for her to have a woman's life." I look at Lucy. It's true that she's childish and, yes, we overindulge her, Jim especially, but maybe marriage will be the thing that helps her to grow up, helps her put away her tantrums and silences.

Georgie strangles his napkin between his hands. "I don't like this. Not one bit."

I catch Lucia waving at me across the table. "Mamma, I'm staying at the Léons' tonight, so you don't need to wait for me."

"Are you dismissing us already, Lucia?" Jim asks.

She lets a brittle laugh. "No, Babbo. I'm just letting you know I'm going to rue Casimir Périer later, not to my so-called home."

Giorgio elbows me, but I refuse to conspire with him against Lucia tonight; this marriage *will* take place. My son sighs, lifts his glass of whiskey, and drains it in one swallow.

THREE DAYS LUCIA SPENDS LYING ON THE LÉONS' SOFA, NOT moving, not speaking, not responding to anyone or anything. Three days I spend on my own sofa, wondering why God has done this to us. Why Lucy has.

"The doctor calls it 'catatonia,'" Georgie says. "She's suspended, locked into her own mind."

"But why?" I whimper. "How?"

"The medics say it's something to do with trauma. Some undealt-with shock or hurt. That's what causes it."

"I've never heard anything so ridiculous," I say. "What shock? What hurt? She's having us all on. This is just nonsense. More Lucia nonsense."

JIM GOES TO RUE CASIMIR PÉRIER TO SIT BY HER. WHEN LUCIA wakes, she asks him, "*Should* every girl marry?"

WHEN LUCIA IS RELEASED FROM THE *MAISON DE SANTÉ* WE PUT her in after the rue Casimir Périer episode, we decide to go back to London. Perhaps the change in air will bring Lucy some peace or sense. At the Gare du Nord, she stands on the platform with her arms folded across her chest, watching the porter lift our bags onto the train; I step into the carriage and hold out my hand to her.

"Come, Lucia."

She shakes her head.

Jim links his arm through hers. "Come on now, daughter of mine, it's time to go. London awaits."

Lucy shrugs him off. "No!" she shrieks. "No!"

I jump off the train. "Lucia, Lucia. What's the matter with you? Don't scream like that. Get on this train now."

"But I hate England! And besides, besides, besides," she babbles and throws her hands about, "if I'm there, in London, and Alec is here, and Hazel Guggenheim is here, in Paris, and Alec is here, and I'm not here, then what will happen? What will Hazel do?" She clutches at her hair. "Don't you see, Mamma? What will Alec *do*? If I'm not here? And Hazel is here, present and waiting and ..." She shakes her head vigorously. "No, no, I'm not getting on that train, no, no, you can't force me to go to horrible England." She looks to Jim. "Babbo, I've done terrible things in my life, but that Guggenheim witch, well, she can do worse, oh yes, very much worse. Madame de Staël plotted against Napoleon and so Guggenheim plots against me."

"Nobody's plotting, Lucia," I say softly, trying to wheedle her back to sense, but she's in a frenzy and has been chewing over this Alec and Hazel problem the whole time, it's clear.

"Madame?" The porter looks from one to the other of us. "Monsieur?"

"I won't go," Lucy roars and I put my hands over my ears, so loud is her sound. I want to cry from embarrassment. "I will *not* go to London."

"Madame?" the porter says, peering into my face. "Monsieur?"

"Take the bags off the train," Jim says.

And so we go home to our flat and Lucy gets her way. No London.

"I can't live here anymore," Lucia says, looking around our salon, "it makes me feel like I'm drowning."

I grind my teeth with irritation. "I'm fed up with these notions of yours, Lucia; you need to grow up and start showing some appreciation. There's nothing wrong with this flat."

"Maybe it's not the flat but the people in it that oppress me."

"I beg your pardon?"

"I'm young! I shouldn't have to live here with old people, as if I'm old too. Everyone else is having a high time and I'm here, sex starved and bored, like a child."

"Such a ridiculous thing to say." I slap the arm of my chair. "You've no idea how charmed your existence is. You have everything. We had nothing at your age. Nothing! I had to borrow a coat to leave Ireland in, I was that poor."

"I don't care what you had or didn't have, or what you think I have or don't have. I can't stay here another day."

Jim speaks softly. "Where then, Lucia? Where do you wish to live?"

"Giorgio and Helen have the baby now and his nurse," I say, impatience gathering, "so you certainly can't stay there, if that's what you're thinking."

"I just have to go," Lucy says, her voice rising to a whine.

Jim spreads out his hands. "But where to, *ragazza mia*?"

"The Léons will have me."

I glance at Jim and he shrugs. "I'll ask them," he says.

༄

LUCIA MOVES INTO PAUL AND LUCIE LÉON'S FLAT, BUT SOON OUR precious girl complains that it's too crowded there, she can't get a moment's peace. At her own request, and with their welcome agreement, she goes to stay with the Colums. Despite my exasperation with her, I visit her there.

"Hullo, Mamma," she says, when I enter the Colum salon, and she's the contained and polite daughter I wish for, not the harridan of home, or the screaming wretch of the Gare du Nord.

"Come here to me, Lucia," I say, hugging her to my breast and she lets me hold her for a few moments before pulling away to sit.

I'm glad to see her placid, but I'm a little put out, too— What does Mrs. Colum have that I lack? Why is Lucia soft and sane with her, but a fluthering virago around me? Molly pours tea for us, but before drinking a drop, Lucy rises out of her seat.

"I'm going to my room to work on my *lettrines*."

"Of course, Lucia," Molly says cheerfully and Lucy wanders off. "It was a good idea of Joyce's to have her paint those illuminated letters—they seem to keep her happily occupied. And calm."

I nod. "Jim says she's a creator, like him, and needs to create. A creator of chaos, maybe." I sigh. "Is she always this quiet with you, Molly?"

"She suffers at night, Nora, as you know. But I lie with her. Last night I pinned our nightgowns together, so she'd know I wasn't going to leave her." She grimaces. "Or she me."

"I never thought of that. Pinning her to me." I worry a teaspoon with my fingers. "You do keep a close watch on her, though, Molly, by day, all the time? She shouldn't be let out on her own; she doesn't know how to keep herself safe and, well, she's become fond of drinking."

"Yes, I'm obeying your wishes on that." She frowns. "I suppose I should tell you that Alec Ponisovsky called a few days past to take her to the theater. Padraic said she couldn't go and she accused him of being a jailer. 'Just like my father,' Lucia said. She didn't fight hard. In the end she said, 'You win.' She's lost some spirit, I think."

"Jailer?" I sigh. "Jim has never curbed her. Nor I. We just want to protect her. She seems so wild in herself. She's either that or half dead most of the time."

"She said something else, too, Nora. She talked of the men who come to see Joyce, the literary men. Lucia said, 'Those men see me as the *hors-d'œuvre* and Babbo as the *plat du jour.*' I thought it an odd remark."

"Our Lucy is an odd girl, Mrs. Colum. She told me she's sex starved, whatever that means. I wonder sometimes if it's all an act. Does she put it on, so we'll notice her? Or did we do something very wrong to her across the years that made her this way?"

"This is a malady of the mind, Nora, it's not your fault." Molly butters the back of a croissant. "My feeling is that Lucia's confused. She just needs to lie low for a little bit, to clear her mind and settle it. And she'll have to decide what direction she wants to take now."

It saddens me that Mrs. Colum seems to see Lucia better than Jim and I do; she appears to know what our daughter is and what she needs. I feel like a dolt, a blind eejit, and a bad mother all rolled together. I sip my tea.

"I was sure Alec Ponisovsky had vanished completely," I say. "That he'd scarpered. And yet you say he called here for Lucy." I shake my head; I know nothing of my own daughter or her life.

Molly leans in and touches my hand. "It may be better to let go of Alec, Nora. The engagement is not going to last. Lucia needs something other than a man to occupy her. These artworks she's doing, they please her. Let her take a painting course."

I nod, relieved to have a small solution to suggest to Lucy, a distraction from the lack of Alec. "Yes, Molly, yes, that's a fine idea. Anything to keep her busy. She must take a course."

LUCIA CHEWS HER LIPS SO HARD AND SO OFTEN THAT THEY BLEED, then she picks off the scabs until the red flows down her chin. Lucia brushes her hair over her face and refuses to look at the Colums. Lucia roars at Molly and Padraic about being their prisoner. She raises her fists but instead of attacking them, as she might me, she punches the walls, bruising her knuckles.

Molly Colum is diagnosed with a tumor. Giorgio and Molly take Lucia to the sanatorium at L'Haÿ-les-Roses. Lucia calls Molly "betrayer."

The doctors at the sanatorium say Lucia needs "therapeutic isolation."

"What does that mean, Georgie? Jim?" I ask.

"No visitors," Giorgio says, and it pains me to think of Lucy without the comfort of one familiar face.

WHEN WE GO TO THE SANATORIUM, DETERMINED TO VISIT OUR daughter, they say Lucia needs weeks of bed rest. They say she needs daylong baths to draw out any badness that may be affecting her mind. They say she might need electric shocks to the head.

I say, "That would surely destroy her brain before it would mend it?"

Doctor Codet, a boil-faced turnip of a fellow, with not an ounce of manly charm, says, "No." He smiles and that makes him look even uglier. "Your daughter is a hebephrenic psychotic, Mrs. Joyce. With a poor future."

Jim gasps. "Can we see her?"

Turniphead scowls. "You may have five minutes with Miss Joyce, no more."

LUCIA IS PALE AS MILK AND HER FACE IS COVERED WITH CRUSTY scabs; I've never seen her look so bad and my guts trounce with sorrow. I hold out my arms, she rushes to me, and I hold her close.

"Oh, my little darling, oh, my peteen."

She stands back and clings onto my arms, her eyes pleading. "They're trying to rip out my soul, Mamma. They watch me every minute of every hour. I see them write things in little books about me. I have to obey them always, do everything they say, meekly, without comment." She lowers her voice. "Or they'll proclaim me mad." She turns to Jim. "Babbo, I'm *not* mad."

"No, *ragazza*, you're not."

"I'm here against my will, Babbo. And I'm lonely beyond reason. Can't you get me out?"

Her father starts to cry.

JIM BREAKS LUCIA OUT OF L'HAŸ-LES-ROSES. WE TAKE HER TO Feldkirch in Austria, with Mathilde, a companion, to where Maria Jolas and her family are staying.

"My soul is gone," Lucia tells Mrs. Jolas.

We travel on to Zürich to see the doctor about Jim's eyes.

We move Lucia and Mathilde to Vence, France, and we stay nearby in Nice.

We walk the Promenade des Anglais and Jim asks me, "Do you think my gift has sparked a fire in Lucia's brain? Is it entirely my fault?"

I don't know what to say in reply. My worry is that between us, we've made Lucia too tender for this world; we've damaged her and now she can't be fixed. I think that all our wanderings and her upset schooling, her lack of a home and friends has upended her. Giorgio has an inner pot of strength that makes life different for him; he's able to draw on that, get on and push through. But our Lucia, our tiny light, has always been sensitive and wayward, soft around the edges, like her father. I think our mistake was that we didn't plant Lucy, let her bud and blossom in one place. We cosseted her for sure but, as soon as she was settled, we ripped her up by the roots and forced her to grow again anew, and it was the growing she found so hard. I say none of this to Jim, I just look at him and shake my head. How can I tell him that between us we may have made our daughter mad?

GALILEE

❧

Paris
1933 AND 1934

WE'VE MOVED TO RUE GALILÉE, NEAR THE ARC DE Triomphe—Lucia with us—reasoning the other side of the river, a fresh place to be in, might do her good. New places always give me and Jim energy and we're hoping it will be the same for Lucy.

Jim takes my hands in his. "Nora, the word 'Galilee' means to roll oneself onto the Lord, meaning to trust him." I nod; Jim cares nothing for God, of course, but he's offering me hope, which heartens me. "Our subtle and barbaric Lucy is quiet in Galilee. Let's trust in that."

Lucia is taking art lessons with Marie Laurencin and Jim is trying to get a booklet of his poems, with Lucia's artworks in it, published. It keeps them busy. He still can't acknowledge that there's something serious wrong with her, something that may not have a cure. Georgie firmly believes his sister to be mad, as does Helen, and the Jolases, too, and I live on the edge of a cliff, waiting always for the next storm that will knock us all into the sea.

❧

DOCTOR TURNIP CODET RECOMMENDS A NEW PHYSICIAN TO US, Henri Vignes, a gynecologist. "Though not a mind man, he knows much about women's brains."

"I am hopeful about Miss Joyce's state," Vignes tells us, but says little else.

Jim nods happily. "Good, good," he says, clutching at anything that might mean Lucy is curable.

"What this Vignes's seawater injection therapy has to do with improving Lucy's condition, I do not know," I say. I'm exasperated with the string of doctors we must see and their contrary reports on our daughter.

"We have to follow every path, Nora," Jim says, glad in himself that he's doing his best for our daughter, trying things out. He thinks he can reverse her malady; he just needs to find the right things to do.

Jim gives Lucy four thousand francs to buy a fur coat. "My wish for you, Lucia Anna, is warmth and beauty," he says, handing over the envelope bulging with notes.

My wish for her is peace and sanity.

PAUL LÉON, NOW THAT HELEN IS OCCUPIED WITH BABY STEPHEN, writes all Jim's letters and deals with the publishers and so forth. We never ask Paul about Alec Ponisovsky and the unspoken dissolvement of Lucia's engagement and he never mentions it either, so Alec lingers like a mote in the eye, there but not there. Jim refers to him as the Russian Elephant Not-in-the-Room.

Jim barely writes a line, he's so preoccupied with Lucia and getting her well. How can I tell him that I'm starting to believe that Lucy may not be fixable? It seems a betrayal to them both. Jim drinks himself into oblivion most nights, out in the cafés and here at home now, too. He slouches in his chair and his cigarettes burn down until his fingertips are scorched.

"You'll burn the bloody place down one of these nights," I roar, grabbing at the latest charred butt that's made a hole in my rug.

Jim decides Lucia needs a companion again and we employ two: one for the early part of the day and one for the evenings. They're grand, capable young women but Lucia, of course, finds fault.

I hear a tussle in the kitchen this morning and go in to find Marie, the daytime girl, clutching her cheek.

"Lucia hit me," she says, "for absolutely no reason."

"There *was* a reason, Marie," Lucia says, "and the reason is that I do not like you."

"Go home, Marie," I say, sure we'll never see her again.

Lucy sits on the sofa and weeps and stays there all day, sobbing and hiccuping, blowing her nose as loudly as a ship's horn, acting as if she's the one who is wronged. She won't speak when I say her name, just sits and cries like a banshee.

"She's trying me sorely, Jim." I hover over him where he sits reading in our bedroom to escape the cacophony of our daughter. "I can't figure out if this is all a game, or if there's something serious the matter with her that makes her act this way."

He shakes his head. "I worry—" he says and, though it's clear he wants to say more, he stops.

At night, Jim's stomach aches and he takes six sleeping pills on top of his wine. Still he doesn't sleep and he paces about, talking to himself in a low, agitated voice.

I start to feel that we're all going mad.

❧

JULY SEES US BACK IN ZÜRICH AND THE EYE MAN SAYS JIM'S SIGHT is getting hopeless. Another strife to add to it all. After a prolonged screaming attack on Bahnhofstrasse, because she does not feel like walking, we have to take Lucia to the asylum at Burghölzli, but the doctor there is optimistic.

"Your daughter is not lunatic, Mr. and Mrs. Joyce, merely neurotic. Though markedly so. There's a man near Geneva who understands cases like this."

We find ourselves traveling with Lucia again, this time to Les Rives de Prangins, an institution at Nyon, and speaking with Doktor Forel. I am weary of all the toing and froing, but I know Jim will go anywhere if he thinks he might find someone to fix Lucy.

"Miss Joyce," Doktor Forel says, "in my opinion, suffers from *dementia praecox*. That is to say, she is schizophrenic."

Jim grips the table. This is what he's been dreading, it's a word he barely dares utter. "Are you sure, Herr Doktor?"

"Quite sure, sir. However, I feel Miss Joyce has a form of *dementia praecox* that can be cured by persuasion. She will stay here and we will treat her."

Back at our hotel, Jim is wretched. "Schizophrenia is a life sentence, Nora. We need another opinion. Let's take her back to Paris."

I rise from my chair. "How many opinions do you want, Jim? Did you not listen to Forel? There's clearly something medically amiss with Lucia; normal girls don't act the way she does, screeching and lashing out at people all the time. Forel thinks he can help her, so let him do that."

"But it's not schizophrenia. Surely not that."

"I know nothing about *dementia praecox*, Jim, but I do know

that ordinary people don't stand in the middle of the street screaming blue thunder, for minutes on end, because they don't want to
walk. They don't throw chairs at their mothers or talk of sex in the
odd way that Lucy does. You'll have to give in to it eventually—
there's something broken in her brain." I hate saying this because
then it might all be true. I get into bed and thump the pillow to
relieve some of my own frustration. "Oh, we can stuff her with
Veronal and phosphate of lime to calm her until it comes out her
nostrils, but Jim, there's always another attack, another scene.
Always someone else who'll be the victim of Lucia's outbursts.
She's not well, Jim!"

"I'm not leaving her here," he says quietly. "Didn't you see
her panic when I told her that Forel used the word 'schizophrenic'?
It sent her into some internal hell."

I get up and stand over him, a hot fury rising in me. "Do you
think I want to leave Lucia in an asylum? Do you think that will
make me happy?" I pull at my collar. "Jim, you know my sister
Delia was sent to Ballinasloe for her nerves and the craythur never
recovered. Mammy's convinced Delia came out of the place mad-
der than she went in. I *hate* institutions, but Lucia needs the help
she can get in Les Rives de Prangins and I want her to get that help
now. It's for her own good." I flump onto the bed and cover my
eyes with my hands.

"Lucia will come back to Paris with us," he says, "and that is
all there is to it."

I sit up straight and glare at him. "You know, Jim, you've never
taken the time to get to know Lucia, not really. Oh, you buy her
things and spoil her to the core, but you don't know the girl, not at
all. You've never spent as much time with her as I have."

"I disagree, but you think what you like, Nora." He lights a
cigarette, then turns to me and shouts: "And allow me, at least, to

say that I was present when she was conceived. At least give me that!"

THE NEW YEAR slides in and at last *Ulysses* is allowed to be published in America. Jim is tickled by the judge's finding and repeats it often: "Nowhere does this book tend to be aphrodisiac!"

The telephone in rue Galilée rings and rings with friends offering their congratulations. Jim sits in his blue velvet jacket, phone in his lap, to quickly answer the calls as they come. Sure enough, the telephone sounds again and he lifts the receiver.

"This'll be Pope Pius," he jokes. "*Ciao, mio caro Papa,*" he says, then holds the telephone away from his ear. "Hello, hello?" He looks at me. "I can hear nothing, Nora." He shakes the receiver. "Hello? This is Joyce speaking."

Lucia comes toward us, the big kitchen scissors in her fist. "I cut the telephone wires," she says.

"You little strap." I run and grab the scissors.

Lucy lunges to try to take them back, but I hold fast and she can't get at them; she leans into me and contorts her face. "Every man that you let into our home had his way with me, Mamma. *Every* man," she screams. "Did you know that?"

"Enough, Lucia!"

She jumps away from me. "I'm an artist, too!" she roars and runs from the flat.

Three days she stays away. We don't know where she goes or who she sees or what she does.

Three long days.

JIM'S BIRTHDAY COMES AND I'M TRYING ON MY NEW LUCIEN Lelong dress for our night out and Jim's complaining that the vee back is too revealing and he has needle and thread out to sew me into it.

"Don't stitch my backbone to my skin, Jim," I say and he laughs.

"Now," he says when he's finished, but the result is such a raggedy mess that I have to undress and pull out the line of stitches.

"You'll just have to put up with my bare back," I tell him and he kisses me from the base of my spine to my neck and, for the first time in a long time, I want to take him in my arms and lie with him. I turn and kiss his mouth and Jim grabs my behind and kneads it but, of a sudden, Lucia is in the doorway and I jump with fright. She lunges forward and starts to slap me hard around my head and I scream.

"Stop, Lucy! Stop! You're hurting me." All my anger rains out and I screech, "Get off me, you little bitch!"

Her father manages to drag her away and we all three stand, panting and staring at one another. Oh my God in heaven, what is happening to us?

"Lucia, Lucia," Jim croons. "Why? Why?"

"That's it, Lucy," I say. "You're going back to Nyon. You'll not sleep another night under this roof." I catch my breath, remorse creeping over me for shouting at her. I grab her into my arms and she sobs. "It's for the best, *a leana*," I croon. "They'll help you at Nyon, they'll help you to get well."

JOB'S PATIENCE, SOLOMON'S WISDOM, AND THE QUEEN OF SHE-ba's coffers, that's what Jim says we need as parents and it's true for him. Lucia is a constant burr under our skin, a worry and a strain and a sadness, and her care at Nyon is costly. And now Giorgio, Helen, David, and darling Stephen are to go to America, to try to launch Georgie's singing career. Though Helen needs a rest-cure, too—she has been feeling highly anxious, apparently—and her family say it will be better for her to have that at home.

"But people never come back from America," I moan, hating the idea of my son being so far from me.

"Don't worry, Mamma, we'll be back," Georgie says, and I cradle little Stephen, for I'll miss his light, sweet presence dreadfully.

Lucia writes to say she spends her days at Nyon staring out of the window—a barred window—and the image lodges in my brain and makes me powerfully sad. What have we done to her that this is how she has ended up, a prisoner in her own mind, as much as in that cage of a room? My guilt is an extra layer of skin that coats me and, every other hour, it seems, I catch myself shuddering with pity for Lucy. And with shame, knowing we may have caused or increased the badness in her.

We leave rue Galilée. The Lord did not, after all, prove that I could trust in him.

FIFTY

❧

Paris
1934 TO 1936

WE ARE BACK ON THE *RIVE GAUCHE*, WHERE WE BELONG, AT rue Edmond Valentin, near the Tour Eiffel; we have five elegant rooms on the fourth floor and, with just the pair of us now, there's ample space. I turn fifty and a motoring holiday with some new friends does me a power of good; it lightens me up, lessens my sorrows.

We visit Lucia at Nyon and she is weepy and sorrowful, but radiant, too, and taut as a tram wire.

"Mamma, I'm so very glad to see you." She wipes at a waterfall of tears. "I'm sorry for all the hurt I caused you, truly I am. Can you forgive your silly girl?"

"Of course, my Lucy." I kiss her head, relieved that she seems, at least, to understand she has behaved badly.

She leaps to Jim. "How is Paris, Babbo? Do you miss me?"

"Horribly, my darling."

She clings to her father and I trail along behind them through the grounds, glad to see them so thick, but wondering if Lucy will ever be right. Right enough to marry or survive in a flat alone, if it comes to it. Doktor Forel says she has too many white blood corpuscles and I nodded along as if I knew what that meant; it's hard, I find, to have conversations with these doctors; they speak in riddles, as far as I'm concerned.

Back at our hotel, Jim is melancholic. "Wise as a serpent and innocent as a dove, that's our lovely Lucy," he says.

I raise my eyebrows and say nothing; I'm not altogether convinced of her virtue. The telephone rings, it's a nurse at the hospital. Lucia has set fire to her bedroom.

WE MOVE LUCY BACK TO THE ASYLUM AT BURGHÖLZLI IN ZÜRICH on the advice of Doktor Forel. She is catatonic, will not talk, will not move. She's like a mannequin in a shop window, rigid and silent, and to look at her that way frightens me to my bones. How does a person get like that? It seems neither real nor right to me. The doctors say she might benefit from the wisdom of Mister Jung at nearby Küsnacht, on the lakeshore. Though Jim disdains the same man since the Mrs. McCormick incident, he's willing to try anything.

"Jung will be the twentieth doctor," I say, hoping by saying it aloud Jim will hear my meaning. It's all too much. For us. For Lucia. We need to stop shunting her from medic to medic and get her settled somehow. But how and where?

LUCY WILL ACTUALLY SPEAK WITH JUNG—WITH HER OTHER doctors she mostly preferred silence. She says she set the fire at Nyon so the nurses would open her door; she says she was too much alone.

"I was horribly lonely," she says, in the voice of a lost child and my heart cracks to smithereens.

She says her father's face is red—from wine—and fire is also red and that's another reason why she burned her room. Lucia says she knows she's spoilt, that her life has been "too nice." She thinks Jim and I should return to Paris because Switzerland is, according to her, "not the worst place in the world" to be. She says she longs to go to Ireland because it is her babbo's place. I, seemingly, am of nowhere.

When we come to visit, Lucy apologizes over and over, tries to figure herself out.

"I'm sorry, Mamma, for all the upset I've caused. Maybe I've eaten too many potatoes in my life," she says. "They're the devil's food, Babbo, you know that, I'm sure?"

"I think not, dear Lucy," Jim says, his face the face of a sorrowing wreck.

JIM CAN'T BEAR TO VISIT KÜSNACHT THIS MORNING, SO I GO alone. When I'm let in, I see that Lucia's in her green beaded evening gown with her opera cloak about her shoulders. She has painted her face with black ink. I stare but say nothing. The whole reason for these dramatics may be to evoke a response, the doctor says, but to me, not to respond seems like further madness.

"Harriet Weaver put the evil eye on me, Mamma," Lucia says. "Devil Harriet."

"No, Lucia. Miss Weaver is the best of women, her gifts of money have kept us alive for a long time. She has been nothing but good to our family, you know that."

Lucy stands and throws off her cloak. "They're all stealing from me here. They took the pen that Babbo gave me."

I get up. "Let me look for your pen, peteen. It's probably here somewhere."

"No!" she screams and I cover my ears.

"JIM, IT'S CLEARER THAN EVER TO ME THAT SHE'S MAD." I TELL him about Lucy's appearance, her inked face, her comments about Miss Weaver, the missing pen.

"They knew it was my pen, whoever took it," he retorts. "They'll try to sell it now and profit from us and us paying ten thousand francs a month to them. The blackguards." He pulls on his beard.

"Jim, have sense. Lucia probably threw the pen into the lake herself."

"No, no, no," he says, his voice breaking.

"Listen to me, Jim. Lucy says she wants to go home to Paris. She raved on about it, saying she'd like her aunt Eileen to come there as her companion. I told her that Eileen has her own three children to worry about, not to mention her job."

He squints at me. "Eileen?"

"Lucy says as she and Eileen are both 'a bit loony' they'd be a good match." I snort. "We actually both laughed when she said that."

Jim looks at me and his mouth curves upward. "Maybe it's not a bad plan."

"Jim! Lucia can sound quite normal, but this is just a mad scheme."

"Maybe not, Nora."

FOR TWO POUNDS A WEEK, EILEEN WATCHES OVER LUCIA IN Paris, then they both travel to London, to stay with Saint Harriet, at her invitation. I'm relieved. Eileen is a no-nonsense sort and Miss Weaver is the same way; between them they'll be able to settle Lucy into some sort of routine until we can decide where she should live and with whom. Eileen telephones us at six each evening. Today she tells me that Lucia asked for a gun.

Eileen laughs. "I said to her, 'Lucy, I'll buy you two guns, in case the first one doesn't go off,' and Lucy and I laughed until we nearly fell over; Miss Weaver didn't see the joke."

I tut and mouth to Jim, *And you think Lucia's all right?* I turn my attention back to Eileen. "But Lucy's in good form, other than that? She seems quiet in herself?"

"She's grand, Nora. And Old Harriet finds her very sane."

But Eileen has to go back to Ireland to tend to a problem with her young Patrick, and when Miss Weaver and Lucia are left alone, Lucy takes to the bed for days on end and won't speak. To cheer her up, Miss Weaver takes her out for the day, but Lucia runs off "to see Piccadilly" and stays out all night. Miss Weaver telephones once Lucy turns up, but Jim is in a red fury with the poor woman.

"We trusted you!" he screeches into the phone.

"Calm yourself, Jim," I say. "Plenty of times Lucy disappeared on us. Don't go falling out with Miss Weaver over this." But Jim loves to lay blame all around him and poor Saint Harriet is firmly in the bold girl's corner now.

LUCIA GOES TO DUBLIN ON SAINT PATRICK'S DAY, SAYING IT'S the only place she wants to be and Jim lets her, because he panders to her every whim. She stays in one half of a cottage in Bray, County Wicklow, rented by Eileen's daughters, Bozena and Eleanora, who are sixteen and eighteen now.

"I'd prefer if Eileen was there, too," I tell Jim, "but perhaps her girls will put some *smacht* on Lucia, tame her a wee bit?"

"Perhaps," he says.

But, no, it's not to be, for who can rein in that girl? Lucy goes missing over and over and her cousins are moidered trying to keep up with her. In the end they contact my uncle Michael and he spends six long days searching for my daughter, which, thank God, we don't hear anything of until afterward.

I read out Uncle Michael's letter to Jim:

Dublin, June 1935

Dear Nora and Jim,

It pains me to write such a letter as this to you but I think—and Eileen Schaurek thinks—it is better for you to know what Lucia has been up to for it might help with her treatment as time goes on. Her cousins are finding Lucia to be a handful and they've related to me some of what she has been getting up to and I admit I was shocked. I will record some of it here so that you have a picture of what has been happening and I apologize in advance if it's very distressing for you:

When she is out and about, Lucia does not wear underwear and lets people know that she doesn't. At home she wears a kimono and nothing else. She also swims naked in the sea at Bray. She talks freely with men she doesn't know and goes to pubs with them. She has been telephoning and telegraphing people she admires, such as Maud Gonne, and gets angry when they do not respond well. This anger manifests itself as setting fires in her bedroom (on the rug, in the corners), drinking champagne until she falls over, and singing all night so that nobody sleeps. (Her entire diet according to Božena and Eleanora consists of baskets of fruit, bottles of champagne, handfuls of aspirin, and undercooked sausages.) Lucia has painted her bedroom black and hung black curtains. Her clothes lie in heaps everywhere. She smokes in bed and tosses the cigarette ends to the floor. The landlady has threatened to evict all of them and the Schaurek girls were nicely settled there before Lucia's arrival so, naturally, this upsets them. Dear Nora

*and Jim, I'm sorry for this catalogue of misdeeds, but I
think it better that you're aware. What am I to do? Please
advise.*

> *Your loving Uncle Michael*

Jim looks at me. "Swimming in the sea is exercise. Isn't that good for her?"

"Jim! Have you not heard another word of what I've just read? Honest to God, are you that deaf, that blind?"

He drops his head almost to his lap and stays bent over for some moments. "Oh, Nora, she's lost control altogether, hasn't she? People will think she's soft in the head."

"You mean they'll *know*," I say evenly.

He looks up at me. "What will be said? All of Dublin must be talking about her."

"Is that what you're worried about, what people will say? Is it your own name being blackened that you're concerned about?" I rattle the letter at him. "Lucia needs to be admitted to an asylum *now*. Before she burns down that cottage, killing herself and taking her cousins with her. She needs minding, Jim, and she needs help. She's our responsibility and we have to help her. Properly help her. That's all there is!"

LUCIA IS ADMITTED TO FARNHAM HOUSE IN DUBLIN.

"And there she can stay," I say to Jim, relieved that she is not able to harm herself now or anyone else.

"No," he replies. "She'll end up as she was after seven months in Nyon. Lucy may have lived like a gypsy in Bray, but I won't leave her in an institution. I won't." He bites his lip. "Miss Weaver must step in again."

I shake my head; he's determined to believe that Lucy is well enough that between our friends, relatives, and ourselves we can somehow fix her. I can't argue it out with him anymore and so, in August, Lucia returns to England.

Lovelands Cottage. Barred windows. Injections of bovine serum. Miss Weaver and Mrs. Middlemost—Scottish nurse—who does a Highland fling to make Lucy laugh, then force-feeds her through her open mouth. Finally, to St. Andrew's Hospital for Mental Diseases in Northampton. Our darling Lucia, inside again. Inside and safe.

ASYLUMS

Paris
1936 TO 1938

Uncle Michael is gone from us, dropped down dead at Mass and sure, maybe, that was a grand way for him to go. He was good to us always, God rest him.

Jim is now in a powerful rage with Miss Weaver for she falsely claimed Lucia had cancer, on top of everything else, after catching a glimpse of the doctor's notes at Saint Andrew's. The doctor says it was merely a questioning note to himself that Miss Weaver saw and it means nothing. But Jim can't contain his anger at her for upsetting us all.

"I am finished with that woman," he says. "By her actions, Harriet Weaver is pushing Lucia further into insanity's abyss."

I close my lips and stay my tongue. Because Jim won't certify Lucia as lunatic, St. Andrew's say they cannot detain her any longer so, in late February, back to Paris she comes, to stay at the Jolases. Living where I am would be unhealthy for Lucia, the doctors say. And for me. My heart is shriveled to a raisin with the burden of everything. Normally I am all go and Jim is all stand still but, now, it's the other way around. I am brought to a halt by Lucy's illness and I stay at home doing little while Jim rushes around, researching this doctor and that, this treatment and the other one. I can't quite fathom how our lives have come to this.

LUCY'S FACE IS ALMOST CONSTANTLY SET IN A DEEP FROWN. It hurts me to see her. I don't go often to the Jolas house. Soon, I don't have to. Lucia violently attacks Maria Jolas with her fists, breaking a tooth in the poor woman's head, and she's straitjacketed and taken away. Doctor Delmas, at the *maison de santé* at Ivry, is her new man.

I'M LIFTED A LITTLE WHEN GEORGIE, HELEN, AND STEPHEN return from New York, though Helen looks peaky and seems to jump when anyone speaks.

I take Georgie aside. "Is Helen all right?"

He scowls. "She's just tired, Mamma."

We sit to table and it's my delight to have little Stephen by me, babbling now in a Yankee accent and grown so big that I stare at him in wonder.

"You're a proper little maneen, Stephen James Joyce." I pet his head. "A handsome lad."

"More goodies, Nonna," he shouts, and I feed him bits of heart-shaped *palmier* from my fingers.

Giorgio asks for the latest news of Lucia and we tell him how she has been—not that I'd know firsthand. The doctors say, because of her hostility toward me, that I should stay away from Ivry. In case she wallops me, I suppose. Or sets fire to the place. Jim goes to see her each Sunday; he finds great comfort in walking with her and coddling her, telling her all will be well.

"We play piano together," he tells Giorgio. "*E balliamo insieme.*" Jim lifts his arms in a waltz.

"Stop speaking Italian," Helen snaps, and we all turn to look at her, shocked by her tone. "You're such a rude family. I'm a Kastor but we don't sit around speaking German. What are you saying when you speak Italian? Is it about me?"

"Babbo just said that he and Lucy dance together at the *maison de santé*."

Helen laughs sharply. "Oh, Giorgio loves to dance, too, don't you? With all the young ladies. All the young beauties." She lights a cigarette with shaking hands. "I'm just the old hag he happens to be married to."

Silence descends and we all, even little Stephen, look at our plates. Anywhere but at one another. I try to think of something to say, to soften the atmosphere, to comfort Helen, even, but not a single sentence will form in my head. The clock ticks into the quiet and eventually I just get up and clear the dishes.

JIM AND GEORGIE GO TO IVRY AND, NO SOONER ARE THEY IN THE room with her, than Lucia leaps from one to the other, trying to strangle them.

Still, that night, Jim dreams that Lucy's cured, that her mind is restored and she is normal again. He wakes unhappy.

Jim and I go to Zürich for his eyes. I light a candle in every church I pass, for our Lucia. I light one for Helen.

JIM IS MY WHOLE LIFE NOW, THAT'S WHAT OCCURS TO ME TODAY. Our children have passed out of our hands, for better or for worse, and there's just we two again. And we have to get on with things as best we can, as a pair, and with Giorgio back and Lucy safe, we can saunter on, me and Jim. There's nobody like him and that's for sure. With things quieter, he's back writing *Finnegans*

Wake. I hear him laughing at night when I'm in bed and he stays up to write; he chortles at his own wit as he scribbles, the soft, silly man.

I knock on the wall. "Stop writing, Jim! Or do a serious bit so you're not hooting like a steam engine at all hours of the night, keeping me from sleep."

He knocks back. "Yes, my goose, yes, yes."

GIORGIO AND HELEN ARE FALLING ASUNDER AND PAUL LÉON makes an enemy of us by suggesting that it's Georgie's fault because he is, according to Léon, heartless.

"Giorgio doesn't seem to care that Helen's mind is fragile, that she needs his support," Paul says. "He needs to show Helen his love. I mean, demonstrate it to her. Physically, if necessary."

"How dare you," Jim says. "How dare you try to direct my son's actions, his life."

"That woman was never right for our boy," I say, acid on my tongue.

WE DINE AT FOUQUET'S OFTEN, JIM AND I. LOBSTER AND CHAM-pagne. *Omelette norvégienne* to finish—ice cream and meringue and sponge in a glorious heap. The sweet has always been our favorite part of any meal. One night I spot Marlene Dietrich nearby and urge Jim to send his compliments to her. She comes over and we say hello.

"My wife admires you enormously," Jim says, and I look at her shyly and smile. "We saw you in *The Blue Angel.*"

"Then, Monsieur Joyce"—she nods to each of us in turn— "Madame Joyce, you saw me at my best."

I grin to myself for a week after this encounter.

❧

Giorgio and Helen go again to New York and I'm not one bit happy about it.

"She's pushing him around," I say to Jim, hovering over him at his desk. "How can Georgie stand to be directed like that?"

"But isn't that what wives do?" he says, his face almost bewildered, and he goes back to his writing.

Herr Hitler annexes Austria in March.

"We're facing another war, Nora," Jim says, gloomily, peering at me above *Le Figaro*.

"But what can we do about it?" I say. "Nothing! We can do nothing about anything, it seems to me." And I start to cry because I feel helpless about how life unfolds in its own pattern and how little we as people can do to stop or sway it.

Gas masks are issued. Candles are in short supply. People raid the shops for tinned goods. We're heading back into the madness of battles and bloodshed again, for sure. I could fall apart thinking about it all—war, Lucy, Georgie—or I can get on with it. I decide to choose the latter.

Our friends try to guess the name of Jim's novel. Mrs. Jolas comes closest with *Fairy's Wake*. Jim is shocked at how near she is. Her husband, Eugene, guesses the correct name. He storms into Fouquet's the evening following Maria's nearly right stab at the title and, before we can even say hello, he whispers fiercely, "*Finnegans Wake!*"

Maria Jolas stands behind him, eyes bright. "Well?" she says.

Jim shakes his head. "You're a pair of clever cats," he says, handing over a pouch of money, the promised reward.

We celebrate with bottles of Moët & Chandon and it feels good to toast and laugh and forget about all troubles for a spell.

GIORGIO AND HELEN RETURN FROM AMERICA, AND HELEN IS clearly under a grim cloud. Before long she's admitted to a mental clinic in Montreux.

"She'll brighten herself, for Giorgio's sake," Jim says. "For her sons' sakes."

"If only it were that easy," I murmur.

WAKE

⌇

PARIS 1939, SAINT-GÉRAND-LE-PUY 1940, AND
ZÜRICH 1941

J IM FINISHES THE BOOK. HE'S IN A STATE OF SIMPLE SATISFAC-
tion with it that gladdens my soul.

"Congratulations, my love," I say. I kiss the top of his head
and lead him away from his desk to sit with me on the sofa.

"Toward the end of the novel," Jim tells me, "Anna Livia says
'how small it's all.'" He pats my hand. "How small it's all, Nora."

"Isn't it true for her, Jim?" I put my arm around him and rest
my head on his shoulder. "The world is a small place, but its sorrows are terribly big."

THE SECOND OF FEBRUARY 1939, AND HELEN, OUT FROM THE
Montreux hospital and doing well, organizes a big do for Jim's
fifty-seventh birthday. Helen goes all out: there's an Eiffel Tower
decanter for the Saint Patrice wine; there's a Nelson's Pillar bottle
full of Pernod, and silver paper along the tables to represent the
rivers Liffey and Seine; there's a huge cake with each of Jim's book
covers on it, right up to *Finnegans Wake*. Best of all, Jim is given
a bound copy of the book by Eugene and Maria Jolas, though it
won't be out officially until May. He asks Helen to read the closing

passage aloud to the company and though, to my ears, an Irish accent would sound more correct, I have to admit she does a good job. I imagine the river, as she reads, running through Dublin town and on out to lovely Howth.

I remember Jim asking me, outside Finn's Hotel, if I understood him, and I recall our days atop Howth Hill, kissing and exploring each other, with the high excitement of new lovers. I look at him now and my heart skitters with pride; I put my hand to my breast. The candlelight catches the beautiful aquamarine ring Jim gave me this morning, telling me it represents the Liffey and our fateful meeting in Dublin.

I stand and speak once Helen is finished reciting. "I mightn't have read *Ulysses* to the end, Jim, but I'll definitely get through the *Wake*, I'll make it my business to."

"Nora, you only managed eleven pages of *Ulysses*, including the cover," he says. Everyone laughs. "I wish you luck getting through this." He holds up the book and we all cheer.

HITLER IS BREAKING UP EUROPE. POLAND FALLS, BRITAIN AND France declare war on Germany. Helen has another breakdown and is back at Montreux. Doctor Delmas at Ivry tells us that for the safety of Lucia, and all of his patients, he's evacuating the hospital to La Baule, south of Brittany. This worries us but, apparently, it's the best course of action.

Every bone in my body throbs and my own doctor says I have arthritis and have had it awhile. The whole of our world is splintering and I can do nothing to stop it. There's no foothold, no handhold. I turn to Jim, but sometimes he seems far away from me, on the other side of some gulf that we've made and yet not made. How has our life come to this: Lucia locked away and Giorgio lost inside a doomed marriage? Is Jim happier inside the words he invents than alongside me in our day-to-day existence? I don't understand anything anymore.

GIORGIO COMES TO US TO TELL US THAT HELEN IS OUT OF HOSPITAL and acting very strangely.

"In what way, loveen?" I ask.

"Well, there's the fact that she's carrying two Persian kittens around Paris with her to attract the attention of men, for example." He grimaces.

I gasp. "Surely not?"

"Have I not just said that she *is*, Mamma?" he barks.

"All right, pet." I glance across at Jim. "Is she more herself once at home?"

Georgie streams smoke out through his nose. "I wouldn't know—I'm staying with Alec Ponisovsky these days. But I'm told she invites strangers home with her and, well, you can guess what else."

"Oh." My head throbs. "Strangers. Men, you mean?"

He nods and his face is miserable. "Helen would be safer back in America, near her family, but she won't listen to me. Perhaps Paul Léon might convince her, Babbo? She usually heeds him."

"So you want me to speak to Léon?"

"If you could. Helen is wild. I'm only glad that Stephen is away at Mrs. Jolas's school at Saint-Gérand-le-Puy, so he doesn't have to see it all. See *her*. Can you imagine?" Georgie fidgets with his matchbox. "There's something else, Babbo. Helen has intimated to the police that you're a spy."

"Oh, for the love of God, does Helen Fleischman want to get your father lifted by the Gestapo?" I shout. "Does she want him expelled like poor Stannie was from Italy? I'll murder her!"

Jim rises. "I'll go and telephone Léon now."

WE GO TO CLINIQUE DES CHARMETTES AT PORNICHET, NEAR LA Baule, to see and settle Lucia. She rises slowly from her bed to greet us and looks to me like a defeated person, the type of woman who used to hawk stolen hares around the streets of Galway, slow and dead-eyed and sad. We hug her and she weeps quietly; angry, hateful Lucia is not here now, but neither is our lit-up, sweet Lucy, our only girl.

"Will I be safe from the bombs here, Mamma?" she asks, creases scarring her forehead.

"You will of course, loveen."

"It's only that I nearly died of fear whenever the planes went over Paris. They were so close, so loud." She looks at the ceiling as if she can hear the thunder of fighters.

"Fret not, Lucia," Jim says, circling her into his embrace and holding her close. I put my arms around them both and hold tight.

PAUL LÉON REFUSES TO INTERVENE WHERE HELEN IS CON- cerned, saying again that Giorgio just needs to be kinder to her, to act like a husband ought to. We're as mad as cats with Léon. Geor- gie sends a frantic telegraph to Brittany asking us to return quickly to Paris; Helen took Stephen from school and Georgie had to go and wrestle the boy away from her. There was a terrible tussle and, of course, the poor child is in bits.

We return to the clinic to say our good-byes to Lucia and she cries silently, her tears a constant river down her face.

"Promise me you'll be back soon, Mamma," she gulps. "Babbo, you'll return to me?"

"We will be back *presto*," her father says, cradling Lucy and kiss- ing her head. "Quicker than you can snap your fingers, *cara mia*."

I hug Lucia to my breast. "Be good, my girleen," I say, and we leave.

HELEN IS AT THE *MAISON DE SANTÉ* AT SURESNES. STEPHEN AND Georgie move in with us, but the place would be too cramped for four mice, let alone four people, so we send Stephen back to the Jolas school at Saint-Gérand-le-Puy and we three temporarily move to the Hotel Lutétia on Boulevard Raspail. We go back daily to the flat to get our papers in order and I tear up all the letters written to me by Jim.

"Why, Gooseen?" he says, a forlorn look to him when he sees the pile.

"Sure, they're nobody's business but our own, Jim. Be sure you get rid of mine, too."

Maria Jolas says we should spend Christmas with her and Stephen at Saint-Gérand-le-Puy and we, and Georgie, decide that we will. What is there for us in Paris now? We arrive on Christmas Eve and stay at the Hotel de la Paix.

"In times of war, we find peace at the Paix," Jim says, tipping the porter; we stand in our room like a pair of orphans, surrounded by bags.

"Lift my trunk onto the bed for me," I say to Jim, but he doesn't move.

In half a second he's bent over in pain, clutching at his stomach. "Oh, for the love of Christ," he calls out and falls onto the bed.

I run to Georgie's room and, by the time we get back, Jim is under the covers and quiet.

"It's his nerves," I say to my son. "We'll leave him be for now, let him rest."

Georgie nods and leaves. I sit by Jim and watch him sleep and wonder, truly, where we'll ever fetch up.

✒

ALL ADVICE IS NOT TO GO BACK TO PARIS, SO WE STAY WHERE WE are. Georgie, though, goes to and fro to the city and Jim warns him to be careful because the German soldiers around Saint-Gérand, or in Paris, could lift him anytime, on any grounds.

"As sure as shit stinks, Giorgio has a woman in Paris," Jim says today when Georgie's gone.

"God, Jim, do you have to be so crude?" I say, wringing my hands, which are knotted from the arthritis and no amount of sitting where it's warm seems to help. The pain creeps up my legs, too, and even my shoulders ache some days. "Anyway, what if Georgie does have a woman? Doesn't he deserve a bit of diversion after all he's been through?"

"As long as she's sane," Jim says grimly.

"She is," I say, then clamp my hand to my mouth for I was meant to keep it to myself.

Jim laughs. "You have to tell me now, Gooseen. The cat's well and truly out. Who?"

"Peggy Guggenheim," I say, feeling guilty for betraying Georgie's secret.

"And how on earth are you privy to this?"

"I think he just needed to tell someone. To confess."

"Ever the Catholic girl, Nora." He folds his newspaper. "Guggenheim collects other people's husbands as passionately as she collects paintings. Let's hope Helen doesn't find out."

"Well, we won't be the ones to tell her anyway."

JIM GETS BLITHERED ON PERNOD BEFORE DINNER EVERY EVE-ning and eats only scraps from his plate.

"I'd prefer to see a glass of wine in your hand rather than that auld stuff," I tell him. He nods but ignores me. "Eat something, won't you?" But he prods at the food with his cutlery and dines on flaky sugared pastries at home instead. "Pernod and cake, and then you wonder why your stomach is crippling you?" I shake my head.

On Sundays we take Stephen away from the school and he plays with his trains and cars and jigsaws on our floor and Jim reads to him.

"Read the one about me, Nonno," Stephen says, and Jim reads out passages from *A Portrait of the Artist as a Young Man*.

"More food, Nonna," Stephen calls to me, and I give him a plate with a chicken sandwich and my own apple tart and a nice dollop of cream. I love to cosset him for he's a darling boy, he got all his father's good parts.

Time passes like treacle in Saint-Gérand, slow and thick the days go, and we dander along inside them.

HITLER STORMS ON. APRIL 1940 AND GERMANY OCCUPIES DEN- mark. Norway falls. In May, Holland and Belgium are taken. In June, Paris. Helen's brother gets her out of the hospital at Suresnes and to an asylum in Connecticut before Paris is occupied, for which we're all thankful.

Paul and Lucie Léon arrive in Saint-Gérand. A shaky peace breaks out between Jim and Paul and, to pass the time, they work together on collating Jim's reviews and so on. Giorgio is back with us, too, and I'm nothing but relieved. I don't ask about Peggy and he offers nothing. Jim is worried about our possessions in the flat in Paris. The war has our money tied up and we can't get the rent to the landlord there; he might destroy our things and let the flat out to somebody else.

Jim writes to everyone he can think of to try to get Lucy out of France and to an asylum in Switzerland. We're worn to a thread with worry about her; she haunts my dreams at night and my breath catches twenty times a day when I think of her. Jim plans every step of Lucia's journey to Switzerland, he secures an exit permit, he recruits escorts. He nearly has her. But then the Germans go back on their word—she can't have the permit after all. We're devastated; Jim takes it worst of all and refuses to get out of bed for a week. I'm moidered with the strain of it all.

A pair of turtledoves take to sitting on our windowsill and I enjoy their happy burble; it takes me out of my own mind and its brew of unhappiness. I go to the grocer's to buy seed for them and meet Paul Léon out for a stroll. He inquires after Jim who is still in the bed with his bad stomach and his upset about Lucia.

"The heat is killing him, Monsieur Léon. It's hotter than Hades here. And we're concerned about dear Lucy and about the flat in Paris, too. Jim is fretting mightily about everything. It does him no good."

"I'm going to Paris in September, Mrs. Joyce. Let me see what I can do."

TRUE TO HIS WORD, PAUL LÉON GOES TO PARIS. BUT HE'S A RUSsian Jew and he lingers too long there. The Gestapo takes him. In our sorrow, we're now also more worried about the asylum at Pornichet and Lucia.

MRS. JOLAS DECIDES TO CLOSE HER SCHOOL IN SAINT-GÉRAND and take her daughters back to America.

"It's too precarious," she says. "Eugene insists that we come home."

"We'll miss you so much," I tell her.

"Come with us," she says. "You'll be safe in America."

Jim looks at me, his face unreadable. "Nora, do you want to

go?" I know he's thinking of Lucia and the distance it would put between us and her.

"All that water, Jim. The wide Atlantic. Jesus in heaven, I couldn't do it."

He looks relieved. "Nor can I."

"Whatever Lucy feels about me, I couldn't bear to be so far from her."

"Lucia loves you, Nora," Jim assures me. "She's just unwell." It costs him to admit it, I know. "She is," I say.

OUR TURTLEDOVES HAVE FLED AND IT'S CLEAR, NOW, THAT WE need to go somewhere other than here too. France is no longer safe for us.

"Zürich," Jim says.

But the Swiss authorities want twenty thousand francs before they'll let us in and no money can get from our bank in London to here, so we can't pay it. Next thing the Swiss say that Jim is Jewish and, therefore, we're not welcome anyway.

"Sure your blood is green!" I say. "What are they on about?"

We get over that by proving our citizenship and, then, with help from old Zürich friends—the Giedions and the Brauchbars—we make up the cash to let us through. We have to plot our leave-taking in secret; Giorgio says we must be unfailingly covert, no one must know we're leaving, and this frightens me.

IN NOVEMBER, MY SISTER KATHLEEN TELEGRAPHS TO SAY THAT Mammy has died. As bald as that. I do not know of what or even when she went.

"I don't think my poor heart can take another shock," I say to Jim, and he holds me on our bed while I blub into my pillow. Poor, poor Mammy. She had a long, hard life and now she's gone back to ashes. "What's it all for, Jim? For the love of God, what is anything for?"

"This life is nothing but a wander through the wilderness of Ziph, Nora, and none of us know what it's for." Jim's at a very low ebb when he's quoting from the Bible and we hold each other and cry fountains of tears for poor Mammy, who loved us both well.

Little Stephen hears us weeping and comes into our bedroom and climbs between us. "Poor Nonna. Poor Nonno," he says, dabbing at our tears with his handkerchief and I thank the Lord on high that life and love go on, in spite of all.

PENSION DELPHIN, ZÜRICH. WE LEFT SAINT-GÉRAND IN THE dead of a mid-December night, Jim's face as gray as his hair with the pain in his gut and the stress of it all. Georgie and Stephen nervous and quiet. But we got here, thanks be to God. We're safe.

We pass Christmas quietly, thinking of Lucy and raising our glasses to her. The New Year steals in and we reacquaint ourselves with the city. We eat once more in the Kronenhalle and Herr Zumsteg welcomes us back as if we are lost family. Jim, of course, piddles with his fork and eats nothing; Giorgio, just like him, does the same. Both drink, wine and brandy. Only Stephen and I eat heartily of the veal and potatoes.

Back at the Delphin, and we're only in the door, when Jim begins to howl and clutch at his stomach.

"Oh God, Nora, oh help me, help me," he bellows.

Giorgio gets him up onto the bed and Jim writhes and grabs at his belly like a woman about to give birth. I get up beside him and hold him.

"You're all right, Jim. Jim, listen to me, you're going to be all right." I look to my son. "Call an ambulance, Georgie, quick."

Jim is taken out on a stretcher to the Roten Kreuz hospital, Stephen running after him calling, "Nonno! Nonno!"

The hospital gives him morphine and, when he comes to in the morning, he's bleary. "I didn't think I'd wake, Nora," he says, when he sees me.

"Well, you did." I try to hold back my tears and disguise my terror. "Sure you're as tough as old boots, James Joyce." I take his hand and it's cold. "A perforated ulcer, they said," I tell him, but he only nods.

I sit by Jim all day, reading bits of the paper aloud and singing "The Lass of Aughrim" to him, slow and low; he slides in and out of sleep. I watch the soft rise and fall of his chest and pray that he will be made well.

Jim opens his eyes. "Is Lucia coming to me?" he says, and I'm alarmed at the question—where does he think we are? I squeeze his hand.

"Take your rest, my love."

Giorgio and Stephen come in for a few hours; Jim is quiet, serene. The doctor tells us to go home, that he'll call if there's any change.

"I'd much rather stay, Doctor, if it's all the same to you."

Georgie puts his hand to my back. "Mamma, you must take care of yourself to be good for Babbo. You need some sleep too."

I nod. "All right so."

We kiss Jim good night in turn and he smiles. "Gooseen," is all he says to me.

I kiss his forehead and say, "I love you, Jim. You're my darling."

THE TELEPHONE BESIDE MY BED BRAYS IN THE NIGHT, CUTTING into my sleep. I have the receiver in my hand before I'm even aware of what's happening.

"Come now," the doctor says.

I rouse Giorgio, dress myself, and ask the landlady to watch Stephen. We rush to the Roten Kreuz.

"I wish today wasn't the thirteenth," I say to Georgie in the taxi. The doctor meets us at Jim's door. "He's gone," he says.

JIM DIED ALONE. PERITONITIS SET IN AND IT KILLED HIM. HE woke and asked for me. I cannot stand the idea of it, Jim calling for me, his fingers reaching for mine and finding nothing but dead air. It wounds me to think of his hand flailing, his voice calling to me and getting no answer in return. I want to go back in time and stay by him, hold his hand in mine, sing and croon to him, to ease him out of this world and into the next. What in God's name will my life be without him? We were like one person with many sides and, now, my best part is gone. Oh Jim, oh my lovely darling, I don't know how to go on without you.

WE BURY HIM IN FLUNTERN CEMETERY, UP ON THE ZÜRICHBERG, beside the zoo. He'll hear the whoops of the monkeys and the bellow of the lions, by day and night, and that'll amuse him surely. I get him a wreath of green, shaped as a harp. Jim would pretend to dislike the wreath, but would love it, really. He'd see it was for music as much as for Ireland. He'd see my love woven through the leaves.

It snows.

"The snow is general," I say to Georgie, and he smiles and tears run down his face.

I don't cry. My heart is frozen to a pit. As the coffin is lowered, I see Jim's beloved face for the last time through the vitrine.

"Jim," I call out, "how beautiful you are."

I can't go to the funeral reception at the Giedions' house; I don't want anyone's eyes on me. Instead, I return to the Pension Delphin alone and sit at my bedroom window to watch the snow falling.

"'Sleepily the flakes, silver and dark, falling obliquely against the lamplight,'" I murmur to myself and finger my ivory necklace that I wore today to honor Jim. I open the window, push out my hand, and let the snow fall faintly onto my fingers.

"Love is unhappy when love is away," I say, into the dark air.

ENDINGS

❧

Zürich
1941 TO 1951

G IORGIO, STEPHEN, AND I GET A FLAT ON DUFOURSTRASSE
and we can just cover the rent. Our money is all tied up with
this war. I'm worried that Lucia will be thrown out of the clinic
at Pornichet if her bills are not paid; it's hard to even get a letter
through to Miss Weaver or to receive a reply, to make sure the
payments are kept up.

"What would the Gestapo do to Lucy if they had her?" I ask
Georgie, over breakfast this morning. "They say Hitler hates the
handicapped as much as he hates the poor Jews. Would that in-
clude people like Lucia?"

"Mamma, set your mind at rest. Doctor Delmas will protect
everyone under his care." He sighs. "If only it didn't cost so much
to keep Lucia there."

"And then there's the worry of that Giedion woman; she's biting at my heels to pay her back the money she put up to get us into
Zürich. How am I meant to pay that without access to your father's
royalties and so on?" I drip honey onto a roll and take a bite.

Giorgio waves his cigarette. "If only I could get some employ-
ment." He can't work without a permit, and if he leaves Switzerland, he'll be enlisted. What would I do then?

"We're in a bind, all right," I murmur.

Georgie sips his coffee. "When does Frau Giedion mean to hand over Babbo's death mask to us, Mamma?"

I tut. "The woman won't part with it until I've paid my debt, that's what she's said to me." Georgie rises. "Oh no, son, don't go causing a riot with the Giedions. Please. My nerves are too flittered for a row."

He puts his hand to my shoulder. "Fret not, Mamma. I'm going to telegraph Weaver again and press on her the urgency of our situation."

I pat his hand. "Saint Harriet will come through with some money, she always does."

ALL BRITISH NATIONALS HAVE BEEN ORDERED TO LEAVE FRANCE. I'm distraught over Lucia. The doctor says all my worry is seizing me up even more, so it's no wonder that some days I can't even go to the shop for our bread, my body is such a weave of pain. I take to the bed and Stephen sits by me to read, sometimes from the newspaper, sometimes my favorite passages from *Finnegans Wake*. He's a dear boy, and but for him and Georgie, I'd be in the ground beside Jim. We get word that Doctor Delmas has safeguarded all those at Pornichet against the expulsion order; he's a man of miracles, surely, and we owe him a great deal.

I go to Fluntern, to the grave, any time my old bones will let me. I take the electric tram up the hill and I like its rackety jaunt and the hours it uses up to go to the graveyard and linger awhile with Jim. I pick away the weeds and make sure there's plenty of greenery around Jim for he always preferred simple leaves to flowers. I sit on the graveside and talk to him.

"Our little Stephen grows more handsome by the day, Jim, and he's off to boarding school in Zug." I tell Jim that Lucia's safe despite Herr Hitler and that Georgie's moving into a flat of his own and I confess my worries about his idleness and drinking. "I don't think either thing does him a pinch of good, Jim." I put my hand to the gravestone. "But sure, at least he's here with me. At least I'm not entirely alone."

GEORGIE AND I MEET IN THE RESTAURANT GLEICH MOST DAYS. They serve only vegetable dishes, but I like it because it's nearby and cheap.

Today I try to get him to eat a salad or some strawberries, but he says, as he always does, "I just don't have your pleasure in food." He plops sugar lumps into his coffee. "Do you think you'll stay in Zürich, Mamma, when the war ends?"

"Will it ever end?" I shrug. "I don't love this city, son, but isn't it a grand place for an old lady, truly?"

"Would you go back to Ireland?"

"The country that burned your father's books on a bonfire? That gave him the cold shoulder even in death?" I shake my head. "I will not, I'll never go back. When we asked that Count O'Kelly if he'd arrange for your father's body to be buried in Dublin, and he sent back a big fat no, well, that ended me with the place." I sigh and press my sore knuckles. I do sometimes think that a cottage in Galway would be nice, but then I think of the soaky damp—bad for arthritis—and I think of the way Ireland doesn't like James Joyce and I smother the idea. "And anyway, Jim's here. How could I leave him?"

"Stephen says he wants to go to New York, when it's all over." Georgie frowns.

"You don't like it, son?"

"I hate to think of the influence of those bloody Kastors on him; I hate to think of him so far away."

I shake my head. "They're his family, too, Georgie. And, no doubt, he misses his mother. And David his brother."

"Still, I don't relish the idea."

"But you'll let him go anyway, the same way your babbo and I always let you do what you wanted."

He sighs. "I suppose I will, Mamma."

NINETEEN FORTY-FIVE. THE WAR IS OVER, THANK GOD. BUT, still, all I think of is money. That and arthritis and Lucia. Jim, too, of course, but less so now. The wires of grief thrum long and loud but the din, and the swallowed-up-ness in sorrow, lessens over time. I never thought grief would ease, but it does, it becomes less of a clamor. And Miss Weaver is sorting our money and we'll soon be in a better position, now that communications are open again.

Stephen is in America, but he'll come back over to see us, all going well. Lucia is safely returned to Doctor Delmas's clinic in Ivry. And Giorgio has a new woman, Asta, an eye doctor.

"Asta might have fixed Babbo's eyes if he'd lived," my son says wistfully.

"She might."

I go to the bathroom and, when I return, Giorgio's sitting by the window in the sunlight, my little cat on his lap, and whatever way the light glints off his glasses, and the side of his face, I cry out, "Jim!" He turns to me in surprise, but my heart is so full and tears are so close that I can only shake my head. "There's no mistaking you as your father's son, Georgie," I say eventually.

MY DAYS NOW ARE GENTLE IN THEIR MOVEMENT, DESPITE THE gnarled bits of trees that are my knees, knuckles, ankles, hips, and shoulders. When I can walk, I go to a bench beside the lake and bathe in the afternoon sun, letting it beam down on me and warm my tired bones. It's hard to believe that it's seven years since Jim left me; time seems to move both fast and slow. I think gently on him and my mind conjures Lucia sometimes, too, but mostly I can't bear to dwell on her, so I lock her into a dark room in my head and keep her safely there.

Today Giorgio joins me on my bench and, from his face, I can tell there's news.

"Is it Lucy?" I say, alarmed.

He touches my hand. "No, Mamma, not that. I got a letter. There's to be an exhibition and auction of some of Papà's things in Paris."

"What things?"

"Manuscripts and so forth. Some of the portraits."

"Oh." I imagine our possessions flung to the four winds. I look at Georgie. "And who benefits from this sale?"

"You do, Mamma. We do. Us."

I brighten. "Well, then. We must go."

"How can Paris look so untouched and innocent after a war?" I ask Giorgio, peering out of the hotel window, down Boulevard Raspail, at the shining facades and the intact window grilles.

"I think the people of Porte de la Chapelle might argue with that, Mamma; the place was destroyed. Over six hundred killed there too."

"Oh, I didn't know."

"Sometimes it's better *not* to know things."

I sit into an armchair and drum my fingers while Giorgio sifts through pages. We're waiting for Miss Weaver to come and help us sort the mounds of papers. I've no joy in the work for I've never liked this kind of thing, but Miss Weaver will know what to do I'm sure. A timid knock to the door and I pull myself up and open it.

Harriet is there, a weird little straw hat cocked backward on her head, looking the same as she ever did. She smiles and embraces me.

"Oh, Mrs. Joyce," she whispers.

"I think we might be Nora and Harriet now, what do you think, Miss Weaver?"

She puts her hand to her mouth and laughs. "Indeed, Nora."

She comes in, sits down, and promptly begins to tell us that, before he was taken and killed, Paul Léon had given items of ours, from our flat, to Count O'Kelly for safekeeping, but they were intended to be sent to the National Library in Dublin.

I'm shocked. "The Lord have mercy on Paul. But can the count do that? Can he take our letters and things and not return them?"

"It seems so."

"Well, that bloody Count O'Kelly seems to have made it his life's plan to annoy me!"

"Nora, there's also the matter of the *Finnegans Wake* manuscripts in my possession," Harriet says. "Might it be an idea to offer them to the National Library also, to keep the papers together?"

"No," I say violently. "If Ireland and the Irish won't have Jim, they won't have his manuscripts. Damn them."

Harriet glances at Georgie. "But to separate the papers, is that wise? Where should the *Wake* manuscripts go?"

I think for a moment. "The British Museum can have them. We got more support from London in our lives than we ever did from Dublin."

"If you're sure," Harriet says, her face a little gray cloud.

GIORGIO AND MARIA JOLAS, RETURNED FROM AMERICA, GO TO visit Lucia at the clinic in Ivry. I, Georgie says, must wait my turn.

"Don't be ludicrous," I tell him. "I'm not sitting here like a fool while you go and visit my daughter without me."

"Mamma," he stays me with his hand. "Doctor Delmas says Lucia is much changed. Let me go to see her first, to test the waters, as it were. Then you shall go."

WHEN HE RETURNS, GEORGIE LOOKS LIKE A MAN WHO'S SEEN AN apparition.

"Tell me," I say.

He tips his chin heavenward and groans. "We walked for an hour in the grounds, just Lucia and I." He sucks his lip, clears his throat. "She is portly now, Mamma, silver-haired. She has hairs on her chin and she says that she worries that they'll prevent her from marrying."

"Oh, the craythur." My eyes sting with tears. "To think she still nurses the notion of a husband."

Georgie winces. "She wants to marry Tom McGreevy, she says, because they both like food. She babbles a lot, Mamma. Refuses to believe that Babbo is gone, then, in the next breath, says somewhat matter-of-factly that she read of his death in the newspaper." He sighs. "I spoke to Doctor Delmas. He says she's still prone to attacking others and that she breaks windows too. They use the *camisole de force* often on her."

"The straitjacket." I hang my head. "My poor Lucy."

Giorgio slips to his knees before me and grips my hands. "Mamma, you can't go out there."

"What? No! After all this time, I must see her. What would she think if I didn't? No, I have to see my Lucy; don't be absurd, Giorgio."

He stares into my eyes. "Mamma, I'm pleading with you. Do this for me. Hold Lucia in your memory, remember her the way she was when she was a girl. She's very much changed, Mamma. Unrecognizable, almost. Preserve her in your heart and mind as she was before any of this." He kisses my knuckles. "Preserve yourself."

My whole body slackens and I feel powerless and sad. "I only ever loved her, Georgie," I whisper. "I only ever wanted to keep her safe."

"I know, Mamma, I know. And Lucia knows and she loves you too."

GETTING DRESSED IS A PERFORMANCE THESE DAYS, I'M STIFFER than a marionette. I have a cozy room in the Pension Neptun and it's easy to keep neat and I don't go out much anymore, save to Holy Mass. So mostly I don't bother to dress. At night, my rosary beads slide through my fingers to the floor and I have to leave the beads where they fall for it'd take me an hour, and a range of shifts and groans, to lever myself from the bed to retrieve them. God will understand.

It's ten years since I lost Jim, which is hard for me to credit. Miss Weaver—dear Saint Harriet—has brought Lucia to England to be near her, to St. Andrew's in Northampton once again.

"She's safe," I say to Georgie. "My Lucy is properly safe now. I can rest easy."

My legs go. I'm so stiff that all the joints seize up and I'm able to walk no more. In April Georgie takes me to the Paracelsus Clinic by Lake Zürich. My days are a blur, I seem to drop into sleep without asking to and I wake for only minutes at a time. I hardly know where I am. Giorgio brings the priest.

"I must be bad if you're here," I say to the padre and he smiles and prays over me.

I can feel my heart slowing, it's been tick-tocking less since

Jim left me, now it lags and loiters inside my breast as if I no longer need it.

My Georgie is here with me, so like Jim, lean and pale and serious.

Lucia comes to me, too, to say farewell and she's brushing her dark, thick hair in long strokes by my bedside and she smiles.

"*Ciao, mammina mia bella,*" she says.

My girl, my girl.

I open my eyes and touch Georgie's cheek. "Ever my babbling Roman baby, ever my lovely, violet-eyed son," I say, and his eyes are wet. "Don't cry, don't cry, Giorgio, my darling. Your father is waiting for me."

Yes, Jim waits for me and I will go to him.

"Gooseen," I hear, "come, Gooseen." And it feels now as if I have sprouted wings large enough to blot out the sun. Up I rise and I follow Jim's voice that I love so well. To Jim I am Ireland, yes, still I am. I'm island shaped, he says, large as the land itself, small as the Muglins, a woman on her back, splayed and hungry, waiting for her lover. I'm limestone and grass, heather and granite. I am rising paps and cleft of valley. I'm the raindrops that soak and the sea that rims the coast.

Jim says I am harp and shamrock, tribe and queen. I am high cross and crowned heart, held between two hands. I'm turf, he says, and bog cotton. I am the sun pulling the moon on a rope to smile over the Maamturk Mountains.

Jim styles me his sleepy-eyed Nora. His squirrel girl from the pages of Ibsen. I am pirate queen and cattle raider. I'm his blessed little blackguard. I am, he says, his auburn marauder. I'm his honorable barnacle goose. His Gooseen.

And I see Jim standing before me now, his cane in one hand,

the other outstretched. He's smiling, the special, crooked smile that is only for me, and I sail toward him, free in my body and in my mind.

I hold out my hand and Jim takes it, I rush into his arms and feel the smother of his love. My only one, my Jim.

Together we walk on.

Author's Note

NORA IS A WORK OF BIOGRAPHICAL FICTION BASED CLOSELY ON the life of Nora Barnacle Joyce. Some small facts have been altered or amended for dramatic purposes, but by and large, I've adhered to what's known of the Joyce family's peripatetic life in Europe.

Nora Barnacle Joyce died of uremia (kidney failure) on April 10, 1951. She was sixty-seven. She was buried in Fluntern Cemetery, but not in the same grave as James Joyce. In 1966, Nora's remains were moved to lie alongside her beloved Jim.

Giorgio Joyce married his second wife, Asta Jahnke, and moved to Germany. He died there of a stroke in 1976 at the age of seventy-one. Giorgio was buried with his parents in Zürich.

Lucia Joyce was moved to St. Andrew's Hospital in Northampton, England, in 1951 and remained there for the rest of her life. Miss Weaver was her guardian and looked out for Lucia until her own death in 1961; after that, Lucia's needs were cared for by Weaver's niece. Lucia died from stroke in 1982 at the age of seventy-five and, at her own request, she was buried in England.

Stanislaus Joyce died on Bloomsday 1955. He and his wife, Nelly, had one son, James, in 1943. Stannie is buried in Trieste.

Stephen Joyce, James Joyce's sole descendant, lived in France until his death in January 2020. Stephen's mother, Helen Kastor Joyce, died in 1963.

ACKNOWLEDGMENTS

THANKS TO MY FAMILY FOR WELCOMING NORA AND JIM, AND MY enthusiasm for them, into our fold. Biggest thanks to Finbar, of course, for endless patience when my writing cabin life means I'm absent from our house life.

A huge *go raibh míle maith agat* to Gráinne Fox for being the kindest, cleverest, most fun agent a writer could hope for. Gratitude also to all at Fletcher & Company for continued stellar work and cheerleading.

Enormous thanks to my editor at HarperCollins USA, the gentle and wise Sarah Stein, who took Nora to her heart like an old friend. And to editors Alicia Tan and Laurie McGee for additional sharp, welcome editing.

To Nora Hickey M'Sichili and all the staff at the Centre Culturel Irlandais in Paris, where some of this novel was written—thanks for gifting me a month in Paris to follow in Nora and Jim's footsteps. My thanks to the Arts Council of Ireland for a Literature Bursary that gave me the time to finish this novel. Thanks also to Paul Maddern of the River Mill in Northern Ireland, for providing the best of writing retreats, where knotty novels can be unknotted in glorious peace. And *grazie mille* to Elizabeth McDonald for valued language assistance.

And thanks, of course, to Nora Barnacle herself, the original and best Galway girl—so beautiful, brave, calm, and strong. I wrote this book to honor you, dear Gooseen.

About the author

About the book

Insights,
Interviews
& More . . .

Read on

Meet Nuala O'Connor

NUALA O'CONNOR GREW up in Dublin,
Ireland. A graduate of Trinity College
Dublin and Dublin City University, she
holds a BA in the Irish language and an
MA in Translation Studies. She is the
author of the biofictional novel *Miss Emily*,
about the poet Emily Dickinson and her
Irish maid, as well as three other novels,
five short-story collections, and three
books of poetry. Nuala is a writing mentor
to new writers, and she is the editor in
chief of the online flash fiction journal
Splonk. She lives in County Galway with
her husband and three children. ∾

About the author

Backstory:
A Conversation with Nuala O'Connor

What drew you to Nora Barnacle's story?
Twenty-five years ago, I moved from
Dublin to Galway city, where Nora
Barnacle is from, and was aware of her as
a strong, vibrant local woman, the life
partner of James Joyce, one who gave him
her unquestioning love and support. As a
teenager, I had read and loved Brenda
Maddox's biography *Nora*, and I often
thought about this feisty Galway woman
who became a true European and amusing
muse to Joyce. I admired the way she had
escaped oppressive Catholic Ireland and
found freedoms abroad. I began to attend
the annual Bloomsday celebration at
Nora's mother's house in Bowling Green—
now a tiny museum—to celebrate both
Nora and Joyce, and I was one of one
hundred readers who read there, from
Ulysses, on the centenary of Bloomsday
in 2004.

It occurred to me to write a novel about
Nora when I was studying Italian by night
and had to write an essay about Joyce's
friendship with the Triestine writer Italo
Svevo. Around the same time, we rescued
a one-eyed cat and I called her Nora
Barnacle. I wrote a short story about Nora,
"Gooseen," which was well received, and
then just found I wanted to spend more
time in Nora's company, to unpick the
whys and wherefores of her life with
Joyce. ▶

You have written biographical fiction before, about Emily Dickinson, as well as the music hall performer and Irish countess Belle Bilton. What is the attraction for you of real lives?

I aim to resurrect these women; I want to reintroduce them to the world as the rounded, wonderful, spiky, real people they were. I don't want to make paragons of them—I aim to get a feel for what their *lived* lives were like. One of the joys of writing biographical fiction is giving the central protagonist an emotional life and a day-to-day existence that is mostly uncharted outside the known facts of their lives. We know that Nora was charismatic, that she buoyed Joyce up, and that she was the inspiration for many of his female characters, including Molly Bloom. But by putting Nora at the center of this novel, I had the chance to get inside her skin and see how she felt about life with her beloved Jim and their children, about what she longed for, and what tried and pleased her.

How did you go about the research for Nora?

There are hundreds of books relating to Joyce's life and work, but I started with Richard Ellmann's superb biography of Joyce, then reread Maddox's *Nora*, and another slim biography by an Irish priest. I then read many other books by and about Joyce, including ones on his father, on Lucia, and also *My Brother's Keeper* by Stanislaus Joyce. I like to do my research in tandem with the writing, which makes for long, busy days, but I love that complete immersion in the work.

I like to walk the ground my characters walked, so I traveled to Trieste and visited the buildings where the Joyce family lived; ate in cafés they frequented; and, of course, visited the Museo Joyce there. I did the same in Zürich, paying a visit to the James Joyce Foundation.

I also secured a monthlong writing residency at the Centre Culturel Irlandais in Paris and worked on the novel there, while trotting around many of the Joyces' twenty addresses, and various cafés and other haunts.

If I see a stage adaptation of any of Joyce's work, I go along, and have been to several Molly Bloom interpretations, including some in Tigh Nora (Nora's House)—a gin bar, named for Nora, in Galway city.

I rewatched Pat Murphy's film *Nora*, but it ends in Trieste, so there was a lot more life after that for the Joyces; their beginnings were crucial and fascinating, of course, but I wanted my novel to span Nora's life.

I also did a course at the James Joyce Centre in Dublin called Ulysses for All to brush up on *Ulysses,* and it was fantastic, and I became a member of MoLI, the new Museum of Literature Ireland, which has a heavy Joyce bias.

The research is one thing, of course, and the writing is another. Generally, I research by night and use my days to get inside the person, to put her on. By being Nora on the page, and feeling how she may have felt, I try to bring her alive for the reader, make her a vivid, breathing woman with a real woman's joys, concerns, and issues, and her responses to them.

What will you work on next?
I am writing about another feisty, historic Irishwoman (I can't resist them!), and the plan, for now, is to write her story as a novella, but my plans may morph and bloom into something else entirely. We shall see. Other than that, I'm planning a contemporary novel and writing short stories. As a flash fiction fanatic, I'm writing those, too, and I also edit an online flash journal called *Splonk.* ᐁ

Further Reading

I recommend the following books to anyone interested in reading more about the lives of Nora Barnacle and James Joyce:

Nora: The Real Life of Molly Bloom by Brenda Maddox

Nora Barnacle Joyce : A Portrait by Pádraic Ó Laoi

Nora by Gerardine Meaney (an appraisal of Pat Murphy's biopic)

James Joyce by Richard Ellmann

James Joyce: A New Biography by Gordon Bowker

James Joyce: A Passionate Exile by John McCourt

James Joyce's Dublin Houses and Nora Barnacle's Galway by Vivien Igoe

Joyce County: Galway and James Joyce by Ray Burke

James Joyce: A Portrait of the Artist by Stan Gébler Davies

James Joyce by Edna O'Brien

Our Friend James Joyce by Mary and Padraic Colum

Reading Group Guide:
Discussion Questions for *Nora*

1. Nora Barnacle and James Joyce were from different social backgrounds. Joyce's family were the fallen genteel, keen on schooling, for boys at least; Nora's people were working class, and education was not a priority. Despite their differences, James and Nora's relationship worked. Why do you think that was? What attracted them to each other? What united them?

2. Nora was fostered to her grandmother at a young age, a common practice in twentieth-century Ireland. Do you think this may have affected her family relationships and subsequent ones, too? In what ways did Nora bond with those closest to her?

3. "I can muddle through with most people and, I think, life's easier on those who can," Nora says. Jim, on the other hand, can be odd around people. What does friendship mean to Nora? Is she a good friend? A competent host? Why does the Joyces' friend group change so often, even when they live for long periods in one place?

4. Nora and Jim, judging by their letters when apart, had a frank, open sexual relationship. Discuss whether you feel this might have been the norm for the era, or if the Joyces were unusual. Who do you feel was driving this openness—Nora or Jim? In what ways did they use intimacy as a way to bond? What did Jim want from the other women he fantasized about? ▶

5. Why do you think Jim will not marry Nora? Is it anything to do with his status as a lapsed Catholic? Why does Nora want to marry? Is Nora happy with the circumstances of her marriage, when it finally happens, after twenty-seven years with Jim?

6. The Joyces' financial situation is, often, precarious. Nora says Jim "sees money only as something to be got rid of." Are the Joyces irresponsible with money? What do you make of Jim's moneymaking schemes—The cinema in Dublin? The idea to import Irish tweed? Why do you think the Joyces spend so freely? What is Giorgio's relationship with money in his adult life?

7. Joyce is supported by women, both emotionally and financially. Nora, Miss Weaver, and Sylvia Beach all play their part. Does Joyce appreciate their help? Does he acknowledge it? What is Joyce's attitude toward women?

8. Nora warns Jim: "If you want to write, you must make the time to write. Boozing and carousing will get you nowhere." Why does James Joyce drink to excess? What damage does it do to his relationships? Is he an alcoholic? Does his devotion to alcohol hinder his writing life? Does Nora aid his drinking in any way?

9. Nora enjoys opera and certain kinds of books, but Jim says that she doesn't "care a rambling damn for art." Is that true? Is Jim snobbish when it comes to literature and art? Is that his right, considering the types of books he himself writes?

10. Giorgio and Lucia both end up as lost souls in many ways—Lucia in an asylum and Giorgio in a bad marriage and then careerless. Lucia was diagnosed with schizophrenia, but do you think any of her other problems were a result of Nora and Jim's style of parenting? What about Giorgio? Do you think the Joyce children's uprooted childhood may have affected them? Were other factors at play?

11. What does Nora want from life? Does she get what she wants and needs? Is James Joyce a help or a hindrance to Nora's hopes and dreams? What rewards in life does Nora enjoy after Jim's death?

12. Home is important to Nora. In what ways is this obvious in the novel? Is Nora adaptable to each new circumstance and, if so, why and how? Does Nora ever find the home she yearns for? Do you think she had a happy life with James Joyce? ∽